DEATH AT THE CRYSTAL PALACE

Jennifer Ashley

Berkley Prime Crime
New York

BERKLEY PRIME CRIME
Published by Berkley
An imprint of Penguin Random House LLC
penguinrandomhouse.com

Library of Congress Cataloging-in-Publication Data

Names: Ashley, Jennifer, author.
Title: Death at the crystal palace / Jennifer Ashley.
Description: First Edition. | New York: Berkley Prime Crime, 2021. |
Series: Below stairs mysteries; 5
Identifiers: LCCN 2021010849 (print) | LCCN 2021010850 (ebook) |
ISBN 9780593099391 (trade paperback) | ISBN 9780593099407 (ebook)
Subjects: GSAFD: Mystery fiction.
Classification: LCC PS3601.S547 D428 2021 (print) |
LCC PS3601.S547 (ebook) | DDC 813/.6—dc23
LC record available at https://lccn.loc.gov/2021010849
LC ebook record available at https://lccn.loc.gov/2021010850

First Edition: July 2021

Printed in the United States of America
1st Printing

Cover art: *Crystal Palace Stairs* © Ernesto Rogata and
NorthScape / Alamy; *Statue* © Brita Seifert / Shutterstock
Book design by Laura K. Corless

For the readers of the Below Stairs Mysteries
who have begged me for more Kat.

DEATH AT THE CRYSTAL PALACE

1

P lease, help me."
 The shaky words came to me from behind a column
copied from those at Karnak in Egypt, lit by a chance beam of
sunshine through the glass roof high above.

I'd met the woman who spoke them, Lady Covington, only
an hour ago, introduced by my friend Mr. Elgin Thanos as the
sister of his benefactor. She had paid little attention to me, as I
was a domestic accompanying her betters in a treat outing to
the Crystal Palace at Sydenham.

Lady Covington had greeted Lady Cynthia Shires, Mr. Thanos, and their friend Miss Townsend with interest, barely reg-
istering me and my eleven-year-old daughter standing slightly
behind them.

After the visit, Lady Covington and her family had moved
off, and Mr. Thanos had escorted the two ladies up to the galleries to take in the view. They had extended the invitation to

me, but Grace wanted to see the Egyptian court, so she and I had wandered toward that exhibit, agreeing to meet up for tea later.

Now Lady Covington came to me furtively around the wide column painted with hieroglyphs. Her family—two grown daughters, two grown sons, and her brother—was nowhere in sight.

"Your ladyship?" I made a deferential curtsy, as did Grace. One always curtsies to aristocrats, even when they are begging for help, in case they take offense if you do not. "Are you unwell?"

"Quite unwell." Another swift glance behind her, then Lady Covington leaned closer to me. "My dear, I have been poisoned."

I felt Grace's hand tighten on mine, and my alarm rose. I offered Lady Covington my arm, leaving it up to her whether she took it or not. "You ought to sit down, your ladyship. Why do you think you have taken poison? Are you ill?"

She looked well enough, if flushed, but it was warm this May day under the glass, with tropical plants and indoor ponds trapping the sun's heat.

Lady Covington's grip was strong when she laid her hand on my arm, but her gloved fingers shook. Grace said not a word, her eyes full of concern as I steered Lady Covington to the nearest bench. It was of stone, made to look as though it had been lifted from Egypt and transported to England, but I knew full well that all the things in the exhibit had been manufactured specially for the Crystal Palace, based on the real items in the British Museum or private collections.

We sank to the bench together, as Lady Covington did not loosen her grasp. Grace seated herself on the other side of me.

Her shoes rested firmly on the floor, which made me realize how long her legs had grown. Soon she would be as tall as I was.

"Would you like a drink of water, your ladyship?" I asked. "Or a cup of tea? I can fetch it while you rest quietly."

"No." Her fingers dug into my arm. "No, please do not leave me. I need nothing."

"If you believe you have taken poison, you must see a doctor. I can call your son, Lord Covington . . ."

"No!" The word was sharper still. "No, I can trust no one. I will be all right, if you sit with me."

My alarm changed to puzzlement. Was the woman fancying things? Or truly in danger? And what had become of her family?

Lady Covington had a sharp face I imagined had once been pretty, though years, loss, and disappointment were etched into her skin. She was not an old woman, perhaps in her late forties at most, and she was slender, her posture upright. Her eyes were light blue and her hair was a rich, chocolate brown, bearing only a few threads of gray and pulled into a simple style under her high-crowned, mannish hat.

I knew she was quite wealthy, the widow of a railroad magnate who had also been a baron, the title going back generations. Her brother, Sir Arthur Maddox, had recently helped open the Polytechnic in London, a school devoted to educating young men in the sciences. Mr. Thanos, my friend and a brilliant mathematician, had been given a post there. Mr. Thanos had told me, in confidence, that Lady Covington was a generous benefactor to the new school. Sir Arthur could never have been involved without her help.

Lady Covington's gown was obviously costly, but

understated—a brown-and-cream-striped walking dress of light material that draped over her legs and gathered over a bustle in the back. The gown bore few frills, but its cut revealed its expense. A fold of fabric touched my brown woolen frock, which though neat and mended was years out of fashion. The contrast between the two of us could not have been more marked.

"Your ladyship, if you are unwell, I must strongly advise you seek a doctor. He can give you a draught to purge you at the very least."

Lady Covington shook her head. "You must think me quite mad, Mrs. . . ." She groped for my name.

"Holloway. I am Lady Cynthia's cook."

"Yes, that is why I sought you out." She regarded me with confidence that I would see the obvious connection.

"Are you worried about something you ate?" I ventured.

"Perhaps. I assure you I am *not* mad, though I understand why you would believe so. They would like to see me dead, Mrs. Holloway."

"Who would?" I asked in bewilderment.

"All of them. Except dear Jonathan, of course. He has been nothing but a help and guide to me."

I remembered the flurry of names that flew by as Sir Arthur introduced his family. Jonathan was the younger of Lady Covington's sons. The older was the current Lord Covington.

"Perhaps I could send for him."

"Not yet." Lady Covington craned to see beyond the crowd clustered about the popular Egyptian court.

We sat facing the hall of columns, which were reproductions of those at Karnak, though in a smaller size. Behind us was a replica of the temple at Abu Simbel in Nubia, and to our right was a tomb from another time in Egyptian history, filled with colorful paintings I'd found quite fascinating.

Lady Covington turned back to me. "I am not mad, and I know have been given poison. Not much, which is why I am able to speak to you and do not appear to be ill. Slow poison is wicked, and I am surrounded by wicked people."

I could hardly argue with her, but I did not understand what she expected me to do. "Why tell me, your ladyship? Your brother could help you—"

"Not Arthur." Her voice changed to steel. "He would never believe me."

"Miss Townsend or Lady Cynthia, then. Both are very capable young ladies."

"I wanted you." Lady Covington's anxiousness had receded a bit, and she once more became the widow of an aristocrat, certain of her place. "I have heard of the goings-on in Lord Rankin's household, and how you made certain the police arrested the correct criminals for heinous things. I want you to call on me. My home is in Park Lane, not far from where you are employed."

Park Lane contained the mansions of some of the wealthiest families in Britain. I worked in a house in Mount Street, around the corner and a short block away.

A cook did not call upon a rich baron's widow to sip tea in her parlor, but I could see that Lady Covington was in some distress. She might be imagining things, in spite of her protests, but then again, she might not. I had observed men and women of all walks of life cruel enough to kill another for even trivial reasons.

"I could pay a visit to your cook, if you like," I suggested. "Or your gardener—do you grow many vegetables or herbs?"

She blinked her pale eyes. "Yes, an excellent excuse. Do come to the garden, tomorrow morning. Ten o'clock. I will speak to you then. But I must—"

"Your ladyship." A stern female voice cut through Lady Covington's breathless words. A rather stout woman wound her way around the columns and sightseers to the bench. She had a severe face and hard brown eyes, her gray hair pinned into a tightly twisted bun. "I have been searching everywhere for you."

The newcomer pinned me with a glare, as though certain I'd waylaid Lady Covington for nefarious purposes.

"Never mind, Jepson." Lady Covington rose, tone brisk, and I and Grace hopped up beside her. "I was asking Mrs. Holloway about one of her recipes. I've told her to bring it to Cook tomorrow."

A plausible reason for me to enter the house. Apparently, she'd dispensed with my idea of approaching the gardener.

Jepson folded her arms in a fair imitation of one of the Egyptian statues behind her. "They are waiting for you, your ladyship."

Jepson was a lady's maid, I surmised. They were usually called by their surnames only, and a lady's maid was the one servant of the household likely to accompany its mistress on an outing. She would look after Lady Covington's things and make certain her ladyship was where she needed to be.

"Let them wait," Lady Covington snapped. "I'll not come to heel for that pack of hounds. They depend on *me*, not the other way about."

"Yes, your ladyship." Jepson's pursed mouth told me she'd heard this rant from her mistress many a time.

Lady Covington gave me a stiff nod. "Thank you for speaking with me, Mrs. Holloway. Please greet Mrs. Bywater for me. I am looking forward to your recipe."

Jepson's eyes narrowed, and she switched her gaze to me. "Recipe for what?"

Lady's maids could be less censured for impertinence than other servants, if they had an understanding with their mistress, but this was rude even so. Lady Covington flushed.

"Lemon cake," she said quickly. "I fancied some. Come along, Jepson. As you say, I should not keep my stepson waiting. George is foul when he's cross."

Without further farewell to me, Lady Covington stepped past Jepson and headed from the exhibit toward the nave. Sunlight through the glass above us caught on the brown satin ribbon around her hat. Jepson, with another suspicious glare at me, followed her mistress.

"Poor lady," Grace said, watching the pair go with sympathy. "She is very frightened."

"Yes, I believe she is." I took my daughter's hand. "You were very good to say nothing. You are a well-behaved young lady."

Grace didn't smile or preen—she regarded me solemnly. "Mrs. Millburn says it's ridiculous to believe that children should be seen and not heard. But even so, she says it's polite to remain quiet when meeting ladies and gentlemen until they speak to me first."

"Mrs. Millburn is quite right." Joanna Millburn, my greatest friend, had kindly taken in Grace and looked after her so I could earn my living. "You are a credit to her."

Grace blushed but accepted the praise with modesty. "Will you help Lady Covington?"

She stated the words without pleading, but I could see that Grace was worried for the woman. As was I.

"Of course I will," I said. "I will visit her tomorrow, as she requests. But first, I must invent a recipe for lemon cake to take to her."

* * *

There you are, Mrs. H." The voice of Lady Cynthia Shires echoed to me as Grace and I wound our way to the transept, as the aisle intersecting the main one was called.

Lady Cynthia was dressed in a gown today that was not much different in cut from Lady Covington's. This was worth remarking upon, because Lady Cynthia much preferred men's suits to wearing frocks. She had conceded to the gown because Mr. Thanos, the dark-haired gentleman hovering behind her, had invited her and Miss Townsend on this outing to meet his benefactor, and Cynthia had not wanted to embarrass him with her eccentricities.

"Time for that tea," Cynthia continued as I reached her. "Won't hold a candle to your teas, Mrs. H., but it might be jolly."

I was happy to partake. Today, Thursday, was my one full day out a week, a condition of my employment, and I wanted to make it last as long as I could. Grace lived with the Millburns, and I resided in the house of my employer, so Thursdays and Monday afternoons were all I had with her.

The tea shop was situated near the indoor garden, enabling us to sit at a table and enjoy the beauty of exotic flowers and Egyptian palms amid the sound of burbling fountains.

The five of us enjoyed tea brought by a harried waitress, my three friends chattering about the exhibits, especially liking the medieval court with its statuary. Miss Townsend, who was an artist, discussed with candor the merits—of lack thereof—of the picture gallery.

As they conversed, I debated whether to tell them about my strange encounter with Lady Covington—my friends had been in the thick of problems I had faced in the past.

But I wasn't certain I should break Lady Covington's confidence. The poison might be nothing but her imagination, that of an overwrought woman surrounded by a family who perhaps preyed on her fortune. The lady's maid, Jepson, had certainly been a dragon. Lady Covington hadn't been at ease with her brother or children, I recalled. She'd stood stiffly next to Sir Arthur when she'd been introduced to us, speaking polite phrases with no warmth behind them.

Whether she was being poisoned in truth or only worried she had been, would Lady Covington thank me for spreading the tale? She might be horribly embarrassed if Lady Cynthia and Miss Townsend charged around to visit her, demanding the entire story.

Well, I would meet Lady Covington tomorrow and assess the situation. I firmly drank tea and kept silent.

"What did you think of Sir Arthur, Mrs. Holloway?" Mr. Thanos regarded me with eager brown eyes. His dark hair, courtesy of his Greek ancestry, was brushed back from his face, exposing sharp cheekbones and the few lines about his eyes inscribed from squinting. Mr. Thanos needed spectacles but was loath to wear them.

"Very . . . zealous." I chose my words carefully. I had no business forming opinions of my betters, but I knew Mr. Thanos truly wanted my impression. Sir Arthur, who looked much like his sister, had spoken at length and with vigor about the new Polytechnic. The younger members of the family had striven not to appear bored.

"He does tend to go on a bit," Mr. Thanos said apologetically. "But he is excited about an institute devoted to science and new discoveries. As am I. It will be wonderful to teach mathematics and theories to young men who have a true interest."

Young men who would understand what Mr. Thanos was talking about, he meant. Mr. Thanos had a brilliant mind, and we lesser mortals could not always follow him. He, however, did not always fathom social niceties, hence his invitation for *me* to join this outing, meet his employer, and render an opinion of a man far loftier than myself.

"Do not worry." Cynthia poked Mr. Thanos with her elbow. "Sir Arthur likes you. I could see that in the way he introduced you to his family. You are his pet mathematician. He expects great things from you, and you will give them to him."

Mr. Thanos's smile dimmed. "I hope you are right."

"Nonsense. He wouldn't have set you up in that lovely flat if he weren't convinced you were the ticket. Cheer up. You'll do well."

"Do you think so?" Mr. Thanos's mouth pulled downward. "My first lecture is Monday evening, right here at the Crystal Palace. I hope I do not work myself into a muddle."

"No fear," Cynthia said stoutly. "We shall all be in attendance. If they admit women to the lectures, that is. What a nuisance if they won't."

Mr. Thanos looked puzzled. "I can't imagine why ladies could not at least listen to the lectures. Scientific advancement benefits all."

"I will make certain of it." Miss Townsend took a delicate sip of tea. "Cynthia and I will be there, and Bobby. Mrs. Holloway, you are welcome to join us."

She set her down her teacup, her fine kid gloves like a second skin to her slender fingers. Miss Townsend was ladylike and elegant to a fault, but I'd come to know that beneath this young woman's modish exterior lay an intelligent mind and a steely will. If she determined that women could attend Mr. Thanos's lecture, they would. She did not command me to accompany them, because she knew that Monday was my half day, and I spent my afternoon with Grace. She would leave the decision up to me.

"Thank you," I said. "I will give it some thought."

"I wouldn't be half so nervous if I knew you were there, Mrs. Holloway." Mr. Thanos sent me a wistful look. "You bolster my spirits. There's nothing you wouldn't face."

"You exaggerate, Mr. Thanos, but I know you are being kind."

I wished he'd said that Cynthia also would bolster his spirits, but he did not notice the omission, and neither did Cynthia. Cynthia and Mr. Thanos were a bit mired in the space between them, and they'd had gone no further than acknowledging they were friends.

Miss Townsend managed to settle the cost of the tea—she had a private conversation with the headwaiter and herded us out soon after, and I never saw money change hands. Again, neither Mr. Thanos nor Cynthia seemed to notice a thing. They were an unworldly pair.

Miss Townsend had us out of the Crystal Palace and heading for the train forthwith. I was grateful—I needed to return Grace to the Millburns' and arrive home before the evening meal so Mrs. Bywater, Cynthia's aunt, would not have reason to chide me. She and I had clashed recently, and I strove to return punctually to avoid further altercations.

As we filed to the terrace overlooking the vast gardens, I glimpsed Lady Covington and her family near the base of the stairs and the great fountains there. Beyond, rose gardens and water features moved gently down the hill to lakes that bore islands full of antediluvian creatures.

Sir Arthur was holding forth, waving his arm at the expanse of the park, probably giving a full lecture about it. Lady

Covington adjusted her parasol against the sun, as though hiding her weariness at her brother's pontification.

I studied Lady Covington's four children with interest. They did not bother to disguise their ennui with their uncle, the younger son, Jonathan, pointedly staring in the opposite direction. The four stood in two distinct groups, the older son and daughter to Sir Arthur's left, the younger son and daughter to his right. Several yards of space separated the groups, giving them the air of strangers who happened to meet in the gardens of the Crystal Palace.

"The youngest two are Lady Covington's son and daughter from her first marriage." Miss Townsend was at my elbow, her low voice in my ear. "The elder are her stepson and stepdaughter—the late Lord Covington's children from *his* first marriage. The stepson, George, is now Baron Covington and lets no one forget it. Jonathan Morris, Lady Covington's son, is a wild young man. Gets himself into scrapes, runs up debts."

And yet, Lady Covington had spoken of him as "dear Jonathan" and said what a help he was. Affection could make one blind to another's faults, I well knew. Perhaps Lady Covington did not realize the extent of Jonathan's misdeeds.

"The younger daughter, Harriet Morris, is very much on the shelf and feels it keenly," Miss Townsend went on. "The stepdaughter, Erica Hume, is the widow of a rather feckless MP. He left her penniless, and she's entirely dependent on her brother and Lady Covington."

Erica held herself rigidly, her parasol at a precise angle. So unmoving was she that I envisioned a blow breaking her into a thousand brittle shards.

The younger woman, Harriet, seemed more at ease, her blue plaid gown rippling in the breeze. Though she must be well into her twenties, she swiveled back and forth, like a child who longed to be elsewhere.

"Why tell me this, Miss Townsend?" I glanced into her shrewd brown eyes and wondered if she'd seen me having the tête-à-tête with Lady Covington.

"You like to know about people," Miss Townsend replied smoothly. "And they are an interesting family. The lot of them live together in the house in Park Lane, as well as on an estate in Kent. Though George is now the baron and could heave them all, including his stepmother, to the pavement, it is Lady Covington who rules the roost."

"Perhaps the new Lord Covington is showing kindness to his stepmother and siblings." I did not believe this was the case, but I always attempted to find good where none seemed to lie.

"There is no kindness in George Broadhurst. He once asked me to marry him, as a matter of fact. I turned him down flat— I shudder to think what life would be, shackled to the likes of him. Now he sneers at me, as though I made the wrong choice. I had my chance to be Lady Covington, his contempt says, but ah well."

I did not press Miss Townsend for further details. Lady Cynthia and Mr. Thanos, who had been discussing a towering specimen of tree that I believed came from the Americas, joined us, and we turned for the railway station.

The Crystal Palace had two stations—the High Level Station, which first-class passengers could reach through a tunnel from the Palace's main entrance, and the Low Level Station, a short walk through the park. Miss Townsend, who'd booked the tickets, had chosen the Low Level, as it was a fine day, and we enjoyed the stroll through the gardens.

As our train skimmed out of the station past the lakes,

Grace pressed her face to the windows to gaze at the models of ancient beasts that inhabited the islands. The giant reptiles glowered at their human observers, though children ran among them fearlessly. We'd not had time to visit the islands today, but I would bring her back another time so we could explore them thoroughly.

At Victoria Station, Grace and I parted ways with my friends. A hansom, generously provided by Miss Townsend, conveyed my daughter and me across St. James's to the Strand and along Fleet Street to St. Paul's and the Millburns' house not far from the cathedral. I visited briefly with Joanna then parted with Grace, again praising her good manners as I hugged her. After this, I ascended the hansom once more to return to Mayfair.

I wiped my eyes as we went—dratted soot in the air. My chest felt hollow, as it always did when leaving my daughter.

I alighted from the hansom in South Audley Street near Grosvenor Chapel and walked around the corner to Mount Street. It would never do for the mistress to look out the window and see me emerge from a cab—she'd lecture me, as usual, on me getting above myself.

The sky darkened with the coming evening as I tramped heavily down the outside steps to the kitchen door. I entered to find Elsie singing in the scullery as she washed a stack of dishes, and the kitchen abuzz with activity.

Tess, my assistant, vigorously stirred something burbling on the stove, sweat dripping down her freckled face. She'd come a long way in the last year from the impertinent waif who'd never chopped a carrot to a competent cook I could leave in charge on my days out.

Mr. Davis, the butler, was lecturing a footman in the servants' hall—from the words that floated to the kitchen, I gathered the new footman had made some sort of gaffe while serving at table during luncheon.

Tess called out a cheerful good evening to me. "Happy to see you, Mrs. H. This sauce ain't thickening for nothing. It needs your touch, it does."

I unwound myself from coat and hat, though I'd need to change my frock before I began cooking. I could not afford to let this one be stained.

Mrs. Redfern, our housekeeper, strode from the passage-way into the kitchen, though she halted just inside the door-way. She would never presume to impede meal preparations.

"I feel I must warn you." Mrs. Redfern's preamble made Tess spin in alarm, the spoon with which she'd been stirring the recalcitrant sauce dripping white stock to the floor.

"Warn me of what, Mrs. Redfern?" I asked, a trifle impatiently. I was tired and still had much work to do before I could rest.

"Of what is happening upstairs—"

"It's a devil of a thing," Mr. Davis cut in as he joined her, having finished his lecturing. "The Earl and Countess of Clifford have arrived."

Mr. Davis's words made me stop in astonishment. "Good heavens." Lord and Lady Clifford were Lady Cynthia's parents. They lived on an estate in Hertfordshire and seldom left it.

"Good heavens, indeed," Mr. Davis said. "They've declared they're here to fetch our Lady Cynthia home."

2

F etch her home?" I asked Mr. Davis in dismay.
       Lady Cynthia's parents were rather weak people, in my
opinion—though I'd never met them—but she was their daughter, and they could summon her home if they wished. Cynthia
was a spinster with no income of her own, entirely dependent
on her family.

She was also my friend. Working in this house would be
terribly lonely without her.

"I know who's doing this is," Mr. Davis said darkly. He
meant Mrs. Bywater, a woman he considered to be hopelessly
middle-class and without taste.

Tess sent me an imploring gaze. "They can't take her away,
can they, Mrs. H.? What are we going to do?"

I made myself move to the table to inspect the greens and
new carrots Tess had washed and chopped. "Do not screech,

Tess, please. There is little we *can* do. Lady Cynthia is a guest in this house, not its mistress."

Tess's mouth hung open, and even Mr. Davis stared at me. Elsie had ceased her singing and peered into the kitchen, her dishcloth dribbling soapy droplets to her apron.

"How can you say that?" Tess demanded. "You must do *something*. Speak to the mistress. Speak to her folks."

"My dear Tess, they will not listen to the likes of me. Now we must get on. Tear the greens next time rather than chop them, though we can shred some cabbage with them and make a tasty salad. I must change my frock. Won't be a tick."

The others regarded me in amazed silence. I suppose they expected me to march upstairs and lecture Lady Cynthia's parents about where it was best for her to stay, but I could hardly do such a thing.

Truth to tell, my heart was breaking. I'd come to be good friends with Cynthia, and I'd miss her dreadfully. Though we were close in age, Cynthia often sought my advice when she was worried, and she'd helped me out of trouble more than once.

But it was no good giving way to despair. I hurried through the passageway with their silence behind me and climbed the stairs to the main house.

I opened the green baize door, intending to nip through the landing to the set of stairs that would take me to my attic room, but raised voices from beyond the drawing room's open doors made me pause. I do not approve of eavesdropping, but the people within were speaking so loudly, I could not help but overhear.

"If you wish me to catch a husband, rusticating in the country will do me no good." Cynthia's strident tones rang. "The only bachelors for miles are a fourteen-year-old boy and Mr. Weir the farmer next door, who is eighty-two. Do you see me as a doting farmer's wife?"

"Cynthia, darling, do not be so droll." A weary female voice floated past Cynthia's adamance, but the words held steel. "Of course there are plenty of young men near Ardeley Hall. Many of our friends have sons, and they've retired to the country for the summer. I cannot imagine how you remain here in London, with the heat and the stink."

"It smells better than endless cowpats," Cynthia said.

"Ha." A man's voice, rather high-pitched and languid, joined in. "Cynthia, darling, you do say the most amusing things. But really, dear girl, how pleasant can it be for you staying here with my brother-in-law and his dreary wife?"

I wondered, wincing, if the Bywaters were at home to hear him. Or perhaps Lord Clifford did not care whom he skewered with his opinions.

"Better than rattling around a manor house with a leaky roof," was Cynthia's rejoinder. "Why you wanted that pile of bricks, Papa, I cannot fathom."

Lord Clifford chuckled breathlessly. "Yes, yes. Highly amusing."

"My friends are in London," Cynthia went on. "But you needn't worry about me enduring the heat and stink this summer—Miss Townsend has a house at the seaside, and she's invited Bobby and me to stay with her for a few weeks."

"Cynthia, you know my views on Lady Roberta," Lady Clifford said, her dying-away voice full of disapproval.

"You barely know her, Mummy. She's a good egg with intelligent conversation."

"She wears trousers." Lady Clifford pronounced the words as though Bobby, Cynthia's closest friend, regularly drowned children. "And cuts off her hair. Please tell me she has grown out of such crudeness."

"Not a bit of it. Miss Townsend's respectable enough. And bloody rich."

"Oh dear. Your language." Lady Clifford's voice held distress. "You are already a hopeless bluestocking, Cynthia. If you become any more mannish, no gentleman will want you."

"Excellent. I'll keep it up, then."

"I do despair of you. Your sister married, and see what she gained?"

"A husband who chased his maids before she . . ." Cynthia trailed off with a cough. Her sister had died not long after I'd come to work here. She's been mistress of this house. Lord Rankin, the husband in question, had moved to Surrey in his grief but allowed Cynthia and her aunt and uncle to stay here and run his London home for him.

Lord Clifford cleared his throat. "What your mother means is that Emily married well, and there's no reason you shouldn't. Be in charge of your own household—wouldn't that be better than gadding about London as an eccentric?"

"*You* were plenty eccentric when you were my age, Papa," Cynthia observed. "Is being lord of the manor better than that? Or has life grown deadly dull?"

Another chuckle. "My dear, you do have a sharp tongue."

"Only when I speak the truth. I don't want to leave London. I am happy here. I have friends—respectable ones—though I can't imagine why either of you have begun worrying about that. Auntie has been going on to you, hasn't she?"

"Your aunt has your best wishes at heart," Lady Clifford said. "However, nothing needs to be decided today. We will stay in London for some time, enough for you to have some summer gowns made."

"Gowns, eh?" Cynthia huffed. "Where will we find the money for that?"

"Now, daughter." Lord Clifford lost his amusement. "Do not twit me about funds. I have plenty."

"Do you? Who did you swindle them from?"

"Cynthia," Lord Clifford said, aghast. "Really."

"Do apologize to your father." The steel in Lady Clifford's voice increased.

"You know Papa is not much more than a confidence trickster, Mummy. Why have you truly come to London?"

"Your mother told you." Lord Clifford's voice hardened. "To fetch you home. Your aunt has given us many stories about you, including you swanning about in gentleman's attire and associating with a *cook*, of all people."

The cook in question was me. I hoped Lady Cynthia would deny our friendship and maintain the peace, but when Cynthia lost her temper, she did not guard her words.

"The cook you dismiss is a fine human being and far kinder to me than you two have ever been. I've watched you drinking with stevedores, Papa, so do not admonish me about speaking to a cook. A damned good cook, as it so happens."

I warmed to Cynthia's praise even as her words alarmed me. Defending a friendship with me was *not* the way to prevent her parents from shunting her home.

"If this cook has taught you the appalling manners I am now observing, I am not surprised Isobel is unhappy you trot down to the kitchen at every chance," Lady Clifford said. "The woman is probably a harpy from the backstreets."

"Honestly, listen to you both. Mrs. Holloway is worth ten of you. Do not bleat to me about the backstreets, Mummy. You know you lived in them before Papa managed to finagle his way into his lofty title and empty house."

"Cynthia, darling . . ."

Lady Clifford's words trailed off as thumping footsteps headed for the hall—Lady Cynthia stamping out in anger.

I quickly rounded the corner to the servants' staircase and started up the four flights to the attic floor, where I had my chamber. I did not pause to catch my breath until I was in my small bedchamber and had shut the door behind me. I leaned against it and inhaled heavily.

My chest was hollow with worry that Cynthia's parents would prevail. Not only would I miss Cynthia, but sequestering her in the country would only break her. She needed independence, a direction, not a foolish husband to stifle her spirit. Nor did she need to molder away in her parents' rather dank household until her youth and looks were gone.

While I'd told those in the kitchen that it was not our place to interfere with an earl's and countess's wishes for their daughter, I had no intention of doing nothing. I would have to be covert and discreet, but I would act. My show of acceptance had been for those, like the footman Mr. Davis had been admonishing, who might carry the tale above stairs.

I unfastened and carefully removed my best gown, fluffed out my petticoats, and donned my gray work dress. I had recently sewn on new cuffs and collar, white and starched.

Back down the stairs I went. When I reached the ground floor, I peered about cautiously, but saw no one. I heard voices murmuring in the drawing room, but the double doors were now closed. Of Cynthia, there was no sign. I hoped she would do nothing drastic. A few months ago, she'd packed a bag and walked out of the house, and would have run away entirely if Miss Townsend hadn't talked sense into her.

By the time I reached the kitchen, Tess had returned to the sauce, and Mr. Davis was holding forth about his dislike for people who considered themselves quality but behaved like spoiled children. Mrs. Redfern regarded him in disapproval, but Elsie and Charlie, the bootboy, listened with interest.

"There isn't time for all that, Mr. Davis," I told him on my way to the stove. "We have work to do. Tess, the sauce is not thickening because you did not cook the roux enough. A little arrowroot will help, but next time, make certain the butter is bubbling but not browning, nor is the roux dry."

"Yes, Mrs. H." Tess scattered in a spoonful of arrowroot from the jar on the shelf near the stove and continued to stir. Charlie ducked into his corner, and Elsie returned to the sink.

"We must convince the Bywaters to allow Lady Cynthia to remain here," Mr. Davis said, not budging from the center of the room.

"How will we do that?" Tess asked over her shoulder.

Mrs. Redfern sniffed. "It is none of our affair, Mr. Davis. I would be sorry to see her go, but—"

"It *is* our affair," Mr. Davis snapped. "They will marry off Lady Cynthia to some insipid sprig to strengthen their family's standing, and I'm certain they'll make sure he's a rich sprig. Lady Cynthia needs to be here, where we can look after her."

"You warm my heart, Mr. Davis," I told him.

I tied on my apron and looked over the recipes Tess had chosen. Salmon with capers, hens in béchamel sauce, artichokes, salad, carrots in dill sauce, and a rhubarb tart. Good choices, if a tad ambitious.

"*You* said there was nothing we could do," Tess reminded me as she whisked the béchamel. "That you weren't even going to try."

"I said I doubted Mrs. Bywater or Lord and Lady Clifford

would listen to me. I did not say I would not give the matter vigorous thought." I began to separate strands of fresh dill. "I wonder why Lord Clifford truly has come to London."

"They said," Tess answered at once. "To fetch Lady Cynthia home."

"Lady Cynthia has been living here for a while now, well before I arrived," I pointed out. "Mrs. Bywater has been complaining about the friendship between Cynthia and me for nearly a year. Why have Cynthia's parents now decided a trip to London is in order? They could have simply sent for Cynthia—Mrs. Bywater would have put her into a coach or on a train without hesitation."

"Ah." Mr. Davis brightened. "I see what you're on about. Perhaps they'll mention the true reason at supper."

"You are there to serve, Mr. Davis, not listen," Mrs. Redfern said, but I could see she spoke the words only because she considered it her duty. "Sara is in charge of unpacking Lady Clifford's things. Her ladyship did not bring her own maid." Her lips puckered with disapprobation. "I will assist her." She rustled out of the kitchen.

"Hoorah!" Tess cheered. "Good for Mrs. R. We'll show 'em."

"We will do nothing of the sort." I set the dill on the cutting board and hefted my knife. "Mr. Davis, I'm certain wine needs decanting."

"Right you are, Mrs. Holloway." Mr. Davis glided out, whistling.

"Did ya have a nice outing, Mrs. H.?" Tess asked, her cheerfulness returning. "The Crystal Palace, eh? My brother and I sneaked off there once when we was tykes. Couldn't pay the fee to go in, but we wandered about the grounds and climbed on the ancient beasts. Fancy those huge things used to walk the earth, and right here in England. Too bad the Flood wiped 'em out, innit? Or maybe a good thing for us." She chortled. "We'd be food for 'em, wouldn't we?"

"Not so much chatter until you've finished that sauce." My knife flashed through the dill, the herb's fresh fragrance soothing. "But yes, it was a pleasant outing. I will take you there one day, once you master the mother sauces."

"Ooh, I'd like that." Tess stared down into her pot, as though determined to master all the sauces on the moment.

Her question about the Crystal Palace reminded me of Lady Covington and her certainty that she was being poisoned. I ceased my chopping and made a note in my book that I must create a lemon cake. I hadn't made one in some time, so I'd have to think about a recipe. I could not give one to Lady Covington's cook that was less than my best. I had a reputation to maintain.

Lady Covington's story concerned me. If she *was* mad or simply had a lively imagination, she'd be all right, but if she spoke the truth, then she was in danger. I disliked to think of her unprotected in her big house, with those four rather odd children, her ironhanded lady's maid who might be deranged, and who knew who else.

I was certain that Jepson had overheard Lady Covington speaking to me. If Jepson was in league with the poisoner, or was the poisoner herself, Lady Covington might not make it through the night.

I realized I was being dramatic, but at the same time, I fretted. I could not rush around and pound on Lady Covington's back door on the moment, which meant I would have to recruit help.

"Charlie," I called into the corner. Charlie ceased playing

with the dice he was rolling and jumped to his feet. "Will you see if you can find James McAdam?" I asked him. "He's bound to be about somewhere."

"Yes, ma'am." Charlie, glad of the excuse to rush outdoors, charged through the scullery. His small legs flashed through the high window as he ran up the outside stairs, then he was gone.

I calmed myself by realizing there was plenty I could do even while tied to the kitchen. James was a resourceful lad. I would bid him hunt up his father, Daniel, and ask the two to invent an excuse to get themselves inside Lady Covington's house and make certain the lady was safe. Daniel, a man of innate charm, had the ability to transform himself into any person he liked. That he'd be able to gain entry into Lady Covington's household, I had no doubt.

He'd certainly gained entry to mine, from the time I'd first met him delivering to a kitchen a few years ago, to the current evenings he stopped by after the rest of the staff went to bed. I knew I should not let Daniel linger while we chatted about our days, his son, my daughter, and anything we could think of, but my heart was always lighter after his visits. The kiss or two we shared before he went could make the drudgery of the next day fly by.

I carried the dill to the stove, scooped out a hunk of butter from a bowl, and began to teach Tess to make yet another sauce.

Late that night, after the staff had gone to bed, I stood at my kitchen table surrounded by broken eggshells and lemon rinds. I'd separated eggs and beat whites until my arm was stiff, but by the time I'd reached the third cake, I thought I'd perfected the batter.

I was folding in the last spoonful of flour on this third attempt when Daniel arrived. I poured the batter into a pan and set the pan carefully in the oven before I went to unlatch the door he'd rapped upon.

A light rain was falling, darkening the gaslights on the street above. Daniel, clad in a rain-spotted jacket, removed his dripping cap and left it on the corner of the sink in the scullery before he followed me into the kitchen.

"Mmm." He closed his eyes and inhaled. "Makes my stomach rumble, that does."

Indeed, I heard the stomach in question growling. Daniel's dark hair glistened with rain, but his blue eyes danced as he slid off his drenched coat. He hung that on the rack near the door, water quickly puddling beneath it.

"Come and eat the failures." I scooped up the eggshells and put them into my slop pail, reserving the lemon rinds to make into candied peel. I cut a slice of lemon cake from a loaf I hadn't considered excellent and thunked it to a plate.

I slid Daniel a fork and a napkin, and he wiped his hands, took up the fork, and plunged in. A very large hunk of golden cake disappeared into his mouth, and he chewed, a smile lighting his face.

"*This* is a failure?" he said after he'd swallowed. "Your failures are splendid."

"Too flat," I said. "It didn't rise properly. For the one I just put into the oven, I beat butter into the sugar before I added the eggs. It will be lighter, and I'll send it upstairs for luncheon tomorrow."

"I will happily consume anything you consider less than

perfect." Daniel took a few more rapid bites, his usual garru-
lousness quenched by cake.

"Have you eaten today?" I asked.

"Not much. No time." The rest of the slice disappeared.

"Well, you cannot survive on cake." I rose and made for the
larder, returning with a plate bearing a large piece of meat pie.
"This was left over from the staff's supper. Shouldn't let it go to
waste."

"You are too good to me, Kat." Daniel pulled the plate to
him and unashamedly dug into the pie. "More than I deserve."

"I know that," I said lightly. "In your very busy day, did you
have time to look in on Lady Covington?"

"Indeed I did." Daniel scooped up a particularly large bite
of meat pie, the gravy dribbling to the plate. He took a full
minute to chew and swallow then wiped his mouth on the
napkin I passed him. "I waylaid their usual deliveryman and
convinced him to take me on as an assistant for an hour. Tim-
ing it to arrive at Baron Covington's household not long after
that, of course."

"Clever." I imagined Daniel giving the deliveryman a long
and touching story of needing work, possibly to feed his son.
Daniel stayed close to the truth in his rigmaroles, though he
embellished without apology.

"The deliveryman and I coaxed a cup of tea out of the cook.
It had started to rain and was dark—she's not as sympathetic as
you are, but she did not begrudge us the tea."

"You are skilled at convincing overtasked cooks to give
you food and drink," I said, reaching for the teapot. "I am surprised you ever need to purchase a meal."

Even as I spoke, I poured him a cup—myself one too—and
slid it to him.

"Perhaps I never do." Daniel winked at me as he lifted the tea.

"What did you discover?" I prompted. "Is the house a hotbed of intrigue? Or is the lady dreaming things?"

Daniel lost his smile. "I am glad you sent me." He slurped tea and clattered the cup into its saucer. "You have reason to be worried, Kat. I believe Lady Covington is in true danger."

3

I had lifted my own cup but quickly set it down, my fingers shaking. "Oh dear. I'd hoped the lady was being fanciful."

"I can tell you only what the cook and one of the house-maids told me." Daniel warmed his fingers around the teacup. "The cook was concerned about her mistress, described her ladyship's digestion as 'delicate.' She said that Lady Covington often took sick in the night, or had stomach cramps early in the morning and was unable to eat breakfast."

"That could be nothing more than a weak constitution," I ventured. Lady Covington's color had been good, however; everything about her robust. "Or overindulgence."

"I suggested this, which brought an indignant reply from both cook and housemaid. Mrs. Gamble—she's the cook—said that usually Lady Covington is quite fit, and only sometimes takes ill. The housemaid says she has powders for her indigestion, which help. Lady Covington never overindulges in anything, according to these two ladies. She takes one glass of sherry before dinner and one cup of coffee each morning. She considers these her treats for the day. Otherwise she drinks tea, flavored only with a little lemon and no sugar. She eats little more than bread, vegetables, and fish, with meat or fowl for supper every once in a while. Mrs. Gamble assured me she prepares an entire feast for the rest of the family but that Lady Covington partakes of only a few dishes."

"Sounds a perfectly sensible regimen. It should keep anyone quite healthy."

"Exactly. So why does she take sick? They could not tell me."

"Continuing the argument, sometimes there is a hidden disease," I said. "One doesn't like to think of it, but some illnesses can render a healthy person sickly quite rapidly. Or, a less bleak situation, a patent medicine that is supposed to clear the skin or aid digestion does exactly the opposite."

"I will remember that." Daniel touched his face as though worried he'd find it breaking out in spots. "The housemaid claims her ladyship takes no medicines except the digestive powders, but who knows whether she has something tucked away she lets no one see?" He lifted a finger. "Before you make a counterpoint, let me tell you what settled the matter for me. The cook said that she sometimes prepares meals specially for Lady Covington, particularly after a bad bout of sickness. Mrs. Gamble makes dishes for Lady Covington alone and carries them up on a tray herself. These meals Lady Covington takes in her chambers, none of the family present. Mrs. Gamble also prepares the tea and brings it with her on those occasions. After these meals, Lady Covington is never ill."

"Meaning someone else has the chance to tamper with whatever she eats for breakfast or during meals with the family," I mused. "She takes sick mostly after supper or early in the morning, you said. But everyone in the house would eat the supper, wouldn't they?"

"I know a little about the process of digestion from listening to coroners and visiting morgues. A person can eat something at noon and not be affected by it until late that night or the next morning. It seems that the stomach empties its contents by then, and some poison—or bad food—does not make itself known until it enters the intestines."

While thinking of such things made me wince, the information was useful. "Meaning she could ingest the substance at luncheon, and only when the cook does not prepare her a special meal." I tapped the table with my fingertips. "I fear then that Lady Covington's misgivings are well-founded. If Mrs. Gamble is simply a careless cook and uses ingredients gone off, then the food she prepares specially would also make Lady Covington ill."

"Exactly. Someone is poisoning the poor lady's lunch."

"Who is in the house at the time?" I asked, fully believing that Daniel would know.

"Mostly the family, but Lord Covington sometimes brings friends home to dine without notice. Mrs. Gamble complained of it."

Always frustrating for a cook to not know exactly how many to expect for supper. One needs to measure ingredients precisely and not have too much left over, or worse, not prepare enough. The cook always takes the blame for a disastrous meal, no matter how chaotic the household.

I sighed. "I am not happy with this. Lady Covington sought me out, and I cannot turn away from her."

"Of course you can't." Daniel covered my restless hand with his. "It is not in your nature."

The warmth of him stilled me. We'd grown closer in the last month or so, he visiting almost every night for a chat that too often led to kisses. I knew Daniel was waiting for a sign from me that I'd like him to court me more vigorously, but I had yet to give it.

I allowed myself to twine my fingers through his, rewarded by a flare of heat in his eyes.

"They are not in a hurry, whoever it is," I observed, turning back to our distasteful topic. "If the poison simply makes Lady Covington ill."

"Slow poison can kill over time," Daniel said. "Arsenic, for instance, can cause nothing more than a bad stomachache until the last fatal dose. A person can even take a tiny amount of arsenic every day and build up an immunity to it, though it's dangerous. One miscalculation and . . ." He shrugged.

"Whatever poison it is aside, I would like to know why someone would wish to kill Lady Covington. For her money presumably."

"You will have to ascertain that for yourself. I couldn't stay long enough to discover the motives of the entire family. The new Baron Covington inherited the estate and his father's post on the board of his railway company, but Lady Covington has plenty of funds for herself, from trusts and so forth, and investments, I gather. She also has influence over the railway company's board, if not an official position on it. A hardheaded lady."

"I like hardheaded ladies," I said.

Daniel's lips twitched. "I wonder why that is? I tend to admire them myself."

My face heated, and I withdrew my hand. Daniel's flattery always embarrassed me. "Go on with you."

Was he contrite? No, indeed. Daniel sent me his flippant grin and returned to his tea and cake.

As he ate, I told him of Lord and Lady Clifford's arrival and what I'd overheard upstairs. Daniel listened attentively, and I was pleased to see his concern.

"It might be worthwhile to look into Lord Clifford's affairs," he said thoughtfully. "He is a crafty fellow—Lady Cynthia isn't wrong about that."

I did not ask Daniel how he knew about Lord Clifford. Daniel knew many things about many people.

"Discover why he is truly in London, you mean?" I refilled his cup. "How would we go about doing that?"

"I have some ideas. You are right to be suspicious of his motives. Though he might only wish his daughter to come home, where he can look after her, why wait until now to fetch her?"

"Precisely. Very well then. I will visit Lady Covington and determine whether one of her family or friends is poisoning her, and you will discover things about Lord Clifford. We can reconvene and pool our knowledge."

Daniel's mouth turned down glumly. "I might not be able to call on you as often for a time."

I should not be bothered—Daniel was not required to come here—but a pang touched my heart.

"Are you off to foreign parts again?" I asked lightly. I lifted the teapot to refill my cup, but the pot was empty, and I set it down rather abruptly.

"No more foreign than Berkeley Square." Daniel cut off the sentence abruptly, disguising his unease by sipping the last of his tea.

"Is this one of your tasks you can tell me nothing about?"

"I'm afraid so." Daniel set down his cup. "I will not be able to make any deliveries for a time. I need to be careful about being seen as anything but an insipid gentleman of leisure."

Daniel routinely became other people, and the fact that he'd disguise himself as a well-to-do young man did not amaze me.

"I suppose this is an assignment from your bespectacled gentleman?"

A few months ago, I'd observed Daniel speaking to a tall, rail-thin man with short gray hair and spectacles. Behind those spectacles lay eyes colder than Arctic ice. Daniel had told me later that he worked for this gentleman, though not by choice.

"It is," Daniel answered quietly.

"Does this gentleman have a name?"

Daniel's gaze flicked to his empty teacup. "It's best you know as little about him as possible."

I shrugged, pretending nonchalance. "I am merely curious."

"Your curiosity leads you into much danger, Kat. I have to wonder—and worry—what you would do with this knowledge."

"Nothing at all. But if you vanish without a trace, I'd like to know whom to ask where to begin looking for you."

Daniel sent me an uneasy look. "Best leave it alone, my love. He is not a man who would take kindly to your blunt questions."

I was excessively pleased by the fact that Daniel had referred to me as *my love*, but he might be trying to disarm or distract me, and I refused to let him.

"You know that if you do not tell me, I will attempt to discover his name another way. I could ask Inspector McGregor, for instance."

Daniel's dismay was almost comical. "Do *not* bring Mc-

Gregor into this. He already despises me, because he knows how foul my master can be."

His vehemence puzzled me. "That isn't your fault, surely."

"My fault because I consent to work for him. I have no choice, but most people don't know that." Daniel heaved a sigh. "Very well, but the name goes no further than you. And I only tell you this so you do not harm yourself blundering about trying to discover it."

"I never blunder about," I said, indignant.

"Forgive me. I should say you ask decided questions and won't be put off." Daniel leaned close, his whisper quiet in the dark kitchen. "His name is Alden Monaghan."

The name meant absolutely nothing to me. "Never heard of him."

"Good." Daniel gave me a nod of relief. "If you had, it would mean you'd come to his attention, and that is not wise."

"Gracious, if this man is so awful, why is he working for the police?"

Daniel lifted his hands. "That is all I can say about him. He is not to be trifled with, and I'd prefer he know nothing about you or my connection to you."

His alarm unsettled me. In some countries, the police could arrest a person and hide him away because he knew too much about the wrong things. I believed it happened in this country as well, though it was not spoken of. If Mr. Monaghan, whoever he was, decided he did not like me knowing about him, he might arrange for me to be arrested, or at the very least require me to move far out of his reach. I had Grace to think of—what would become of her if her mother was accused of hindering the police, or worse?

"I will say nothing to anyone," I promised. "I understand."

Daniel looked relieved. I believe he knew exactly why I'd curb my curiosity.

He pushed aside his teacup and stood, and I rose beside him.

"I will miss you," Daniel said softly.

I would miss him too. I could not ask when he'd be able to return—I was certain he didn't know or would refuse to tell me even if he did.

"God keep you," I said.

Daniel touched my cheek and leaned to kiss my lips.

The kiss went on rather longer than it should have, and I was in his arms, resting against his chest by the time it finished. Daniel brushed moisture from my lip.

"God keep *you*, Kat."

And then he was gone.

I spent the breakfast preparations wondering how I would slip away to visit Lady Covington, but after the meal, the excuse was made for me.

While I sorted through the vegetables Tess had brought from the market, Mrs. Bywater strode into the kitchen, a paper in her hand and an excited light in her eyes.

"Well, Mrs. Holloway, it seems your talents are requested in high places. A letter arrived this morning from Lady Covington, who wishes you to personally deliver a recipe Cynthia raved about to her. I do not remember your lemon cake, so it must be something you prepared for Lord Rankin."

Mrs. Bywater's thin face puckered as she pondered, but I could see the delight in receiving a letter from an aristocratic lady outweighed her confusion about when Cynthia would have eaten my cake. I'd finished up the recipe last night—the third cake had been as airy as I'd predicted—but I had not yet served it upstairs.

"I see," I said carefully. I longed to know what Lady Covington had written, but Mrs. Bywater clutched the letter, not about to hand it to me.

"You should go quickly," Mrs. Bywater said. "Tess can take over your duties until you return."

Tess, whose head had popped up from where she chopped the spring onions for meat pies, stared, mouth a round o. No one else lingered in the kitchen at the moment, the staff busy in various parts of the house. The room was quiet but for the stock bubbling away on the stove.

"Do hurry," Mrs. Bywater said as I stood uncertainly. "Her ladyship should not have to wait for you. The address is 94 Park Lane, near Upper Brook Street. If you walk swiftly, you will be there in no time."

I glanced at my apron, which was spattered with grease. "Perhaps I should change into a better frock."

"Nonsense." Mrs. Bywater's impatience was mixed with elation. A lofty woman personally requesting a recipe from *her* cook would elevate Mrs. Bywater's status in her circle. "You won't be taking tea with her ladyship—you'll speak to her cook. Your work dress will be fine. Go on with you now."

She flapped the paper at me then rushed away.

I untied my apron. "It seems I will be visiting Lady Covington's home in Park Lane."

"Ooh." Tess assumed a false highborn accent. "Ain't we a toff?" She burst into laughter. "Good on you, Mrs. H. Perhaps this lady will offer you a position. If she does, you'll take me with you, won't you?" Her laughter trailed off. Tess ever feared I'd leave my post, subjecting her to the mercy of a new and unknown cook.

"She will not offer me a position," I said as I unpinned and hung up my starched cap. "Mrs. Bywater is right. I will deliver the recipe and that will be that."

"Then why'd she ask for you special?" Tess said in suspicion. "Charlie could nip 'round and take her ladyship's cook a piece of paper."

"Perhaps the cook can't read, and I will have to explain." I removed my coat from its hook, slid it on, and tucked my recipe into the pocket. "Not many cooks know their letters. A great advantage if they do, which is why I have you practice reading."

"I know, I know." Tess returned to the green onions. "Don't let all those nobs turn your head, Mrs. H."

"Of course not. I will be back as quickly as I'm able."

"I'll be fine. I'm only doing meat pies. Off you go."

It spoke of how far Tess had come since she'd first stamped in here, terrified and sullen, that she didn't mind putting together the luncheon herself. Now she made bread, pies, and other dishes without coaching.

I climbed the stairs to emerge into a fine rain that was cool but not bothersome and made my way along Mount Street toward Hyde Park, rounding the corner at the massive Grosvenor House and into Park Lane.

The two blocks to Upper Brook Street passed quickly—not many people were out and about at midmorning in the rain. A nanny herded two small children across the road to Hyde Park, admonishing them to keep their coats well buttoned and their hats on. I smiled, remembering Grace at their age—she'd wanted to dash about without hat and coat too.

Number 94 was a five-storied brick house with many windows and a good number of chimneys, which boasted that the inhabitants could afford to have a fire in most of the rooms. A half-round portico with Greek-style columns shaded the front door. The room above the portico sported a huge bow window jutting out over the porch. I thought I saw a woman's figure there, but lace curtains and the rain confounded my gaze.

The likes of me did not approach the front door of such houses and knock. I rounded the corner, searching for the stairs that would lead down from the street and into the kitchen, but found instead a gate that led to a walk behind the house.

The gate was unlocked, and I strolled through it into a green and pleasant land. The noisy road, smoke, and fumes faded as I wandered under trees just leafing for spring. A cherry tree flowered in pink splendor in the middle of the green, like a lady in a gauzy wrap, and rhododendrons, trimmed against the walls, were just putting out brilliant scarlet blooms. Flower beds full of daffodils, irises, and other bulbs lent vibrant color to the green.

The walk skirted the house, which was a typical mansion of Park Lane, far larger than the homes in Mount Street. In one corner of the garden I found neat beds of vegetables, stakes indicating that the thin shoots would become radishes and carrots. Beyond that, a greenhouse stood against the garden wall.

"Can I help you, miss?"

A young man approached the kitchen garden as I stood admiring the mounded rows. He was obviously the gardener, in mud-spattered breeches and thick boots, a wool coat against the rain, a flat hat, and a spade over his shoulder. He had chestnut hair, thick like Daniel's, brown eyes, and a lean face tanned by wind and sun.

"I am Mrs. Holloway," I informed him. Best to let him know

right away that I was no idle stranger. "I am cook to Mrs. Bywater on Mount Street. Her ladyship asked that I bring her a recipe."

The young gardener pushed his hat askew and scratched his forehead. "That so?" he asked good-naturedly. "She told *me* you was coming here for advice on starting a kitchen garden. Which is it, missus?"

4

+———————+

Before I could answer the gardener's question, Lady Covington herself strode down the path. Dressed in a long coat and hat with veil, she tapped the stones with a tall walking stick held in an elegant gloved hand.

She paused without surprise and studied the gardener with an imperious gaze. "Symes, have you given Mrs. Holloway the fresh herbs Lady Cynthia asked for? Be quick about it, man."

"Of course, your ladyship. They'll be ready for you in the kitchen, missus."

I curtsied to Lady Covington, a bit unnerved by her arbitrary change of story, and prepared to move to the outside stairway I'd spied at the rear of the house, which I presumed led to the servants' area.

"Mrs. Holloway, I believe you should come inside with me. I do not want any interruption in the kitchen. I'll send someone for the herbs. This way."

Lady Covington gestured to me with stiff fingers then

strode on, stick tapping, toward a door with an oval glass window. I glanced at Symes, who raised his brows, shook his head, and walked away.

I said nothing as I caught up to Lady Covington. The door opened for her, held by a footman who'd no doubt sprung to assist as soon as he'd seen his mistress approach. He stared in perplexity at me in my cook's frock.

"This is Mrs. Holloway," Lady Covington said, as though I were any other guest. "We will require tea in the sitting room."

The footman bowed, strove to keep his face blank, and hurried away.

A maid dressed in black with a stark white apron and cap came forward to take her mistress's coat, hat, gloves, and walking stick. Lady Covington, once free of these burdens, moved briskly across the wide but dim front hall, me following, our footfalls deadened by the thick carpet.

The house was immense, the sitting room in similar proportions. Tall windows lined one wall, but what should have been a fine view of the garden was obscured by panels of opaque lace. Heavy blue velvet draperies, tied back, additionally swathed the windows. A small coal fire glowed in the walnut-paneled fireplace that took up one wall, but the blaze could scarcely warm all this space. The ceiling rose at least twelve feet above us, pseudo Gothic fan vaulting punctuating the room's vastness.

Unlike sitting rooms and parlors that managed to be crammed full of as many pieces of furniture, plants, and objets d'art as possible, this room had but a few groupings of tables, sofas, and chairs, very little bric-a-brac, and no potted plants.

The furniture was upholstered in a dark blue that matched the drapes, with splashes of yellow via cushions for contrast.

The few paintings depicted vast landscapes and a fine manor house, possibly the Covington country estate. Only one portrait graced the collection, of a bearded man with a stern expression, whom I took to be the late Lord Covington.

No other portraits. No photographs on the tables, nothing but impersonal elegance, and several buttons on the paneled wall that could summon individual servants.

"Sit. Do." Lady Covington indicated a chair of stiff blue damask. I perched on its edge, still in my coat and hat—the maid had not offered to take my things, and Lady Covington had not asked her to, a signal I would not stay long.

Lady Covington paced until the maid returned with a tray bearing a teapot and teacups. Lady Covington waved her away with a languid hand, seated herself on the chair next to mine, and poured out tea for both of us.

I hesitated to take a cup in a house where Lady Covington—and Daniel—feared poison, but I cautiously sipped. I tasted nothing but tea.

"Do not worry," Lady Covington said, seeing my hesitance. "It is never in the tea."

"Why would anyone wish to poison you, your ladyship?" I asked in a quiet voice. I noticed Lady Covington had settled us far from the door, which was now closed.

"To kill me, of course." She sat rigidly upright, back straight, her silver-gray gown in the latest fashion, her hair pulled in a simple style away from her face. "But you mean, what motive has anyone for doing away with me? My wealth, I would guess. My first husband left me well off; my second husband, even more so. My stepson now chairs our railway company, as the late Lord Covington did, but he is not as sound in business as his father. George is a spoiled brat, quite frankly—his mother indulged him far too much from what I understand. He inherited the title and the entailed estate, but Covington left a large amount of *un*entailed money to me. If I had not married his father, George would have received much more cash, and he resents me for that. He does not hide the resentment either." Lady Covington took a decided sip of tea.

"Then you believe the new Lord Covington is the culprit?"

Lady Covington sighed and set her teacup on the table between us. "I would if he had the wits. George has much arrogance but is not overly gifted in intelligence." She fell silent, as though waiting for me to explain all.

I had no idea how to proceed—I was well out of my depth. The only thing to do, I told myself, was ferret out as much information as I could and try to discover evidence that someone was indeed poisoning the poor woman. I would then take this evidence to Inspector McGregor, an intelligent and respected man at Scotland Yard, and have him properly deal with it.

Feeling a bit more confident, I continued my questions. "What brought you to the Crystal Palace yesterday? Your brother, Sir Arthur? I understand there will be scientific lectures there next week."

"Indeed, but that is George's idea, not my brother's. George has many shares in the Crystal Palace, and he's always trying to revive it to its former glory. It's a bit run-down for my taste. But we scurry there as often as possible to make certain all is well. George is convinced more tickets will be sold if he makes an appearance and drags his entire respectable family with him. He decided that since I am giving Sir Arthur funds for the Polytechnic, Sir Arthur can take his scientists to the Crystal Palace to entertain paying attendees."

"I see."

"You do not." Lady Covington lifted her teacup. "But I will

try to make things clear. Everyone in this house is in need of money. Erica, my stepdaughter, married one Jeremiah Hume, who died in a coaching accident. The trouble was, when the coach struck him, he was nowhere near home but very near the house of a woman he was reputed to be carrying on with. He left Erica penniless—everything Hume had, and it was not much, went to an heir in Canada. Hence Erica had to return here to live or starve. She feels the humiliation."

I did not blame her. As one who'd been left penniless by an unfaithful husband, I understood Mrs. Hume's mortification. I at least had the chance to earn my living, while Erica would be dependent on her family if she found no other man to marry her.

"Do your stepchildren and own children get on?" I asked tentatively.

"Of course not. My daughter, Harriet, despises Erica and George. Not that Harriet has had much luck in matters of marriage herself. She was nearly engaged to a young man who then decided to marry another. Harriet pretends not to mind, but she too was humiliated. Oh, do not think she was in love with the idiot. She simply wanted to be married and out from under my thumb."

Lady Covington's death might give Harriet a bit of money, depending on how Lady Covington left things. She'd be out from under her thumb that way.

"You think me a hard woman to suspect my own flesh and blood—my own daughter," Lady Covington said. "But if you lived in this house, you would not consider it odd. It's rather fetid in here. Simmering anger, jealousy, resentment. In an earlier age, we'd have all killed one another by now, by the sword or pistol, in old-fashioned duels."

She spoke with no fear. Yesterday, at the Crystal Palace,

she'd been worried and tired, but today she was robust, her tongue sharp.

"You have not mentioned your son," I ventured.

Immediately, her eyes softened. "No, no, Jonathan has nothing to do with any of this. He does not stay much in the house, which I think is wise. George hates him. But Jonathan is as concerned as I am."

Miss Townsend had mentioned that Jonathan got himself into scrapes, probably helped out of them by his mother. If she favored him in her will, here was another person who might not be sorry if she died. Jonathan absenting himself often from the house would keep suspicion from him and protect him from ingesting any poison accidentally.

"Is there anyone else you suspect?" I asked. "Someone close to you—your lady's maid, perhaps?"

"Jepson?" Lady Covington gazed at me in unfeigned astonishment. "Jepson would no more poison me than she would a child. She has a soft heart."

I recalled the pinch-faced woman who'd charged to us at the Egyptian exhibition, with her impertinent words and disapproving glare. I'd never connect her with the phrase *soft heart*. She'd certainly chivvied Lady Covington without apology.

"It would be easiest for one of your staff to put poison into your food," I explained. "They have the most access to your meals, while the upstairs—your family—might not. Do any of the family cook?" Some ladies and gentlemen dabbled in the culinary arts for enjoyment.

"My children and stepchildren?" Lady Covington gave me a mock-astonished look. "Heavens no. They couldn't be bothered to lift a finger. The cook is in charge of all meals, and the footmen serve them. I do understand what you mean—it would be easy for a maid to slip something into a dish while it sits in the dumbwaiter downstairs, or a footman could while the food waits on the sideboard. But the odd thing is, only I take ill. None of the others do—they are rather complacent about that. They believe I am simply weak and sickly. I once mentioned that I worried about poisoning, but they dismissed it as a flight of fancy."

She glared at me, as though daring me to tell her I agreed that she was in less than vigorous health.

"This person is clever then," I said. "Or, they have access to things only you eat or drink. Do you take powders for sleeping or other ailments?" Daniel had told me she took powdered medicine, but I wanted to hear the answer from her lips.

"Only when I am ill from the food." Lady Covington lifted her chin. "I am not subject to ailments. I have a very strong constitution. That is why I *know* I am being poisoned."

"But you are unsure who is doing it. If you were certain of the culprit, you'd confront them, or summon the police."

"You have grasped things precisely. I know I am not imagining things, but I do not know who is undertaking this or how. Now, what can you do? I have heard of you delving into the truth of matters, especially in the goings-on at the house of Sir Evan Godfrey, but speaking to you now, I wonder if you are up to the task."

I was not offended, because I agreed with her. I'd solved the mystery in the Godfrey home—a few houses away from this one—with the help of my friends. Unless I sat in a corner watching everyone in this household, I doubted I could discover who was putting noxious substances into her meals.

"I can only do my best, your ladyship."

"I suppose—"

"Mama?" A rustle of skirts drew my attention to the doorway, through which a young woman strode. She was Harriet, Lady Covington's daughter. "Jepson told me you were in here. What are you doing entertaining a *domestic* in the sitting room?"

Her tone and her pinched lips implied that finding me here confirmed her opinion that her mother had gone completely mad.

Lady Covington regarded her daughter coldly. "I asked Mrs. Holloway to provide me a recipe. I thought it kind to give her tea for walking all this way when she has work to do."

Harriet exuded displeasure. "You could have had Mrs. Gamble give her tea in the kitchen."

Lady Covington rose and faced her daughter. I quietly set aside my tea and came to my feet.

Lady Covington and Harriet possessed the same stance and shape of face, glossy brown hair, and blue eyes. Their expressions of willfulness were similar as well. But I saw that the older woman was the stronger. Harriet began to wilt under her mother's steady gaze.

"This is my house," Lady Covington stated. "If I wish to entertain a pack of monkeys in my own sitting room, I will."

"It's George's house now." Harriet's mouth turned down sourly. "But never mind. Do as you like. I hate George."

"Harriet . . ." Lady Covington's admonishment wasn't because of Harriet's sentiment, I surmised, but because Harriet had said such a thing in front of me.

Harriet ignored her mother and turned to me. "What sort of recipe?"

I curtsied to her. "Lemon cake, miss."

"Ooh, I love lemon cake. Have Cook make it for tea."

"The menus have already been set for the day," Lady Covington said frostily.

"Well, do forgive me." Harriet's tone matched her mother's. "When George marries, you know, the new Lady Covington will set the menus. Like as not, she'll boot us all out, and then where will we be? Not that anyone would marry George, the ass."

On the heels of these words, another woman hurried into the room, her face blotchy red with anger.

"*Harriet*," she admonished. "You take that back."

Erica Hume, née Broadhurst, dressed as fashionably as the other two ladies, but she managed to make her frock frumpy. The skirt was twisted, her collar soiled, strands of hair escaping their pins. Her coloring was pallid compared with the other two, with her sand-colored hair and light brown eyes.

"Well, he is an ass, Erica," Harriet stated. "I know you dote on him, but he's a stuck-up prig who believes he's more intelligent than he is."

"Stop!" Erica shouted, raising her hand to strike Harriet. "You stop. He's better than *your* brother, who is a lying, thieving—"

"Ladies, cease this at once." Lady Covington's voice boomed through the room. "What will Mrs. Holloway think of us?"

Lady Covington likely didn't worry about my opinion of her family, but I was a servant, and who knew what tales I'd pass along?

"I do not gossip, your ladyship," I told her primly.

Lady Covington ignored me, her focus on the two younger women. Erica flushed. "Beg pardon, Stepmother."

"Yes, all right, I beg your pardon, Mama." Harriet wrinkled her nose at Erica and stuck her tongue out at me once Lady Covington turned away. Then she grinned as though she'd made a joke. As I'd observed at the Crystal Palace, Harriet was much like a child in grown-up clothes.

"Thank you, Mrs. Holloway, you may go," Lady Covington told me. "The footman will show you the way to the back stairs."

I curtsied once more, not that any of the three noticed, and exited the room through the double door Harriet had left open.

No footman was in sight, nor was the maid who had served us, but I guessed the back stairs would be under the grand, polished staircase in the main hall.

I was struck by the quiet as I crossed the expanse of carpet. In the Mount Street house, Mrs. Bywater regularly had callers or hosted one of the many organizations she was a member of. The sound of female chatter constantly filled the main floor. Cynthia's laughter rang, or her voice and Mrs. Bywater's rose in disagreement, which happened frequently. In my kitchen, Elsie sang, Tess chattered about anything that came into her head, and Mr. Davis and Mrs. Redfern were free with their opinions as they passed to and fro. Here, dust motes swam in the air, caught in the feeble light from the high windows.

Silence sat upon this house like a shroud. Even the women in the drawing room could barely be heard from here—the carpet and space muffled all. More rooms opened behind the staircase, including the dining room, which was reached by a set of five steps next to the main stairs. Its doors were open to reveal a massive table and solid chairs.

I moved through this soundlessness to the door under the stairs and reached for the brass doorknob . . . to have it wrenched out of my grasp as the maid Jepson yanked open the door from the other side.

Jepson's lip curled when she saw me, her eyes like flint. She wore no cap—lady's maids, who had high status in the household, often did not. Her gray hair had been severely tamed into a knot, her black brows telling me the color it had been originally. Jepson was a few inches shorter than I was, but the way she peered up at me in complete distrust did not give me an advantage.

I regarded her with the same lack of trust. Here was a woman who could easily poison her mistress—Jepson handled Lady Covington's food, tea, coffee, or any other drink, as well as her medicines.

Jepson opened her mouth, likely to demand what I was doing there, but was interrupted when the front door flew open, banging harshly into the wall. The footman leapt from the shadows of the vestibule to catch it, but too late.

A young man strode past the flustered footman, tossing the lad his hat. The footman caught it without fumbling, showing he'd performed this ritual before. The young man also threw the footman his walking stick, then gloves, which the footman scooped up, a grin on his face.

"Jepson," the intruder called. "What the devil are you doing hiding so furtively under the stairs? And who are *you*?" He halted directly in front of me and sent me a very impudent grin.

5

————✦————

Jonathan Morris, the ne'er-do-well son, wore a dark suit of fine fabric—I'd seen enough of Daniel's tailor-made clothes to realize these had been crafted by the best in Bond Street or Savile Row. His morning coat buttoned to a tie that peeked modestly from under his collar. Above that tie was a flushed face, light blue eyes, and the dark brown hair of his mother.

"I am Mrs. Holloway," I answered him with dignity. "Your mother sent for me."

"Did she? Why?" Jonathan's question held lively curiosity.

"Mrs. Holloway is a cook," Jepson supplied. "She is delivering a recipe."

"Jolly good." Jonathan beamed at me. "Something tasty, I hope."

"Lemon cake." Though I'd not had a chance so far to hand anyone the recipe I'd labored over.

Jonathan rubbed his hands. "Excellent. I hope I can try it

soon. That is, if our cook can manage it. Where is my mother, Jepson? I must report in like the dutiful offspring I am."

"Sitting room." Jepson's disapproval rang in her voice.

Jonathan did not respond to her chill tones. I could see he was a charming young man—his smiles and way of speaking directly and without hauteur were disarming. If I had not become used to Daniel's constant charm, I might have succumbed.

"Well, the maternal love calls. Best be getting on, Cookie," he said to me, "or Jepson will boil over. She hates strangers in the house."

Jepson looked as though she'd boil over on the moment. I gave Jonathan a rather stiff curtsy.

"Mrs. Holloway," I said.

"Pardon?" Jonathan blinked ingenuous blue eyes.

"I am Mrs. Holloway," I repeated. "Not Cookie."

He stared at me a moment longer, then his grin returned. "Cheeky little devil, ain't you? And so young to be a cook. I do look forward to this lemon cake. Maybe Cook—*our* cook—will let you stay and make it yourself. I would be delighted."

I wanted to let him know his familiarity was not acceptable, but I must take care not to offend him. Sons of wealthy widows and stepbrothers of aristocrats could make life difficult for me.

Before I could decide how to answer, Erica emerged from the sitting room. "Jonathan," she snapped. "Cease bothering the servants. Your mother wants you."

Jonathan turned back to us and rolled his eyes so comically that I wanted to laugh. A treacherous young man, I concluded, far too winsome and forward.

"Coming, dear sister." Jonathan put on a falsetto and trotted across the hall to Erica. He pinched her cheek as he passed and sailed into the sitting room. I heard a squeal of delight from Harriet within.

Jonathan banged the sitting room door closed behind him, shutting Erica out. Erica glared at the door then gathered her skirts and marched stiffly up the stairs, ignoring us completely.

"He is a handful," I said, nodding at the sitting room. "Quite boisterous."

Jepson's baleful stare told me she did not care for my observations. I also saw she agreed with them. "Mr. Morris is right that you had best be off."

"I do need to give your cook the recipe."

"Give it to me. Cook can't read."

I withdrew the paper from my pocket and handed it to Jepson, as she continued blocking my way downstairs. I wondered if the cook would even receive it.

"Good day to you," I said.

Jepson barely gave me a nod. She would not move, so I exited the house through the oval-windowed door that led to the garden, feeling Jepson's cold gaze on me all the way.

The gardens were refreshingly open and peaceful after the stifling atmosphere of the house. I took a few breaths to steady myself before I walked on.

When I passed the stairs that led down to the kitchens, I decided to descend and speak to the cook myself, Jepson notwithstanding.

I took care on the steps, which were steep and damp, and let myself in through the door at the bottom. Beyond a square foyer I found a kitchen that was far more spacious than mine.

Light flooded the room from the high windows that faced the garden, rendering the space cheerful. The kitchen was fitted out with plenty of shelves and cupboards as well as the latest in stoves, with eight burners plus a warmer, and three ovens below. Baskets hung on one wall, and between them, a grainy photograph of an older man, possibly the cook's husband, or brother, or father—someone she wanted to gaze at fondly as she worked.

How fine to have a large, well-stocked kitchen with fresh herbs and vegetables just up the back stairs—the garden would save running to the market every day. It was difficult to grow vegetables in London because of all the soot and smoke, but it could be done by a competent gardener and a hothouse.

Mrs. Gamble was what most people thought of when they heard the term "cook," a plump woman with gray hair, a flour-dusted apron, and a round, pink face. She was rolling out dough at her work table, her hands as floury as the pastry.

"Good morning," I called to her. "I am Mrs. Holloway."

Mrs. Gamble blinked at me, frowned, and blinked again. We were alone in the kitchen—no kitchen maid evident, no housekeeper or male servants going in and out.

"Oh, right, love. You are that cook what was coming to visit the mistress. Have you seen her?"

"Indeed. I gave Jepson the recipe—a wonderful lemon cake. It's simple, really. Eggs, lemon, flour, orange-flower water, sugar, and butter." I went on to explain, knowing that cooks who couldn't read had prodigious memories for recipes, and I did not trust Jepson to read the thing out to her. "Separate the eggs to keep it light. Beat the whites with the orange-flower water, sugar, and a bit of lemon rind, then beat the butter in a different bowl, add the egg yolks to it, and fold the egg white mixture into that. Then you stir the flour into the whole thing.

The cake must go into the pan immediately after or the batter will deflate before it can bake."

Mrs. Gamble listened attentively. "The proportions?"

"Three quarters of a pound each of sugar and flour, and a quarter pound of butter to ten eggs. The lemon and orange-flower water as you like."

She nodded. "The mistress will be expecting me to make this, I suppose."

"Possibly." Lady Covington had been inventing so many excuses for my presence that she might have forgotten about the cake. "Can you remember the recipe? In case it slips Jepson's memory."

Mrs. Gamble's lips twitched. "Aye, I'll remember. Jepson doesn't always come to the kitchen."

"Her ladyship praises your cooking," I said. "Says everything you prepare specially is sweet as can be."

Mrs. Gamble nodded without hesitation. "Aye, she has a finicky digestion. I make her soothing meals, as what I make for the family sometimes disagrees with her. Lemon cake will be just the ticket."

"If you have any questions about it—or if you would like other suggestions to help her ladyship's digestion . . ."

Mrs. Gamble returned to rolling the dough, a bit too harshly in my opinion. Pastry wants a light touch.

"If those four children let her be, her insides would be well," Mrs. Gamble declared. "I know I'm talking out of place, but 'tis true."

"I met three of them upstairs," I said to encourage her to continue.

"Three leeches, you mean. Young Lord Covington's not a pleasant man either, but at least he has much to keep him occupied out of the house. The young ladies need marrying, and

so does the younger gentleman. Places of their own to give
them something to do. Idle hands are the devil's tools, you
know."

If one of the younger generation were poisoning Lady Covington, it was the devil's work indeed.

I waited, in case Mrs. Gamble was more forthcoming about
the secrets of Lady Covington's relations, but she pursed her
lips and continued rolling her pastry. The piecrust would be
much too tough if she continued to abuse it as she did.

"This is a fine kitchen." The dresser brimmed with plates
and bowls and the shelves with foodstuffs, and polished copper pots hung over the stove.

Mrs. Gamble gave me a modest nod. "This mistress knows
how to fit out a kitchen. So many don't, and then they expect
perfect meals made on a smoky stove that won't boil water and
a table too small for anything but setting down a teacup."

"Too true, Mrs. Gamble," I agreed. "We are fortunate to
work in good houses."

"Well, the mistress is all right. She's the second wife, as you
know. The first, I hear, ran this house like a martinet but
couldn't put together a menu to save her soul."

"You weren't here when she was alive?"

"Lordy, no. I was in Oxfordshire. Didn't come to London
until last year."

"Has her ladyship always had a delicate digestion?"

Mrs. Gamble sent me a peculiar glance, as though wondering at my interest. Daniel had pried much out of her, but then,
Daniel had a warm smile and handsome eyes.

"It's a trial when our ladies and gentlemen can only stomach certain foods," I extemporized. "I wondered if you had
any advice, seeing as her ladyship is a bit dyspeptic."

"She wasn't always," Mrs. Gamble said. "Didn't start until,

oh, six months ago? Nothing to do with my cooking." Her gaze was hard.

"It wouldn't be, would it, if all of the household eats your food but only her ladyship has troubles?" I said quickly. "No doubt she is grateful for your soothing dishes."

"She is, indeed. I imagine that when the leeches leave for their own lives—if they ever do—she'll be fine again."

"Worry does affect the stomach," I said. "Well, I must be off. I hope you enjoy the lemon cake, Mrs. Gamble."

"Huh. Won't be me that's eating it, will it?"

"An extra pan with leftover batter never goes unwanted in the kitchen. Good day, Mrs. Gamble."

She nodded at me, then she banged down the rolling pin as though remembering something, snatched up a basket, and thrust it at me. "These are for you, love. Picked by Symes—said her ladyship instructed it."

I remembered Lady Covington demanding of Symes whether the herbs Lady Cynthia had asked for were ready. I did not need the herbs, and I knew Cynthia had never asked for them, but I took the basket without question.

Mrs. Gamble and I exchanged another farewell, and I exited via the stairs leading up to the garden.

When I'd reached the top of the staircase, I saw the young gardener, Symes, leaning on his hoe, studying the greens at his feet. He glanced up as I emerged, and pulled off his hat.

"All well, Mrs. Holloway?"

"Yes, Symes, thank you." I hefted the basket. "And for the herbs."

He grinned, showing white teeth. "Aye. Seems the mistress was a bit confused on why you were coming."

I sent him a small smile. "Lords and ladies don't have to have reasons for what they do, you know."

"Too true. Not like you and me, eh, Mrs. Holloway?"

I did not like the familiar way he looked at me or that he lumped me into a class of human being with him, but I could be civil. Besides, I did not want to spurn any resource that might help me discover who was trying to poison Lady Covington.

"No, indeed, Symes. Good morning."

He gave me a friendly nod, waiting until I'd exited through the gate before he resumed his cap.

When I returned to the Mount Street house, I was struck by the contrast between it and Lady Covington's. Even the kitchen had been quiet, Mrs. Gamble working by herself in the large and well-appointed room.

My kitchen was cramped, with pots, pans, and crockery taking up every available space. But it was cozy with Elsie singing in the scullery, Charlie playing a game with one of the footmen in the corner, Tess joining her voice with Elsie's from time to time, an upstairs maid sailing in to fetch a cup of tea for Mrs. Bywater, and Lady Cynthia, planted at the table, her elbows on it, looking morose.

Cynthia wore trousers and frock coat today, a garb not much different from that of Jonathan Morris. I knew Cynthia's clothes were tailor-made for her—I wondered what the tailor thought when she came in for fittings.

I set down the basket of herbs and removed my coat, then carried the basket to the table and began to sort through the greens, their fragrance pleasantly clean.

"What's all that?" Cynthia asked in a dull voice.

"Thyme, a bit of basil—too early for it, so it must have come from the hothouse—tarragon, and chervil." I lifted the tarragon, my favorite, and inhaled its fragrance. Some said it smelled of anise, but I thought it had a bright scent all its own.

"Oh." Cynthia rested her chin on her fists, which slid the skin of her face upward.

"Should you be downstairs?" I asked her as I tied on my apron. "Did your parents go out?"

"I shall never go upstairs again," Cynthia said. "I'm certain a cubby can be fixed down here for me to sleep in."

Tess sent me a tense look that told me Cynthia had been here for some time.

"You would be vastly uncomfortable," I said to Cynthia. "Not to mention hot."

"A bit of sympathy would not go amiss, Mrs. H.," Cynthia said crossly. "You know they've come to drag me back to the country. I can dig in my heels, but they'll drag me all the same—I'll leave grooves behind me. I can't stick it, so I'm not moving."

She leaned back in the chair and propped her boots on a low stool.

"I do sympathize." The herbs I sorted were in very good condition and quite fresh. I would use them for dishes today. "I have been pondering a way to keep you here."

"Have you?" Cynthia brightened a fraction. "What shall we do?"

"How well do you know Baroness Covington?"

Cynthia considered. "Slightly. Miss Townsend knows her better. Why?"

"Perhaps you could stay with her for a time. This house is becoming a bit crowded with your mother and father and the Bywaters. Perhaps Miss Townsend could persuade Lady Covington to take you in. It's a very large house. I've just come from there."

Cynthia eyed me in surprise then with misgiving. "Why on earth should I? What's it all about, Mrs. H.?"

I waited until the maid hurried out with Mrs. Bywater's cup of tea, and the footman and Charlie moved their game to the servants' hall. Elsie was belting out a tune and splashing loudly in the sink.

In a quiet voice, I told Cynthia and Tess about my encounter with Lady Covington at the Crystal Palace and all I'd learned from her and the cook today, as well as what Daniel had reported. Now that I was certain something foul was happening, I had no hesitation in recruiting Cynthia and Tess to help.

Both listened in disbelief, which soon became concern. "You think the lady's maid's doing it?" Tess asked when I finished. "Poisoning the poor woman? Nasty old bat. The lady's maid, I mean."

"That I do not know. If Cynthia were there to keep an eye on things . . ."

"Delighted to," Cynthia said at once. "Not only can I watch this maid and the other members of Lady Covington's ghastly family, but I can clear out of here. Papa bleats on about having me at home or respectably married off, but I don't trust him. He's up to something."

I did not admonish her for speaking so of her father, because I agreed with her. Lord Clifford had lied his way into his title, claiming to be next in line when he'd in fact been a few spaces removed, but the heirs had been scattered across the globe and difficult to track down. Time had made Lord Clifford now the correct heir, as the others had passed on, but he had taken advantage of distance and the time it took for legal dispatches to arrive to stake his claim. He'd apparently undertaken other swindles in the past, though I did not know the details about them.

"He cannot do much while staying here with the Bywaters," I said, hoping this was the case.

Cynthia scoffed. "Auntie Isobel dotes on Papa. She does love a peerage. Uncle might have a thing or two to say, however. He's a plain-speaking man."

Mr. Bywater was an upright middle-class gentleman who went to work in the City, read his newspapers in the morning and evening, and preferred easy comfort to extravagance. His sister, Cynthia's mother, had been a famous beauty and far more frivolous than her brother, eloping with Lord Clifford long ago.

"Will your mum and dad let you stay with another lady?" Tess asked. "If they're trying to catch you a husband?"

"They might not notice. Haven't said a word to me all morning. Papa was at the table when I went in to breakfast, deep in the racing news, never even grunted when I greeted him. Mummy, of course, is still in bed."

I pretended not to notice Cynthia's hurt at her parents' disregard. "Mrs. Bywater is more likely to object to you going. But if Miss Townsend asks her, I am certain all will be well. Your aunt likes Miss Townsend."

"Dear Judith does know how to wrap people around her fingers." Cynthia slapped the table with both hands, rattling the cutlery there. "I'll do it. Anything to escape this beastly house, *and* I'll be doing a good deed."

"If you don't get poisoned yourself," Tess said, eyes round.

"Might put the poisoner off, having a guest in the house," Cynthia said. "A widow growing ill and passing on is one thing. A healthy young woman turning up her toes on the dining room carpet is another."

"Oh dear," I said with a qualm. "Perhaps you shouldn't go, after all. It isn't fair for me to put you in danger."

"Nonsense. If no one else in the house is taking ill, then I won't either. The cruel fellow—or lady—seems to be targeting Lady Covington."

"While that is true, they might resent you poking about."

"I will have a care, Mrs. Holloway. If Lady Covington truly is in danger, we can't abandon her."

"I agree." I subsided. "It could be she is not ingesting the substance inside the house at all. When the cook takes her a private meal, she is fine. Perhaps you should try to discover if Lady Covington goes out for tea or some such, say, at a friend's home. Or secretly devours chocolates from a certain shop, or is taking some sort of remedy for beauty or slimness."

"True, there are foul concoctions out there purporting to make you young, lithe, and free of blemishes," Cynthia said cheerfully. "Plenty of women sicken themselves trying to look different from what they do."

She spoke with the confidence of one who'd never had to worry about excessive plumpness or spots on her face. Cynthia took her very fine looks from her mother.

Lady Covington, approaching fifty, might have begun to feel her age and worry about her attractiveness, turning to the remedies we'd mentioned. I doubted this, as she was such a steely lady, but all of this was only my conjecture.

Cynthia's moroseness fled. "I'll alert Miss Townsend and bring her in to help me confront Auntie. Then I'll storm the battlements, as it were. Never fear, Mrs. H. I'll report in every day, like a good soldier."

Cynthia came at me, and I thought she'd embrace me, herbs and all, but she only gave me a hearty pat on the shoulder before skimming out on light feet.

I knew Tess would want to continue discussing Lady Covington and Cynthia's parents, but I forestalled her.

"You are ready to learn something new, my girl." I lifted the aromatic strands of dill. "I will teach you to make green mayonnaise."

"Green?" Tess wrinkled her nose. "Why would you want mayonnaise to be green?"

"It is simply an herb sauce, but wonderful with fish and meat. Gather a half-dozen eggs and separate out the yolks, and we'll make a batch. Put the whites aside to save for meringues."

Tess had come to know me well enough to obey my orders without lingering to ask questions.

While she gathered up the things, James came in from the street, giving Elsie a cheery greeting.

"Message from Dad, Mrs. H.," James told me as Tess competently broke open an egg and slid the yolk from shell to shell to drain off the white.

I reached out a hand so James could put whatever letter into it, but he shook his head. "He didn't write nothing down. Just wanted me to tell you he couldn't be reached for a time. I know where he is, and I'm to linger nearby once every day or so, in case he can slip out. But he's well lodged inside the mansion of a prominent gentleman, and will remain there for a while."

6

I did not like the idea of Daniel out of reach. I admonished myself that I had no business expecting him to be nearby whenever I wanted him, but emotions do not always respond to logic. I knew his life was not always his own, and I understood, but my heart felt heavy all the same.

"Thank you for telling me," I said to James. "Before you run off, I have a missive for you to deliver."

Instead of being annoyed I wanted to employ him as the post, James scrunched his cap in his hands and told me he'd be happy to wait.

I slipped down the hall to the housekeeper's parlor, which was empty, as Mrs. Redfern was busy supervising the maids upstairs. I seated myself at the desk and scribbled a note on paper torn from my notebook. I folded it neatly and left the parlor, briefly visiting the larder before carrying the letter to James.

"To Mr. Fielding," I said as I handed it to him. "At All Saints Church in Shadwell."

James's mouth popped open. "Uncle Errol?"

He referred to Mr. Fielding as "Uncle," but Errol Fielding and Daniel were not blood-related brothers. They'd been raised by the same man, a Mr. Carter, who'd been a criminal of some sort but apparently kindhearted enough to take care of two homeless boys.

"Indeed. I know it is a long way, but do not rush. Take this for fortification." I gave him the wrapped piece of seedcake I'd taken from the larder.

James flushed with pleasure. "Thank you kindly, Mrs. H. He'll get the letter, no worrying."

"I am not worried. If you do see your father, please greet him for me."

"Right you are, Mrs. H."

James was a good six feet tall now, almost a man at seventeen years old. His voice had deepened in the few years since I'd met him, and he'd sprung up like a weed. His clothes, a secondhand suit I hadn't seen before, fit him a bit better than his last set—his rapid growth seemed to have slowed somewhat this year. I had become quite fond of James, and I gave his strong shoulder a pat as I said good-bye.

"Why are you sending for the vicar?" Tess asked me as soon as James had gone. "He's a handsome man, I'll say, though nothing as fine as Mr. McAdam."

Mr. Fielding was indeed handsome, far more so than a man of God ought to be, but like Tess, I preferred Daniel.

"Mr. Fielding is clever at finding things out," I said. "Now to the mayonnaise, which should be in every cook's repertoire. If you master it, you have a dozen sauces at your beck and call.

You never know when the mistress will demand a rémoulade for the meat or a creamy dressing for the salad."

Tess subsided, knowing I expected her to concentrate on the task at hand. I showed her how to stir the eggs with a bit of mustard and vinegar, and then to whisk, whisk, whisk while I poured in the oil, bit by bit, never letting it be more than a thin stream.

"Ow!" The bowl rang as Tess whipped the concoction. "Me arm is going to fall off."

"Constant whisking is key," I said. "I've had many a day of aches from this sauce, but it is worth it. Mrs. Beeton says that patience and practice are essential."

"Well, let her come here and do all this stirring, then."

"The poor lady died young," I said. "Very sad."

"Yeah, that is sad." Tess had a tender heart. "But look, it's all creamy now." She pulled out the whisk, showing me globs of true mayonnaise.

"Excellent. The trick is to add the oil as slowly as you can."

"I thought it were constant whisking," she said cheekily as she rubbed her arm. "And patience and practice."

"All of those things. Now we'll beat in the herbs and have a nice green sauce."

I added the dill and parsley I'd chopped, and then we fetched clean spoons and had a taste. "Oh." Tess's face lit. "This is wonderful. Can we have some with our supper?"

"We have made so much, a few spoonfuls won't be missed." I separated them into a smaller bowl. "Now this goes into the larder to keep chilled, and it will go up with the fish. Don't forget."

"How can I?" Tess rubbed her right arm again. "Me poor muscles will remind me."

"You did well, Tess."

Tess said nothing, but her cheeks were pink, eyes shining as she turned to her next tasks. I carried the mayonnaise to the larder to set over the bowl of ice I kept in the coolest corner. Ice was an expense Mrs. Bywater agreed to, mostly because Mr. Bywater was happier when his salads and sorbets were cool and not unpleasantly warm.

As I exited the larder, I halted in surprise when a gentleman emerged from the door next to the butler's pantry. That room was the wine cellar, which was nothing more than a niche used to store bottles from Lord Rankin's collection. Mr. Davis guarded them like a watchdog, but Mr. Davis was nowhere in sight, and this gentleman had a bottle under each arm.

He jumped guiltily when he spied me, then took on a look of false hauteur. "You there. Cook, is it?"

When Jonathan Morris had called me *Cookie*, I'd been annoyed, but he'd said it as a jest, trying to rile me. This man said *Cook* with condescending sniff.

He was Lord Clifford. I had never seen him, but I recognized the voice that had argued with Cynthia upstairs.

I curtsied politely. "I am Mrs. Holloway." I was growing weary of reminding people I had a name.

Lord Clifford was in his fifties, with receding light brown hair just touched by gray. Pencil-thin sideburns met an equally thin mustache under his nose, and he wore no beard. His eyes were hazel—Cynthia's clear blue eyes came from her mother.

Lord Clifford looked me up and down. "You don't seem a decadent chit who's leading my Cynthia astray. You look respectable."

"I hope so, sir," I said stiffly.

"Hmm. Perhaps Old Biddy Bywater reads you wrong. She

believes Cynthia would straighten up and be a sweet gel if not for you. But I rather think Cynthia is simply high-strung. Like her mother. And me." Lord Clifford sent me a crooked grin, meant to disarm me.

I could see why this man would be a successful swindler. He appeared as a harmless twig of the aristocracy, happy to read his racing news and sip whatever beverage his valet set in front of him. A gentleman who'd never mislead others into giving him an inheritance he didn't deserve.

I imagined him blinking his eyes as he did at me now, declaring that he of course was the second cousin of the deceased, and so sorry for the old chap, and all that, but only too chuffed to realize he was now a peer.

"You'll do," Lord Clifford said. He observed my glance at the bottles he clutched and sent me an impudent wink. "Saving old Davis the bother of tottering down here for me. These wines belong to Rankin, my son-in-law, you know. Rankin won't mind."

With a tip of his head, Lord Clifford turned and leapt up the back stairs, his well-made leather shoes ringing on the rough boards. He so easily balanced on the steep staircase that I imagined he'd more than once run down to grab whatever bottle he liked.

Lord Rankin, who'd never approved of Lord Clifford, probably would not be happy that Lord Clifford helped himself, but it was not for me to interfere. Mr. Davis would be incensed—he kept the wine cellar in pristine order and would be blamed for any missing bottles.

I hid my misgivings and returned to the kitchen to continue preparing dishes with Tess.

Mrs. Redfern entered a few hours later, her back stiff and her lips quivering.

"Mrs. Holloway, whatever you have decided to create for supper, you must cease. Mrs. Bywater has declared that her ladyship will take over deciding the menus."

Mrs. Bywater had been leaving the cooking decisions to me, once she'd realized this was best. I was to serve simple meals and keep to a budget, but otherwise, I was free to cook as I pleased. I liked basing each day's menu on what I could find at the markets—much better to see what was available and fresh than to fixate on a certain dish and then not be able to locate the ingredients.

"What sort of menus does she have in mind?" I asked, hiding my trepidation.

"She will send down a list when she is ready. I tried to explain that the household already runs smoothly, particularly the meals, but her ladyship decided she must have the food to her taste. Lady Clifford's digestion is delicate, apparently."

I had the sudden fear that some mad person was out to poison aristocratic ladies in general, but I told myself this was nonsense. Perhaps Lady Clifford did need a specific diet for her health.

I surveyed the beans, carrots, and potatoes I'd already chopped and the lemon tart Tess was finishing up for the oven. If Lady Clifford suddenly wanted a meal of only bone broth and watercress salad, the rest of this would go to waste.

"I will do my best, Mrs. Redfern." I kept myself from heaving an exasperated sigh. Venting my frustration in front of Mrs. Redfern and Tess would do no good.

Mrs. Redfern turned and stalked out. Her rigid anger told me that Lady Clifford was busy making difficult requests upstairs as well.

Tess, who'd been listening in apprehension, burst out, "What we going to do?"

Holding my anger was becoming more difficult by the minute. "We will do what we are told. It is what we are paid to do."

"But—"

"You will have to learn, Tess, that whatever the mistress of a house wants for her meals, you prepare it. It is *her* house, her food, her wishes."

"But Lady Clifford ain't the mistress, is she?" Tess slopped lemon custard onto the table as she filled the tart shell. She hastily wiped up the drops with one finger, which she popped into her mouth.

"She is a guest of the mistress. Besides, this house belongs to Lord and Lady Clifford's son-in-law, as his lordship reminded me when he came down to purloin the best burgundy."

I snatched up the cut potatoes and dumped them into a bowl. They'd keep if I filled the bowl with cold water—I could use them for a shepherd's pie or perhaps a bubble and squeak for the staff if Lady Clifford did not want them. The rest of the vegetables would make a salad or soup, and I knew the servants would make short work of a lemon tart. I saw no benefit in throwing away perfectly good food.

"Well, it ain't right." Tess carried the tart carefully to the oven and set it inside. She closed the door without banging it, as I'd taught her, but made her annoyance known by slamming down the towel she'd used to shield her hand from the heat of the oven. "We work hard and then it's not wanted."

I shared Tess's frustration, but it was part of my task to keep her calm. "We don't yet know what she wants." I filled the bowl of potatoes with water from a pitcher, then sat down, suddenly tired. "We have to wait and see."

"And then prepare the entire meal at the last minute."

"Too true, my girl. So we might as well pause a moment and refresh ourselves."

Tess plopped herself onto a stool and snatched up a bit of carrot, chomping on it. "Don't mind if I do."

"Is Caleb well?" I asked her.

Tess had been walking out with Caleb Greene, a young constable whose beat included Mount Street, since last autumn.

Her cheeks went pink. "He is perfectly well. A good soul, Mrs. H. But don't worry. I won't be rushing off and marrying him. I'm not daft."

"Marriage is not always a bad thing, Tess. With a kind man, you'd be happy and have no worries." Though my marriage had been awful, I'd observed good ones, like that of Joanna and Samuel Millburn, and knew they were possible.

"Rot that. I'd be cooking and cleaning, like I do here. But here I get paid." Tess crunched another carrot. "I prefer working with you, Mrs. H., to looking after a man. Why can't men look after themselves, anyway?"

"Because it's put into their heads from the time they are born that only women can make their lives comfortable. Or so I believe. I never had a brother, so I really don't know how they are raised."

"I'd say you're right. My brother's not right in the head, so he's a different case. I need my wages to take care of him. A husband might not be so understanding."

"Caleb might." I'd met the lad, and he seemed to have a sensible head on his shoulders.

However, I did not trust myself to be the best judge of male persons. Daniel, for instance. I'd first met him when he'd delivered goods to a house I worked in several years ago. I'd thought him only a deliveryman who did odd jobs for whatever he could earn, a personable, winsome fellow with a good heart.

Later I learned that not only did Daniel have a son, but that he could change his persona at will. He might become a City gent, or a dandy who frequented the ballrooms of Paris, or a scruffy tramp. He did this on jobs for the police—he was not part of the police, he'd tried to explain, but I was not supposed to know that, or anything about this part of his life, in fact.

I did know Daniel's job was perilous, and I'd been pulled into the danger with him from time to time. I had lately been thinking it would never do to put my daughter in the same sort of danger.

"Speaking of marriage," Tess said, as though reading my thoughts. "Mr. McAdam ought to marry you. Take you away to that house of his in Kensington. You could look after him and James, and I could come cook for you."

She'd suggested this before. In fact, it had become a favorite topic, Tess's dream of a better life.

"Mr. McAdam is too busy for a wife." I rose. Idleness did not suit me. I'd make a start on the shepherd's pie, which would take time to bake.

"You could help him," Tess said. "You could find out things, as you do. Be a detective or some such, like those Pinkertons, or in the stories Caleb reads."

"Nonsense." I bustled to the larder for butter and cream so I could start mashing the potatoes. "I am a cook," I said when I returned, "and this is all I'll likely ever do. I am fortunate that I do it well, so that I can be hired in good houses."

"Just wait." Tess watched me with a smile. "When Mr. Mc-Adam goes down on one knee, you'll change your mind."

I doubted very much that Daniel had marriage in his thoughts. He liked my company, and that was all. I kissed him

far more often than I should, but we were not young innocents. We knew exactly how far any spooning could go before
it became shameful and scandalous. Both of us had raised
children out of wedlock, and neither of us was in a hurry to be
in such a situation again.

"That will be enough of that," I told Tess severely. I pushed
a bowl heaped with fresh green peas at her. "Shell that lot. I'll
need them for the shepherd's pie."

Tess good-naturedly pulled the bowl to her and reached in
for a handful of pods. "I do love a good shepherd's pie. Put in
lots of juices, Mrs. H."

"I intend to."

I heard a bang of the outside door, and Elsie scuttled into
the kitchen, her cheeks flushed. "It's that handsome vicar, Mrs.
Holloway. Upstairs in the street. He's asking for ya."

7

❖━━━━❖

I quickly rinsed and wiped my hands, snatched up my coat, and charged up the stairs.

I found Mr. Fielding, resplendent in his vicar's suit and dog collar, waiting patiently a few houses down, in the direction of Hyde Park. The day had turned fine, blue breaking through the hovering clouds.

"Mrs. Holloway," Mr. Fielding greeted me. "How lovely to see you. Shall we stroll? Have a chat about charity and good works?"

Blue eyes twinkled in a face with a neatly trimmed beard, Mr. Fielding's dark brown hair equally as neat beneath his understated hat. He wore gloves and carried a walking stick, his ensemble perfectly depicting a middle-class gentleman who watched over a parish in an East End slum. He'd recently been granted the post of suffragan bishop, which was a sort of an assistant to a higher bishop, with other parish vicars answering to him.

I hoped whoever had given him this position did not regret it. Mr. Fielding had begun life as a confidence trickster and, according to Daniel, had not much changed since.

"I have a kitchen to run," I told him.

"Your mistress would be pleased for you to be seen with a vicar. She's a sanctimonious prude, and she likes me. Shall we?"

He held out his arm. I did not take it, but I fell into step with him as we walked toward the park.

"How are the children?" I asked abruptly.

The smug grin left Mr. Fielding's face. "They are ungrateful brats, and I have you to thank for saddling me with them. At least Michael has ceased trying to climb the chimney. He's taken to being underfoot in Mrs. Hodder's kitchen. She'll give notice, mark my words."

Mr. Fielding, earlier this year, had taken in a half-dozen children varying in age from six to sixteen, rescued from an unspeakable life.

It spoke much of him that the children were still with him. He'd promised he wouldn't send them to a workhouse or turn them out, and he'd kept his word.

"Your housekeeper is a good woman," I said with confidence. "All will be well."

"My dear, you have no idea what it is to look after six children from the streets. Like wild dogs, they are. Ah well. My sins have come home to roost, and I am paying penance."

Mr. Fielding looked so morose I couldn't help laughing. "Mr. Fielding, if you were so miserable, you'd have sent them away long ago."

"I'd never do that." Mr. Fielding glanced about as though afraid of being overheard by the few on the street. "Tell no one. I'll be labeled a soft touch and be the target of every fraudster in the metropolis."

"I am certain it won't come to that."

"Perhaps not. But do keep my secret, I beg you. Now, dear lady, I was delighted to receive your missive. Pleased that you requested help only I could give. What can I do for you?"

Now that he'd asked me bluntly, I hesitated. Mr. Fielding, as Daniel frequently pointed out, was not the most trustworthy of men, his collar notwithstanding. He'd become a member of the clergy, Mr. Fielding had admitted to me, first to remove himself from a foster father, a marquess's son, he loathed, and second, for ambition's sake.

However, I did not know many others I could take into my confidence. Mr. Fielding could at least keep things to himself.

"Do you know anything about the Earl of Clifford?" I asked. "Lady Cynthia's father?"

"Never met the man. I have heard he's a reprobate. Or was. Has been living quietly in the country for a number of years, I gather."

"He is now in London. I wish I knew why."

"Ah," Mr. Fielding said in delight. "And you would like me to find out."

"I would have asked Daniel, but he is very busy these days."

"Busy doing the police's dirty work for them—yes, I know. Daniel asked me to look in on you from time to time for him."

"He did?" I halted in surprise. Not because Daniel wanted someone to make certain I was well, but because he'd asked Mr. Fielding to do it.

"Shocking, is it not? My dear brother doesn't trust me an inch—not that I blame him—but he has decided to give me a task looking after the most important person in the world to him."

My face grew warm, and I resumed my steps, speeding them a little. We reached Park Lane, and Mr. Fielding led me across the road when we found a break in traffic. We went through a gate into Hyde Park, which lay wide and green on this May afternoon.

"James is the most important person in the world to Daniel," I corrected him.

"Of course," Mr. Fielding said cynically. "Fatherhood is all. Or so I am told. Living with the hellions for the past few months has made me realize such sentiments are all puffery. Fatherhood is devilishly hard. Instinct makes us protect the children so our species will survive, and that is the whole of it. The noble ideals imposed on us about it are balderdash. I'd use a stronger word if I weren't with a lady."

I'd believe him if he weren't so adamant and red in the face. "So our *species* will survive?" I repeated. "Are you a follower of Mr. Darwin?"

Mr. Fielding squeezed my arm and hopped a step, his humor restored. "I wouldn't be a good ecclesiastical if I wasn't," he said with mock solemnity. "I do believe we descended from apes—why else would I know so many fellows who are the spitting image of monkeys? And some ladies too. Whether God had anything to do with that, I don't know."

"Gracious, I do hope you do not speak these alarming ideas from your pulpit, Mr. Fielding."

"Never." He flashed a grin. "I give them the epistles for the day and take my sermons from them. Or I read out a sermon another bloke wrote—I tell them it's by the other bloke so no one comes 'round later and thumps me over the head with their book of collected sermons. But if I find one that's clever, I read it. Saves me the bother of writing my own."

At least he studied the sermons and the lessons, I reflected. Perhaps some of the ideas in them would rub off on him.

"We are straying from my question," I said, "which I believe you have done on purpose. I am interested in what brings Lord Clifford to London, and if his presence poses any danger to Lady Cynthia. Her parents claim they have her best interests in mind, but I am not so certain. If they take her home to the country, she will be more or less a prisoner there. There are not many choices in life for a spinster."

"Even a stunningly beautiful one. She *is* a stunner, you will agree, Mrs. Holloway, especially in those trousers. If I had any inkling toward marriage, I'd do her the honor." He shrugged. "Which she would turn down in a flash, so we are both safe."

Mr. Fielding spoke glibly, but I saw a flicker of pain in his eyes. He'd lost a woman close to him recently, a good-hearted one, and while he never spoke of her, I knew he grieved.

"Mr. Fielding . . ."

"I agree with you, Mrs. Holloway." Mr. Fielding raised his hands. "They'd shut her away, fearing her oddity—or more likely, her blunt tongue. Lady Cynthia is their only surviving child, and she's an unmarried woman with strong opinions and scandalous friends. Her ma and pa will either keep her stuck at home or try to marry her to a boring aristocrat who will squash her spirit. I don't mind at all helping you save someone so original."

"Good." I let out my breath. "I have no idea how you will go about discovering their motives, but I must beg you to be discreet."

"My dear woman, I am a master of discretion. I convinced the Church of England to let me take orders, didn't I? They had to have been mad to do it, but I tend my flock well enough, and they don't regret it thus far."

Mr. Fielding stood still and gazed across the massive park toward the Serpentine. The original Crystal Palace had stood on the vast green, erected the year I was born, for the Great

Exhibition of science and technology. Less than a year later, the Crystal Palace had been dismantled and rebuilt—and expanded upon—in Sydenham, south of the Thames. The place had been a marvel when first opened, I'd heard, and the current incarnation was larger and even more impressive than the first.

"I will discover Lord Clifford's scheme," Mr. Fielding said. His exuberance faded, and his expression became serious. "If *you* worry, then there is cause to. I learned that lesson. I will discover his business and impart all to you, and then we will decide how we can stop him."

M r. Fielding walked me home. I quite enjoyed my short stroll—it was a fine day, and Hyde Park was one of the few places in London a body could find a breath of fresh air.

Mr. Fielding bowed and tipped his hat to me when he left me at the head of the outside stairs in Mount Street.

"Thank you, Mrs. Holloway," he said loudly. "Your interest in charitable works for the destitute is heartening. I only wish more domestics were as compassionate about their fellow souls."

"You rather overdo things, Mr. Fielding," I admonished him in a quiet voice.

"Only giving what's expected of me." He dropped his volume to match mine. "Also, my speeches will keep you in the good graces of your mistress. Carry on with your fine cooking, Mrs. H. And no worries."

He winked, straightened his hat, and strode off, assuming a countenance of extreme piety.

I smiled to myself as I descended to the kitchen. I liked Mr.

Fielding, despite Daniel's warnings, but I knew I could not let myself soften completely toward him. He was indeed a reprobate, which is why I'd sent him after Lord Clifford. A fraudulent man would recognize another fraudulent man's activities.

I entered the kitchen to find Mrs. Redfern, who relaxed in relief when she beheld me. "Thank heavens, Mrs. Holloway. Lady Clifford is on her way down."

"Down?" I blinked as I shrugged off my light coat and hung it on its peg. "I thought she'd send a list of changes she wanted."

"As did I, but she has decided to come herself." She broke off abruptly as a light patter on the slates announced the arrival of her ladyship.

As Lady Clifford halted languidly in the passage outside the kitchen, I was struck by how much she resembled Cynthia's younger sister, Emily, who had first hired me to work in this house.

Lady Clifford had the same pale hair as her daughters, a delicately boned face, light blue eyes, and an air of being too fatigued to keep herself upright. I recalled my first interview with Lady Rankin—Emily—and how she'd peered at me tiredly over her writing table and said she supposed I'd do.

Her mother now regarded me with a similar weariness. Her gown, a cream-colored organdy, was adorned with lace on the high collar, cuffs, and placket of the bodice. The gown reminded me of those Emily had worn, and I wondered if Lady Clifford's choice had been a deliberate one.

Lady Clifford peered vaguely into the kitchen as Mrs. Redfern, Tess, and I quickly curtsied.

"Mrs. . . . ?" She gazed at me, eyes half-closed as though trying to see me in the dim light.

"Holloway, your ladyship. How may I help you?"

"Come with me." Lady Clifford beckoned and wandered down the passageway, me behind her, until she came to the larder.

She gazed into the room—a long chamber lit by one high window, filled with shelves of crockery and boxes of food-stuffs, as well as empty crates that had held today's vegetables stacked neatly, ready to be returned to the vendor. Lady Clifford entered and glanced about as though she'd never seen a larder before.

"The meals," she said, not looking at me. "Too heavy. An herb salad and a bit of rice. That is all I require."

"I am happy to cook a special meal for you, your ladyship. To serve you at supper or on a tray, or however you like."

Lady Clifford's fair brows arched. "This is for the entire family, my dear. It is growing far too warm to continue with the fare we had last night. Whole roast chickens and beef and potatoes." She made a delicate shudder.

"Mr. Bywater prefers it," I explained. "He is hungry after his day in the City."

"Neville ought to stay home then." For a moment, Lady Clifford's languor slipped, and she spoke as a sister irritated with her younger brother. "And the meat pies." Another shudder. "My dear, my brother might like them, but I loathe them. It reminds me of a horrible boardinghouse I stayed in when I first married. That was long before Reginald—his lordship—came into his inheritance."

"I understand, your ladyship." I thought it unfair she decided that no one would eat what *she* loathed, but it was not my place to say such a thing.

"Good. Then we'll have no more of that. No gravies, no sauces. Simple salads, perhaps some fish from time to time, but only with lemon and a little minced herbs on the top. His lordship doesn't like his meals fussy."

I knew that if I served Mr. Bywater salad, rice, and a tiny portion of dry fish with a smattering of thyme, I would have to quickly look for another post. He preferred plain fare to anything complicated, which I agreed with—food does not have to be complicated to be good—but Lady Clifford was taking things a bit far.

"Mummy?" Cynthia's voice floated down the back stairs, followed by the arrival of Cynthia herself, her hurry stirring the tails of her man's frock coat. "Mummy, what are you doing down here? Papa is searching for you."

"Saving his digestion from these awful meals," Lady Clifford said, as though I weren't standing a few feet away.

"There is nothing wrong with the meals, Mummy. Uncle likes Mrs. Holloway's cooking. He's cross as a bear when his stomach isn't happy. He'll be impossible to live with if she does not carry on as usual."

"We should all give in to my brother's whims, should we?" Lady Clifford asked in annoyance.

"Better than existing on leaves and rice. Papa washes down his meals with so much port, he never worries what he eats, if he even notices."

"*Cynthia.*" Lady Clifford became a mother now, admonishing her wayward child.

"I'll not be sitting down to a parsley salad every evening. I prefer more robust victuals. Whatever you are cooking for supper is fine, Mrs. Holloway."

"Cynthia, you are not the mistress of this house. Of any house."

Cynthia let the dig at her unmarried state float by. "Auntie

is at the moment, and she'll fight tooth and claw to keep Uncle
happy. It really is the best way for peace in the house. You
must see that."

Lady Clifford's brows slammed together. "Your uncle and
aunt are trumped-up nobodies."

"Careful, Mummy. You are Uncle's sister, so you were a
trumped-up nobody right alongside him at one time in your
life."

Lady Clifford flushed, but she seemed to have forgotten my
existence. "I married well. That is the difference."

"If you are waving your choice of Papa as an example
of how well I can do, I will pass on marriage altogether,
thank you."

Lady Clifford drew herself up, facing Cynthia squarely. I
did not move, keeping as still as I could in the shadows.

"Cynthia, if you believe you have a say in the matter, you
are mistaken. Your father and I can no longer bear the keeping of you. You are well past the age when you ought to be
married with a husband looking after you. You now exist on
our charity, and that is running out. You cannot expect your
aunt and uncle to keep you either."

Cynthia's face lost color, but she kept her voice steady.
"Papa has run through the last of the money already, has he?
Only yesterday he was telling me he was in funds."

"For important things," Lady Clifford said. "Not for paying
the bills of a girl-child who prances about in men's clothing
trying to be shocking. You are nothing but a spoiled chit, Cynthia. If you were a son, things would be different. You'd be the
heir. As it is . . ."

Lady Clifford abruptly ceased speaking, her shoulders sag-
ging. She pressed her hands to her face as grief broke through
the wall she placed between herself and it.

Cynthia lost her derisiveness and gathered her mother into her arms. "There now." Her voice went soft. "Don't take on so." She sent me an apologetic glance. "Go on with the cooking, Mrs. H. Leave her to me."

I nodded, my heart squeezing in sympathy. Cynthia rubbed Lady Clifford's back as her mother sobbed on her shoulder.

Cynthia's brother had taken his own life years ago, and Lord and Lady Clifford had not recovered from it. *Who could?* I asked myself as I slipped past Cynthia and along the passageway to the kitchen.

No one at all. The tragedy would cling to them for their lifetime.

T ess and I finished supper and placed the dishes in the dumbwaiter to be sent to the dining room. I gave them potato and leek soup, asparagus braised and sprinkled with lemon zest and parsley, slices of roast beef with a green salad—to show Lady Clifford I acknowledged her taste—and finished with the lemon cake I'd perfected last night. All plates came back empty, including Lady Clifford's.

"She ate every crumb," Mr. Davis reported as he returned from supervising the serving upstairs. He slid off his coat and hung it on the back of a chair in the servants' hall, where Tess and I were taking our evening meal, and slumped into the chair. "His lordship, if you please, told me the wine he took—and opened far too soon—did not go with the beef, and he didn't think much of the vintage. If Lord Clifford had asked me instead of helping himself, I'd have decanted a nice Côtes du Rhône, which would have done splendidly."

He shook his head and snatched up a newspaper that lay askew on the table.

"I'm sorry, Mr. Davis," I said around my mouthfuls of shepherd's pie—which had turned out well, the potato crust browned and tasty. "I tried to stop him."

"Nothing you could have done, Mrs. Holloway." Mr. Davis began turning over the leaves of the newspaper. "He's a lordship, and we're not. Perfectly fine if *they* steal things, innit?" Mr. Davis's polished tones often slipped when he was angry. "Speaking of aristocrats, it seems the police have begun rounding up the blokes who assassinated those gentlemen in Dublin last week. What's the world coming to?"

"What have Irish murderers to do with aristos?" Tess asked. She'd already made short work of her shepherd's pie and lingered over a cup of tea. "Seems like the men what did the stabbings were the opposite of genteel. Fenians and their like."

Last week, in a place called Phoenix Park in Dublin, the chief secretary for Ireland and the Irish undersecretary had both been brutally and shockingly murdered, stabbed to death in the early evening as they walked home through the park.

"I mean the police are talking to some of the peerage." Mr. Davis tapped the page. "Doesn't say whether the aristos were helping the assassins or are friends of the deceased." He peered more closely at the paper. "This fellow here seems familiar, but I can't place him."

I rose to look over his shoulder at the small photograph he indicated. It was blurry, but the man Mr. Davis had his finger on was clear enough, with a short gray beard, a tall hat, a severe suit, and an even more severe frown. His name was not stated in the text around it, but if the man was a peer, the newspaper would hardly wish to be sued for libel for implying he had a hand in the murders.

It was the man half behind the first who caught my eye.

He'd turned his face away from the camera, as though not wanting to be seen, so only a part of his jaw and slicked back hair under a top hat could be viewed. However, I knew that curve of jaw, the thick dark hair, and the manner of standing very, very well.

He might not wish to show his face, but the man behind the stern aristocrat was Daniel McAdam.

8

Mr. Davis did not notice my unease as I peered at the photograph, nor did he recognize Daniel. *I* would not have had I not been as familiar with Daniel as I was. His guise as a gentleman completely absorbed him.

I resumed my seat as Mr. Davis perused the article. "Seems funds have moved from England to Ireland, but they don't know from whom. The Irish Home Rule question is so heated I wouldn't put it past some of our gents to sabotage it. Or help it along. It's hard to say."

Usually, when Mr. Davis started going on about political doings, I let my mind wander. Now I lifted my teacup and slurped a good bit of tea without noticing the taste. What had Daniel to do with this peer? And the assassinations in Ireland?

I knew Daniel got himself involved in dangerous undertakings, but this one was truly terrifying. The anarchists responsible for these killings—a group named the Invincibles—would stop at nothing to murder Daniel if they thought he hunted them.

But why on earth should Daniel be after these assassins at all? The police in Dublin had already arrested several men, and the newspapers had reported that even more culprits had been found. The photograph Mr. Davis pointed out had been taken here in London, outside the Houses of Parliament, nowhere near Ireland.

No, Daniel must have been with this gray-bearded man for other reasons, and a journalist had taken the opportunity to snap their photo as they emerged from the building.

The question gnawed at me. When Mr. Davis abandoned the paper and focused on the shepherd's pie I'd fetched him from the kitchen, I read the entire article.

The journalist remained vague about what English or Irish peers they suspected had given the anarchists help and instead concentrated on the assassins involved—one with the interesting moniker of James "Skin-the-Goat" Fitzharris—and the grief of the murdered men's families. The fact that the victims were gentlemen prominent in the government caused very real concern. Would the prime minister be next? The queen herself?

When the article wound into wilder and wilder speculations, I set it aside. Daniel had not been mentioned, either by name or as the lordship's companion. He'd been ignored. That was a relief.

Daniel had enemies, and I did not want those enemies to realize that the man in respectable gentleman's clothing and the good-natured deliveryman with holes in his gloves were one and the same. That would be a very real disaster. I could only hope that Daniel was taking many more precautions than usual.

* * *

That evening, Cynthia had Sara, the upstairs maid, pack a bag for her, and she left home for a stay with Lady Covington the next morning.

Mrs. Bywater, as I had predicted, approved. Cynthia explained she'd met Lady Covington at the Crystal Palace and Lady Covington had taken a liking to her. Mrs. Bywater believed that Cynthia making friends with Baron Covington and his family was an excellent opportunity. After all, Baron Covington was single with no heir and ought to be looking for a bride. Even if he did not choose Cynthia, perhaps one of his friends would.

Lady Clifford was less certain, but she did not object. I uncharitably mused that Lady Clifford did not mind someone else taking care of Cynthia for a time.

Mr. Bywater was the only one who raised an objection, saying it strange that Lady Covington had any interest in Cynthia, but Mrs. Bywater and Lord and Lady Clifford overruled him. Cynthia's father was all for the scheme, saying it might teach Cynthia to wear decent clothing and stay far from her more scandalous friends. Leave the scandals to *him*, Lord Clifford had finished jokingly.

"Don't get yourself poisoned, your ladyship," Tess advised when Cynthia came down to the kitchen to say her farewells.

"Not a bit of it," Cynthia answered jovially. She'd dressed as a respectable young lady in a blue gown with tight sleeves, black buttons, and dark blue braid for trim. Her hat with a small brim perched on the back of her head. "Lady Covington's family has not taken ill so far—I'll eat only what they do, and I'll be well. If there's any doubt, I'll nip out to a vendor's cart and munch on whatever they sell."

"I will miss you," I said suddenly. I hadn't realized it, but as Cynthia tugged her gloves straight and prepared to leave, I knew I'd looked forward each day to chatting with her or hearing her laughter ring through the kitchen.

"And I you, Mrs. H." She blinked and touched a finger to the corner of her eye. "I'll be back, though, and I'll write, to tell you how I am getting on."

"Do take care."

"Of course." Cynthia shook my hand, patted my shoulder, and strode out through the scullery.

"I hope she'll be all right," Tess said as we watched her march up the stairs.

"As do I, Tess." I let out a long breath. "As do I."

The remainder of the weekend passed uneasily. I saw nothing of Mr. Fielding or James—or Daniel. I would attend Mr. Thanos's lecture with Lady Cynthia on Monday evening—she had already persuaded Mrs. Bywater to let me accompany her. I was surprised Mrs. Bywater had sanctioned this, as she did not like me being friends with Cynthia, but I supposed she weighed the damage to Cynthia's—and her own—reputation if Cynthia ran off to the Crystal Palace alone. Cynthia would go regardless, and I would at least be with her to guard her reputation.

When Cynthia had settled in with Lady Covington, she wrote me a letter, which was hand delivered to me on Sunday afternoon by an errand boy who expected tuppence for his trouble.

Well, I am here. I already see this entire house is poison-
ous, and by that I mean that the inhabitants, with a few
exceptions, loathe one another. The only one rather re-

moved is Sir Arthur, who is preoccupied by his Polytechnic, but good old George (which is what I call young Baron Covington) does not like Sir Arthur and considers him a parasite.

The family gathers every evening for a meal. Good old George sits at the head of the table, trying to be pompous, with Lady Covington—the real head of the household—at its foot. The various other members—Miss and Mr. Morris (Harriet and Jonathan, Lady C.'s daughter and son) sit on one side with Mrs. Hume (Erica, the stepdaughter), Sir Arthur Maddox, and me on the other.

I face Jonathan, who needs to be watched. He's the very devil. Dear Jonathan is up to his neck in schemes and scrapes, lending friends money that is never seen again. He will not admit who these friends are or what the money is for—highly suspicious.

The maid, Jepson, distrusted me entirely at first, but I think she is warming to me. That means she carries me a cup of tea without such a severe frown. The frown is still there, but it has softened a small amount. Lady Covington puts her well-being into the hands of Jepson, which I also think is highly suspicious.

Lady C. believes Jonathan can do no wrong, suggesting the strange sort of maternal blindness that afflicts some women. On the other hand, her poor daughter, Harriet, can do no right. Lady C. mimics my parents in her adamancy in finding a husband for Harriet, but there is some difference. My parents have no idea what to do with me, while Lady Covington is determined Harriet shall marry none but the best.

Harriet has a hard time of it, not coming from a titled family herself—being a baron's stepdaughter takes her off the lists of the most finicky families. Her own father was no aristo, but I gather quite wealthy in his own right. One of these railroad magnates. Lady Covington met her second husband via her first—they were both on the board of the same railway company. I gather Lady Covington's first husband died in some tragic circumstance, but I haven't been able to find out what happened to him. The subject is abruptly changed whenever the man's name comes up (he was also Jonathan Morris).

No one has taken sick thus far, but there was a near thing. Lady Covington yesterday afternoon said her stomach ached slightly. Jepson was about to mix her a large glassful of some powder from an unmarked packet, but I happened to be passing the bedchamber and jumped in to offer a set of powders I'd found jolly good at passing off indigestion. I managed to foist them onto Lady Covington, who was willing to try them, before Jepson could grab them and throw them in a rubbish pail. I mixed the powder—which was bicarbonate of soda I'd procured at the local chemists for just this circumstance. Lady Covington drank it up, with Jepson hovering like a disapproving bat, and after the lady belched heartily, she declared she felt much better. She continued in roaring good health all night and continues this morning. It was after this episode that Jepson's frowns grew less fierce.

This makes me wonder: is Jepson on Lady Covington's side or is she not? Surely she'd be less happy with me for curing her mistress's dyspepsia if she were trying to murder her. Then again, she might be buttering me up so that next time I do not interfere.

It is difficult for me to read people, Mrs. H. I am not certain how you do it so well.

I will continue posting you my observations of the family, which so far have shown me that they are spoiled and ungrateful. Makes me ashamed of my own pique with my family, but then, my family can be overbearing.

Erica has been disappearing from the house often, I gather, but where she goes, I have no idea. Neither does anyone else. She takes a maid, but the maid is always sent home with the excuse that Erica is meeting with a friend and doesn't need her. Erica returns in a hansom and is vague about where she's been. I suspect a liaison, but with whom, I do not know. Erica is not a beautiful woman and is rather stiff mannered, but perhaps with her paramour she is sweet and loving. I have difficulty imagining it though.

The whole lot of them are keeping things from Lady Covington. Good old George sits on the board of the aforementioned railway company—a private line. George likes to talk about his business, but I gather he's rather bad at it. Lady C. is constantly holding up his father as a prime example of a brilliant businessman, which must rankle him.

In my family, and in Bobby's and Miss Townsend's, talking about money and business, especially at the supper table, is considered rather gauche, but then Lady C. wasn't raised in the peerage. Her father, somebody-or-other Maddox, was an entrepreneur, and Sir Arthur, his only son, is as well. Sir Arthur too twits dear old George on his lack of business sense.

George points out that Sir Arthur now runs a school, as though that is a horrible scandal—like a brothel—at which Sir Arthur only looks weary. I try to like Sir Arthur, as he was kind enough to give Mr. Thanos a fine flat and a job as a lecturer, but he can be a tedious bore, I'm sorry to say. I will never express this opinion to his face, however, because I do not want to endanger Mr. Thanos's position in any way.

Harriet is quite a frustrated young lady, I'd say. She does wish to marry, I think, but any mention of a suitable gentleman is brushed aside with a scoff. When Erica, who had a bad marriage as you know, complained that Harriet was an ungrateful harridan for turning up her nose at perfectly good gentlemen, Harriet threw a spoon at her. Lady Covington banished Harriet from the table, and Harriet stomped off with her nose in the air.

I found Harriet later, crying her eyes out. I tried to comfort her, saying marriage shouldn't be entered into lightly, and I agreed she ought to be picky, but Harriet stared at me as though I'd run mad. This morning, she disappeared from the house for a time, though she returned before anyone raised the alarm. She was much happier then, and I suppose she simply needed a bit of time to herself, perhaps for a brisk walk. She was flushed and windblown when she returned.

There you have what I know so far about the family. When we dined, all dishes were served by the footmen, and we ate the same thing. The cook is nowhere as talented as you, but she turns out some decent grub. If any member of the family refused a dish, I did as well, eating only what was taken by all. Lady Covington is always served first. Apparently, the late Lord Covington paid her this courtesy, and the custom remains. Dear George tried to look gracious when she took the first helping, but I saw his resentment.

His resentment stems from the fact that she is given deference by all the staff, not because she is greedy with *the food. Lady Covington, though she has a good appetite, takes far less on her plate than the younger ones. Sir Arthur eats like a horse. It is interesting that only Lady C. takes ill, because the others consume enough for an army. If the poison were put into the food in the kitchen, everyone at the table would be writhing in agony.*

I will try to find out more about Erica's and Harriet's mysterious outings, where Jonathan's money actually goes, and how poison gets into the house. I managed to purloin one of the powder packets that Jepson tried to feed Lady C., and I will take it to a chemist to see what he believes is in it.

I must finish now to send this to you. I wish I was in your kitchen, nattering away with you, but I will be a good soldier, and remain on duty until the poisoner is uncovered.

Yours in haste,
Corporal Shires (saluting)

O n Monday, I returned from my half day out with Grace, helped Tess prepare supper, and then changed into my best frock and boarded a train with Cynthia, Bobby, and Miss Townsend to Sydenham and the Crystal Palace.

Cynthia had procured my ticket, and I found myself in a first-class carriage with the three young ladies. I never felt comfortable traveling first class—servants rode third class—but Cynthia saw no reason I should not journey with her. I sat on the corridor side of the coach, my hands folded in my lap, trying to be unobtrusive.

Bobby, dressed in a gentleman's suit with a high hat, so resembled a male that the conductor did not realize she was a lady—he called her *sir*. Unlike willowy Cynthia and Miss Townsend, Bobby was a bit plump around the middle and was the very image of a young gent who liked his pudding. She cut her hair short—couldn't be bothered with it, she'd told me—and slicked it back with pomade. If she pasted on a mustache, none would be able to tell her from a man.

Miss Townsend, with whom Bobby now lived, was an artist, and did not dress in the restrictive, highly fashionable clothing other young ladies of her class did. I liked her simple close-fitting chocolate-colored gown with cream lace. Her hat was the same shade as the gown, its front brim adorned by a short cream lace veil.

Cynthia had forsaken male dress tonight for a maroon gown with black trim and a delicate bon bon of a pillbox hat set on her carefully curled fair hair. She did not wear a veil, as she'd once declared she hated the things. If this hat had originally had a veil, she'd torn it off.

"Couldn't let Thanos down," Cynthia said when Bobby chided her for looking like a fashion plate. "It's his debut, as it were, and I'd hate for him to be embarrassed because his best woman chum is shocking the audience by dressing as a gent. No one minds you doing as you like, Bobby," she added hastily.

Bobby nodded, not offended. "They're used to me. Shock has worn off. Or, like the conductor chappie, they have no idea." She chortled.

Miss Townsend drew out a box with glasses and a bottle of brandy, and poured out for all of us. I accepted a goblet politely and took the barest sip, though I was not one for spirits.

"Mr. Thanos would never be embarrassed by you," Miss Townsend told Cynthia. "He likes you too well."

Cynthia's cheeks grew pink. "But his new employer will be

nigh, and I now take meals with Sir Arthur. I must come off as demure and ordinary, so I won't be banned from the house before Mrs. H. can wrap up the investigation."

Bobby and Miss Townsend knew all about Lady Covington's troubles, and in fact had eagerly inquired if we'd made any progress when Cynthia and I had entered the compartment.

"They're coming, you say?" Miss Townsend asked.

Cynthia took a deep gulp of the brandy. "The whole lot of them. Wouldn't miss dear Arthur's presentation about his new Polytechnic. Well, Lady Covington said that, and the rest of the brood had to agree they'd toddle along with her. They were happy when I said I'd be traveling down with friends—I think the younger generation is glad to see the back of me for a time."

"Be careful George doesn't propose." Miss Townsend raised her glass in a toast. "I'd have to start calling you Baroness."

Cynthia scoffed. "No fear. I know Auntie hopes that good old George will fall hopelessly in love with me and offer me an immense engagement ring, but I see no sign of it. Not the least bit interested in me, is old George, thank heaven." She wiped her forehead in relief. "Young Mr. Morris, now, has tried to corner me several times, *not* to propose, if you take my meaning, but I rebuff him. I'm not averse to punching him in the nose if I have to. He takes my rejection amiably, but I've learned not to be in a lonely corner when he is in the house."

"He is rather handsome," Miss Townsend pointed out. "Perhaps Auntie Bywater wouldn't mind if you married the younger fellow, who's bound to inherit a fortune sometime."

"Rot that." Cynthia shuddered. "I'd kick you if I didn't know you were teasing. Besides, I suspect young Jonathan has his hand in the jam pot. Stealing from his own mother—I ask you."

"Sounds a right hellion," Bobby agreed. "Besides, Cynthia prefers a gent who wears spectacles."

Cynthia flushed a bright red while the other two ladies guffawed at her expense. I sipped more brandy, pretending not to notice.

When we arrived at the Crystal Palace, the weather good for walking the short distance from the station, I was pleased to see a crowd. Fountains played in the gardens, and the interior of the Palace was lit by gaslights, rendering it a shining beacon in the night.

The walkways inside looked odd at night without the sun beaming on them, as we made for the space in the nave where Mr. Thanos and others from the Polytechnic would lecture.

We reached the south end of the building near the natural history exhibitions. A platform for the speakers had been erected in front of the screen of the kings and queens of England that adorned the very end of the Palace, the statuary making a regal backdrop. Rows of chairs had been placed before the platform, though a long fountain rather butted into the space, and seats had to be divided around it. Potted plants and live trees framed the dais, as though the lecturers sat in a slice of jungle.

I spied Lady Covington and family. They were already seated in the front, which told me they must have arrived by an earlier train. Lady Covington sat upright, with Erica beside her. Jonathan lounged on Lady Covington's other side, with Harriet fidgeting next to him. George sat next to Erica, a look of disapproval on his face as he studied the crowd around him. Sir Arthur Maddox lingered near the platform, bouncing on his toes as he waited for the program to begin.

Mr. Thanos, his dark hair combed flat, his spectacles flashing in the lamplight, stood with a clump of gentlemen similarly clad in dark suits. Mr. Thanos clutched some papers, possibly his speech, and was crumpling them absently. He brightened when he caught sight of us, lifted his hand in greeting, dropped his papers, and scrambled to retreive them.

Miss Townsend led us to a row behind Lady Covington's family. As I filed in to my seat, apologizing to those I passed, I caught sight of a man in the back. No mistaking his neatly trimmed beard, clerical collar, and beatific expression. Mr. Fielding. I was busily wondering why he'd come when the man beside him turned around.

I stopped, treading on a older gentleman's foot, and my skirts, which I'd held out of the way, fell from my slack hands. The gentleman I'd tripped over bit back a curse and glared at me.

The man next to Mr. Fielding was Daniel. He saw me—I know he did—but he looked right through me as he turned to speak to a gentleman on his right. That man was the unnamed aristocrat from the newspaper, the one who might have something to do with the brutal murders in Dublin.

9

After a hasty apology to the gentleman I'd stepped on, I took my seat between Cynthia and Miss Townsend, my hands trembling.

I forced myself not to look back. I knew I'd seen Daniel, and he'd very carefully not acknowledged me.

What on earth was he doing here? He'd known I planned to attend Mr. Thanos's lecture, and that Cynthia and the others would be here too. Perhaps this aristocrat he followed about had decided that listening to lectures from tutors in the new Polytechnic was just the thing. I chafed with my ignorance. I hoped James would visit me soon and let me know more about what Daniel was up to.

The presentation began. Sir Arthur Maddox stepped up to the platform, where the lecturers now sat in a line of chairs behind a podium. The iron girders of the Crystal Palace soared above him and the medieval-style screen lent the scene dignity. The Palace's dark glass reflected gaslights that winked like stars.

Sir Arthur cleared his throat and spoke loudly.

"My friends, I welcome you. We stand in a cathedral of learning, originally built to exhibit the many scientific wonders of the world. It was rebuilt to show us not only natural marvels but also cultures of exotic places and historic sites such as Pompeii and ancient Egypt. All the learning of the globe, placed into one magnificent building."

He indicated the arched glass and vast space around us with a sweeping gesture. We applauded. Even Jonathan pounded his gloved hands together and shouted, "Hear! Hear!"

"London's new Polytechnic, funded by generous donors, while not housed in such a magnificent building as this one, will also encompass the science of the world, the newest findings and theories put into practical use for the benefit of all ladies and gentlemen of Britain."

More applause. Jonathan added a loud "Huzzah!" before his mother admonished him to silence.

Sir Arthur went on about the sorts of things that would be studied—mathematics, experiments on scientific ideas, photography, electricity and its oddness, and other blindingly new disciplines I knew little of.

He finished to rousing applause, Jonathan springing to his feet. Harriet pulled him back down with a scowl.

The speakers began, the tutors from the new school explaining what they'd be lecturing on and expounding upon some of their theories. Most was beyond me, and I suspected beyond much of the audience. But Sir Arthur and the other founders of the Polytechnic were hoping to raise funds tonight, and a gentleman or lady didn't have to understand the science to be fascinated and open his or her purse.

As the lectures continued, I fretted about Daniel. I longed to turn and gaze at him, but this would be foolish. I did not want to give away that I was acquainted with him, and I could only hope that Cynthia, Bobby, and Miss Townsend would not expose him either.

Amid applause for a speaker on the luminiferous aether departing the podium, Sir Arthur announced Mr. Elgin Thanos, lecturer in mathematics.

Cynthia stiffened beside me as Mr. Thanos stepped forward, setting a sheaf of papers on the stand. He cleared his throat and adjusted his spectacles, nervously trying not to notice the audience waiting for him to begin. A slate blackboard stood behind him, and Mr. Thanos fiddled with a piece of chalk in his hand.

"I will be giving lectures in theoretical mathematics," Mr. Thanos began as the crowd quieted. "Theory, yes, though the Polytechnic is keen to research practical matters, because from theory comes many scientific advancements."

He paused. The audience rustled programs, some interested, some already wishing they could move to the refreshments promised after the lectures. Cynthia wrapped her hand around my wrist and squeezed.

Mr. Thanos cleared his throat. "For instance, because of a theory on how light could be etched onto a metal plate if the plate was coated in some substance, photography was born. Now we can all have a portrait done without hiring an expensive artist."

He paused, as though waiting for laughter. A few titters came, including one throaty chuckle from Miss Townsend, an artist who occasionally painted portraits.

"Oh," Mr. Thanos said, catching sight of her. "My apologies to the artists in the room."

This did bring a laugh, which surprised him. Mr. Thanos beamed at everyone and continued.

"Another stride forward in science happened in electromagnetism, long thought only a theory of mathematics, batted about by scientists sitting in comfortable chairs, but these theories made possible the telegraph, which sends messages through lines across the world in an instant, and now can vibrate a diaphragm to send a human voice along the same sort of lines. A business in Manchester is now using such a device to convey messages every day."

This received more attention, and Mr. Thanos warmed to his subject. He continued talking about inventions involving electricity, then moved back to theory.

"There is a conundrum that has been dogging mathematicians since the seventeenth century, known as Fermat's Last Theorem. Monsieur Fermat wrote an equation in the margin of a manuscript, stating that he knew the equation to be true, but the proof of it was too long to write in that space. No one has ever found a way to prove this theorem, though mathematicians have tried for two centuries. What a wonder if a student or teacher at the Polytechnic could solve the conundrum. It is a very simple idea . . ."

He started for the board, trying to juggle chalk and papers and continue speaking at the same time. Mr. Thanos predictably dropped his papers, which scattered every which way as the audience chortled.

Mr. Thanos collected the sheets, but could not manage to hold them and write at the same time. Cynthia released my arm—thank heavens, as she was gripping it rather tightly—

sprang to her feet, and pushed her way to the aisle. She held her skirts out of her way as she hurried to the platform and up on it.

Mr. Thanos regarded her in some alarm. The audience began to clap again, especially the gentlemen, who were pleased to see such a lovely young lady before them.

Cynthia firmly took the chalk from Mr. Thanos's hand and whispered something to him. He looked startled but thrust one of the pages at her. He watched worriedly until Cynthia began to write on the board, then he returned to the podium, removed his spectacles, dabbed his face with a handkerchief, and looped the spectacles around his ears again.

"My . . . er . . . friend, Cynth—er, Lady Cynthia Shires—will write out Fermat's theorem. It is quite simple, and that is what is perplexing."

I heard whispers around me, and Jonathan leaned back to peer at me. "*Friend?*" he stated in a soft voice. "Of course. Dear Cynthia is an enigma, is she not?"

"Hush," Lady Covington said. "Cynthia is a fine young lady, and you will not gossip about her."

Her tone was admonishing but not sharp, as though she couldn't bear to speak harshly to Jonathan. Jonathan winked at me but closed his mouth.

I expected Cynthia to write a string of numbers on the board, but it was a sentence: *For integers n > 2, the equation $a^n + b^n = c^n$ cannot be solved with positive integers a, b, and c.*

That was all. What it meant, heaven knew.

Cynthia finished writing, but she remained poised by the board, chalk in hand, waiting for Mr. Thanos to signal her. As Mr. Thanos explained what the statement meant—I was never clear exactly what—she noted what he indicated.

They'd done this before, I realized, though I'd not observed it. Cynthia often met Mr. Thanos, along with a group of ladies and gentlemen, at a public house near the British Museum. These people of learning gathered in an upstairs room to read or lecture to one another or discuss art, music, or science of the day. I imagined Cynthia had begun writing equations for Mr. Thanos so he could pontificate on them without having to stop and scratch things on a slate or blackboard.

Mr. Thanos continued his lecture, most of which I did not understand. He tried to tie in the obscure equation, which only had one number in it, as far as I could see, to the scientific discoveries certain to be found at the new Polytechnic.

The listeners hung on his words, though privately I did not believe they understood any more than I did. Mr. Thanos was a handsome young man, however, which must have pleased the ladies, while the gentlemen enjoyed watching Cynthia scribble, her body swaying as she did so.

Mr. Thanos finished and received enthusiastic applause— I clapped until my hands tingled.

Cynthia returned to her seat, flushed and breathless. "He never can write and speak at the same time. I have no idea how he'll manage when he begins his classes."

"You can attend with him and help, as you did tonight."

Cynthia scrunched up her face. "*If* the Polytechnic admits women. Wouldn't want the walls to fall in. Ha."

"You'd be his assistant, not a student," I said. "However, they could not stop you acquiring knowledge while you were at it. Others might control where your body goes, but they cannot hinder your mind."

Cynthia laughed, her good humor restored. "Always the philosopher, Mrs. H. Well, now, the lectures are done—let us go have a large slice of cake."

Refreshments had been set up a little way down the walk, among a statue garden outside the Pompeian Court. The Pompeian Court consisted of a replica of an entire house from that unfortunate city, its door open to welcome visitors, though none went inside at this time. The refreshments tables were dominated by statues around the main fountain, one of James II of England, said its plaque, another of Dr. Johnson, who, according to the notice on the statue's base, had written a great dictionary in the previous century.

The food and drink were indifferent, and I nibbled a few dumplings that were meant to be Chinese—they were not—and part of a seedcake that Cynthia plunked on my plate. She herself took a large portion, as she was fond of seedcake. I sipped tea, which was watery.

Lady Covington remained at her brother's elbow, greeting ladies and gentlemen and thanking them for attending. Lady Covington and Sir Arthur were close in age, his hair the same shade of brown just going to gray, with a full mustache and no beard. I watched from a short distance away, close enough to hear Lady Covington assure the guests that investing in the Polytechnic was a good use of their income.

The rest of the family wandered about in a bored manner, none of them together. Harriet drank tea and stared at flowers around the fountain. George tried to engage gentlemen in conversation, but most quickly withdrew from him to speak to his mother and step-uncle. Jonathan darted down a dark row, and Erica entered the Pompeian house.

I came alert when Daniel and the gentleman he'd arrived with approached Sir Arthur.

Daniel had dressed in a dark suit that fitted him exactly, a discreet tie tucked behind the high vee of his waistcoat. His coat flowed neatly to dark trousers that gave only a glimpse of polished black shoes. The suit was adorned only with a watch chain and small gold stickpin.

He swept his gaze across the crowd as they neared Sir Arthur and Lady Covington. The gray-haired gentleman greeted them, shaking their hands.

Daniel saw me, but as before, his eyes registered nothing, and he returned his focus to Lady Covington and Sir Arthur. He spoke—nothing more than saying good evening—his manner that of a lethargic gentleman of wealth, his voice a fading drawl. If I'd never met Daniel before, I'd have labeled him a spoiled, pampered young man condescending to accompany his older friend to a tedious engagement.

I turned away, my heart pounding. My Daniel wasn't visible within the weary young gentleman resting his walking stick over his arm. Could I ever grow used to Daniel assuming personas in order to spy for the police?

"He is the Duke of Daventry," a quiet male voice said behind me. I turned to behold Mr. Fielding sipping tea from a delicate porcelain cup, a twinkle in his eyes. "Old title, rich as Croesus. Has a mansion in Berkeley Square. Our Daniel is chumming up to him for some reason."

"Has it anything to do with the murders in Ireland?" I asked in a whisper.

Mr. Fielding started. "I should not be surprised that you already know all. But yes, the duke's enemies are putting it about that some of his money floats across the Irish Sea to those who want Ireland out from under Britain. Sounds barmy to me. Why would a duke of ancient lineage want to help rabble-rousers?"

"Is the duke Irish himself?" Some noble families had been granted titles to land there generations ago.

"Absolutely not. A more blue-blooded Englishman you'll never meet. Makes you long to bloody his nose and see what color comes out. Daventry has businesses in Liverpool, which employ many laborers working themselves to the bone to line his pockets. Liverpool is a hop and skip across the water to Dublin. So his enemies say. I think it's all . . . balderdash."

"Then why is Daniel staying so close to him?"

"I am trying to find out, but Daniel is not letting me near."

I studied Daniel again. "He unnerves me, the way he can take on a role."

"Indeed." Mr. Fielding sipped tea again, the very picture of a distressed vicar.

"You are a humbug, Mr. Fielding."

His smile flashed. "Yes, but I know it. I have, however, thoroughly embraced my role as vicar, delivering sermons, sheltering those demon children, visiting the sick, giving the last rites to the dying." He sobered. "*That* has turned me from a pure villain into something like a man. The comfort some take in me mumbling words over them is unsettling. All my schooling in theology did not prepare me for that."

"It will be the making of you," I assured him. "So will the demon children."

"Dear lady, you are always determined to find the good in a person, including that reprobate, Daniel. Mark my words, I was never the villain he was. He's reformed, it seems, and the world should heave a collective sigh of relief."

I glanced at Daniel, now conversing with Sir Arthur. Mr. Fielding had told me in the past that Daniel had been far worse a rogue than he. At times I believed it, but then reminded myself that Mr. Fielding was a confidence trickster and an easy liar.

Sir Arthur faltered suddenly, his leg bending as though it had given out on him. He put a heavy hand on his sister's arm, and his face took on a peculiar tinge of gray.

"Arthur!" Lady Covington's cry rang through the vast space.

I hurried to them, Cynthia and Mr. Fielding joining me.

Daniel caught Sir Arthur, and he and Lady Covington escorted him to a chair. The duke, on the other hand, backed hastily away, as though fearing Sir Arthur had some contagion.

Mr. Thanos pushed through the crowd. "Sir, are you all right?"

"No." Sir Arthur sank heavily to the seat Daniel steered him to. "I do not know what's come over me. I was perfectly well a few minutes ago."

Lady Covington hovered near, her face ashen. "Is it your heart?"

"No." Sir Arthur folded his arm across his stomach. "Cramps. Horrible ones. And I can't catch my breath."

"He needs water." Daniel spoke in the languid tones of an upper-class gentleman, one who was somewhat agitated but didn't want to bestir himself too much. "You," he said to me. "Fetch this man some water."

I answered this demand with a derisive look. I knew that Daniel was not simply fortifying the idea that he had no idea who I was, but also attempting to send me out of danger.

"I'll go." Cynthia turned abruptly and made for the refreshment table.

Daniel must have warned Mr. Thanos and Cynthia and her friends that he was attending tonight, and in what guise, because they pretended to regard him as a stranger.

"A doctor," Daniel continued. "There must be one in all this crush."

"No need," Sir Arthur wheezed. "I've eaten something that disagreed with me, is all. Take me home—I'll be well."

"You came by train, did you not?" I asked Lady Covington as she wavered indecisively.

"Yes, yes. We already have the tickets for a late train back."

"Perhaps the railway will let you on an earlier one, or you could hire a coach."

"The train will be much more comfortable. They will certainly let us on—my husband ran the railway board." Lady Covington's imperious manner returned.

"Shall I find your stepson for you?" Neither he nor his siblings were anywhere in sight.

"Ah yes, George." Lady Covington seemed to have forgotten she had a stepson. "Please, Mrs. Holloway, find my children. We must convey Arthur home."

Her agitation showed she hung between concern and real fear. Sir Arthur's symptoms could be those of poisoning—had he drunk or eaten something meant for Lady Covington? However, I'd seen neither of them eat or drink a thing. They'd been shaking hands and flattering potential donors to the school since the lectures ended. Sir Arthur's illness could be perfectly natural.

"A doctor, I say." Daniel raised his voice. "Is one about?"

I turned from him and pushed through the gathering crowd in search of Lady Covington's brood.

I saw none of them hurrying worriedly to their uncle to see what had happened. I cursed the lot of them under my breath as I rushed past the long fountain toward the lecture area, where I'd seen Jonathan nip down a side aisle. While I did not trust the lad, Lady Covington would be happiest with him to comfort her.

I followed the path he'd taken and found myself in the natural history exhibits, which housed replicas of animals, plants, and dwellings from all over the world. I passed the Amazonian rain forests then across to Africa and through more space to Borneo and New Guinea, all the while searching frantically for signs of Jonathan.

A rustle of skirts and light laughter towed me past New Guinea to Australia, where a woman's figure solidified in the darkness. I heard more laughter and then a man's low tones.

I scuttled forward, ensuring I made plenty of noise. The woman gasped and turned, and the man she was with— I glimpsed only a tall person with a beard—vanished past the clump of Australian plants.

"Miss Morris?" I called softly.

Harriet strode abruptly out of the shadows. "What do you mean, spying on me? What are you doing here?"

Her words did not sting, because I sensed great fear beneath them. I wondered who the man was, and why Harriet had arranged to meet him here in a part of the Palace not lit for the gathering.

"I was sent to look for you, miss," I said. "Your uncle has taken ill, and your mother wishes for you to all go home."

"Does she?" Harriet shook her skirt free of a bramble-like plant. "Drat it. What is the matter with Uncle Arthur? What have you to do with it? You are a maid, are you not?"

"Your uncle fears he ate something that disagreed with him," I said, ignoring her mistake about my profession.

Harriet glanced in concern toward the wider aisle, then she rounded on me and seized my arm in a firm grip. "Not a word, do you understand? You say nothing about what you saw, or I'll have you sacked."

"You have no need to threaten me, Miss Morris. Now, before you race off, let me help you pin your hair. It is greatly mussed."

Harriet released my arm to clap a hand to her hat, crushing the lace curled on top of it. The hat had slipped sideways, and dark tendrils of hair drooped haphazardly to her shoulders.

I quickly slid a few hairpins from her complicated braid, tucked in the stray locks, and smoothed the entire coiffure.

"Much better," I declared.

Did she thank me for my trouble? No, the young lady glared at me and rushed away toward the gathering point.

I scanned the darkness for the man, but he'd gone. I wondered if he'd been one of the guests this evening or if he'd traveled here furtively to see Harriet.

I left Australia and moved back across the globe to the refreshment area. Harriet was hurrying toward her mother, the very picture of worry. A man bent over Sir Arthur, holding his wrist—I assumed Daniel had managed to find a doctor. George had joined them, but Jonathan and Erica remained absent.

I recalled Erica wandering into the Pompeian house, so I turned my steps that way. Bobby and Miss Townsend were scouring the guests for the missing family members, and when Miss Townsend caught my eye, she shook her head. No luck.

The door of the Pompeian house stood ajar, and I stepped inside.

It was dark here, but enough light leaked over the open roof and doorway to provide faint illumination. An atrium filled the front of the house, a square pool of water in its center. Doorways grouped around this led to small cubicles. Red and yellow walls held painted scenes of people reclining on couches, playing lyres, or dancing.

I glimpsed all this only in passing, my eyes drawn to what lay the floor of the atrium. Erica sprawled facedown and motionless next to the pool, one hand outstretched as though she'd tried and failed to reach the cool water.

10

M rs. Hume." I raced forward, dropping to my knees. I turned her over, Erica's body flopping limply onto my lap.

Her face was gray, her half-closed eyes glinting in the dim light. I had little idea how to find someone's pulse, but I lifted her hand and peeled back her glove.

Her skin was warm, and as I touched her, Erica dragged in a hoarse breath.

Not dead, but very, very ill.

"Mrs. Hume." I patted her face, but she only groaned and did not acknowledge me. I spied a handkerchief peeking from her sleeve, pulled it out, dunked it into the pool's water, and dabbed her face. "Wake up, my dear, please."

I needed to fetch the doctor. I started to rise but was pulled down by a surprisingly strong grip.

"Henry," Erica whispered. "You must–" She broke off with another moan.

"Do not move. I will bring help."

"Don't leave me." Her plea was heartbreaking. "Henry . . ." She began to silently cry.

I pried her fingers from me and hurried to the door. "Bobby!" I shouted, seeing her nearest.

Bobby immediately started for me, Miss Townsend following.

I realized as Bobby reached the house that I'd neglected to call her *Lady Roberta*, but I was too worried to be bothered by niceties. Bobby didn't seem to notice, in any case, as she charged over the threshold.

"Oh, good Lord," she said, stopping short when she saw Erica. "Is she all right?"

"She is not. Please help me get her off this floor, and then she must have the doctor."

No chairs stood in this house, only a bench against a wall in the open room beyond the atrium. Bobby leaned to Erica, who blinked at her in confusion, and wound an arm under the ill woman. I supported Erica's other side, and together Bobby and I heaved her to her feet and a few tottered steps to the bench.

Erica collapsed to it, her head dropping back to the wall, her pale face filmed with perspiration. I quickly removed her hat and dabbed her face with the wet handkerchief once more.

Miss Townsend had arrived as we moved Erica, and now she studied the woman, her expression grave. "Bobby, run for the doctor," Miss Townsend ordered. She took a seat on Erica's other side, and Bobby made her swift way out the door. "Mrs. Hume, what did you eat?"

Erica dragged in a few ragged breaths. "Nothing."

"Nonsense, it had to have been something. Or drank? What did you take tonight?"

"Only some tea."

We'd all drunk tea out of communal pots that round-cheeked waitresses had carried about. My heart beat swiftly—had whoever wished to poison Lady Covington dropped a dollop of something into the tea?

Miss Townsend guessed my thoughts. "If it was in the tea, many more people would already be ill. She must have ingested it at home before they departed."

"Cynthia." My fears surged. Cynthia had said she'd eaten and drunk only what the whole family did. Had the noxious substance been served before or after she'd left the house this evening?

"Cyn appears to be fine," Miss Townsend said, but her face creased in worry. "Miss Morris seems all right as well. I've not found Mr. Morris."

Was Jonathan lying in a moaning heap in some aisle in the darkness? I clutched the lip of the wooden bench to keep myself from racing away to find him. I would wait for the doctor, as Erica seemed to be quieter with me next to her.

"Henry." Erica's hand found mine. "Please look after him for me. Promise me."

"Who is Henry?" I asked her gently. I'd not heard the name from anyone in the family, nor had Cynthia mentioned him.

"Promise . . ." Erica's eyes were losing focus.

"Yes, I promise." I patted her hand.

Erica's grip went slack. I touched her face in alarm, but she still breathed, if shallowly.

A commotion at the door announced the arrival of Bobby with the doctor. Daniel followed them, along with Mr. Fielding, Cynthia, and Mr. Thanos, and behind them, a wide-eyed Jonathan.

I vacated my seat, and the doctor, without paying much attention to me, took my place. He pried open one of Erica's eyes, pressed fingers to her pulse, loosened her jaw, and examined her mouth and tongue.

Daniel halted by my side, but like the doctor, he behaved as though he stood next to empty air. I knew he'd taken the position deliberately, however, and I felt better with the warmth of him beside me. He wore scent, a light spice that smelled costly.

Jonathan shoved rudely past Mr. Thanos, but his face was drawn with concern. "We'll see to her. Mama has sent for a coach to take us to the train."

The doctor turned to him gravely. "It is too late for that. She must not travel. I will take her to my surgery, which is not far from here, and try to purge her. You have a coach, you say?"

Jonathan acknowledged this impatiently, and the doctor and Miss Townsend pried Erica to her feet between them. It was clear the young woman could not stand, let alone walk. Daniel made a move to her, but Jonathan cut him out and lifted Erica into his arms himself.

Jonathan strode out with Erica to the cooler air of the nave. Lady Covington rushed to them, snapping orders for all to clear out of the way.

"Vicar," the doctor said in a low voice as he passed Mr. Fielding. "We might need you."

Mr. Fielding did not look happy, but he nodded, gave me a pat on the shoulder, and followed him.

The others had gone, and I was left in relative privacy with Daniel. We stood in silence. I did not want to betray Daniel by any familiar gesture or even by turning to face him fully. A person's ease with another tells much about what is between them.

Daniel likewise made no sign that he knew me. He straightened his gloves and, as he bent his head to do so, murmured, "I will speak with you later."

If I had not been so focused on him, I'd have missed the words. They relieved me, but even refraining from giving him a nod took all my strength. I was not comfortable with subterfuge.

Daniel adjusted his coat with an air of a man who did not know me from a rock in the road and walked away.

Cynthia approached. "Lady Covington is asking for you."

"For me?" I deflated. "Probably to demand to know why I haven't found the poisoner yet."

"Well, how could you?" Cynthia balled her hands. "That's what you sent *me* to do, but I've failed, haven't I? Jove, Mrs. H., I ate luncheon with them today. The poison can't have been introduced then, or the rest of us would be rolling about in agony."

"Then we must discover how it was administered and when. That should help us discover who put it in whatever Erica imbibed."

"I certainly hope so," Cynthia said somberly.

She led me after the retreating crowd, the Palace growing eerily silent. I heard only my footsteps and Cynthia's and our harried breaths.

We caught up to the guests who were milling outside the entrance. Carriages clogged the road, coach lights glowing in the darkness.

Cynthia towed me to Lady Covington's hired coach. Lady Covington, who waited beside it, barely glanced at me before she was herding me and Cynthia inside.

We took a seat facing Harriet, who twined her fingers together and gazed at anything but me. Someone handed in Lady Covington and slammed the door for her.

"Where is Mrs. Hume?" I asked in bewilderment.

"Jonathan procured a carriage at the front of the pack. He and Erica, the doctor, the vicar, and my brother have gone in that. Jonathan is a resourceful lad." Lady Covington said it with pride, even in her agitation.

"Did you eat luncheon with the others?" I asked her.

"Of course I did. As did Cynthia and Harriet. Erica's and my brother's illnesses could have nothing to do with the luncheon." She sounded very positive.

"Then it was something they took after they arrived at the Crystal Palace," I said. "Perhaps nothing to do with *your* illnesses at all."

"The symptoms are the same," Lady Covington said. "Only much worse in Erica's case. What my brother described is exactly how I have felt on occasion."

"Clumsy to do it here," Cynthia remarked. "When every person attending took things from trays and drank out of the same teapots."

"Unless they ate something different from the others." I stared out at the night, the glass reflecting a ghost of my face. "Perhaps apart, in secret."

"In secret?" Lady Covington's tone snapped my attention to her. "What absolute nonsense. Why would Erica consume food in secret?"

"Perhaps not food." I strove to retain my patience. "A medicine or potion, either for digestion, or the complexion, or some such."

"Erica is a vain thing," Harriet said decidedly. "Always looking for lotions or creams to put on her face. She's getting long in the tooth."

"I know Arthur has no worries about his complexion," Lady

Covington said. "He and Erica would hardly take the same concoctions."

I fell silent. True, the only connection between Erica and her step-uncle was the fact that he had taken luncheon with the family, and they'd attended the gathering at the Crystal Palace tonight.

My mind went back to Miss Townsend producing a box in our first-class coach and handing around glasses of brandy.

"They could have eaten something on the journey," I said. "Did you have refreshments along the way?"

Harriet sat forward. "Oh yes. I'd forgotten. Cook packed a hamper. It was supposed to be for Mama, so she wouldn't have to risk eating at the lectures. But Mama did not want anything, and the rest of us nibbled. Erica ate rather a lot."

I came alert. "What became of the hamper?"

Harriet scowled. "I'm not to know. I'm not a servant."

"Harriet." Lady Covington's sharp word had Harriet flouncing back into her seat. "I will find out. When Cook makes things for me, they're always all right. No one should have taken ill."

"That is so." I groped for words, trying to put things delicately, but Cynthia had no such qualms.

"Then the poisoner jolly well had a go at the hamper," she said. "When your back was turned, they bunged in the poison, but Erica and Sir Arthur ate it instead of you."

"I do not know how they could have done so," Lady Covington said.

"Did you have your eye on the hamper the entire time?" I asked, glancing to Harriet to include her in the question.

Spots of red appeared on Lady Covington's cheeks, burnished by the lamplight inside the coach. "Of course not. Forgive my brusqueness, Mrs. Holloway. I am quite worried about Erica."

"I et some of the strawberries," Harriet said. "And I feel quite fit. No, I did not watch the hamper at all times. It was passed around, wasn't it? We ladies shared one compartment, and a porter came and took it to the gentlemen once we'd had our fill. As I say, Erica ate much of it, greedy thing."

"Then it was out of your sight in the corridor," I said.

"My brother's compartment was the next one along," Lady Covington said. "But I see what you mean. The porter brought in the hamper, which had been loaded alongside our small amount of baggage. Arthur insisted on carrying a change of clothes in case his suit became soiled, and we always bring cushions and things to make train compartments more comfortable. Anyone could have tampered with the food between the time it left our coach at the railway station and the time it appeared in our compartment."

"Or before it even entered the carriage from your house," Cynthia said. "Did you see anyone with the hamper before you departed?"

"It came straight up from the kitchen," Harriet said. "I watched Peter—he's one of our footmen—bring it up the back stairs and shove it into the coach."

"Then anyone could have introduced poison at any time," I said glumly.

"Not Erica, obviously," Lady Covington said.

"I would not be so certain, Mama." Harriet made a sour face. "She is beastly to everyone. She might have decided she'd take a dose of the poison to show *she* wasn't trying to harm you. But miscalculated the amount."

"I highly doubt that," Lady Covington said crisply. "She'd

be very foolish to do so. She would never think of such a thing, in any case."

"No, she's not very clever." Harriet's face softened. "I'm not fond of Erica, but I do not wish to see her so ill. She looked horrible, poor thing."

"What exactly did she eat?" I asked. "Did either of you notice?"

"I had the strawberries, as I said," Harriet answered. "Not many of them. I wasn't very hungry, and they were a bit tasteless."

"Too early in the season," I said.

Harriet clearly had no idea why this mattered. "Erica ate about a dozen of the things, along with cream, a scone with currants, and two slices of your excellent lemon cake—the one whose recipe you brought Mama. I told you Erica was greedy. I am surprised there was anything left when the hamper reached the gentlemen."

"Please ask Sir Arthur what he had," I said to Lady Covington. "Mr. Morris and Lord Covington did not seem to be ill at all."

"Jonathan never takes sick," Harriet said, waving her brother away. "Neither does George, but that's because he's too pompous."

Lady Covington frowned but did not reprimand her. "Jonathan was good to help."

I recalled Jonathan's stark worry as he lifted his stepsister and carried her from the Pompeian house. I wondered—did he have a tendresse for her? They were not related, after all, and their respective parents had married when they'd already been adults, or near to it.

Or was Jonathan the poisoner, and his concern for Erica remorse that he'd poisoned the wrong woman?

And who had been the gentleman Harriet had met in the dark? Did he have anything to do with trying to harm Lady Covington, and why? The man might be a suitor Lady Covington disapproved of, and with her death, the path might be clear for him to marry Harriet. I glanced at Harriet in speculation. She caught my eye and resolutely turned to look out of the window.

In another quarter of an hour, we reached the doctor's surgery, a cottage set back from the road behind a garden gate. It was a small place, almost lost in the dark and shadows of tall trees.

No one appeared to assist us, and Cynthia, never liking to wait for that sort of thing, shoved the door open and leapt to the ground. She released the catch on the coach's side to yank down the steps, and served as footman to hand us down. She shouted at the coachman to wait and opened the gate to lead us through the tiny garden.

The front door of the surgery was unlocked, and we entered a large and pleasantly furnished room with an open doorway leading to what looked like a consulting room. A staircase led upward on the left wall, and voices floated down from above.

Lady Covington hastened up the stairs, followed by Cynthia and then me. Harriet remained below, mumbling that she was useless in a sickroom.

The first person we saw in the narrow corridor at the top of the stairs was Jonathan. His face was chalk white, his eyes red rimmed. "Mama, it is bad."

Lady Covington drew a breath. She put her hand on his shoulder, squeezing it as though trying to comfort him. Then she straightened her back and walked to the door at the end of the hall.

"Your sister is downstairs," I said to Jonathan.

"Is she?" Jonathan scowled at me. "Bloody Harriet. Damn the lot of them. Oh, sorry, Cyn. I need a drink."

He pushed past Cynthia and clumped down the stairs. I heard the front door bang, sending a draft up the stairwell.

Cynthia peered after him. "*Curiouser and curiouser*, as Alice said."

I did not have time to wonder about Jonathan, because Mr. Fielding emerged from the room at the end of the corridor. He had a prayer book in his hand, his expression uncharacteristically sober.

"She'll not last," he said. "The poor little thing. Who would do this? It's monstrous."

"A tragic accident," I said. "Inflicted on her by a cruel person."

Cynthia folded her arms, her pale hair glistening like spun flax. "I know that look, Mrs. Holloway. Whoever did this will not be safe."

"Not if I have anything to say about it," I agreed softly.

Cynthia gave me a decided nod. "Or I."

The doctor opened the door. "Vicar. Quickly." He gazed past him at me. "Are you the cook? She's asking for you."

I swallowed. Like Harriet, I did not relish sickrooms, but I did not want one of Erica's last wishes to go unfulfilled. I gathered my skirts and followed Mr. Fielding into the room.

I knew at once that Mr. Fielding's assessment of Erica's condition was correct. Her breathing was swift and shallow, her face a bloodless gray. Lady Covington held her hand, a look of vast pity on her face. Mr. Fielding moved to Lady Covington's side, opening his book and clearing his throat.

I went to the other side of the bed and took Erica's ice-cold hand in mine. "Mrs. Hume?" I said softly. "You asked for me."

"Cook?"

"Yes, dear." Unlike when Jonathan or Lord Clifford had addressed me by my title, I was not in the least offended by Erica's pathetic gasp. "I'm here."

"You promise?"

I recalled her plea for me to look after Henry, whoever he was. I doubted she'd be able to tell me more about him now.

"Of course. I promise."

Mr. Fielding was already speaking, reading words of comfort. "Depart, O Christian soul, out of this world, in the name of God the Father Almighty . . ."

Erica let out a breath. "Thank you. I won't tell. It's not your fault . . ." Another breath. "I love you, Mama."

It was the last thing she said. The exhale became a rattle, and she lay very still.

Mr. Fielding continued to read. I'd never observed him in his full role as vicar, but now he intoned the blessing in a deep and soothing voice. Whether he believed the phrases he spoke or not, he showed nothing but calm sincerity. Lady Covington bowed her head and whispered along with him.

The doctor closed Erica's eyes, and there was nothing more to do.

L ady Covington remained in Sydenham for the night at a nearby hotel, which had been built to house the tourists who came to visit the Crystal Palace. The doctor kept Sir Arthur at his surgery, which was also the doctor's home, to keep an eye on him. Sir Arthur had recovered somewhat, but was still pale and sickly.

Cynthia and I would be journeying to London—Lady Covington had sent us away, saying she'd not be poisoned by the hotel's food. Cynthia had argued, but Lady Covington had been firm.

Jonathan and Harriet remained with their mother, but George declared without inflection that he'd return to London alone and begin preparing for Erica's funeral.

"He's a chilly cove," Mr. Fielding said to me as Cynthia and I rode with him in the hired coach Jonathan had commandeered. No one balked at a respectable vicar volunteering to accompany a young lady and her domestic to the train. "Covington's behaving as though his sister's sudden death is simply another business matter."

"Some people hide behind a cool mask," Cynthia said charitably, "when they lose a loved one."

"You did not see him in the room when I was finishing the last prayers. *Oh well, nothing to be done,* says he. *Perhaps it's for the best.* Bloody cold fish. A man who doesn't value another's life is a dangerous one."

"He said it was probably for the best?" Cynthia's brows rose. "Ah, I see. She was unmarried, a widow, yes, but her husband hadn't amounted to much. Better she's out of the way than continues living, a burden to her family for the next decades."

"Exactly." Mr. Fielding removed a flask from his pocket and drank deeply.

"Who is Henry?" I broke in.

Both Mr. Fielding and Cynthia stared at me blankly.

"Henry?" Cynthia repeated.

"Mrs. Hume asked me to look after someone called Henry," I explained. "Had she mentioned anyone by that name, Lady Cynthia?"

Cynthia pondered a moment. "No, I'm sure she didn't. I've not heard the name Henry mentioned in the house."

"Could be anyone then," Mr. Fielding said. "Her secret lover? Her budgerigar?"

"She has no pets," Cynthia said. "No one in the family does. Lord Covington—the deceased one—couldn't abide them. Didn't like animals unless they were useful, mostly as meat. There was a lively discussion about it the other evening."

"Lover then," Mr. Fielding concluded. "Widowed Mrs. Hume had hidden depths."

I could not picture the rather brittle Erica slipping off to meet a lover. Harriet, yes, and in fact I'd caught her with a man who might be such.

"One doesn't ask another to look after a lover, though, does one?" I mused. "She'd bid me to tell him of her fate, or make certain he was well, but not look after him."

"True," Mr. Fielding said. "But she didn't supply a surname, didn't call him 'Mr. Whomever.' Perhaps she did keep a dog in secret, poor mutt."

I and Cynthia would have to find out.

The lower railway station at the Crystal Palace was quiet, most of the guests already gone. I was happy to see Mr. Thanos, however, waiting for us.

His kind face fell as we told him of Erica's death. "The poor woman." Mr. Thanos shook his head, sadness in his dark eyes. "You must stop this person, Mrs. Holloway."

"The police should," Mr. Fielding said grimly. "Not that I have much use for the constabulary, but your pet inspector can unravel this case of poisoning now that it is obvious what happened."

"Difficult to prove," I told him, discouraged. "Unless the coroner finds it is definitely poison, and not simply bad food, they might rule it an accident. Many poisons mimic the symptoms of food gone off, and unless a coroner looks for a poison specifically, they won't find it."

Ever since poor Mr. Thanos had been laid low by a dose of poison, I'd read up on such things and how they were detected, in case the information would be useful in the future.

Mr. Fielding let out a harsh laugh. "Do remind me to avoid your cooking, Mrs. Holloway."

"I would never spoil my own meals, Mr. Fielding," I said, appalled.

He laughed again, but the sound was anything but mirthful.

We rode to London in silence, the four of us sharing a first-class compartment. Miss Townsend and Bobby had gone back before us, Mr. Thanos told us, and I found that I missed their company.

It was very late by the time we arrived at Victoria Station. Mr. Fielding and Mr. Thanos saw us home in a hired hackney, Mr. Thanos holding Cynthia's hand a bit longer than necessary when he shook it to say good-bye.

Mr. Fielding's roguish look returned as he waved Mr. Thanos back into the hackney, and I hoped he would not tease Mr. Thanos too much.

Cynthia entered the house through the front door one of the footmen held open for her, and I turned for the back stairs.

When I was halfway down, a voice whispered in the blackness, "Kat."

He was there. I did not know how he'd come to be there or how he'd known I would need him, but I did not question.

As I halted on the steps, unable to move, Daniel came to me and enfolded me into his arms.

11

---◆————◆---

I hadn't realized how much I'd longed for Daniel's comfort until he stood against me in the darkness, his body a bulwark between me and the world.

He stroked my back, his breath warm on my cheek, and I clung to him while emotions chased one another in chaotic abandon.

"I'm so sorry, Kat."

"It was not your fault." My words were muffled by his shoulder. He smelled of warm wool, soap, and hint of the scent he'd worn earlier tonight.

"I mean for having to keep away from you. For behaving like a lout tonight and pretending you did not exist."

"You were acting the part. I understand." Daniel hadn't released me, and I saw no reason to break his hold.

"This gentleman I'm pretending to be disgusts me. He's a self-centered prig only interested in his own prestige. But it helps me get close to people."

"Like the duke."

I felt Daniel start. "How do you know who he is?"

"My dear Daniel, why do you ask these questions?"

His soft laughter vibrated beneath my ear. "I ought to know better. But please, keep this information to yourself."

"Do you think I would not? But what am I to do?" I held him more tightly. "That poor young woman died, Daniel, and I could not stop it."

"I know, love. But there was nothing you could have done."

"No?" My head popped up. "I could have stayed at Lady Covington's house and browbeaten the lot of them until I found out who was trying to poison her. Instead, fearing for my position if I stayed too long, I fled home and sent Lady Cynthia to worm her way into Lady Covington's family's confidence. *Cynthia* could have been the one to eat the poisoned food. Lady Covington might very soon be next—and what about any other unfortunate who eats or drinks something meant for her?"

Daniel clasped my hands between us. "Dearest Kat, what do you expect to do? You must earn your living, and Cynthia is no fool—she knows how to take care of herself."

"Even so, I had no business sending her. I doubted myself as soon as I asked her, but there was no stopping her then."

"Take heart, love. Now that this terrible thing has happened, the police will be involved. No coroner will let the sudden death of a healthy young woman go unquestioned. There will be an inquest. If it is ruled a deliberate poisoning, Scotland Yard may well be called in, and Inspector McGregor will be interested. You need not worry about this any longer—in fact, I wish you *would* leave it alone." Daniel shuddered. "If someone came to me to tell me gently that *you* had been poisoned . . ." His grip tightened. "I'm not certain what I would do."

I stilled, hearing the catch in his voice, feeling the answering squeeze in my heart.

"If the police become involved, they will simply blame the cook," I said with conviction. "She prepared the hamper of comestibles the family ate on the train. *I* know that anyone in the house could have drizzled a substance onto the scones or the cake. But the police will say the cook did it accidentally, reaching for the wrong bottle. At best, she'll lose her job, and at worst, they'll arrest her."

"I can have a word with McGregor. He's not one to fix blame until he knows exactly what happened."

"Only if Inspector McGregor is assigned the case. A cook adding the wrong ingredient to a dish won't gain much priority at Scotland Yard, I'll wager."

"Possibly not, but my point is that you have no need to look into this further." Daniel studied my face and heaved a resigned sigh. "Not that you will listen to me. This is dangerous."

"Oh, is it? What about chumming up to a duke who might be funding assassins?" I whispered the last, and Daniel's eyes widened.

"You frighten me, Kat. You truly do." He lifted my hand to his lips, kissing my palm through the glove. "Promise me you will be careful. Send word to me through my dratted brother, whom you have recruited, it seems."

"Mr. Fielding has been very helpful."

"Errol never does anything that won't benefit him. Please remember this."

"I have taken his measure, believe me."

I wished I could stand here on the stairwell for as long as I liked, speaking to Daniel and having him kiss my hand. But people walked by on Mount Street, carriages creaked not far from us, and it was late. I'd have to rise in the morning and prepare breakfast for the household. Working-class women did not have the luxury of lying abed, even after an evening of tragedy.

"Good night," I said softly. "I must beg *you* to take care. The men who struck in Dublin were brutal."

"I know." Daniel caressed my cheek. "Hence my mission. You are a good woman, Kat Holloway. Sleep well."

I knew I would not, but I appreciated the sentiment. I kissed his cheek, withdrew from his grasp, and moved around him in the darkness down the stairs to the kitchen door.

I slept poorly, as I'd suspected I would. I could not banish the image of Erica's gray face, nor her weak whisper, *Henry. Please look after him for me . . .*

"I will," I said quietly to the darkness. "As soon as I find out who on earth Henry is."

I rose and washed my face in chilly water, pouring the waste into my slop pail, which I carried with me to the kitchen.

I'd have to discover exactly which foods both Sir Arthur and Erica had consumed, I thought as I trudged down the many flights. Plus what sort of poison it was and how a person would obtain it, let alone add it to the food.

Neither Jonathan nor George had been sick at all, but Jonathan had been very upset that Erica had taken ill. Remorse because he'd not meant the poison for her? Or more tender feelings, as I'd speculated last night? Harriet had eaten only a few nibbles of strawberries, she'd said, but if she'd known which food was tainted, she could have simply avoided it.

I tried to think it through clinically, but the knot of worry in my stomach tightened whenever I realized how easily Cynthia could have been poisoned. If she'd decided to take the train with Lady Covington's family instead of joining me, she might have enthusiastically partaken of the offerings in the hamper.

Downstairs, Tess, oblivious to the happenings of the night, was her usual cheery self as she kneaded dough for bread. "Did you enjoy the Crystal Palace again, Mrs. H.? Could you understand a thing Mr. Thanos said?"

She was the only one in the kitchen at the moment—Charlie had lit the fire in the stove but was nowhere in sight, and Elsie hadn't come down yet. I quietly told Tess what had happened.

Tess's face lost color as she listened. "Oh, Mrs. H. How very awful. What are you going to do?"

"What I have to." I tied on my apron and approached my table to beat up a batter for crumpets. "Find out who used the poison and stop them."

"Good for you." Tess continued her kneading, flour scattering across the table. "What can I do to help?"

I hardly wanted Tess to be in the position, like Cynthia, to be hurt by this poisoner, but I knew she wanted to see things put right. "You could ask Caleb to keep you informed about what he knows about Mrs. Hume's death. There is sure to be an autopsy and an inquest. I know he is only a beat constable, but he can find out things, can't he?"

"Oh, Caleb's a good one for gossip." Tess finished with the dough, plopped it into a bowl, and covered it with a towel. "I don't mean he spreads tales or that sort of thing. But he tells me."

Her confidence in him was touching if naive. "I would not want him to get into any trouble, so he is not to go nosing about."

"I will explain. Caleb's good if someone tells him exactly what to do."

I hid a smile, the first one that had crossed my lips since Erica's death.

We continued to cook breakfast—boiled eggs and toasted crumpets, plenty of bacon, and leftover meat pies. I poured off cream into a jug that I set in a cold part of the larder to save for an idea for custards based on the flavors of the Lesser Antilles. I'd come across a vendor from Antigua as I wandered the markets a few months ago and tasted a custard flavored with cinnamon, anise, and coconut. I'd long wished to replicate it, and after many notes and a few failures, I thought I'd cracked the formula.

When I was upset, I let myself grow obsessed with cooking and creating recipes. Some part of me found it soothing to focus on exact measurements and techniques, and trying to discern ingredients in a dish I'd never made before solely by tasting it. Chopping, kneading, stirring, basting—all cleared my mind and allowed me to unravel other problems.

I would have to find an excuse to go to Park Lane so I could quiz the cook, Mrs. Gamble, about exactly what had been in the food hamper and through whose hands it had passed before it left the house. I had a tiny idea about where the poison had come from in the first place, but I couldn't be certain until I returned to Lady Covington's house.

Mrs. Redfern entered the kitchen as Tess and I finished buttering the last of the crumpets to be sent up for breakfast. Tess licked butter from her fingers and reached for a towel.

"Mrs. Holloway."

Mrs. Redfern's quiet tone caught my attention. I paused from my wipe-down of the kitchen table and gazed at her inquiringly.

"I do not like tittle-tattle, as you know, but I must tell you that some has begun about you."

As I stared at her, Tess burst out, "What sort of tittle-tattle? Mrs. Holloway never done nuffink. Who has been saying so?"

I hushed her. "Please explain, Mrs. Redfern."

Mrs. Redfern flushed, uncomfortable. Her discomfort rose as Mr. Davis strolled in, newspaper in hand. He'd heard us, because he raised his brows at Mrs. Redfern and said, "Yes, I think you ought to explain."

"I am only passing on knowledge," Mrs. Redfern returned with a sniff. "One of Mrs. Bywater's neighbors came to her early this morning to relay that she'd seen you, Mrs. Holloway, in the arms of a man. On the stairwell outside the kitchen. A scoundrel, she claims, though she could hardly see what sort of man he was in the dark."

My stomach knotted in dismay. Mrs. Redfern gazed at me sternly while Mr. Davis fell silent, but before I could stammer an explanation, Tess interrupted.

"What neighbor?" she demanded. "I bet it was old Mrs. Beadle, what moved into the house next door. She's a busybody if I've ever seen one. She dismisses maids left and right, *after* she spies on them."

"Never you mind who it was, Tess," Mrs. Redfern snapped. "And hold your tongue about your betters."

I guessed, from Mrs. Redfern's evasive answer, that the visitor *had* been Mrs. Beadle. She and her husband had leased the house next door once the previous owners, the Harknesses, had gone.

Mrs. Beadle hadn't seen wrong—I'd clung to Daniel shamelessly, needing his strength.

"Mrs. Bywater is not happy," Mrs. Redfern went on. "She is

prepared to come down here and question you about it after breakfast."

Meaning she'd wait until her husband had gone to the City and could not interfere. I swallowed, wondering how I would explain myself. Mrs. Bywater was ever waiting for an excuse to give me the sack.

Mr. Davis stared hard at me. He'd in the past claimed that Daniel was "sweet on me" and opined that I could do better than a scruffy deliveryman. I expected Mr. Davis to tell Mrs. Redfern exactly who the man had been and make it clear he did not approve.

Instead, he let out a snort. "Preposterous. Mrs. Holloway is not walking out with anyone."

I almost argued with him—he knew Daniel came to visit me often—but I held my tongue.

"I told you, Mr. Davis, I know nothing of the matter," Mrs. Redfern answered. "I came to warn Mrs. Holloway what is being said of her. She is free to defend herself."

"Meddling Mrs. Beadle saw nothing of the sort," Mr. Davis went on. "Mrs. Holloway was very upset last night—there was a death at the Crystal Palace, where she went to hear improving lectures." He waved the newspaper, indicating that a story about the death lay within its pages. "I was comforting her. The man Mrs. Beadle saw was me, and no, I have no amorous intentions for poor Mrs. Holloway, nor does she for me."

Tess listened with avid interest, and my mouth dropped open, but I could not speak.

Mrs. Redfern regarded Mr. Davis with surprise. "Mrs. Holloway returned very late. I heard her come up to her room after one o'clock."

"I was up very late myself. Checking the wine cellar to

make sure his lordship didn't have another go at it." Mr. Davis finished with a growl.

Mrs. Redfern gazed at Mr. Davis for a moment in deep skepticism then she let out a breath, deciding to accept the explanation. "Thank you, Mr. Davis. Well, I shall go up and tell Mrs. Bywater there's nothing in it. I am very happy the neighbor was mistaken." She shot me another look, still uncertain, and strode from the room.

"Mr. Davis," I began, my voice quavering.

Mr. Davis held up a forefinger, silencing me. With a glance at Tess, who bounced on her toes, a grin on her face, he stalked out, heading for the butler's pantry.

I abandoned the kitchen and followed him. Mr. Davis tried to close the door on me, but I pushed into his sanctum.

"Mr. Davis, why would you—?"

Mr. Davis slid out of his tailed coat and turned from hanging it on a hook. "Because I do not wish you to lose your post, Mrs. Holloway. I doubt any cook Mrs. Bywater hired would be anywhere near as good as you, and my stomach would not thank me. Besides, aren't we friends?"

"I'd like to believe so." I wet my dry lips. "And I do not wish you to think less of me. I—"

He lifted his forefinger again. "No need to explain, Mrs. Holloway. We all make mistakes, and I know you are a respectable woman. But I am curious. Was it the vicar?"

I blinked in amazement. "Mr. Fielding? Good heavens, no."

"Ah." He deflated. "I had hoped. A vicar of a poor parish could do worse than taking a cook to wife. Not, again, that I wish you to leave. That means it was McAdam." Mr. Davis looked displeased.

"Mr. McAdam is a fine man," I stated. "Not a scoundrel. He

is more than what he seems." Mr. Davis did not know the extent of that, nor could he ever find out.

"Too many women have been taken in by a gentleman's disarming manner." Mr. Davis shook his head. "It usually ends in tears."

"I assure you, there is nothing untoward between Mr. McAdam and me." I conveniently forgot the many times Daniel had kissed me. "He was, as you say, comforting me, because yes, I was upset about the death. Lady Covington's stepdaughter. It was a terrible thing." I faltered.

Mr. Davis took up the newspaper, his glance sympathetic. "We shall say no more about it. I am happy to look after you, my friend, but please do not allow Mr. McAdam to comfort you again within sight of the neighbors."

"I will bear it in mind, Mr. Davis."

We exchanged a glance of understanding, and I left him.

I returned to my intention of visiting Lady Covington. I would have to invent an excuse to placate Mrs. Bywater—I could not simply tell her I wished to pay my condolences, as cooks were intended to carry on with their duties even if the sun fell out of the sky.

I opened my notebook after Tess and I had sent the breakfast dishes up in the dumbwaiter, and I looked over the ingredients list for the spiced custard. Cinnamon, cloves, star anise . . .

"Oh dear," I said in a loud voice. "I am out of bay leaves."

Tess glanced up from mixing the batter for my lemon cake. Those upstairs had liked it so much, Mrs. Bywater had sent down a request that I serve it again.

"I can run to the market for you," she offered.

"No, indeed. You must finish the cake. I know where to procure some quickly."

So speaking, I stripped off my apron and cap, snatched up my coat and hat, and was out the door before Tess could answer.

A warm breeze blew down the street, promising hotter weather to come. June could be quite pleasant in London, and I looked forward to it, but July and August turned stifling and smelly.

The Bywaters stuck it out through the summer instead of retreating to the country, because of Mr. Bywater's position in the City, but that was fine with me. If they shut up the house during the summer months, I'd have no wages, and if they took me to the country with them, I'd not be able to visit Grace. London born and bred, I could put up with the stench and heat, and Grace was worth any discomfort.

I walked quickly along Mount Street and turned to Park Lane. Lady Covington had implied I could use anything I liked from her kitchen garden, and I pounced on that invitation today.

I passed the house on Park Lane and turned the corner to Upper Brook Street and the gate to the garden. The gate was unlocked, and I slipped inside.

I heard the sound of a rake on gravel and saw Symes behind a hedge, hunched over his work. The back of the house showed blank shades drawn over the windows, a sign of a bereavement.

Did I see the edge of a shade twitch? I studied the window where I'd glimpsed movement, but saw nothing more.

I did not wish to attract Symes's attention, so I headed down the stairs to the kitchen. The smell of green and growing things faded behind me as the damp of the stairwell over-came it.

The door at the bottom of the stairs was wrenched open, and Jepson, the dragon of a lady's maid, glared out at me.

"What do *you* want?" she demanded. "Haven't you caused enough trouble? Miss Erica is dead, and it's all your fault."

She raised a hand, preparing to strike me.

12

❖———❖

I seized Jepson's wrist and pushed her back across the threshold just as Mrs. Gamble stepped from the kitchen into the small foyer.

"Whatever are you doing?" She directed her words to Jepson. "Good heavens, woman, what is the matter with you? Come in, Mrs. Holloway, and have some tea." With a scowl at Jepson, Mrs. Gamble headed back into the kitchen.

I released Jepson's hand. We studied each other with narrowed eyes, then Jepson backed away stiffly.

"Have your tea," she snarled. "But you get no thanks from me."

She turned on her heel and marched up the stairs and into the garden, a bright white petticoat flashing beneath her dull black skirts.

"Never mind her," Mrs. Gamble said as I shut the door and entered the stuffy kitchen. "She's blaming everyone and the moon for Mrs. Hume's death." Mrs. Gamble moved to a dresser where she shoveled tea leaves into a pot. "It's me she's blaming most," she said mournfully. She sniffled and carried the teapot to the table, waving me to a stool while she fetched a steaming kettle from the stove. "After all, it's me what prepared the food." Another louder sniffle as she poured a stream of bubbling water into the teapot. "She says she'll have the police on me, the dreadful old biddy."

"Anyone could have tampered with the basket once it left you," I said soothingly. "From the footman who put it into the coach to the porter at the train and anyone who went near the baggage cart before the hamper was fetched."

Mrs. Gamble nodded, only a little relieved. "That is so. But it's servants who are always blamed when things go wrong."

She was unfortunately correct. Cooks, maids, and footmen could so easily be sacked or even arrested for something not their fault, because we were convenient scapegoats.

"I will find out," I said. "I promised Lady Covington. Now, tell me what was in the hamper."

Mrs. Gamble returned the kettle to the stove and settled herself on a stool at the end of the table. The rest of the table's surface was strewn with her accoutrements set out to make meals today—a rolling pin for pies, mortar and pestle plus bottles of oil for various herb sauces, a slicing knife for vegetables. "It is good of you, dear, though I'm not certain what you can do. I made that hamper special for Lady Covington. I didn't know she'd not want it, or I wouldn't have bothered, and Mrs. Hume would be alive." She wiped away a tear that trickled down the side of her nose.

"You couldn't have known," I said.

"That's not what the police will say." Mrs. Gamble drew out a large handkerchief and mopped her face. "I made up a nice basket, full of things her ladyship enjoys. A couple of boiled eggs, a few slices of ham and soft cheese, strawberries—I found a good lot of them at the market—a few currant scones, some cream for them, and the lemon cake."

"What became of the hamper last night? Was it brought back home?"

Mrs. Gamble nodded. "A porter from the train returned it this morning. Everything was gone—apparently, Erica tucked in when none of the others wanted much. Thanks heavens Sir Arthur only nibbled a little. He's on the mend, her ladyship says."

"That is good to hear," I said in relief. "A pity there's nothing left in the hamper. The remaining food might have been tested."

"Aye, that's true. But I know it were all right when it went into the hamper. I tasted the lemon cake myself." Mrs. Gamble softened into a smile. "It is excellent cake, Mrs. Holloway. The family think me a genius. Thank you ever so much for sharing the recipe."

"You flatter me, Mrs. Gamble." The tea had finished steeping, and I forestalled Mrs. Gamble by reaching for the pot and pouring out for her. The trickle of steaming tea into the cups was calming as always. "It is only a question of mixing up the right ingredients."

"And in what measure." Mrs. Gamble took a noisy sip of tea. "That's the true nature of cookery."

"An oven that bakes evenly also helps. The dearest desire of every cook." I blew on the tea to cool it and drank. The tea was very weak—she'd likely reused the leaves until they did little more than color the water.

"Well, we can only have what those upstairs decide to give us. I've been in places where I was expected to cook ten courses a night on a stove the size of this stool I'm sitting on. I ask you."

"Some mistresses have no idea what is required, do they?" I gazed about the large room and at the gleaming stove, the myriad of hanging pots ready for any recipe, and a shelf holding pudding molds, a coffee grinder, and various long spoons. "You are well fitted out here."

"Aye, the first Lady Covington understood she'd not have fine meals unless her kitchen had the latest in contraptions."

"What was she like?" I asked. Perhaps the person wishing Lady Covington dead resented her for replacing the paragon of the first Lady Covington.

"A hard woman, by all accounts," Mrs. Gamble said. "I didn't work here when she were alive, as I told you, but I've heard much from the other staff and the family. She was the one behind Lord Covington's success, everyone says. He inherited his position on the board, but when his first wife got her claws into him, he suddenly expanded the railway line and made money hand over fist."

"What railway line is it, do you know? Does it go to Sydenham?"

"Heaven knows." Mrs. Gamble shrugged. "They go all over, I think. I'm not one for riding trains."

"I don't like them much either, truth to tell. The present Lady Covington met Lord Covington through the railway, did she not?" I asked, remembering Cynthia's letter of information. "Her first husband, Mr. Morris, was on the board as well?"

"Yes, indeed. A bit of a scandal when it first came out." Mrs. Gamble rested her elbows on the table and warmed to the gossip. "Mr. Morris had died suddenly in an accident. The first Lady Covington was already gone by then—she took sick—a year before that. Mr. Morris was in a train crash."

I jumped. "Oh dear." I recalled Cynthia stating that the family did not like to talk about what happened to Lady Covington's first husband. "That is tragic, especially as he worked for the railway."

"Funny the way things happen, ain't it? Rich as anything, Mr. Morris was, and her ladyship copped the whole lot. Miss Harriet and Mr. Jonathan inherited a small amount, but her ladyship has the lion's share. Holds the purse strings tight, she does. Anyway, Mr. Morris wasn't in his grave a year, Lady Covington still in widow's weeds, when it's announced she's marrying Lord Covington."

Mrs. Gamble leaned closer, her large bosom nearly in her teacup. "If you want my opinion, it weren't a love match, but a business one. Lord Covington needed Mr. Morris's money put back into the railway business, and the new Lady Covington wanted to influence the railway board's decisions, just like the first Lady Covington did." She gave another shrug. "But who knows? They might have been potty about each other. Anyway, Lady Covington and her brood moves in here, and a few years later, Lord Covington pegs it—his heart gave out from overwork, his doctors said. Now young Mr. George is Lord Covington, but it's his stepmum who runs this household. Maybe if the young master marries, the new wife will put the dowager in her place, but I doubt it. Lady Covington knows her own mind. Besides, Mr. George shows no sign of wanting to marry." She shook her head, despairing of Mr. George.

"Not everybody rushes into marriage," I said, thinking of Cynthia's struggles.

"He's hardly rushing anything. He's nearing forty. It might be the making of him. Mr. George is letting the railway line lose money, which displeases Lady Covington no end."

I remembered Miss Townsend telling me that George had asked her to marry him. Miss Townsend's family was quite well off, I knew from Cynthia. Had George been hoping to bring still more money into the family business? In addition to marrying a strong-minded young lady who might take him out from under his stepmother's thumb? I did not blame Miss Townsend for turning him down. I wondered if he'd admitted his defeat to anyone in the family. Had he asked other young ladies with the same result?

"What about Sir Arthur?" Cynthia had said George considered him a parasite. "I am glad you say he is faring better."

"Aye, he's resting upstairs, but he et fine this morning. His breakfast plate came back clean."

"He lives here?"

Mrs. Gamble shook her head. "Not any longer. He's recently taken rooms in Cavendish Square, near his new school. Excited as a boy about that, he is. But he's here most nights, his feet under the supper table. Doesn't have anyone to cook for him. Between you and me and the doorpost, he's trying to keep in Lady Covington's good graces. *She* is funding much of his precious school."

"So I gather." Perhaps that was why George considered his step-uncle a parasite. If Sir Arthur persuaded his sister to pour all her money into the Polytechnic, would there be any left for her children and stepchildren?

Sir Arthur, I mused, could have little cause to murder Lady Covington—unless she'd made a will bequeathing him a vast sum for the Polytechnic. I would have to inquire. Plus he'd have taken a great risk if he'd purposely ingested the poison himself to throw off suspicion. Poisons were tricky. Some could remain in a body long afterward and do damage years later.

The rest of the family *did* have a strong motive for wishing Lady Covington dead. Barring a will in favor of the Polytechnic, her children and stepchildren would presumably inherit all of Lady Covington's wealth. I wagered Jonathan, as he was her oldest son, would get most of it, but I imagined she'd provided something for the others. Erica's share now would be divided among them.

"Mrs. Gamble," I said after another thoughtful sip of tea. "Do you know anyone called Henry?"

Mrs. Gamble looked blank. "Henry? No one here by that name. All our staff is called John and Peter and James, ain't they?"

"Including the gardener?"

"Symes?" Her perplexity grew. "His name is Algernon. Who is this Henry?"

"I wish I knew. Erica—Mrs. Hume—mentioned the name . . ."

I did not want to break Erica's confidence, but I could hardly uphold my promise to look after the fellow if I had no idea who he was.

Mrs. Gamble shook her head. "No one I know. Mrs. Hume's husband's name was Jeremiah. They didn't have no children. One would have been the making of her, I think. But from what I hear, he wasn't home enough for her to have the chance. Gallivanting, he was. Almost every night, different lady each time. Such a shame."

A cheating husband explained some of Erica's brittleness. I remembered my own shock and disbelief when I'd learned that my husband, now deceased, had raised an entire other family, unknown to me. The betrayal, humiliation, and self-deprecation had laid me low for a long while. I'd berated myself for being a fool, especially when I'd discovered that my marriage had not been legal. He'd wed the other woman first. Gradually I'd understood the fault was his, and I now blamed him squarely, but it had taken a long time for me to forgive myself.

Erica must have known about her husband's mistresses even while she lived with him. Horrible. I wondered if his death had brought her grief or relief.

"Mr. Hume were an MP." Now that Mrs. Gamble was full of tea and comfortable with me, she held forth. "Lord Covington—Erica's father, that is—helped Mr. Hume win his seat in Parliament. Put his might behind it. Perhaps that was why Mr. Hume played away, couldn't stand facing the constant reminder that he owed everything to his wife and her father."

"Perhaps," I said without commitment. Some men needed no excuse.

If Erica had found herself home alone every night, maybe this Henry had indeed been a lover, someone to comfort her in her loneliness.

It wasn't done for a lady to take a paramour, although plenty of society women did. Everyone knew of these ladies' affairs, but no one spoke of them. A woman was more censured for being obvious about her lovers than for having them at all.

Erica did not seem the type. Not a woman who graciously greeted her husband's friends, all the while smiling to herself that she'd met a handsome man in secret who fulfilled her desires.

Harriet, now. She was unmarried, but with her prettiness and youth, she likely had young men on a string, including the one I'd caught her with at the Crystal Palace. I would have to find out all about him. If he was someone her mother disapproved of, Lady Covington's death might free Harriet to go to the man. Another idea I'd have to explore.

"It's a shame," Mrs. Gamble said, her chin trembling. "Mrs. Hume was not the most pleasant lady, but it's unfair she passed so suddenly. It ain't right."

I reached across the corner of the table and laid my hand on her plump one.

"It isn't right, no. I intend to find out what happened, Mrs. Gamble, and bring whoever did this to justice."

It was a bold statement, and an overly dramatic one, but it made Mrs. Gamble wipe her eyes and give me a nod. "I'll help as best I can, Mrs. Holloway. The fact that someone tainted *my* food ain't to be borne."

I'd hoped to ascend to the main house to speak to Lady Covington, but the housemaid who came down to refresh her ladyship's tea said she wasn't receiving anyone, including me.

Because I'd failed her? Or because the lady simply couldn't bear to see any person who would wish to speak about Erica's death?

I would leave her be for now. I told Mrs. Gamble to sit and rest while I poured hot water into the teapot the maid carried, using the kettle Mrs. Gamble had heated for us. Lady Covington asked for nothing to eat, the maid reported, but I had a sniff and small taste of the lumps of sugar in their bowl on the tray. They tasted of only sugar, so I waved the maid off.

"Thank you for the chat, Mrs. Holloway," Mrs. Gamble said as I resumed my coat to leave. "It did me good."

"It did me good too, Mrs. Gamble. Thank you for the tea."

"Anytime, love."

I left her puttering about her kitchen and made my way up the outside stairs to the garden.

The sun breaking through the clouds warmed me. I loosened the top button of my coat as I looked around the green paradise.

One would never know this garden was here if one did not

walk in through the gate. A high wall separated it from the street, and the gate had close-set gratings that blocked the view from without.

The garden wound through land between Lady Covington's home and the house behind it on Upper Brook Street. I walked along, admiring the low hedges and rows of herbs and flowers, impressed by how the meandering path made the garden appear larger than it was. The walkway ended at another gate, which led to the mews between Upper Brook Street and Upper Grosvenor Street.

"Morning."

I jumped and spun to find the gardener behind me. He smiled, teeth showing behind his dark beard.

"Didn't mean to give you a fright, Mrs. Holloway. Did you come for more herbs?"

"Not at all," I said coolly. "I wanted to give her ladyship and family my condolences."

"Aye, a bad business." Symes took another step to me. "Poor Mrs. Hume. No one really liked the poor woman, which is even sadder."

I had to agree. "Have you heard of anyone named Henry, Mr. Symes?"

Symes took off his hat, rumpled his thick hair, and clapped the hat on again. "Can't say that I have. Who is he?"

"This is what I do not know. I believe Mrs. Hume left the house now and again, dismissing her maid before she returned. Do you have any idea where she went?"

Now Symes's gaze turned suspicious. "Why do you want to know that?"

Cynthia had described these absences, which were strange. They might have nothing to do with the poisoning—or everything to do with it.

"It might not matter at all. But then again . . . who knows?" I lifted my palms.

"It's police business now," Symes said. "Not ours. Lady Covington is not happy about that. She won't have police in the house."

"Not even to discover who killed Mrs. Hume?"

"That's why her ladyship sent for you in the first place." Symes was even closer now, not in a threatening way, but one a little too familiar for my liking. "I know all about that—not much goes on in this house the staff don't know. Her ladyship thought you could help, but you couldn't. Not your fault," he added quickly. "What do the likes of you and me know about these things?"

His tone exuded sympathy. Our betters asked too much of us, it said. He and I should draw together over this tragedy I'd been expected to prevent.

I took a step back. "What sorts of plants do you grow here, Mr. Symes?"

Symes grinned, not offended, and waved a hand over the garden with a glow of pride. "All sorts. We have carrots coming up, lettuces, and I've planted the tomatoes and peppers in the hothouse." He motioned me to follow him, and against my better judgment, I did.

The hothouse sat on the south side of the property, against the wall that separated it from the mews. It was a long, low building open at either end with many glass windows to trap the sun's warmth.

I stepped inside after Symes, close air surrounding me. In any other circumstance, I would be delighted. Large pots of tomato plants lined a bench, and below those, the large green leaves of peppers showed. None of the plants had any flowers or fruit at the moment, but that would come later, in July and

August. If the plants thrived, the household would have all the tomatoes and sweet peppers they wanted.

Several flats held seedlings, each carefully labeled as beans, cucumber, courgettes, and spring onions. All specimens looked healthy. From this bountiful hothouse and the lush grounds, I concluded that Symes was an excellent gardener.

"Anything you want from here, you just say, Mrs. Holloway. As soon as I harvest, I'll set things aside for you."

"You ought to ask Lady Covington first," I admonished. "These are her vegetables and herbs, after all."

Symes shrugged. "She said I should give you what you like. She's taken with you, is her ladyship."

"She *was* taken with me, you mean. She might not be now."

"Aye." Symes nodded. "They expect too much." He gave me a hopeful look. "Maybe I do as well?"

I straightened. "Mr. Symes, you are a kind man and a talented gardener. But I am very busy."

Symes's face fell. I did not like to disappoint him, but I truly had much to do, not to mention a daughter to look after and a man I was falling in love with. I did not need the complication of a well-meaning gardener who wanted to walk out with me.

"Ah well. Don't think too harshly of me, Mrs. Holloway. You are a fine-looking woman."

"I appreciate the compliment," I said politely. "I will take you up on the offer of the herbs and vegetables. They are excellent specimens."

"Thank you." Symes accepted my praise as his due. "I do my best."

"Well, good day, Mr. Symes. If you happen to discover who the person called Henry is, will you please tell me?"

"As you like." Symes clearly wondered why I'd fixed on this Henry, but he nodded.

He remained in the hothouse, taking up a trowel, as I departed. I let myself out of the gate to the mews and walked through a tiny passageway that led between coach houses. I emerged into the mews, which were busy with coachmen grooming horses or repairing harness or carriage wheels, the scent of horse pungent. The mews led out to Park Street, which roughly paralleled Park Lane, and I turned down this to walk home.

When I entered the kitchen, Cynthia sprang up from the table where she'd been chatting with Tess. She wore a suit, and thrust her hands into its pockets.

"The chemist told me what was in Lady Covington's powders," she said. "The ones Jepson was so angry at me for not giving her." She bent closer, though there was no one else in the kitchen but Tess, and confided, "Magnesium hydroxide."

13

❧————❧

O h." Cynthia's words arrested me in the act of lifting off
my hat. I took it all the way off and hung it up with my
coat, hiding my disappointment.

"What's magnees . . . ?" Tess asked. "Whatever you said?"

"A common substance," I answered, retrieving my apron
and moving to the table. "Sometimes it's known as magnesium milk, and it's nothing more than a laxative."

"Not poison, then," Tess said, deflating.

"I suppose it can be if you take too much," I answered. "But
the symptoms would be different."

Cynthia rocked on her heels. "Chemist said there wasn't
anything but the laxative in the powders, so that wasn't how
the poison was given. Anyway, we do know Erica took sick
from what she ate from the hamper."

"As did Sir Arthur," I said as I resumed my apron. "We can't
know which food was dosed, however. The hamper was empty

when someone from the railway returned it to the house, Mrs. Gamble says."

Cynthia's eyes widened in alarm. "Lord, I hope none of the porters nicked leftovers from it."

"That would indeed be terrible," I said with a shiver. "Though I think any porters falling ill would have been reported in the newspaper."

"That's somefink I could find out," Tess chirped. "Can tell Caleb to, I mean. Whether any porters on that train got sick. Be more evidence the food was tainted, wouldn't it?"

"That is true," I said. "Thank you, Tess. I appreciate the help."

She beamed, pleased.

"What do you want *me* to do, Mrs. H.?" Cynthia asked. "I'll go back to Lady Covington's tomorrow—I'm giving her family a day to themselves. What sorts of things can I ferret out?"

"Please, do not go," I said quickly. "It is obviously *not* safe to eat food from that house."

"Nonsense. The hamper was meant for Lady Covington alone. The poisoner couldn't have known it would be passed around." Cynthia paused. "Jove, if the poisoner *is* one of the family, and he or she sat calmly and watched Erica down the lot . . ." She trailed off grimly. "I'll go back so I can wring his neck. Or hers."

"Anyone on the train could have had the chance to doctor it," I pointed out.

Cynthia dug her hands deeper into her pockets, slouching like a languid young man. "True, the hamper would have sat with the luggage on the platform, then been loaded into the baggage car and carried from there to the compartment. An enemy who didn't live in the house could have seized the opportunity. He'd not have guessed Lady Covington wouldn't eat a thing."

"But how would someone from outside the house poison the family meals Lady Covington has taken sick from?" I carried my spice boxes from the dresser to the table and began laying out ingredients for the Antiguan custard. "They'd have to find a way to slip into the kitchen and sprinkle the substance into the dishes, and I'm certain Mrs. Gamble would notice. A good cook never lets a meal go up without having a taste to make certain all is well."

"Has the cook ever been sick?" Tess asked Cynthia.

"Not that I've heard. None of the staff either. Hmm."

I sniffed a fragrant star anise and set it into a bowl. "Then the poison must be introduced *after* the food leaves the kitchen. Everyone below stairs would sample a bit of what goes upstairs—I always make extra to feed the staff if I do not cook them a separate meal. Or I have Tess taste things to give me her opinion. Depend upon it, if the food was poisoned in the kitchen, someone else would fall ill, mostly likely Mrs. Gamble herself."

"I'll just have to catch them at it." Cynthia bounced on her toes with the eagerness of a pup. "Don't worry, Mrs. H. I'll eat very little and smuggle in biscuits to keep myself nourished in the middle of the night. Now that Erica has paid the price, I'll wager the rest of the family will take Lady Covington's fears more seriously."

"*If* they find poison in Erica," I said, recalling my discussion about this with Daniel. "After all, bad food lays people low or kills them all the time. Not always the fault of the cook—ingredients can go off, with none the wiser until it's too late."

"Miss Townsend has some leverage with the police," Cynthia said. "Her father is in the Cabinet and does something or other in the Home Office. She can encourage them to look for poison. Look carefully, I mean."

I was not optimistic. Erica belonged to a wealthy and prominent family, that was true, but I did not have much faith in a police coroner if the poison wasn't obvious. I was not an expert on such, but the coroner could decide that Erica's symptoms came from a bad egg or a spoiled strawberry. The police might dismiss Lady Covington's conviction about poison out of hand, labeling her a hysterical woman.

"Or I could speak to Inspector McGregor," I said. "He does not welcome my interference, but he knows by now that I do not cry wolf."

Tess grimaced. "He frightens me, does the inspector. Caleb's terrified of him, though he says Inspector McGregor is a good policeman." She added the last reluctantly.

"I will speak to the inspector as soon as I can." I did not relish hunting him up—McGregor could be intimidating, though I agreed with Caleb that he was a good policeman, if a bad-tempered one.

Cynthia let out a breath. "I feel ineffectual shuffling about this house. Every time I see Mummy or Auntie, they immediately open their mouths to tell me about some young toad they want to pair me up with. It's galling. My father is chumming up to some prominent chaps while he's here—I imagine to fleece them somehow—and I live in terror he'll convince one to throw his son at me. It's becoming stifling."

"Do you not want to marry at all, Lady Cynthia?" Tess asked. "You'd have your own house and your own servants. Maybe me and Mrs. H. could work for you." She gazed at Cynthia, her freckled face hopeful.

"Marriage is all right for some," Cynthia conceded. "But I won't do it if I have to be paired with an idiot."

"Maybe Mr. Thanos will propose," Tess suggested brightly.

Cynthia's flush rose all the way to her fair hair. "Why should he? Bachelor's life is good for Mr. Thanos. Besides, he hasn't got two pennies to rub together. He can't afford a wife. Well, must get upstairs before Auntie realizes I'm here and drags me away by the ear."

She turned and nearly ran out of the kitchen, banging her way up the stairs. The slam of the door at the top echoed down the corridor.

Tess drooped. "Oh, I shouldn't have said nothing. Didn't mean to put me foot in it."

I calmly laid out a few cinnamon sticks. "Not your fault, Tess. I think Cynthia would be deliriously happy living in a cramped flat with Mr. Thanos and making certain his socks match. I must do something about that."

Tess clapped her floury hands. "Can I help?"

"Perhaps." I had no wish for her to go blundering in with some mad scheme in her enthusiasm. "Now, pay attention, and I will teach you a new pudding."

I had procured the meat of a coconut from a vendor not long ago. It had been a bit dear, but I'd kept it wrapped in paper and now shredded it into a jug of cream.

Now to combine the spice mixture. "Star anise, a bay leaf, cinnamon, vanilla, and a scraping of nutmeg," I said, dropping each into a pot. "Mixed with a little cocoa powder and water. Grated chocolate would be best, but I could not find any that did not cost the earth. We warm this on the stove for a time, and then add it to our custard."

Tess was fascinated by the coconut. She prodded the shredded, wet mass with her spoon. "I saw a coconut tree once at Kew Gardens. Big, tall palm, it was, with nuts as big as me head."

"A wonder of the world," I agreed. "We are lucky to be able to have such foods from all parts of the planet."

"Sun never sets on the British Empire, they say," Tess said, then she let out a laugh. "And it never shows its face in London."

I finished the spice infusion, simmered it a time on the stove, then let it cool. Meanwhile I had Tess combine the coconut mixture with cream I'd boiled and sweetened a few days before. I strained the infusion into the creams and added a beaten egg, then the whole thing went into a pudding basin and into the oven.

"We have to watch it carefully so it doesn't scorch," I warned.

Tess, busy licking the spoon and bowl, couldn't be bothered to answer.

The custard did turn out, and I sent it up for supper in individual cups nestled in a bowl of ice to keep them cool. For the rest of the meal, I did salmon, a soup of thinly sliced vegetables, filets of beef with asparagus, a salad, and a whole chicken. As usual, the plates came back empty.

Sometime later, as the kitchen calmed and after Tess had gone up to bed, I drew a much-needed breath and set a kettle on for tea.

I truly did not wish Cynthia to return to Lady Covington's and endanger herself, but on the other hand, she was my eyes and ears inside the house. I did not trust the servants there—Symes might be sweet on me, but if he was loyal to whoever was poisoning Lady Covington, he'd hardly give the person up to me. He might even be pretending interest in me to steer me wrong.

A step brought me out of my contemplation. The figure of a man emerged from the cavernous darkness of the hall, a chance beam of light gleaming on his thinning hair, sharp face, and lines of narrow sideburns.

"Your lordship?" I curtsied, but kept near my table, aware of how alone I was. The kitchen echoed my words.

"Mrs. Holloway." Lord Clifford entered, his shoulders slightly stooped under his tailor-made coat. "I came to tell you how much I enjoyed your pudding—the custard with the unusual spices. Most excellent."

I curtsied again. "Thank you, sir."

"Don't be stiff-necked, my girl." Lord Clifford came closer without unease, a man used to making his way into anyplace he liked. "I often descend to praise a good cook. And give her a token of my appreciation." He dipped his hand into his frock coat and emerged with a coin.

A gold sovereign. Quite a lot of money for a tip. A cook could expect to be given a penny for her trouble, or perhaps a shilling if the person decided to be generous.

An entire pound was unheard of. If I tried to spend that, I might be taken for a thief or a counterfeiter.

"You are very kind, your lordship, but I cannot accept so much."

"Absolute rot." Lord Clifford opened his hazel eyes wide. "Of course you should have this. You earned it."

I could discern where Cynthia obtained her casual charm. Lord Clifford obviously thought nothing of wandering downstairs and chucking high-value coins at a cook.

When I said nothing, Lord Clifford tossed the coin onto the table. It rolled across the flour I'd spread out to knead the piecrust for tomorrow's breakfast tart. The coin teetered, spun, and clattered to rest on the flour-dusted board.

"Thank you, your lordship," I said, as he seemed to be waiting for me to acknowledge the gift.

"And perhaps you won't say a word to your supercilious

butler about a bottle or two finding their way to my chamber."
Lord Clifford winked at me and touched the side of his nose.

So that was his game. Butter up the cook so she'll let him
abscond with Lord Rankin's best vintage.

"Papa?" Cynthia's voice rang down the passageway, and
Lord Clifford winced, like a boy caught out of school. "What
are you doing down here? Nicking more wine, are you?"

Lord Clifford flushed as Cynthia strode into the kitchen
and halted beside him. Her suit was a mirror of her father's.

"I was simply rewarding Mrs. Holloway for a meal well
cooked," he protested. "You are far too distrustful, my dear."

"I know you well, is all." Cynthia tucked her arm through
Lord Clifford's. "Mummy is searching for you."

Lord Clifford glanced heavenward. "She wants to drag me
to some dreary play in a musty theatre. Why aren't you going
with her, daughter? It's the Season, isn't it? The time when
young ladies swathe themselves in jewels and try to catch a
man's eye. You'll never marry at this rate, and you know you
must."

Cynthia kept her tone even. "I am exhausted and shocked
from the events last evening."

"Oh, right. The young lady dropping dead in the middle of
the Crystal Palace. Was all over the newspapers. Poor thing."
To Lord Clifford's credit, he did sound sad.

"It was awful. Yet Mrs. Holloway came home and made
spectacular meals all day for us. You ought to give her a thousand guineas, Papa, not one small sovereign."

Cynthia was being ridiculous, but I appreciated the sentiment.

"I would if I could, my love." Lord Clifford squeezed Cynthia's arm fondly. "Where have you been disappearing to, eh?
Your aunt and uncle are dull as ditchwater, and your mother

leaves me to them, pretending to need to rest all the blasted time. You ought to rescue me."

"I've been staying with Lady Covington, remember?" Cynthia said. "Mummy did tell you."

"I didn't realize they would absorb you and leave you no time for your poor pater. Covington." Lord Clifford's brow furrowed. "That name calls something to mind, besides the poor woman who died. Hmm. Railways—that is it."

"The late Lord Covington owned a railway," Cynthia said. "The family still owns it, and the new Lord Covington sits with his stepmum on the board of directors. Dear old George has no idea what to do with this railway, according to Lady Covington."

"No, that wasn't it." Lord Clifford tapped his lip in thought. "Ah, I have it. A jolly big crash some six or seven or so years back. Train was mangled, about seventy or so people killed. Tragic. Faulty wheel or some such thing. It was Covington's railway, I'm certain."

"Lady Covington's first husband died in that railway accident," I said, startled into joining the conversation.

"Did he now?" Cynthia asked. "Explains why none of the family wants to mention it. How safe are a man's trains when one kills him?"

"Quite," Lord Clifford agreed.

I had to wonder, in light of this discussion, whether Harriet or Jonathan blamed their mother for their father's death. Perhaps they were taking their revenge on her. Why they'd suppose Lady Covington would have anything to do with the railway accident, I did not know, but emotions are not always logical. Or perhaps their mother and father had quarreled and he'd rushed off to be away from her, taking the fateful train.

"I shall be sure to find out more about that," Cynthia said

with a nod at me. "Now, Papa, let us leave Mrs. Holloway to it. She cannot concoct her wonderful meals with us in the way. Take Mummy to the theatre and enjoy it."

"Ghastly." Lord Clifford shuddered. "It is some horrible melodrama."

"Use the time to ingratiate yourself to the London *ton*. That should entertain you."

"True." Lord Clifford pursed his lips. "It might help with—" He broke off, darting a guilty glance at his daughter.

Cynthia's mouth tightened. "Do rein in your tendency to dupe others, Papa. Simply make friends with them."

Lord Clifford sent her a lofty look. "I told you, Cynthia—those days are well behind me. I was a rogue in my youth, yes, but now I am a staid old man."

"Hardly." Cynthia rolled her eyes. "Good night, Mrs. H. I'll take him away."

So saying, she tugged her father from the kitchen. He went out with every sign of reluctance, his thin voice floating back to me as he continued his complaints about being dragged to the theatre.

I eyed the gold sovereign that lay forgotten in a puff of flour. I could call to Lord Clifford and insist he take it back, but how foolish would I be to chuck away so much money?

I lifted the coin, dusted it off, and dropped it into my pocket.

"Have they gone?"

I stifled a shriek. "James. Good heavens, lad." I pressed my hand to my chest as James materialized out of the shadows of the scullery. "How long have you been there?"

"Since just before his lordship arrived." James crushed his cap in his lanky hands and did not appear one bit ashamed. "Thought I'd better keep quiet while the quality were about."

He sent me a rueful look. "Wish gentlemen would toss *me* gold sovereigns. Most I get are farthings, and that's to make me go away."

"Don't be so silly." I took a breath, trying to calm myself. "How are you faring, James?"

"I'm well, thank you. Don't you want to hear why me da sent me to you?"

"The thought had crossed my mind." I stifled my eagerness by gathering up the flour where the coin had lain and tossing it into the dustbin—coins, as dear as they are, can be dirty things.

"He wants to see you, Mrs. H. At Grosvenor Chapel, where you usually meet. Now, if you're able."

14

———◆———◆———

I'd already had a very long day, but I assured James I would meet Daniel in the designated place. James said he'd wait for me, and not long later, he and I walked arm in arm along Mount Street to South Audley Street, then south to the tasteful building that was Grosvenor Chapel.

The chapel's columned front and octagonal steeple were faint in the darkness, the brick facade fading into the night. James and I turned left into the lane that ran alongside the chapel, our walk ending at a large iron gate between two white pillars.

The gate was unlocked. Beyond was the churchyard, a very pleasant place to stroll on a sunny summer morning but a bit unnerving at eleven o'clock on a dark night.

Daniel solidified from the shadows of a tall tree. He wore his deliveryman's clothes—wool coat patched at the elbows, breeches and thick socks, heavy boots, a cloth tied around his neck in lieu of a cravat.

Daniel seized my hands and, in the cover of darkness, dared kiss my lips. The houses of Mount Street rose behind us, and I hoped that Mrs. Bywater—or more likely, our busybody neighbor—did not peer from an upper window.

Daniel's breath fogged, the air chilly. "The chapel is open for us. Shall we adjourn somewhere more comfortable?"

"Your vicar friend is quite accommodating," I said as the three of us moved to the side door of the chapel. We'd met in the sacristy before, on another dark night, when I'd first met Mr. Fielding.

I half expected to find Mr. Fielding waiting for us, but the sacristy was empty except for a candle flickering in a holder on a shelf. Robes peeked from a closet with a half-open door, and stacks of prayer books reposed on a table.

"I did the man a favor once," Daniel said. "We became friends."

Great friends, I reflected, for him to give Daniel the run of the chapel in the middle of the night. The favor must have been a large one.

James showed no sign of leaving. He leaned against the wall and folded his arms, his frown not reassuring.

"What has happened?" I asked Daniel. I was not one who liked others to dance gently around a subject. I preferred to get it over with in one blow.

"Nothing." Daniel took my hands again as we stood in the center of the underlit room. "Nothing disastrous anyway. I have come from Inspector McGregor."

"Excellent. Is he investigating? Does he believe Erica was murdered? What killed her?"

Daniel stifled a laugh. "Bombard me with one question at a time, please. McGregor was not investigating, because it is not his case. The Sydenham police did the postmortem, and they have not called for any assistance from Scotland Yard. I gave McGregor all the details so he can insist on looking into it if he sees fit after he reads the reports."

"I see." I stemmed my impatience with effort. "What did the postmortem find?"

"The conclusions have not yet been written up." Daniel released me. "On the other hand, I have acquaintances in the coroners' offices, and I was able to discover the preliminary results. Mrs. Hume did die from ingesting a noxious substance, that is clear. What that substance is, they do not yet know. They've ruled out the most obvious poisons—arsenic, strychnine, prussic acid."

"Then it is something much more obscure. I feared it might be."

Daniel nodded. "The coroner wished to call it accidental food poisoning, as Sir Arthur had also been ill. Tainted food not well cooked, the hamper passed from hand to hand, left to sit in foul air. Death by misfortune."

"You say he *wished* to. Did he not do so?"

"McGregor wired the Sydenham coroner and told him to search more diligently. To look for more exotic poisons. It might take some time, but rest assured, the true cause of Mrs. Hume's death will be uncovered."

"You mean you bent Inspector McGregor to your will." I sent Daniel a warm look. "He'd never have bothered otherwise."

Daniel rubbed his forehead. "*Bent him to my will* is going a bit far. But yes, I persuaded him. You should be flattered that he resisted until I said *you* thought there was something untoward going on in Baron Covington's household."

I gazed at him in surprise. "That convinced him? Inspector McGregor dislikes me entirely."

"No, he does not. McGregor realizes that when you get a whiff of something, so to speak, then it is a true problem. He grumbles and growls, because he knows he will have to work harder on an obscure crime. You've been proved right too many times."

"I must always catch him in a bad temper, then." I was not certain whether to be gratified or alarmed by the inspector's faith in me. "I suppose he does know how to smile?"

"If so, I've never caught him at it."

"Well, perhaps one day." I rubbed my gloved hands. Summer was still a month away, and the unheated room was cool. "Now then, Daniel, you did not expect me to meet you in secret, in the dark, simply to tell me that no one knows what killed Erica Hume. Or to tell me you have convinced Inspector McGregor to help. What else has happened?"

"How well you know me." Daniel began his crooked smile, the one that had made my knees weak the first time I'd met him. "I do have a favor to ask."

"I might have known."

By the way James scowled, folding his arms tightly, I assumed he did not approve of this favor. Strange, because James usually stood by his father in all things.

"It is delicate." Daniel rubbed his forehead once more, a sign he was uncomfortable. "You know I am watching a prominent man."

"The Duke of Daventry."

"I suppose Errol told you his exact identity," Daniel said. "My brother has been turning up wherever I go, playing the harmless and somewhat dim-witted vicar."

"Mr. Fielding agrees with me that I should be more informed." I had asked Mr. Fielding to find out what Lord Clifford was up to, but so far he'd told me nothing of that.

Daniel cleared his throat. "Well, I will have to tell you all, if I am to ask you to help me."

"You ought to, yes."

"Please cease the reproving stare, Kat. I hate being less than honest with you, and your looks can skewer me to the bone."

"Serves ya right," James put in.

Daniel did not admonish his son, which told me more than anything else that Daniel was worried.

"Daventry is a family man," he began. "Very keen on it, is a devoted husband and has grown children he is very fond of. He is believed to be funding anarchists—as Errol no doubt told you—but his enemies might be touting this idea to ruin him. My guv'nor sent me in because I can be careful about these distinctions."

"Commendable." I made an approving nod. Daniel was always fair.

"On Thursday, the Duchess of Daventry is hosting a lavish garden party at their estate in Surrey. They also have a house in Berkeley Square, which is where I am living at the moment—as far as the duke is concerned, I am the young cousin of an old school friend who is now in Canada and out of touch. The weather is fine enough that the duchess wants a garden party at the Surrey estate for several hundred guests. The duke and duchess give generously to several charities and are celebrating the success of those endeavors. They extended the invitation to me, but the duchess is keen that I bring a young lady. She believes I ought to be married by now, with a wife to look after me."

"It is the fashion this month," I said, even as my misgivings grew. "Mrs. Bywater and Cynthia's mother have renewed their wish that she be wed as soon as possible. Did you wish me to ask Cynthia to accompany you? Pretend she is your fiancée or the like?"

"No, no. Lady Cynthia is known to the duke and duchess, and probably to many of the guests who will be there. Her presence would raise far too many questions and cause a scandal." Daniel avoided my gaze. "I am asking *you* to do it."

My dismay, which had begun when he began his explanation, now struck me sharply.

"My dear Daniel, I cannot possibly." My voice rang to the dark corners of the room, and the words whispered back to me under the wavering candlelight. "Apply to Miss Townsend. She has played your lady before."

"Miss Townsend too would be recognized. In Paris she could bring off the deception, but she never could here. Her father is high in the government, close friends with Gladstone. If the duke is guilty, I do not want to put him on his guard."

My heart thumped, my throat closing. "Surely you must know other young ladies in your . . . line of work."

"None that I trust. I trust *you*, Kat. And you are unknown."

"I am a cook," I said firmly. "If you are thinking to dress me as a grand lady, you are mad. Even in a costly frock I could not be mistaken for anything but a domestic." I removed my gloves in jerks and spread my hands. "You see?"

My fingers, plump and capable, were flecked with burns and nicked here and there, the palms dry and calloused from hard work and strong soap. Though I kept my nails neatly trimmed, they were a far cry from the soft manicured ones of ladies like Cynthia and Miss Townsend.

Daniel took one of my hands and kissed it. "They are beautiful to me. It will be an outdoor event, so you will have your gloves on at all times, in any case. A large hat with a veil will help."

"Until I open my mouth." I snatched my hand from his grasp. "I have taught myself to smooth out my speech, but any member of the upper classes will know as soon as I converse with them that I am a fraud. There are nuances I will never be able to mimic."

"It is only a matter of practice." Daniel must have had all the nuances correct if he pretended to be the son of a man from a well-known public school like Eton or Harrow. But he'd been practicing a lifetime, and I'd have a few days. "I can claim that you are Dutch or Flemish, which will explain away any slips you make. I won't have you be French, because too many people know that language, but I've never met an Englishman who confessed to speaking Dutch. However, plenty of Dutch are fluent in English."

"For heaven's sake, Daniel . . ."

"Hear me, please. It is for a few hours only, though I know it will rob you of your beloved Thursday. I will make certain you are finished in time to spend some of your day out with Grace." Daniel let out a growl of exasperation. "I tried to put them off the idea, but the duchess then promised to introduce me to several eligible young ladies if I arrived on my own. That would indeed be a disaster."

I quailed. "You are mad. Mad, mad, mad . . ."

"Believe me, I thought long and hard before I came to you with this, Kat. You would help me immeasurably, and I will be forever in your debt."

His remorse was true, but I saw something in his dark blue eyes behind the pinprick of reflected candlelight. Fear?

Tamping down on my panic as I pictured myself walking into the garden party and being instantly exposed—which would either expose Daniel as well, or at least subject him to censorious ridicule—I tried to decide what he was *not* saying.

"If you fail at this task you've been set, your guv'nor, as you call him, will be unhappy," I stated.

Daniel nodded, quiet. "He will be."

I remembered the ice-cold man with the spectacles I'd seen outside a prison when the prison's wall had been breached—Monaghan was the name I'd pried from Daniel a few days ago. He had a hold on Daniel I did not understand, and I knew Daniel had little say in what jobs he did for this man.

I turned abruptly and paced the room, uttering a few words that were definitely unladylike.

"If I ever meet Mr. Monaghan," I said as I returned to Daniel, "I will have things to say to him."

"Then I will do my best to keep you from him. He is a dangerous man."

"One on our side of the law?"

"For now." Daniel set his mouth in a flat line.

"I see." I paced a few more times, turning over in my head all the possibilities of what could go wrong with Daniel's scheme. So many things could.

I knew, however, that Daniel would never have come to me if he'd had any other choice. He wanted to bring a lady to the garden party so that his hostess wouldn't foist an innocent on him. Daniel's disguise would never stand up to close scrutiny by a young lady determined to catch herself a wealthy and socially acceptable husband.

I could be an outsider, met on his travels, respectable enough to be presented to a duchess, but one who could disappear once Daniel was finished with this case and not be missed.

If Daniel displeased his hostess, and she turned him out,

he'd have to go to his guv'nor and tell him he'd not been able to collect more evidence for or against the duke. If Mr. Monaghan grew angry, what would he do? Send Daniel away to some awful and perilous place? Banish him, even jail him?

All because I was too timid to help.

I heaved a sigh that came from the depths of my soul. "I will need a frock," I said. "The ones I have will hardly do."

Daniel relaxed. "Thank you, Kat." He took my hands once again. "Miss Townsend has agreed to provide you clothes and guidance and make certain you know the role you are to play."

Very practical of him. "We will have to be careful. Most visitors to a house never see the cook, but if one of my former employers appears at the garden party, they will know that your young lady from Amsterdam is a fraud."

"I have already scrutinized the guest list, and no one you have worked for in any capacity will be there."

I gave Daniel a level stare. "You know who all my former employers are, do you?"

He flushed. "Yes."

I was too worried about my upcoming ruse to be unnerved. "Well, I still believe you mad, and I am not one for playacting. But nor do I want you to suffer at the hands of your guv'nor. If he sends you to the ends of the earth, James and I might never see you again."

Daniel's brows rose. "If he tried to do that, I'd tell him to go to the devil."

"And what would be the consequences of that? Much the same result, if I read the situation aright."

Daniel grimaced. "Possibly. You, of course, will know nothing about the duke and this Dublin business. Nothing to do with you."

"I do understand. I will be polite but uninterested in anything not on the surface."

The corner of Daniel's mouth quirked. "I knew I chose right to ask you. You will be perfect, Kat."

"Let us hope so," I said darkly. "And let us hope the duchess's cook is up to scratch. Or I might be tempted to remark strongly upon it."

J ames saw me home after I took my leave of Daniel. He slumped along, hands in his pockets, a glower on his young face.

"You do not like it," I said as we walked. "I do not either, but I see that Daniel doesn't have much choice."

"He shouldn't be putting you into danger," James growled. "Bad enough he does it for himself."

"I agree, but I understand his predicament." I admitted to myself that not only did I wish to save Daniel the embarrassment of his hostess thrusting young ladies at him, I did not want those young ladies hanging on him and becoming enchanted by him. Or he becoming enchanted with *them*.

"Be careful." James's warning broke through my silent tirade. "This bloke dad works for is a hard one. I don't know much about him, and Dad keeps him well away from me—if he even realizes Dad has a son—but I know he's bad, even if he does things for the police."

"Yes, I've seen him. Not someone I want to encounter any closer." I patted James's arm. "I will take care, love. I will be the polite but not bright stranger and never see the lot of them again. No one looks hard at a servant, so even if I pass them in the street as myself, I doubt they'll notice."

James fell silent, but his uneasiness and anger simmered. I was touched that he cared so much for my safety—I had come to care greatly for him.

Thus it was that when Thursday came and I left for my day out, Cynthia met me around the corner in South Audley Street. She hailed a hansom, which took us to Miss Townsend's home, where I was to be transformed.

15

❖━━━━━━━━❖

I'd visited Miss Townsend's Mayfair home before, a tall town house on Upper Brook Street, not far from Lady Covington's mansion.

Miss Townsend's quiet butler admitted us, and a maid led us upstairs to a lavish bedchamber and attached sitting room that took up the entire floor. Bobby was there, resting in an armchair near the fireplace with her feet on an ottoman, but she banged down her boots and rose as Cynthia and I entered.

A gown rested on a chaise, a plum-colored creation lined with darker purple braid and lace. Its fabric was sateen, which was cotton with a satin sheen, good for walking about gardens. The gown caught the light as Miss Townsend held it up to me.

"I have a friend about your build," she said. "A few alterations will be needed, I'm certain, but I actually can wield a needle."

"As can I," Cynthia said. "Taught before I had the wits to protest."

I was positioned in the middle of the room, well away from the windows, while the three ladies remade me. Off came my worn brown frock, petticoats, and stockings, until I stood bare legged in my corset cover and pantalets, my skin prickling with cold and embarrassment.

"This too." Miss Townsend tugged the sleeve of the corset cover.

"What on earth for?" I asked in alarm. "No one will see it. I certainly hope not anyway."

"The manner in which a gown lies betrays what's under it," Miss Townsend explained. "When I learned to paint human skin, I first studied the muscle and bone beneath. We are many layered."

"I would like a few layers to remain between myself and the world, thank you." I rubbed my cold arms. "I refuse to part with the corset itself; I will tell you this at once."

Miss Townsend sent me a patient smile. "Your corset should be fine. Although I did have my corset maker do one up for you. Yours to keep should you decide to wear it."

Bobby let out a laugh. "Give in at once, Mrs. H. Judith will have her way, and she'll kill you with kindness until she gets it."

Miss Townsend, ignoring her, opened a box on a nearby chair. Inside, nestled in tissue, lay an ivory-colored corset with panels of silk moiré, thin shoulder straps, and silken white lacings.

"I'd dirty that the moment I put it on." The words came out

of my mouth in a whisper, and I reached a finger to the smooth fabric. My own corset was made of practical stiff cotton, the shafts that held the boning much mended.

"You could keep it for special occasions," Miss Townsend said. "I agree it is not practical for work. I have an old one myself for my outdoor painting sessions."

"Or you could shuck it entirely, Judith." Bobby resumed her chair and sent Miss Townsend a pointed look. "The skirts too."

"I have not yet taken to Bobby's and Cynthia's enjoyment of male dress," Miss Townsend said, her smile in place. "If women's things are designed correctly, they are not as restricting as they could be."

"One has to have a pile of cash and a trustworthy dressmaker for that," Cynthia said. She had worn her coat and trousers for this outing, and she lounged on a chair, legs over its arm, as though to prove the ease of the garments.

"Shall you try this corset, Mrs. Holloway?" Miss Townsend touched the new one with a light fingertip.

I heaved a sigh. "Very well. But I will change behind a screen."

"Use my bedchamber. The doors roll shut." She lifted the corset box and carried it into the bedroom beyond, laying everything on the bed. "I have new stockings in the box as well. Emerge when you are finished. If you have trouble with the lacings, I'm certain Cynthia will assist you."

"Be happy to," Cynthia said with no signs of moving.

Miss Townsend left me alone, pulling the double pocket doors closed behind her.

I had no idea what I was doing standing in an elegantly simple bedchamber in Mayfair, laying aside my sensible work clothing for the garments of an upper-class lady. I'd been born within hearing of Bow Bells—the bells of St. Mary-le-Bow, in Cheapside. In fact, my mother had been living in Bow Lane, not far from the back of the church. I was Cockney to the bone, and I always would be. Daniel was the same—a boy of the London streets would never be a gentleman, no matter how much he pretended to be.

Setting aside these philosophical musings, I unlaced my corset—I could do this myself from long practice, enough to wriggle out of it—and quickly donned the new one over my chemise. At least Miss Townsend hadn't insisted I relinquish *that*.

I *would* have to have Cynthia's assistance, I realized. I'd never manage on my own. Before I called her in, I slid on the stockings, gauzy silk that was like rainwater on my flesh. I tied the garters, also provided, and held the corset to me while I peeked out and beckoned Cynthia in.

Cynthia good-naturedly laced and tied the corset—not too tightly. She then helped me with the corset cover, a sweet, light shirt of silk that reached to my waist.

"Bit of a shame to hide these," I remarked, touching the corset cover. "They're the most beautiful things I've ever worn."

"Judith has taste," Cynthia agreed. "Now then, ready for the outer layers?"

"Let me put on my shoes. I would hate to ruin these lovely stockings." The stockings were so light I barely noticed I had them on.

"Oh yes, Judith found you these." Cynthia lifted a box from the dressing table. Inside lay a pair of high-heeled boots of soft white leather.

It was a pleasure to don the shoes, which supplely cupped each foot. They fit suspiciously well.

"How did she know what size to obtain?" I asked in amazement.

Cynthia cleared her throat. "I might have slipped into your chamber and stolen your spare pair of shoes. Miss Townsend took them to a cobbler and had this pair made to order. I put your shoes back as soon as he'd taken the measurements."

I hadn't noticed them missing, but then I was usually too exhausted when I went to bed to check all my belongings. I kept my extra shoes in a box on a shelf.

"Daniel only asked me to do this on Tuesday evening. How did Miss Townsend have them made so quickly?"

Cynthia hesitated. "Well, truth to tell, I nicked 'em a bit before this. Wanted to surprise you. As a gift."

I stood up, learning the balance of the new heels. "Cynthia," I admonished her.

"Do not put your back up. You're a proud woman, and so am I. Shouldn't a friend purchase a friend a gift?"

"A book or a small trinket. Not a pair of shoes."

"Books are devilish expensive, even secondhand ones. Besides, good thing I did, eh? Now you have something to wear for your adventure."

I shook my head but decided to say no more. Cynthia was kindhearted, and I would not scold her for her generosity.

We returned to the outer room. Miss Townsend helped me into a crinoline with a bustle that would smooth the skirt, then a creamy and rustling petticoat. She proved she could indeed sew as she altered the waistband to fit.

Finally, the skirt went on with a few more tucks to settle it around me. The slick purple fabric caught on my work-worn hands as I stroked it in wonder. The skirt gathered over the bustle in back—a small one, not the enormous things I'd noted ladies wearing lately—decorated with lace tied into bows.

The bodice came last, fitting me closely and buttoning up the front. The side seams had to be let out a bit so I could breathe, but with a snip here and there and a tightening of my laces, the whole thing became neat and even.

Black buttons made a nice contrast to the light and dark purples, and the lace and braid finished the look. The gown's color brought a pinkness to my face, and my eyes were starry as I beheld myself in a tall looking glass.

"Oh my," I said.

Even Bobby became interested as Miss Townsend fussed about, taking in a seam or sewing down an errant bit of braid. Cynthia stood back, arms akimbo, and surveyed me.

"Excellent. McAdam's eyes will pop out."

"I certainly hope not. He will need them."

The jest was made absently, because what I saw in the mirror stunned me. My hair was mussed, half out of its braid, but otherwise, I could not believe that the beautiful creature I beheld was me.

The gown fitted me well after Miss Townsend's alterations, hugging my figure, which I had always thought a bit too plump. The shimmering fabric flattered me, as did the new corset, trimming my body to the correct proportions. The high heels lifted me and straightened my back, giving a regal tilt to my head.

I still thought a cook's face gazed back at me. Before I could voice my opinion, Miss Townsend was pulling pins from my hair and wielding a hairbrush through my long, dark tresses.

She called in her lady's maid, who thought nothing of sitting me down and pulling my hair this way and that, braiding some parts, curling others. She complimented me on having such thick and abundant hair that she didn't have to add switches, then went to work pinning it all in place.

The result was a style that swept my hair from my face to the back of my neck, where it wound in braids and curls up to the crown of my head. The final touch was a hat, a small one the same color as the gown, with a purple dotted lace veil that hung from the hat brim to my upper lip. Kid gloves softer than my own skin went onto my hands.

"Perfect," Cynthia declared.

Miss Townsend clasped her hands, admiring her work. Bobby, who'd retreated while the maid worked on my hair, gave me a jaunty bow. "I'd be proud to have you on my arm, Mrs. Holloway."

"As will McAdam." Cynthia danced a little jig, kicking her heels up at the end. "I'd love to be there to see his face."

"You must tell us absolutely everything," Miss Townsend said.

"Yes, about how far his mouth falls open," Bobby said. "We have so little entertainment."

"Shush, Bobby," Miss Townsend said, but Bobby only guffawed.

I wondered how much Miss Townsend actually knew about what Daniel was doing and why. Daniel trusted her, but his situation was delicate. I would ask him, but for now I concluded he'd told her just enough to recruit her help, which she was eagerly giving.

Because of Daniel's mission? Or did these ladies have another intent in mind? They were very keen to know what Daniel would think of me.

"You are all very romantic," I told them severely. "I am assisting Daniel to save him from embarrassment. That is all."

"Of course," Cynthia said quickly. She winked at the other two.

I gave up. "I must hasten, or I will be late."

Daniel had arranged that I would be driven to Waterloo Station, where he would meet me and escort me to Surrey. A hansom pulled to the door, driven by Daniel's cabbie friend, Lewis. James, dressed in a trim dark suit, waited inside to assist me.

He opened his brown eyes wide as Bobby handed me in. "Love a duck. Is it you, Mrs. H.?"

"It is indeed. No need for such language." I settled the skirts, pulling a dust blanket over them. I didn't always bother with the blanket, but I wanted no soot, mud, or horse dung on this beautiful skirt.

The ladies had come outside with me and now waved me good-bye, like three aunties sending me off to my debut. I nodded graciously at their beaming faces as the hansom jerked away.

I busied myself trying to keep the gown clean and holding on to the small beaded reticule Miss Townsend had thrust at me as Lewis drove us out of Mayfair and across the river to the edifice of Waterloo Station. A train there would take us directly to Esher, where Daniel had arranged a coach for the remainder of the journey.

Daniel, in the persona of his upper-class man-about-town, waited languidly in the middle of the entrance hall of the station, turning his hat in his hands. He was the very portrait of a bored young man tired of waiting for his lady.

"At last," he said as James led me forward. James was to play Daniel's servant, as a man of Daniel's status would not roam about without someone to fetch and carry for him. "How are you, my dear?" Daniel kissed my cheek, his lips barely brushing my skin. "Well, hurry up, lad, take that to the compartment." He gestured to a small portmanteau resting next to him. "We must get a move on."

James, as good an actor as his father, moved blank faced toward the waiting train on the nearest platform, as though used to being ordered about by impatient gentlemen.

Daniel took my arm and led me onward. "Very fetching," he said as he eyed my gown. "Astonishing hat. I thought you'd miss the train, darling. You'd have watched me disappearing down the track, the train huffing and puffing, if you had left it any later."

I definitely preferred the affable man-of-all-work to this jackanapes. I could not say so in the crowd—Daniel's speeches were for the benefit of anyone listening. No one seemed to pay much attention to us, all hurrying toward their own destinations, but Daniel was cautious.

I was nowhere near late, as the train was not due to leave for another twenty minutes. I clutched Daniel's arm and tried to look contrite.

"Here we are." Daniel pulled open a door and helped me up into the train carriage. A first-class compartment once again. My head would be turned by all this luxury. "Mind your skirts, darling. Where is that boy?"

James loped along the corridor and entered the compartment. He heaved the bag to the shelf above and slammed the door, shutting us in to privacy.

"Want me with you, Dad?" James asked it with a tone of one who would rather be elsewhere. The plush luxury of a first-class car filled with two well-dressed adults was likely not what he thought of as excitement.

"Explore as you like, but stay out of trouble." Daniel gave him a father's frown. "I do not want the conductor tossing me off the train because you decided to climb on top of it. You have a third-class ticket if you want to take a seat, or you can come back here."

James grinned. "Right. I'm off. It ain't far, so no time for me to do much." He slammed open the door to the corridor and rushed out. Daniel closed it gently behind him, and then we were alone.

16

‧—◆————◆—‧

D aniel regarded me across the compartment in silence. A whistle blew, a man on the platform waved a flag, and the train jerked forward. Soon we were chugging steadily free of the station, a wave of smoke and steam blanketing the windows and cutting off the outside world.

"It is not like you to say nothing for such a stretch of time," I said as the train gained speed and the smoke cleared a bit, showing we rattled through the suburbs. "You are usually chattering away before you have even said good day."

"Forgive me." Daniel made a mock bow in his seat. "I am admiring the lavish beauty I see before me. It has stolen my breath."

My face heated, though I knew he teased. "Fine feathers make a fine bird." I waved my gloved hand dismissively. "Miss Townsend was clever to find the gown for me."

"Miss Townsend has great flair for the art of costuming. The stage lost a talent in her. When she assisted me in Paris, she played the empty-headed wealthy hostess without flaw. She knew exactly how to present you."

"As an empty-headed widow from Holland?" I sent him a smile. "You are flattering."

"And you are lovely." Daniel said the words in all seriousness. "Thank you for helping me."

I shifted uncomfortably, wishing my giddy gladness would vanish. I should not let Daniel's praise please me so.

"I am attending this garden party to deter debutants eager to hunt down a husband," I said. "I am not merely helping you; I am saving your life."

Daniel laughed. "That you are. Remind me to be in your debt forever." He broke off as the conductor entered to check our tickets.

I noted that the conductor kept his manner deferential, taking both tickets from Daniel and barely glancing at them before handing them back with a bow. He tipped his hat to me and withdrew. Very different from a conductor who jerked open the door of a third-class compartment, snapping, "Ticket, missus," before slamming the door and continuing on his weary duties.

I was the same person, and yet in this dress and hat with a young man to handle the tickets for me, I suddenly deserved the conductor's politeness. It made one think.

"While we have a few moments to ourselves," Daniel said, "let me tell you what you will need to know to survive this day."

My name would be Katharine Holtmann, he said, widow of a Dutch businessman I'd married only a few years before he'd died of illness. I'd met Daniel—whose name for this sojourn was Mr. Lancaster—in Amsterdam through my late husband when Daniel had done business there. I could be vague about what business, because I didn't bother myself with the technicalities of what my husband had done. "Shipping" would cover many possibilities.

Daniel and I were now affianced, but we had not set a wedding date. I, the young widow, was enjoying my freedom and inherited wealth, and young Mr. Lancaster wasn't certain he was ready to settle down.

"Plausible," I said when he'd finished. "As long as no one digs too deeply."

"I've already fed the duke and duchess much about Mr. Lancaster's background. The man I am supposed to be cousin to is conveniently in the wilds of Canada. By the time anyone inquires—if they bother—I hope this business to be over, and it will no longer matter."

I spoke in a near whisper. "Do you truly believe the duke had something to do with those terrible murders?"

"I do now." Daniel was somber. "Though what I believe doesn't matter. I need proof. He's a duke, which is not only the highest title of the aristocracy, but his family is distinguished, containing many soldiers who fought bravely in wars throughout history. His family was given the title by Queen Anne, for valor under the Duke of Marlborough against Louis XIV."

"Not a man you can simply arrest and bang up in Bow Street nick, then."

"You have grasped the problem. If I prove he funded the murders in Ireland, it's treason, but making it stick will be the devil of a thing. Even if the charges do take, he'll likely be let off by those who can't afford to let him embarrass them. Exile will be the worst thing the duke suffers, and it won't be official exile."

I could see Daniel was unhappy about this, and my own anger stirred. If a man's support and money led to the brutal deaths of others, should he not pay? It was the same situation as the conductor behaving politely to me while I rode in a first-class carriage in an expensive frock, and dismissing me when I rode third-class in my working-class garb.

"I will try to help as much as I can," I told Daniel.

He viewed me in alarm. "You will do nothing today but say polite inanities to the duchess and her guests. No tearing through the duke's home searching for incriminating documents."

"I had no intention of doing so," I said loftily, though truth to tell, I had already been thinking of ways I might slip into the house and find something that had eluded Daniel.

"For heaven's sake, Kat, do nothing. These are men who thought nothing of striking down well-known gentlemen in broad daylight in a public park."

"I saw the story in the newspapers." I shivered. "It was gruesome. I do promise to take care."

"You don't, you know." Daniel adjusted the curtain against a beam of sunlight that struck his eyes. "Take care, I mean. You should leave the problem of the poisoner to Inspector McGregor, but I know you won't."

"His hands are tied, as you told me. So are yours. That leaves mine free."

Daniel's voice turned hard, and he flicked the curtain from his hand. "It doesn't have to have anything to do with you."

"My dear Daniel, poor Lady Covington sought *me* out, very worried about what was going on in her household. Then her stepdaughter died before I could find out who would be wicked enough to put poison in the food. I cannot now tell her it's none of my affair and turn my back."

"I know." Daniel deflated. "And I like you the better for it. But damn you, Kat, you worry me to distraction."

"But it is all right if you worry *me*? You are living in the house of a man who might have paid assassins in his pocket. What happens if he finds you out? I should go on baking bread and saucing roasts without a thought to your fate, should I?"

"I'm used to this sort of thing, and I know how to defend myself. That is the difference."

"I see. Fine if I fret and stew, but if *you* are a hair concerned, then I must stop everything and sit in my kitchen until you come to call?"

"Not what I meant . . ."

"I know." My nervousness made me sharper than usual. "Forgive me—but you drive *me* to distraction too. When will you give up all this madness?"

Daniel's mouth flattened. "When I have paid my debts."

"Have you many of these debts?"

His nod made my nerves tighten. "Errol is not wrong when he tells you I am worse than he ever was. In the past, that is. I have reformed."

"I understand. More things you refuse to tell me about."

"More things I *can't* tell you. One day, as I keep promising."

"One day might not come soon enough," I snapped.

I turned my face from him, my breathing rapid, my tight lacings cutting into my ribs. I usually wore my corset looser than this, much more practical for having a good row with my beau.

Daniel slammed himself back into his seat, highly annoyed with me. In this sorry state, we arrived at Esher, eighteen or so miles, as the train journeyed, from London.

Once alighting in Esher, I had to bury my frustration and become Daniel's—Mr. Lancaster's—bride-to-be.

A landau waited in front of the station, the top pulled down for the fine weather. Blue sky stretched overhead, dotted by a few puffy clouds. The landau belonged to the duke, Daniel said. He conveyed this information by exclaiming how kind it was for His Grace to send us, mere nobody guests, his personal carriage. Others leaving the station stared at him, which was Daniel's intent.

We were not the only guests heading for the duke's country estate. A stream of landaus, coaches, and light phaetons made their way along the road that led from the town and up a drive under a stand of tall trees to the duke's home.

Having lived and worked in London all my life, I rarely had glimpses of vast estates, except in paintings hanging in the few drawing rooms I entered. I tried to pretend I'd seen plenty of these houses in my frivolous, pampered life, as the landau took us toward the enormous abode.

The wide manor rose three stories, each corner flanked by a four-story tower. A profusion of chimneys dotted the flat main roof, which sported a railed walkway. The towers bore scrolled gables, very much like those I'd seen in pictures of Dutch houses. I hoped I wouldn't be called upon to compare the architecture of both countries.

The grounds sloped from the house to a river that glittered at the bottom of the hill—the Thames, I surmised. In the distance, on the other side of the river, I could see a large, crenellated, towered structure.

"That's Hampton Court, darling," Daniel said as he leapt to the ground and turned to hand me down. "Home of our jolly King Henry. You know, the one who chopped off all his wives' heads."

"Oh," I said in true astonishment. Not about Henry and his wives—we all knew the stories, and I'd sung funny songs about him when I'd been younger—but I'd never seen a true palace aside from the ones in London, which were now more like government offices. This was a proper palace from long ago. My first thought was that Grace would love to see it.

"The view is better from the roof of the duke's house. I've only been up there once, more's the pity, but perhaps we can sneak upstairs. Come in and meet our host and hostess. They've been showering me with constant questions about you. So exhausting."

The double front door stood open, and people wandered through it. Daniel led me in, leaving James with the coachman.

We entered a massive hall of stone walls lit by many-paned windows. A staircase wrapped around the entire hall from the back of the house to the front, with two wide landings in between. I imagined it took ten minutes to traverse the whole thing to the next floor. Paintings covered the walls, as did weapons of old, lances and swords, that sort of thing. A few suits of armor lurked in shadowy corners, and an upright glass case full of gleaming silver bits reposed beneath the bulk of the staircase.

"It's Tudor," Daniel said, waving at the expanse. "Or Stuart. Or . . . something. The duke didn't inherit it. He bought it lock, stock, and barrel from a nabob who bought it from an earl of very old family who'd run out of money. It's the new aristocrats who have all the blunt these days. Ah, here's the duchess."

Daniel led me out through another set of double doors to a wide terrace, its steps descending to a parklike garden, with plenty of people milling about in it. I liked gardens very much, so I was pleased I'd spend the majority of my visit here.

The Duchess of Daventry was a tiny woman, I'd say in her early seventies. Her face was lined with fine wrinkles, most of them from smiling, which she was doing as hard as she could. She clasped my hands to welcome me.

"So pleased you could come, my dear. I have been plying Mr. Lancaster for details about you, and he has been most cryptic. Very glad to finally meet his mysterious fiancée."

I fought and lost the habit of a lifetime. I curtsied. I could no more not do it than not swallow a mouthful of food.

"Thank you kindly, Your Grace," I said, a bit breathlessly.

I was terrified I'd given myself away, but the duchess increased her smile. "Such pretty manners. Quite unlike some of the rude girls of today. I commend you, Mr. Lancaster."

"You see why I kept her hidden, don't you, Duchess?" Daniel chortled. "Didn't want any other lads stealing her away. She is a treasure." His knowing wink told us he meant me as a person as well as the wealth I'd supposedly bring to our marriage.

"Do enjoy your morning, Mrs. Holtmann," the duchess said, ignoring Daniel. "We have a fountain walk, and the roses are just blooming. And a tea tent in case you grow faint with hunger. Tell Mr. Lancaster to let you rest there."

"Thank you." I couldn't help curtsying again. I'd been raised to bend my knees to those above me in station, and a duchess was as high as I could find besides the queen or her princess daughters. I'd also learned that a show of humility kept a bad-tempered mistress from striking me.

The duchess laughed and shooed us away, turning to greet her next guest.

"She is rather lovely," I whispered as we strolled on. I hoped she had nothing to do with murders in Dublin. I could not picture the small, beaming woman funding a conspiracy to assassinate government leaders.

"The duchess is a fine lady," Daniel said, keeping to his Mr. Lancaster persona. "Knows how to organize a do. Let us admire the flowers and fountains, shall we?"

If my only task was to accompany Daniel, my hand on his

arm, around beds of early roses, pansies, and irises, this day would be pleasant. None of the couples or small clumps of ladies and gentlemen regarded me with the least dubiousness as we passed. They said good morning and little else, intent upon admiring the garden and making certain others noticed they had been graced with an invitation to this gathering.

"Who are all the guests?" I whispered.

"Oh, acquaintances of the duke's. From all over." Daniel kept his voice pitched normally. Explaining these things to a foreign young woman would not be considered odd. "Politicos and others. No gathering in England is only about gazing at flowers. There are favors to be exchanged, decisions to be made. What happens on the floor of the Houses of Parliament or in Cabinet meetings is only part of what goes into running the nation."

"It is too bad, as the gardens are so beautiful." I had known from working for the wife of an MP that politics happened in clubs and at suppers, far from the buildings of power. The wife had rarely seen her husband, and had taken up with a young man to entertain her, which had led to the MP banishing her to the country and me having to find another post.

"Well, we can enjoy them," Daniel declared. "*I* am never going into politics. A fool's game, that."

A stiff gentleman ambling by with his equally stiff wife sent Daniel a sneer, even as they both nodded cordially. Daniel tipped his hat, and I managed not to curtsy.

"What are these flowers?" I pointed to a line of tall stalks with deep blue flowers bursting from them. "They are so pretty."

Daniel glanced at them with the bored air of a man who didn't understand what women saw in such things. "Dashed if I know. Duchess might, but she's up to her ears in guests. Perhaps we'll find a gardener."

He did not quicken his pace, as though having no interest in either plants or gardener.

I paused to admire the blooms. I recognized the skill in this garden—it was full but tidy, each plant given room to grow but close enough to its neighbors that the beds were a riot of color.

I knew what the plant was, it so happened. Larkspur. It was a bit early for it, but if the seeds were started in a hothouse or nurtured with row covers, a good gardener could make them bloom to the duchess's schedule.

What made me pause was that I knew larkspur was poisonous. A cook needs to fathom what plants *not* to put into a dish—for instance, the leaves and stems of pepper plants are poisonous, while the peppers themselves can be eaten without worry, unless one is sensitive to spicy foods.

It occurred to me as I stood there that Lady Covington's Park Lane house had a beautiful and well-tended garden, including a hothouse that raised all sorts of vegetables and herbs. Many plants were partly edible, or edible at certain intervals in their life-span, while at the same time, many could be deadly. A salad of the wrong kind of greens or beans could kill the unwary.

Not all gardeners knew these things, so I did not immediately suspect Symes of sending in poisonous leaves to the kitchen. Even if Mrs. Gamble couldn't tell the difference, Cynthia would have noted it if some unusual vegetable or fruit had been served for supper. And again, Mrs. Gamble would taste everything before sending it up.

Of course, anyone in that house could go out into the garden and pick flowers or herbs without any question attached to the action. They could equally well slip a few deadly leaves into a pot of soup in the dining room. Only when Mrs. Gamble made certain the food went directly from her hands to Lady Covington were no ill effects felt.

"You're miles away, darling."

"Pardon?" I snapped back to Daniel. "Very sorry. I thought of something, is all."

Daniel looked curious, but he knew I could not speak openly here. I uncharitably thought it only fair that he should wonder what was going on inside *my* head for a change.

"It is warm, I agree," Daniel said, raising his voice for benefit of those around us. "Perhaps we can adjourn to the tea tent. Or the house. The duke won't mind if we wander about looking at his paintings."

"The house." I was rather warm, and the shade inside had been pleasant. I did not fancy a crowded tea tent where I might be more closely scrutinized.

Daniel and I strolled back the way we'd come, nodding to more guests as we went. We circled a large fountain of stone cupids pouring large pitchers of water over each other, and headed for the terrace.

As we reached it, I heard a voice I recognized.

"Delightful of you to let us come, old boy." A slender man in a dark suit, with thin sideburns flowing to an equally thin mustache, shook the hand of the silver-haired duke, the two standing just outside the entrance to the house. "Would love to continue our little chat."

I halted, pulling Daniel up short. "Oh dear."

"What is it?" Daniel's voice was in my ear, low, urgent.

"That is Lord Clifford," I whispered. "Cynthia's father."

17

◆————◆

What the devil was he doing here? I hadn't realized Lord Clifford was acquainted with the Duke of Daventry. Cynthia must not know either, because she'd have not sent me straight into the lion's den. Nor had Mr. Fielding reported such a thing.

Daniel's arm tightened around mine. "Does he know you? Has he seen you?"

"Yes, he jolly well has. He's come down to the kitchen several times. Lady Clifford as well."

"Damn." Daniel straightened, resuming his languorous stance. "The tea tent it is, then, darling."

"You said there was no one I knew on the guest list," I hissed as we turned and made our way quickly back toward the fountain.

"He isn't on it," Daniel said adamantly. "I would have noted that immediately, believe me."

"Then why is he here?"

"If I knew, I'd not be cursing."

We quickened our steps toward the tent beckoning us at the edge of the garden. Then I stopped abruptly. Daniel followed my gaze to see the duchess, her arm locked through that of Lady Clifford, entering the tea tent.

"We slip away," Daniel said, his gaze on Lord Clifford and the duke. "And you go to the train station."

"What will you say to the duke and duchess?"

"That you were feeling ill and wanted to return to London. You've done exactly what was needed. The duchess has seen you and will cease trying to pair me off with her friends' daughters. I know this was a risk." Daniel let out a breath. "I can only thank you."

He was correct. I'd played my part, as brief as it was, and had no more need to stroll a duke's garden in finery. That suited me. As pleasant as it was to wander among the beautiful flowers with Daniel, I'd prefer to shuck this gown for my own sensible clothes and spend time with my daughter.

The duke and Lord Clifford moved down the steps of the terrace to the garden. Daniel and I circled around and climbed up the terrace's far side, scooting into the house behind their backs.

"Wait here," Daniel whispered, stationing me in a shadow under the monstrous staircase. "I'll find James, and he can escort you back to London."

"I am certain I can find London on my own," I told him. "It is a rather large city, and my train will be marked *To London.*"

Daniel's smile made his face even more handsome. "You won't go on your own dressed like that without causing a scandal. James will make certain all is well."

He had a point. As myself, I could walk about with impunity, but a lady of the middle or upper classes would mar her reputation, or at least be talked about heartily, if she dared go anywhere alone. Best I did not draw attention to myself or Daniel.

I backed into the cool gloom under the staircase while Daniel hastened out the front door. The glass case filled with ancient-looking spoons and a knife or two helped shield me. I could study the interesting antiquities and ponder the possible ways a person could harvest and use poisonous plants while I waited.

Steps echoed in the hall, followed by male voices. One man mumbled in a low voice, and the tones of Lord Clifford rose over his.

"Do think about it, dear chap. It would save me no end of bother."

Oh Lord. I pressed myself beneath the corner of the staircase and peered around it as the small, silver-bearded duke and taller Lord Clifford halted in the middle of the hall. Something sparkled and winked in Lord Clifford's hand.

"May I see it again?" The duke stretched out a hand, and Lord Clifford spilled what looked like a diamond necklace onto the duke's palm.

The duke brought the necklace to his eyes, studying it carefully. The strand dangled, catching what little light filled the hall.

"It's been in the family for donkey's years." Lord Clifford glanced about and lowered his voice. "My wife gets worried . . . well, you know. Women grow fond of things, don't they?"

"Indeed." The duke slid a loupe on a chain from his pocket and examined the diamonds with an air of expertise.

I remained fixed in place, staring hard at the pair until my eyes began to dry. Cynthia had told me many times how Lord Clifford had run through the money of the estate and lived on nothing but what he could charm from his friends. Was the necklace part of the jewels of the earldom? If so, why hadn't Lord Clifford sold them long ago? Why was he offering them now, to this particular duke?

My hands tightened as worry squeezed me. If the duke was involved with the anarchists, and Lord Clifford was found to be giving him diamond necklaces, he could be implicated as well. Which would destroy Cynthia.

Lady Clifford truly seemed to wish to get Cynthia married, but Cynthia—and I—suspected Lord Clifford of an ulterior motive for his journey to London. Had Lord Clifford simply planned to sell a valuable necklace to a rich duke and pocket the cash, or did he sympathize with the Irish cause? I read Lord Clifford as a selfish man who likely cared for no cause but his own comfort, but he might be coaxed into the duke's schemes with the promise of reward.

"It certainly is beautiful." The duke continued to peer at the diamonds while Lord Clifford again scanned the hall, as though ready to bolt if anyone appeared.

My greatest fear was that Daniel would dash back inside. I doubted Lord Clifford would recognize him—Daniel hadn't been around much since Lord and Lady Clifford had arrived—but Daniel would be looking for me, the duke would ask Daniel where his companion had got to, and lies would tangle with lies.

Lord Clifford paused when his gaze reached the shadows of the stairs. I drew back silently. Had he seen me? Would he call me out of hiding?

I held my breath, but nothing happened. Lord Clifford either hadn't seen me or thought me a harmless young lady gazing at a case full of spoons.

"May I leave it with you, then?" Lord Clifford asked. "I'd be chuffed if I could. I'll be in London awhile. Staying with my brother-in-law in Mount Street."

The duke slid the magnifier into one pocket and the diamonds into the other. "Yes, I will be happy to help."

"Excellent. Well." The earl clapped the duke on the shoulder, nearly overbalancing the man. "I will find my wife and partake of your generous tea. Haven't got anything a bit stronger than the old British beverage, have you?"

The duke chuckled. "I believe I do." He removed a flask from his pocket. "Dollop that in your tea, and I'm certain you'll be a happier man."

Lord Clifford laughed merrily. He took the flask, dropped it into his pocket, gave the hall one last scrutiny, and followed the duke out the door to the terrace.

Daniel entered through the front in the next moment. I gathered my skirts and scurried to meet him.

"Forgive me," Daniel said, sotto voce. "I had to wait until they'd gone. Did they see you?"

"I don't believe so." We left the house and crossed the gravel drive to James, who opened the door of the landau that had driven us here. I remembered the chill of Lord Clifford's gaze falling on me, but he could not have known who I was even if he'd seen me. A woman in the darkness, hidden by a hat and veil? I'd been well concealed.

"I will make certain they did not." Daniel pressed my hands and drew me closer. "Thank you, Kat. And do take care."

I nodded. I did not dare kiss him, though I suppose young Mrs. Holtmann might kiss her fiancé good-bye. But I did not want to draw more attention, and I was supposed to be feeling unwell.

I hated to withdraw my hands and climb into the carriage, not knowing when I'd see Daniel again. I hoped he'd swiftly discover whether the duke was guilty or not and have done with hunting down anarchists. And then have done with doing anything for the cold-eyed Mr. Monaghan.

Daniel gave me a faint smile and assisted me into the landau.

"Do take care, darling," he said for benefit of the coachman and anyone else nearby. "I'll call upon you later, shall I? Not certain when."

"Of course." I leaned back on the seat and pretended to be wilting from the heat.

"Look after her." Daniel spun a coin in his fingers and tossed it to James, who deftly caught it. "Do whatever she says, and be quick about it."

"Yes, sir." The coin quickly disappeared into James's pocket, and he leapt onto the back of the landau.

The coach started. Daniel raised his hand in farewell, and I feebly waved back.

It was over. I'd successfully made certain all believed shallow Mr. Lancaster had a fiancée, and now I could return to being Kat Holloway, no-nonsense cook.

I watched the house and gardens disappear behind the trees, knowing it could be many years before I saw such splendor again.

I was not able to speak to James until we were seated in a compartment—first-class again—for the return journey. I had the compartment to myself, which I thought entirely frivolous, so I insisted James stay with me. We feasted out of a basket of tea things James had procured at the station.

The cakes were not as good as what I could bake, but I was hungry and I made do. James downed the pasties included in the basket, but I declined, as I feared marring the dress with their juices.

"I do not like that your father recruited you for this deception," I said as I nibbled a scone that was far too dry.

James shrugged around a mouthful of meat and gravy. "No one else he could trust, was there? He'd have used a constable or some such, but he said with you, he wanted me only."

I supposed there was sense in that decision. A constable would ask questions about me or report my existence to Daniel's boss, and Daniel wanted Mr. Monaghan far from me.

"I do appreciate the effort." I reached across the space of the compartment and gave James's knee a pat. "Besides, you look fine in that suit."

It was a footman's garb, slim trousers and coat with a cravat. It fit James's form far better than his usual woolen jackets and breeches and made him quite handsome.

James fingered his collar. "It's stifling. I don't know how toffs do it."

"I too will be happy to resume my usual clothing."

I touched the skirt with my gloved hand, trying to suppress the wistfulness that came over me. I'd never owned something this beautiful.

No reason to be sentimental, I told myself. *It's only a frock.*

I forced myself to put aside any regret and continue with the scone. When Daniel and I had traveled down, I had been angry with him, and he annoyed with me, and we'd not had much appetite or opportunity to eat at the garden party. Now I finished off the sandwiches and unwrapped two small seedcakes and passed one to James.

"This basket." I studied it. "Lady Covington's family had a large one, a hamper, and a porter took it while they boarded."

James chewed, listening while I ruminated.

"What happens to bags the porter takes?" I continued. "Are they ever out of someone's sight? Or does he carry them directly to the compartment? If they are put in a baggage car, are they left alone until called for?"

"I can ask." James leapt to his feet. He was out the door before I could say a word, air rushing into the compartment in his wake.

I tidied up the things and put the papers and scraps back into the basket. I thought of Daniel still at the duke's, and Lord Clifford handing the duke a fortune in diamonds. A simple transaction to raise money for Lord and Lady Clifford? Or something more sinister?

The bright, green countryside, meadows awakening from winter, had given way to buildings on London's outskirts before James returned. He plumped down into his seat, pleased with himself.

"Porter says bags not loaded directly to a toff's compartment are put aside in a room at the end of the first-class car. When a toff asks for it—usually ringing for it, or sending a servant trotting down to fetch it—the bag is taken out and goes to the compartment. Returned to the room when done. That's for small things like a food hamper or a lady's toiletries case. Larger bags go into the baggage car. Baggage car is locked up and guarded, to keep thieves from strolling in and helping themselves, but the smaller room in the first-class car isn't locked. Porter or conductor is usually near it, but not always. Thieves don't ride first-class," he finished.

"Well." I thought about Mr. Fielding and Lord Clifford. "Often they don't. Thank you, James. That is very helpful."

It would have been easy for any member of Lady Covington's party to move down the car, enter the room at the end, open the hamper, and sprinkle poison into Lady Covington's food. The fact that Erica ate it instead was their misfortune.

Or was it? A new idea formed. Lady Covington had only ever been slightly ill by the poison, never taking enough to kill her. Sir Arthur likewise had only been ill and was recovering, according to Mrs. Gamble.

Perhaps Erica had been the target of the killer all along. After all, anyone could have eaten out of the hamper that night, but Harriet had said Erica, who liked her food, had eaten quite a lot. If the poisoner had known Erica would, and had even encouraged her, he or she could have chosen that moment to strike. All would assume Lady Covington was supposed to die, and no one would search for a motive to kill Erica.

But why *should* anyone wish to kill Erica? I wondered. She'd been married to an MP who hadn't been good to her and had not left her well-off. She scarcely had been a threat to anyone in the family.

A more horrible thought entered my head. Perhaps the killer wished to inherit *all* of Lady Covington's money and not share it with any of the others. I did not know what was in the lady's will, though I could find out, but perhaps Lady Covington had left fortunes to all four children.

George—Lord Covington—had inherited his father's title, but not his gift for business. What if George, knowing he was losing money, coveted Erica's share of Lady Covington's fortune? Or perhaps Jonathan believed that he, as her only son, should get the lion's share? Or Harriet, who had a secret beau and seemed to long for freedom, would find that freedom if she had a great deal of money.

If I was right, how long before any of the other heirs would die by "accident"?

Then there was the problem of Henry. Was he a man Erica loved, but possibly he did not love her? An affair gone on too long? Did Henry find it easier to kill Erica than free himself from her clutches?

I rubbed my temples. I would have to return to the house and talk further to Mrs. Gamble, who knew much about the upstairs. It wouldn't hurt to have another chat with Symes either, to find out which of the family liked the garden.

We reached London and the throngs of Waterloo Station. James, acting the part of my lackey, rushed out and waved down a hansom cab. He instructed the cabbie to take me to Upper Brook Street, and climbed in beside me.

At Trafalgar Square, James deserted me. He'd paid the cabbie already, he said, with coins his dad had given him, and all I had to do was alight at Miss Townsend's. James waved as he disappeared into the crowd milling before the National Gallery, and was gone.

The cab clopped through Haymarket to Piccadilly and up through Regent Street past the building where Mr. Thanos had rooms. We turned at Hanover Square, passing beside Hanover Church, and so to Brook Street, Grosvenor Square, and Upper Brook Street.

I gave the cabbie an extra penny for a tip, which he took gratefully. Miss Townsend's butler, spying me, helped me descend.

"They're upstairs in the studio, Mrs. Holloway," he told me as he ushered me into the cool, quiet house and closed the door behind me.

The butler treated me no less respectfully than did Mr. Davis, though he must wonder at Miss Townsend dressing me like a doll and sending me off to Surrey. He seemed to take Miss Townsend's eccentricities in stride, including her invitation to Bobby to live with her.

I climbed the polished staircase to the top of the house, my feet in the high-heeled shoes aching somewhat, and entered the studio, which was flooded with light from skylights and large windows. Stacks of canvasses lay everywhere, and finished paintings leaned against the walls.

The sharp smell of varnish assailed me. I found Miss Townsend in a smock, gliding a large brush over a finished painting. Cynthia and Bobby lounged on the far side of the room, reading newspapers.

A strange blatting sound emerged from the wall, and I jumped. Miss Townsend coolly reached for a speaking tube without looking up and applied it to her ear.

"*Mrs. Holloway has returned.*" I heard the butler's voice hollow and small inside the tube.

Cynthia and Bobby came to their feet, Cynthia tossing aside her paper. Miss Townsend turned, a drop of varnish splashing to the paint-splotched floor.

"Why are you back so soon, Mrs. H.?" Cynthia sang out. "Everything all right? Or were you found out?"

They surrounded me, Cynthia's light blue and Bobby's and Miss Townsend's brown eyes avid, the three wanting to know everything.

I set down the reticule and unpinned the hat. "My visit was cut short because your father turned up, Cynthia."

Cynthia blinked in astonishment. "Papa? At the Duke of Daventry's? Papa doesn't know him—I'd have heard him boast of acquaintance with a wealthy duke. Jove, I'd have warned you if I'd known. Did he recognize you?"

"I do not believe so." Again I felt that fleeting touch of Lord Clifford's gaze, and I had to wonder. If he *had* recognized me, he could have easily exposed me then and there, which would have exposed Daniel as well. I shuddered to think of what Daniel's guv'nor would say if Daniel was betrayed because he'd brought me to the duke's house.

"What the devil was my father doing there, do you know?" Cynthia asked me.

I told her what I'd seen and heard, and how her father had handed the duke a diamond necklace. "The transaction does not seem to be complete. Lord Clifford told the duke to contact him when he was ready, I suppose to purchase the necklace . . ." I trailed off as Cynthia covered her face. "Whatever is the matter, Lady Cynthia?"

Cynthia shook her head, still buried in her hands, and groaned. "Oh, not the diamond necklace. Not *again*. He promised."

18

Miss Townsend, Bobby, and I regarded Cynthia in bafflement.

"What are you going on about, Cyn?" Bobby demanded. "What necklace?"

Cynthia raised her head. Her cheeks were flushed, tears standing in the corners of her eyes. "Something my father trots out from time to time. Did he arrive there with anyone, Mrs. Holloway? Besides my mother, I mean. Or did you see him speaking to anyone else?"

"Only the duke," I answered. "Why?"

"He needs a partner, but I didn't think he had many cronies left in London. I'm sorry, Judith, I must go. Good-bye, Bobby, Mrs. Holloway. I will speak to you later."

This last Cynthia said to me as she hastened out of the studio. We heard her clatter down the stairs, calling out to the butler below.

Miss Townsend raised her brows but held up a hand as Bobby started forward. "Best to leave her be, I think. It's none of our affair and will be a family matter she needs to face alone. Was the gown suitable, Mrs. Holloway?"

Neither Bobby nor I protested her change of subject, though Bobby was as curious as I.

"Indeed." I was loath to part with the gown, though I knew I could not wear it to Cheapside to visit my daughter. "Please give your friend my thanks when you return it."

"It is yours," Miss Townsend said. "She had planned to send it to a secondhand shop, as she was finished with it anyway. Now that it fits you, you might as well retain it."

I paused in the act of tugging off the gloves. "Good heavens, if Mrs. Bywater found such a gown hanging in my room, she'd think I was some man's fancy piece."

Both Miss Townsend and Bobby laughed, thinking me joking, but I did not exaggerate. Mrs. Bywater so far had not stooped to searching her servants' rooms, but if any of the maids or Mrs. Redfern saw it, and Mrs. Bywater heard of it, I would be hard-pressed to explain.

"Never mind," Miss Townsend said. "I will keep it here for you. Whenever you wish to wear it—perhaps Mr. McAdam will take you dining—send word, and you may don it here."

I touched the skirt, the smooth fabric cool to my bare fingers. "You are very kind, but—"

"No buts, Mrs. Holloway. You have earned this. You gave up your day out to help Mr. McAdam on one of his hunts, and you ought to have something for it. I will keep the gown, and we'll say no more about it."

She could do as she liked, of course. I gave Miss Townsend a nod, then I took myself downstairs to her bedchamber to change into my own clothes.

I felt much more myself in my plain corset and brown dress, years out of fashion by now. But this was the frock I wore to visit Grace, and donning it always made me lighter of heart. No beautiful gown with a dozen frills could compare to that.

Miss Townsend and Bobby walked downstairs with me, Miss Townsend's butler having procured another hansom.

Bobby pulled a coin from her pocket. "For your daughter," she said, handing me a shining copper penny. "She can buy whatever toys she likes with it. You are lucky, Mrs. H."

She looked wistful. I realized that Bobby, though she eschewed the dress, manners, and restrictions of a woman, liked children and envied me mine. I doubted she yearned after them enough to don a frock and marry a man, but if she ever had young ones to look after, I thought she'd do well by them.

I thanked her and Miss Townsend again, climbed into the hackney, and left to ride across London to Cheapside.

This, I thought as I sat in Joanna's parlor sipping tea with Grace while Joanna's four children read books or played games, *is much better than walking through a duke's garden ignoring the rude stares of haughty people.* They might have finery and riches, but I had warmth and friendship, and a daughter I loved with all my heart.

Grace and I went for our walk, not far today. We wandered about St. Paul's Churchyard, admiring the huge dome that dominated our skyline. I told Grace about the duke's home in Surrey, his lovely gardens, and interesting bits and bobs inside the house. I'd been honest with her and Joanna, telling them I'd be late because I was helping Mr. McAdam.

"Perhaps you could be a cook in a place like that," Grace

said when I'd finished describing the huge staircase and the displays of antiquities beneath it. "Wouldn't that be grand?"

"It is not likely to happen. I'd have to live outside London, and then I couldn't visit you so often."

Grace, nearly twelve now, gazed at me with wisdom in her brown eyes. "I'm happy living with Mrs. Millburn, you know. And Jane." She named Mrs. Millburn's oldest daughter with whom she was now as close as a sister. "Even Matthew, though he likes to tease something awful." Matthew was the Millburns' youngest son. "You do not have to stay in Town for me, Mum. If there's a splendid house that would pay you lots and lots, you should go."

Her words held sincerity. Warmth washed through me, not only from pride at how selfless she was but partly from a twinge of sadness. Grace was growing up swiftly, becoming less in need of my presence.

"It is a kind thought, but neither here nor there at this point," I said. "No splendid house is offering me employ, and I do well in Mount Street. I like Lady Cynthia, and I enjoy the cooking."

"Lady Cynthia is rather beautiful," Grace said. "Will she marry Mr. Thanos soon?"

I let out a breath, recalling how Mr. Thanos had gazed at Cynthia after his lecture at the Crystal Palace. "He is shy. But I hope he'll come around one day."

"He will if you tell him to, Mum." Grace nodded with confidence. "I like Lady Bobby too. She makes me laugh. Please tell her thank you for the penny." She patted her pocket where the penny reposed.

"I will." I barely heard Grace's last words, because an idea was taking shape in my head about Cynthia and Mr. Thanos.

Mr. Thanos might not fall on his knees and propose to Cynthia because of it, but my idea would throw them together, which might lead to a more permanent arrangement.

I walked Grace back home, parted from her with my usual reluctance, and returned to Mount Street on foot, wanting the exercise and the time to work out how I'd persuade Mr. Thanos to accept my idea.

T ess wanted to demand every detail of my day out to a duke's house, I could see, but I'd scarcely relate anything to her while the kitchen was full. Lord and Lady Clifford dined in tonight—they'd returned from Surrey—and footmen, Mr. Davis, Mrs. Redfern, and maids hurried to and fro on various duties as Tess and I prepared supper.

I made my Antiguan custards again, as Mr. Davis told me Lord Clifford had requested them. Tess had done so well preparing most of the meal that I had plenty of time to cook the custard and chill it while she roasted a hen, made gravy, and finished up the salads.

"A fine night's work," she said cheerfully, once everything had gone to the dining room.

Tess was growing in talent, and I would lose her one day when she sought employment as a cook in her own right. That was the way of the world, but I'd become very fond of Tess and did not like to think of her leaving.

I and the staff ate in the servants' hall after service. As I had at Joanna's home, I reflected that the banter of the maids and footmen, including the complaints, made for a cozy time of it. I'd had my taste of being a toff, and I decided I preferred to be me, hard work and all.

Tess had labored much today, so I sent her to bed early and finished cleaning the kitchen myself. The others drifted away to other tasks or bed, and as usual, I remained alone as things quieted down. I treasured this time to myself, to sharpen my knives, to reflect on what I'd done during the day, to make notes on recipes, and to hope Daniel would drop by.

Lord Clifford turned up instead.

"Good evening, your lordship." I rose hastily, setting down the fillet knife I'd taken up to sharpen. I curtsied, my heart banging. "I hope you enjoyed the puddings a second time."

"They were superb, my dear." Lord Clifford strolled toward the table, hands behind his back. "I must say, you create wonderful dishes in here." He glanced at the dresser stacked with crockery, the copper pots hanging above the stove, and my clean work table strewn with knives and the sharpening stone. "The kitchen at our country house is much, much larger."

Not unexpected, as only so much could fit beneath a London town house. "Yes, your lordship."

"I imagine the Duke of Daventry's kitchen is even larger." Lord Clifford sent me a pointed look, and then I knew. "Were you there trying to convince him to hire you? Or for some other ruse?"

I stood very still, though I felt my body rocking slightly. What to tell him? I could not betray Daniel or endanger him, and I was uncertain whether Lord Clifford was in league with the duke.

"I know it was you." Lord Clifford halted a few feet from me, his gaze straying to the knives. "You wore a lovely purple ensemble—it quite suited you. I'm good with faces, you see, and the way people walk and move. I never forget. I saw you in the garden with that twit, Lancaster. Were you trying to fleece him? Don't blame you if you were. If ever a fatuous idiot needed to be fleeced, it is the Honorable Mr. Lancaster."

I relaxed a fraction. Lord Clifford hadn't realized Daniel was anything but the empty-headed fop he pretended to be.

"I am a cook, your lordship," I began.

Lord Clifford snorted. "You are far more than that, my dear. You are a very clever young woman. No one but me noticed you—why should they? But I am quite good at spotting a fraud."

I wasn't certain how to respond. Should I deny I was there, and insist he was mistaken? Or admit it and beg him to say nothing? Either way, I was at a firm disadvantage.

Lord Clifford had descended here to blackmail me, I surmised. What would he want? Money? Or something more sordid? I needed to make him understand right away that I would not put up with that sort of nonsense.

I wet my lips. "Your lordship . . ."

Lord Clifford chuckled. "My dear, do not look so terrified. Your secret is safe with me." He tapped the side of his nose. "As I say, young Lancaster deserves to be swindled. All I ask is that you tell me exactly how you do it. I love a good story."

"I . . ." It was a rare day that words failed me, but they failed me now.

"There you are, Papa." Cynthia charged into the room. "I have been trying to run you down all evening, but I didn't want to say anything in front of Mummy."

Lord Clifford beheld his daughter, whose fetching pink tea gown fluttered around her like rose petals, in some alarm. "Say anything about what?"

"I told Lady Cynthia about the necklace," I said quickly. Lord Clifford had not yet reached the conclusion that while he'd seen me, I'd seen *him*.

His face lost color, his cheeky expression gone. "Now, Cynthia. Darling . . ."

"You promised, Papa," Cynthia said severely. "There was to be no more of that."

Lord Clifford folded his arms tightly across his chest. "For God's sake, Cynthia, don't tell your mother."

"That rather depends on what you tell *me*. Why did you trot it out? Strapped for cash, are you? You told me you had plenty of funds."

"Well, I do not," Lord Clifford snapped. "Keeping up an estate is a devilish thing, which you'd understand if you ever stopped at home. The outbuildings are ever in need of repair, the bloody roof leaks, and I don't want to talk about the state of the drains. The Duke of Daventry has more money than the Queen of Sheba, and now that the government is looking at him askance, I'd be doing the country a favor relieving him of some of his wealth. Less for him to send to nuisance-makers in Ireland."

His words relieved me a bit. At least Lord Clifford had no intention of assisting the duke in his nefarious activities.

"Who are you working with?" Cynthia demanded.

Lord Clifford flushed. "Pardon?"

"The necklace scheme takes two. Who is your partner this time? Don't let it be a beautiful woman again and break Mummy's heart."

"No, no, nothing of the sort. Besides, I'd never look twice at another woman—you know that. I love your mother without reservation."

"Then who?" Cynthia persisted.

"You need not worry. He's harmless, probably doesn't even understand what I'm up to. He's highly respectable. A parson, dog collar and all."

"Oh." My syllable cut through whatever Cynthia had drawn breath to say. "Your lordship, did you by chance meet this parson recently?"

Lord Clifford blinked at me. "As a matter of fact, I did. Here in London." He slanted Cynthia a guilty glance. "I nipped out of the theatre when I was there with your mother the other night to take some air. He was wandering about the portico, as weary of the horrible play as I was. We began chatting."

"Tell me," I continued in growing disquiet, "is his name Mr. Fielding?"

Lord Clifford's mouth dropped open. "Jove. How did you know?"

I shook my head, my dismay complete. "You might be the one who's been had, your lordship. I do hope the necklace doesn't make its way into his pocket."

"What does she mean?" Lord Clifford asked Cynthia. To me he said, "The necklace the duke has is worthless, my dear. I have a dozen of the things."

"You were trying to sell the Duke of Daventry false diamonds?" I asked in alarm. "He'll have the law on you."

Cynthia was shaking her head. "It's not so simple, Mrs. H."

Lord Clifford looked rueful. "What I showed him was the real thing, a family heirloom, as I told him. Then after he pocketed the necklace, I took it back, substituting one of paste. I certainly wasn't going to leave my wife's favorite necklace with him in truth."

I recalled how Lord Clifford had clapped the duke forcefully on the shoulder, which now I realized had been to distract him while he'd done what my old pals had called a "dip."

Cynthia heaved a sigh. "Let me explain, Mrs. H. You see, my father finds a man—or woman, he's not particular—who wants money, lots of it. Papa trots up to him, usually at a large do, like the Duke of Daventry's garden party today, and says either that his wife is worried about losing her necklace, or that he's bought it for her as a surprise and worries about losing it himself. Would the duke hold on to it for him? Perhaps somewhere secure in his very secure home?"

I nodded as she seemed to want a response, but I wasn't certain how this would make Lord Clifford or the duke any money.

"Exit Papa. Enter the friend—Papa's friend, that is. He or she will purport to be a total stranger to Papa. He—in this case, Mr. Fielding—notices the necklace in the duke's pocket or perhaps says he saw Papa handing it to him. Mr. Fielding asks to see it. He's a trustworthy cleric, so the duke finds no harm in it. Mr. Fielding examines it, exclaims that it's a masterpiece, and very costly. Would the duke sell it to him? Or perhaps to a wealthy friend or relative of Mr. Fielding's, as vicars can be notoriously poor. Duke says, *Sorry, old chap, it's not mine. Holding on to it for a friend.* Mr. Fielding says his relative or rich friend would pay several thousand guineas for it. He then hands the duke his card, saying if the duke changes his mind or convinces the owner to sell, then write or wire. Mr. Fielding toddles away. Then Papa turns up again. He's sorrowful, with some story about debts, and if only he could sell the necklace, he could cover them. Would the duke be interested?"

"Oh," I said. "I am beginning to understand."

Lord Clifford broke in. "Yes, it's all up to the duke, don't you see? If he's an honest man, he'll offer me the several thousand guineas Mr. Fielding did, knowing that's what the necklace is worth. But if he's a scoundrel, which I suspect the duke is, he'll say he feels sorry for me and will offer me a fraction of that, perhaps a few hundred quid. He can easily part with that much. Then when I'm gone, he writes to Mr. Fielding, says he now owns the necklace, and he'll sell, thinking to himself he'll reap several thousand guineas without having done a day's work." Lord Clifford shook his head, disparaging of the duke's chicanery.

"Then Mr. Fielding never answers," I said slowly. "The duke is out a few hundred pounds and is the proud owner of a paste necklace."

"She's got it," Lord Clifford said approvingly to Cynthia. "A clever young lady, as I suspected."

Cynthia scowled at him. "And if Daventry decides to seek you out and demand to know what the devil you meant by it?"

"Why should he?" Lord Clifford opened his hazel eyes wide. "I've done nothing wrong. He's the greedy toad who tried to cheat me out of several thousand guineas. If he discovers the necklace he has now is fake and upbraids me about it, I can claim I had no idea. A very good copy is worth a bit anyway, so he'd have paid a fair price. Mr. Fielding has done nothing wrong either. He never promised to buy the thing, only asked the duke to write him."

I could see the cleverness of Lord Clifford's plan, but only if their victim did not put together that he and Mr. Fielding knew each other. Knew each other well by now. I ought to have known two rogues would get on together.

"Tomorrow, you will go back and fetch that necklace." Cynthia shook a finger at her father. "You will thank the duke for keeping it safe and you will say nothing about needing to sell it. Bring the damned thing home."

"Such language in front of the staff, Cynthia—"

"No." I cut into the argument. Father and daughter turned to stare at me. "No, I believe your lordship could do some good with this. *Do* return to the duke, and do try to sell the necklace to him. Let him contact Mr. Fielding and have Mr. Fielding actually purchase the necklace. If the police are right, and the duke is trying to fund anarchists, he will be happy for a quick way to make several thousand guineas. The police can watch what happens to those funds, and perhaps catch him in the act."

19

M y, my." Lord Clifford looked me up and down in admiration. "I was right about your cook, Cynthia. An uncommonly clever young lady. *And* she can turn her hand to a decent pudding."

"You are trusting in my father a great deal, Mrs. H.," Cynthia said in warning. "I think I should just tell Mummy and let her have a word with him."

"Now, Cynthia, darling, do not be so hasty." Lord Clifford tried a laugh. "Mrs. Holloway is correct—I can do some good here. Help out jolly old England. Your mum never needs to know *how* I go about it."

"Because you promised and promised her you'd never do this again." Cynthia glowered. "You promised me as well."

"Dash it all, we truly are hard-pressed, Cyn. I am not exaggerating when I say the house and lands are an appalling expense. I do not tell your mother all this, because I don't want to upset her."

"But you are willing to go along with her scheme of marrying me off to a wealthy simpleton?" Cynthia demanded. "One with enough money to help you, but not enough brains to understand you are gouging him."

"As to that . . ." Lord Clifford laid gentle hands on Cynthia's shoulders. "You do not need to worry about marrying right away. Plenty of time, my dear. You are a beautiful young lady. Any chap would leap at the chance to take you to wife."

"Only because they believe an earl's daughter will bring them wealth and position. More fool they." Cynthia's tone softened. "I think we can come to some sort of arrangement, don't you, Papa?"

"Indeed. Indeed." Lord Clifford released Cynthia and rubbed his hands. "Of course. Be entertaining to use my powers to do some good, what?"

"Not on your own." Cynthia became stern again. "Mrs. H., I think we need to let him be guided by Mr. McAdam."

"I agree," I said. "He will instruct you, but you must do exactly what he says."

Lord Clifford blinked. "Who the devil is Mr. McAdam?"

"The fatuous idiot, Mr. Lancaster," I said.

I admit I drew great satisfaction from the astonishment on Lord Clifford's face.

Daniel must have remained in Surrey, because he did not visit that night. I chafed, needing to tell him about Lord Clifford and how I thought his ruse could assist Daniel's mission. I wanted to put my hands on Mr. Fielding as well, to shake him soundly.

But whatever went on in the world, I had to cook breakfast for the household the next morning. Tess and I poached eggs, fried ham, and toasted bread, and I made up a hollandaise sauce for the eggs. I was so distracted by my thoughts that the sauce almost turned—reverting to eggs and butter. Tess relieved me of it and beat in a squeeze of lemon juice and cold water, as I had taught her, and all was well.

Once the staff had finished their breakfast of the hash I made from the extra ham and leftover potatoes and had gone about their duties, the kitchen quieted. I sent Charlie, when he could be spared, to find James, who had likely spent the night in his father's rooms in Southampton Street, judging from the direction he'd run when he left the hansom. I gave Charlie a note and strict instructions to deliver it into James's hands.

While he was gone and Elsie was up to her elbows in suds in the scullery, Tess approached me.

"Caleb dropped by on his beat this morning," she said in a loud whisper. "He says the police know what the poison is."

I ceased kneading bread dough and stared at her, flour drifting from my hands. "Do they? Inspector McGregor must have chivvied the Sydenham coroner."

"Suppose." Tess leaned closer, smelling of the fresh herbs she'd been chopping. "Inspector McGregor didn't say nothing about it, but Caleb had a butcher's at the report when no one was looking."

"He ought not to have done that," I said in worry. I wanted very much to know what was in the report, but I did not wish Caleb to get into trouble.

"He's very careful, and besides, he could always say he's interested and wants to help. The poison was . . ." Tess's brow puckered. "Something with a long, fancy name. Caleb didn't know what it was either. He copied it out for me." Tess drew a scrap of paper from her pocket and handed it to me. "I don't even want to try to pronounce it."

I studied the long scientific words, carefully written in block capitals: CARBOHYDRATE ANDROMEDOTOXIN. "Means nothing to me," I said, studying the paper. "I will have to look it up."

"Can you? Where would ya look up things like that?"

"In a medical textbook. Or I could ask a chemist. Or consult with a brilliant man who knows almost everything."

Tess relaxed. "You mean Mr. Thanos, don't you? Give him me best. Is that helpful?" She pointed at the paper.

"I believe it will be, once I know what it means."

"Good." Tess grinned and skipped back to her herbs. "I hope you find whoever's doing this. How's a cook to keep her post if people drop dead in the dining room?"

She had a good point.

Once we had luncheon prepared enough that I could leave Tess to it, I took up my basket and headed for the greengrocers. I walked a circuitous route that put me on Regent Street in front of the house where Mr. Thanos now had rooms.

For all my pains, Mr. Thanos was not in. His landlady told me he'd gone to the Polytechnic.

That building was closer to the markets than Mr. Thanos's abode, so I'd come out of my way for nothing. I held my basket closer and trudged up Regent Street toward Cavendish Square.

I gazed for a long time at the many-columned structure that was the Polytechnic and wondered how on earth I'd find Mr. Thanos inside it. This was a place of learning, and not even open yet—they'd commence in September. For now, lecturers were preparing their curriculum and the building was being repaired.

I decided to do what I'd do in any house, and walked around to the back and down a short flight of stairs to the servants' entrance.

"Can you tell me how to find Mr. Elgin Thanos?" I asked a

passing maid, who carried a broom and duster. "I have an important delivery for him." I patted my covered basket.

The woman was stout and red-faced, her hair damp under a limp white cap. Not much air moved in this corridor, and it was warm.

Her surly expression at my interruption softened at the mention of Mr. Thanos's name. "Ah, he's a one. Such a kind young man. He's in his rooms, dear. Want me to take it to him?" She reached out a work-reddened hand.

I carefully backed a step. "No, indeed. It is very sensitive, and I was told to deliver it in person." I changed my stilted tones to the ones I was born with. "Do help me out, love. I'll be in a world of trouble if this thing don't reach Mr. Thanos unbroken."

The woman nodded sympathetically. "Aye, they're particular about their machines, ain't they? Up you go. He's on the second floor, back corner on the right as you're looking from the street. His digs ain't large, but he don't seem to mind. Not like some of the others."

"I imagine there's much fighting over the big rooms in this new place," I said, to be conversational.

"Aye, you're right, there. Men of learning can be like children." The maid shook her head.

"Well, thank you, love," I said, deciding our chat had wound to its close. "I'd best be getting on."

The maid nodded to me cordially, and I hurried away. The back stairs were wide and steep, and I was puffing by the time I'd reached the second floor. I followed the maid's instructions through the empty halls to the rear of the building where an open door spilled sunlight into the corridor.

I peeked into this chamber and saw Mr. Thanos hunched over a desk, face in his hand, as he read papers spread before him.

The desk took up most of the tiny room, and the rest of the space was crammed with bookcases. Books of every size and shape filled the shelves, some lying across rows of others. Papers hung out of boxes stacked on the same shelves, and the desk was awash with paper and more books, some opened over others.

Mr. Thanos abruptly seized a pen and made a swift note, muttering under his breath. "No, it does *not* follow that sequence. Where did you learn mathematics, Elgin, old fellow? Blast it, I shall have to rewrite half of this bloody—"

I cleared my throat.

Mr. Thanos jerked his head up, sunlight from the small window catching on the thick lenses of his spectacles. Another man might have snarled at the interruption, from a servant no less, but Mr. Thanos, after a startled look, leapt to his feet, a wide smile spreading across his face.

"Mrs. Holloway, what a wonderful surprise. I say, you've come in time to save my sanity." Mr. Thanos tossed down the pen, splattering ink across his pages, then tore off his glasses and sent them after the pen. The spectacles landed solidly in a splash of ink.

"I've brought you a delivery." I set the basket on the least-cluttered corner of the desk and lifted out a wrapped parcel. "Lemon cake, a large hunk of it. I made more today and decided you likely weren't feeding yourself."

"That's what Cyn—Lady Cynthia says. So does my landlady."

"Well, you'll be able to nourish yourself with this."

"You are too kind." Mr. Thanos lifted the parcel and took a sniff, closing his eyes. "I will be quite ready to tuck into that. Thank you for thinking of me, Mrs. Holloway."

"I do confess it was not only kindness that brought me." I left the basket and drew Tess's paper out of my pocket. "I came to see you about several things. One is, do you know what sort of chemical this is?"

Mr. Thanos took the paper and peered at it, then groped behind him for his spectacles. He brought them to his face, pursed his lips when he saw the ink on them, and thrust his hand into his pocket for a handkerchief, losing hold of the paper in the process.

I retrieved the scrap from the floor and held it until Mr. Thanos had cleaned the glasses, returned the handkerchief, and looped the spectacles around his ears.

"Now." He stared at the words on the paper. "Hmm."

"Do you know what it means?"

"Can't say that I do." Mr. Thanos held the paper up to the light, as though that would give him the answer. "But let us see, shall we?"

He turned to his bookshelves and stepped onto a small ladder, eagerly scanning the books' spines. "I inherited this lot from the last chap who had this office, before the old Polytechnic shut down. Chap went to South America to study the stars. Just imagine . . ." Mr. Thanos drew a breath, letting his mind wander to the joy of staring at the heavens from the southern latitudes. "Ah well. Plenty to do here. His library has a bit of everything in it. I swore I saw some excellent tomes on botany."

"Botany?" I moved closer to the bookcase and scrutinized the titles, all of which were very long and printed in minuscule type.

Mr. Thanos shook the paper. "*This* is a chemical found in plants. I'm certain I should know it, but botany is not my field, and neither is chemistry. Mathematics is very consuming. Ah, here we are."

He extracted a tome and flipped it open, quickly becoming absorbed in a page.

"Does it tell you what the poison is?" I asked after a few minutes had ticked past.

"Hmm?" Mr. Thanos's head popped up. "Oh, no, I beg your pardon. This is an essay on the history of pi. Pi, the number." He chuckled. "Not your excellent pastries."

"I see," I said, a trifle impatiently.

"I will save it for later." Mr. Thanos tossed the book to the desk, where it landed across the pages he had been working on. "These shelves are a treasure trove of knowledge." He seized another book and thrust it in front of me. *The Taxonomy of the Flora of Britain, Native and Introduced*, the title on the front said. There were more words, but Mr. Thanos whipped the book away and leapt from the ladder.

He laid this book more carefully on the desk and opened it to an index in the back. I thought he'd consult the scrap of paper again, but Mr. Thanos ran his finger along a column, paused at one line, and then flipped pages. He stopped at one and slapped it.

"There. You see?"

An entry for *andromedotoxin* started in the middle of the page and filled one column with very small print. I skimmed the words but understood perhaps one in three.

"Could you explain, please, Mr. Thanos? Botany is not my field either, apart from what growing things I can put into sauces."

"Of course." Mr. Thanos paused and gave a breathy laugh. "Very good, Mrs. Holloway. Now, this toxin is pretty nasty—apparently in minuscule amounts it causes nausea and loose bowels. In greater amounts, the victim will have convulsions then slowly lose function of the body and become paralyzed, while the heart rate drops dramatically. They will slip into unconsciousness and die if the poison is not removed from their system within six hours." Mr. Thanos shuddered. "How awful."

As he spoke, I remembered Erica becoming more and more ill, unable to move at the last. The doctor presumably had tried to get her to vomit but too late to save her.

"It *was* awful," I said quietly. "What is the plant?"

"Oh, er . . ." Mr. Thanos read on. "It's rhododendron." He looked up. "Disturbing. Jove, those plants make up everyone's garden hedge."

Yes, indeed, and many well-tended, dark-leafed specimens lined the large garden behind Lady Covington's house.

20

M r. Thanos continued reading aloud, but I scarcely heard him. That the plant was so ready to hand in Lady Covington's garden cemented the fact that the poisoner was someone in her house. Every member of the family and all of the staff had access to the garden. Symes, of course, more than most.

It was one thing to have a supply of the plant, I told myself, trying to quell my zeal, quite another to know how to harvest it and introduce it into Lady Covington's food. One would have to grind up the stems or leaves or boil them down, and it would have to be done in secret.

Mr. Thanos continued to read. "It says the honey that bees make of the flowers is poisonous. Beekeepers must be aware of what pollen their bees feed on." He grimaced. "That will make me look at a pot of honey a bit more warily, to be certain."

"Indeed, it will me too. Thank you, Mr. Thanos. Will you mark that page and put the book where you can find it again?"

Mr. Thanos blinked up at me. "Pardon? Oh, right. Is this helpful?"

"It is immensely helpful."

I waited until Mr. Thanos found a folded paper to mark the place in the book—I hoped the paper did not contain some important breakthrough in a mathematical problem—and tucked the book into the bottom drawer of his desk, which was remarkably empty.

"Now to the other point," I said. "Lady Cynthia."

Mr. Thanos's face became a dark shade of red. He unhooked his spectacles and held them nervously. "Yes? How is she?"

"Quite well. Now, listen, please. I noted how ably she wrote out your equations for you when you were explaining formulas at your lecture at the Crystal Palace."

Mr. Thanos took on a faraway look. "Yes, she did it splendidly."

"She tells me she often helps you write things when you are distracted."

He nodded. "She has been a boon to me. I'd never have finished my paper for the mathematics society if she hadn't aided me."

"Excellent. Why not, when you begin your lectures here at the Polytechnic, take her on as an assistant? She can write your equations on the board or hand you papers you need or find books for you . . ." I had no idea what Mr. Thanos did during his lectures or for his research, but he and Cynthia would.

Mr. Thanos brightened a moment, then his excitement dimmed. "I'd be chuffed to, but Lady Cynthia is a woman." He pointed this out as though I was not acquainted with the fact. "The Polytechnic is for young men."

"She will be keeping your equations neat, not enrolling," I argued. "Besides, I hear of plenty of young ladies—wives as well as unmarried misses—who assist in scientific endeavors, here and in America." Mr. Davis had been reading me bits about ladies who were helping astronomers study the nature of stars and planets. Some of the women had become quite learned and highly regarded.

"That is true." Mr. Thanos brightened again. "The ladies compute things, which takes much skill, more than most believe." He fell silent, staring through the dusty window at the brick backs of houses in Cavendish Square.

"I am certain you can convince Sir Arthur, once he has fully recovered, that Lady Cynthia would be of great help to you. He has met her and seen that she can write things out without making a mistake."

"She can." The warmth in Mr. Thanos's eyes was gratifying. "She makes fewer mistakes than I do. I get into a rush, my mind is on the next thing and the next, and my hand cannot keep up."

"There, you see? Speak to Sir Arthur. Be insistent if he objects. Dear Cynthia is a clever young woman, and she should be able to exercise that cleverness. If she can be useful, perhaps her parents and aunt will cease pushing her at unsuitable young men."

I had more in mind than simply finding Cynthia something to do, but I saw no need to worry Mr. Thanos about my ideas at the moment.

Mr. Thanos squared his shoulders. "Right. I will persuade Sir Arthur. You can depend on it."

"Thank you, Mr. Thanos." I breathed an inward sigh of relief. Task accomplished. "Please enjoy the lemon cake."

"I will, I will. Thank you, Mrs. Holloway. You are kindness itself."

"You exaggerate, Mr. Thanos, but I will take the compliment. Thank you very much for your help, sir, and good day. I will tell Lady Cynthia you give her your regards."

I visited the markets in Oxford Street, filling my now empty basket with greens. I remembered Lady Covington's offer to take what I wanted from her kitchen garden, but I would not have time to visit it today. I would return there soon, however, and look closely at the rhododendron shrubbery. Would I find traces of cuttings? Or would I be able to tell a surreptitious cutting from the usual trimming the gardener did?

Thus musing, I returned home and began preparations for supper. I saw no sign of Lord Clifford as I went to ask Mr. Davis for a bold red wine to add to my braised beef. He brought out a rich burgundy and uncorked it for me.

"His lordship should have all the bottles he needs in his chamber," Mr. Davis said dryly. "One entire shelf is gone." He gestured to the dark interior of the wine cellar.

"Then he won't be back for more right away," I said, trying to soothe him. "Perhaps he'll retire to the country again soon."

Mr. Davis sighed. "Lady Cynthia is an honest and good-hearted girl. Such a pity about her relations."

"I agree." I paused, thinking through all that I'd learned about Lady Covington and her family as well as Mr. Thanos's revelations. "Do you recall, Mr. Davis, an account of a train accident about some years ago? It would have been in all the newspapers, presumably. I'm not certain exactly when. Or even where."

"You mean the one in Oxfordshire?" Mr. Davis closed the wine cellar's door and locked it with a key on a chain attached to his waistcoat. "About seven years, as I recall, if it's the same accident. There are so many, unfortunately. But you are speaking about Lord Covington's railway."

"Indeed, I am," I said in surprise.

"I heard Lord Clifford discussing it in the dining room," Mr. Davis explained. "He brought it up, as Lady Cynthia has been staying at the Covington house. Not the sort of conversation I'd think agreeable over the fish course, but Mr. Bywater seemed interested. I had a friend who had meant to travel on that very train from Oxford to London and decided at the last minute to go the following day. Made his hair white when he read the accounts, he said."

"Lady Covington's first husband perished in that crash. Do you remember if Baron Covington was blamed?"

Mr. Davis scratched his head then absently straightened his hairpiece. "It was a bad one, as I recall. Killed, oh, seventy-five people, and maimed others for life. Apparently, a set of wheels failed on one car. The brakeman tried to stop the train, but the brakes weren't connected from car to car, and the back carriages uncoupled. Those were all right—they glided to a stop, but the front five or six carriages kept going while the bad wheels pulled them off the track. Twisted the carriages right around before the engineer noticed and could halt. By then it was wreckage, with people trapped." He shivered. "Horrible. Lord Covington's company was sued by many and almost was shut down, but apparently, they talked their way into staying in business. Promises to make improvements, payments for the funerals of those who didn't survive, pensions for the injured."

"Terrible," I said feelingly. Trains were practical and had their uses, but they were unpredictable machines.

"Covington's railway line did truncate," Mr. Davis went on.

"They lost the western region, I believe, and now their trains run mostly in the south and southeast."

Such as the trains I'd taken to Sydenham to visit the Crystal Palace. I shivered. "I imagine few wanted to travel on their line after that."

"Not necessarily. Most of us don't know who owns the trains we board, or care, as long as they take us in the right direction. And people forget, or reason that trains are safer now. Which is true. Improvements were made to connect brakes across cars because of that wreck."

I wondered, though, about the victims, or those who'd lost loved ones. Did they forget? Harriet and Jonathan had lost their father, though why they'd blame their mother or try to murder her for it, I did not know.

"Thank you, Mr. Davis. You have been very helpful."

Mr. Davis tapped his temple with his forefinger. "You'd be surprised what's up here, Mrs. Holloway, after a lifetime of experience and reading my newspapers."

We parted, me with wine ready to use with my beef. I braised it and added potatoes and carrots, a hearty meal, such as Mr. Bywater liked. In deference to Lady Clifford's preference for lighter eating, I made a salad and clear soup to be served alongside it.

While I shoveled the night's loaf of bread into the oven, James turned up.

"I'm famished." He gazed in longing at a pan of beef Tess stirred with a long spoon and the strawberry tart waiting on the dresser. "Went all the way to Surrey and back to deliver your note."

"Sit down there." I pointed to the end of the table. "Tess, cut off a bit of the ham left over from luncheon and a spoonful of hash. The lad needs feeding."

Tess grinned and disappeared to carry out my orders.

"Your father understands what I wrote him?" I asked.

James nodded. "Seems to. Was right angry at Uncle Errol. Heard the two of them having a bit of a barney."

A barney was a loud quarrel. "I hope the Duke of Daventry didn't hear them."

"Nah, they were out in the park a long way from the house, by themselves. Standing still, like any two gentlemen enjoying nature, but hammering away at each other. With words, I mean."

"As long as Mr. Fielding agrees to help."

"I think he will. He was long faced when they came back to me, and said he knew *you* were behind everything. I don't know what it's all about, but I said I reckoned that was true."

"Good." I gave a decided nod. "I hope Mr. Fielding plays his part and all goes well." The duke was a dangerous man, I was coming to understand, but Daniel and Mr. Fielding were too. The one not prepared to deal with real danger was Cynthia's father.

Tess brought the ham and hash and set it in front of James. James lost all interest in machinations between me and his father and tucked in.

Lost in thought, I finished preparing the beef and the rest of the meal.

After the upstairs had eaten their supper, Mr. Davis returned to the kitchen and told me what had been discussed at table—Lord Clifford declared he'd return to Surrey in the morning for the Duke of Daventry's house party that continued through the weekend. Lady Clifford had decided that she preferred the theatre and other outings to walking in the country, and would remain in London.

Lady Cynthia had expressed her wish to return to Lady

Covington's to help her through her difficulties, and would leave in the morning. There was no talk at all, Mr. Davis said gleefully, of Lady Cynthia and marriage.

Good, I thought with satisfaction. Lord Clifford was holding up his end of the bargain.

In the morning, Tess took her day out. I sent her off with extra crullers to give to Caleb, to express my thanks for his help.

I learned, however, that Caleb hadn't been as discreet as he could have been. When Tess returned late that afternoon, Caleb entered with her, and behind him came Inspector McGregor.

21

Few things unnerved me more than a policeman in my kitchen. When my husband had died at sea, a policeman had come to the house where I'd worked as an assistant cook. The police sergeant had found one of my letters to my husband and realized I'd borne his daughter. The sergeant had not visited me to break the news gently, but to demand to know if I had any of my husband's possessions, which by rights belonged to his wife.

Since I'd believed *I* was his wife, the report had been a double blow.

When I beheld Caleb in his smart uniform, brass buttons up to his chin, I had a moment of light-headedness. Ten years dropped away, and I was the frightened young woman wondering how on earth I would raise my child with no husband and no widow's portion.

I drew a deep breath and willed my heart to beat normally again. Caleb was a good soul, not the sneering sergeant who'd insisted on searching for my husband's belongings in the rooms I'd let at a boardinghouse.

Inspector McGregor, in his usual rumpled suit, removed a faded hat and eyed me in annoyance over his thick mustache.

"Mrs. Holloway, if you will lend me a few moments."

I had no time at all for him, but Tess sent me a look of apology as she reached for her apron.

"I'll take over, Mrs. H. The inspector promised he'd not keep you long."

"Very well." I wiped my floury hands and, without removing my apron, beckoned the inspector to follow me down the hall to the housekeeper's parlor.

Mrs. Redfern spent little time in this parlor, as she insisted on being upstairs to direct the maids in their work. Very conscientious, was Mrs. Redfern, never shirking her duties to sip tea with her feet up.

The parlor was empty. Inspector McGregor had been in this room before, but these days it was painfully neat, Mrs. Redfern having organized the previous chaos. My few cookbooks were lined up on one shelf in the corner, untouched by all but me.

"Will you sit, Inspector?" I waved him to the soft wing chair that was a recent acquisition.

He waited like a gentleman until I perched on the edge of the Belter chair before he took his seat.

"Mrs. Holloway, you are corrupting my constables," he rumbled.

"I beg your pardon, Inspector." I faced him without flinching, resting my hands on my knees, and forced myself to meet his keen stare. "I am naturally curious to find out what truly happened to Erica Hume."

"Yes, McAdam informed me you were there when she died." Inspector McGregor scowled as though I'd planted myself at Erica's side to make things difficult for him. "And that you believe she was killed by mistake, the poison meant for Lady Covington."

"Precisely," I said crisply. "Lady Covington is still in danger, and as far as I can see, the police are doing little about it."

"Because the police believe the death is accidental." McGregor's mustache bobbed with his words. "Poisonous leaves from the garden got into the food, and Mrs. Hume consumed enough to kill her."

"Which is nonsense . . ."

Inspector McGregor held up a hand. "I said the police in general are convinced, not me. I would have been, if McAdam hadn't told me of your interest. You are a confounded busybody, Mrs. Holloway, but I have learned you are usually right about things."

I was pleased he thought so, but I did not feel clever allowing Erica to die. "Not always."

"Often enough. That is why I've come. Instead of throwing yourself in front of a crazed poisoner, tell me everything you've discovered, and I'll make an arrest before you are killed."

"Very amusing." I knew he was correct that I had been reckless in the past, but then, I'd more than once had to lay hands on a killer when the police were nowhere in sight. Not alone, of course—Daniel had obligingly assisted. "Unfortunately, I have been able to find out very little in this case. I have toyed with the idea that Mrs. Hume was the intended victim all along, but I confess I have given up the notion."

"Lady Covington is the more likely target," Inspector McGregor said with a decided nod. "She has wealth that can buy Park Lane ten times over. In fact, her first husband, Morris, owned several unentailed properties across England, and

Lady Covington inherited the lot, held in trust for her son until she dies. She'd live well on the rents even if the late Mr. Morris hadn't also left her a huge sum in the bank. The new Baron Covington doesn't have half as much. When the present Lady Covington married Lord Covington, all assumed she'd pour her money into his railway, but she did not. The cash and property were tied up in trust so her new husband did not automatically take over. Morris knew what he was doing."

"Mr. Morris died tragically in a train accident," I said. "He'd certainly prepared well for his wife's living."

"Yes, the Heyford crash of January 1875." Inspector McGregor settled himself more comfortably in the chair. "Morris was in one of the first-class carriages, traveling from Coventry southeast to London. He'd made a business trip, as part of his position on the railway board. He was partly blamed for the wreck, but exonerated, as he would never have taken that train himself if he hadn't believed it perfectly safe, and also because he wasn't alive to make amends."

"I had wondered if someone resented Lady Covington enough over that to kill her."

Inspector McGregor shrugged. "Lady Covington always avowed her husband had done no wrong. Many lawsuits were leveled at the railway company, but it paid out, and all was finished. They had to cease operation on that branch of the line, but within a few years began to make back the money they'd lost concentrating on travel to the southeast."

All as Mr. Davis had told me. "You have been thorough, Inspector," I said admiringly.

"As soon as I found out who this Mrs. Hume was, I made my inquiries. Never hurts. The railway might have nothing to do with anything, but I wanted background on the family. *You* will give me more." He pointed a stubby finger at me.

"I don't know much more." I didn't mention Harriet's paramour, because I wanted to learn further details about him first. If he was an innocent, lovelorn swain, I did not want Inspector McGregor to pounce on him.

"But you will find out. Anything you discover about Lady Covington's household, you will tell me. If you have to send me reports through McAdam, I'll put up with it."

"Mr. McAdam is very busy," I said hesitantly.

"So it would seem. I am not to know what he is doing, though I can guess. Not my case. Not my area." He sounded vastly irritated by this. "Send word through Constable Greene."

"Constable . . . ? Ah, Caleb."

"Yes, the one who's attached himself to your assistant. She has him wrapped around her finger."

I regarded him primly. "A man could do worse than marrying a cook."

"I hope to all that's holy he isn't thinking of marrying anyone. He's not a bad policeman, and could go far."

"I am pleased to hear it. You mean that when he has a detective inspector's salary, *then* he might be able to marry?"

"Touché, Mrs. Holloway. I'm interested in this case, because I know there's more than meets the eye, or else *you* wouldn't be involved."

"Possibly true, but did you not interview them about Erica's death? Considering poison was found."

Inspector McGregor's expression turned sour. "I tried to speak to the family, and the servants, but the whole lot of them froze me out. No one in that household, whether upstairs or down, will deign to talk to the police. I was scum on the bottom of their shoes—they would not even let me in past the downstairs back door."

"The staff is very protective of her ladyship."

"I imagine she pays them a fair amount. A rich woman can buy loyalty."

I thought of Jepson, the dragon who guarded—or at least seemed to guard—Lady Covington. She had been with Lady Covington a long time, from what I understood. There was more than riches keeping that household together, but whether it was love or hatred remained to be seen.

"Very well, Inspector. I will save you the mortification of being treated as though you are dirt on the bottoms of their shoes and speak to Lady Covington's family and staff. Would you like me to write to you, or would you prefer I give the constable a verbal report?"

"A letter is fine." Inspector McGregor slid to the edge of his chair. He wanted to rise and depart, but he was enough of a gentleman to not simply stand and stalk out before I was ready to say my farewells.

I stood up, relieving him of his impatience. "Would you like to take home some lemon cake, Inspector? I have made several batches."

"You are very kind, but no."

I saw sudden hunger flicker in his eyes and his fingers twitch, but he was trying to be the correct policeman who did nothing untoward while he was on duty, including indulging in sweets offered by a helpful cook.

The poor man needed a wife, I thought. One to make certain his collar was straight and he was well-fed enough to not be tortured by the thought of cakes.

"I'll wrap it up for you anyway," I said. "You can have it with your supper."

Before he could protest, I strode back to the kitchen and lifted an already wrapped bit of cake I'd intended to send to Bobby and Miss Townsend. I could give them another.

I thrust the packet at Inspector McGregor as he made his way through the kitchen to the back door. He could do nothing but take it and tuck it into his pocket, though he scowled as he did so.

Inspector McGregor said a curt "Good day," and opened the door, sending a cold gust into the kitchen. He slapped his hat firmly onto his head, slammed the door until it rattled, and trudged up the stairs into the wind.

The next day, Sunday, I woke early and worked hard alongside Tess to make certain the Sunday dinner would be a fine feast.

Mrs. Bywater, who walked down the road to attend services at Grosvenor Chapel most Sundays, allowed the staff to attend church with her if they wished. I decided to go with her today, as did Sara and Mrs. Redfern. The three of us followed at a discreet distance behind Mr. and Mrs. Bywater, and surprisingly, Lord and Lady Clifford.

I slid into a back pew with Mrs. Redfern and Sara. As always, I found the white-columned interior of the chapel with its galleries and arched ceiling soothing. Grosvenor Chapel had no stained glass, and while I thought stained glass pretty, I liked how the clear windows flooded the chapel with light. God was in nature, after all, and letting in the sunshine—what there was of it on a London spring day—admitted His presence.

The vicar, a slim man with a calm, almost liquid voice, conducted the service. I could doze off listening to him, but I remained awake to study him with interest. This was Daniel's friend who allowed him to enter the sacristy in the middle of the night and entertain guests there. Daniel had said he'd done the man a favor, and I was curious to know what.

I switched my gaze to Cynthia's parents, who sat in the front of the chapel. From this angle, I could see Lord Clifford, who'd returned from Surrey late last night, on the end of the pew, gazing in a bored manner at the gold-leafed cross hanging over the altar.

Lady Clifford, next to him, had her head bent as though in prayer, her lips moving. It struck me as I observed her that she was an aging woman. Though she dressed smartly, much more so than Mrs. Bywater, her slim frame drooped, and her shoulders possessed a thinness that spoke of waning strength. Sunlight touched her hair, which was fair like Cynthia's, but in this chapel, it appeared more white than flaxen.

I recalled Lady Clifford collapsing against Cynthia when she'd come down to my kitchen, sobbing when she'd thought of her children. She'd lost a son under horrible circumstances, and a daughter under not much better ones.

Cynthia easily grew exasperated with her parents, but I saw her hurt that they regarded her as a nuisance to be foisted off on a husband while they grieved her much-lauded brother and sister.

My mother had rarely had two coins to rub together, and she'd spent all day and many nights charring to keep food on our table. But I'd never had any doubt that she loved me deeply, and I'd loved her in return.

She'd made sure I learned my letters, and when I was fourteen, she'd found me a position as a cook's assistant, hoping I could begin a profession in service. A cook in a proper household could make a living and have a decent roof over her head far easier than a woman who scrubbed floors piecemeal.

When my mother had died, having worked herself into an early grave, I'd felt nothing but pain for a long time. I'd become an under-cook in a large house in Grosvenor Square shortly before her death, *moving up in the world*, my mother proudly told her old cronies in Bow Lane. It was in this vulnerable state that I'd met my husband.

The service ended with one of my favorite hymns—

Holy, holy, holy, merciful and mighty
God in three persons, blessed Trinity

I sang loudly, still thinking of my mother, and ducked outside after the music ended, without waiting for the final blessing. I wanted to make certain the dinner Tess and I had begun would be finished for the family when they arrived home.

I found Lord Clifford at the end of the chapel's porch, lounging against the last column, he having slipped away during the last hymn. He lifted his hat and fell into step with me as I walked toward Mount Street.

"It happened as you said, Mrs. Holloway," he told me in a low voice. "The duke has paid me two hundred guineas for the necklace. I'd only asked a hundred, but he was moved to assist me." Lord Clifford chortled his triumph before he caught my look and amended his expression. "Anyway, I toddled back to London, telling him I wanted to rejoin my wife—which is true. I don't much like being away from her long. Reverend Fielding has taken over. He is going to give the duke four thousand for that bloody—er, dashed—paste necklace." Lord Clifford trailed off admiringly. "Lancaster—or, no, he's McAdam, isn't he? He came up with the cash for Mr. Fielding to pay over. A dashed clever chap is McAdam. I truly believed him a vacuous fop whose head was only good for holding his hat."

"Thank you for your help, your lordship," I said with relief. "You might be exposing a very treacherous man."

"Well, I don't approve of thugs stabbing gentlemen in

broad daylight. It could have been *me*." Lord Clifford glanced about as though fearing an anarchist would charge through the sunlit May morning and plunge a knife into him there and then.

"Perhaps you ought to take her ladyship home to the country," I ventured. "It will be a bit safer than London. And she seems sad."

"That she does, the poor old girl." Lord Clifford lost his cheerfulness. "It's a hard thing, losing a child, Mrs. Holloway."

I thought of Grace, and knew he spoke the truth. If anything happened to Grace, I would want to die myself.

I could hardly blurt out to Lord Clifford that I had a daughter, so I said, "I can imagine, your lordship."

"A damned hard thing." This time he did not stammer over his expletive. "My wife feels it keenly. It's one reason she's fussing about Cynthia—wants to see her settled, with children of her own. Seems to think she'll be protected that way. Didn't help Em, though, did it? But my wife is beyond logic on the subject."

"I believe Lady Cynthia understands. I have grown to know your daughter well, and I'm very fond of her. She is no fool. When she is ready, she will settle herself. I think you will be agreeably surprised."

Lord Clifford nodded, his eyes softening. "She's a good gel, is Cyn, in spite of her eccentricities—which she inherited from me, don't you know." He laughed weakly. "I am happy she has such a friend in you." Lord Clifford paused, and I ceased walking.

He watched a chestnut horse pulling a black buggy past us, the horse's hooves clopping, the pungent odor of manure in its wake.

"I am grateful to you for looking after her," Lord Clifford finished.

"Not at all, your lordship."

"Please, continue to do so. Cynthia needs friends. My sister-in-law . . ." He trailed off and shook his head. "Well, you know her."

"Mrs. Bywater means well." I believed she truly did, in spite of our disagreements.

"Does she?" Lord Clifford scrunched up his face. "Don't know what old Neville sees in her, but I'll behave and be civil to her. Good day for now, Mrs. Holloway. I will await the ladies—ah, here they come."

I gave him a polite curtsy and continued along South Audley Street, pleased with the conversation.

A fter I sent up the midday meal, I took my basket and walked to Park Lane.

Cynthia had returned to Lady Covington's yesterday. I used the excuse of obtaining more greens from Lady Covington's garden to visit there, stopping on the way at the house in Upper Brook Street to leave a lemon cake with Miss Townsend's butler for the two ladies.

I entered the garden through the gate at the end of Upper Brook Street to see Harriet Morris taking cuttings from the rhododendron bushes that lined the wall.

22

W hatever are you doing, Miss Morris?" I demanded.
Harriet jumped and whirled to me, dropping deep
pink blossoms onto the ground.

"You!" she said dramatically. "What are *you* doing creeping
about, terrifying me?"

The gate had squeaked loudly when I'd swung it open, so
I'd hardly been creeping.

"Why are you cutting rhododendrons?" I asked.

Harriet stooped to retrieve the blossoms, which she thrust
into her basket, crushing them as she did so. "To create a
pretty arrangement for the table. Lady Cynthia's here. We
should make some effort in this morose old place."

I debated telling Harriet that poison from that plant had
killed her stepsister, but she had a fairly sharp set of pruning
scissors in her hand, and I decided to keep my silence on the
matter.

"Why do you stay, then?" I asked. "If it is so morose?"

Harriet glared at me, her lace-trimmed bodice rising with her sharp breath. "Where would I go? What would I live on? I am stuck here . . . forever."

"Does your young man not have money? Or a house to take you to?"

Harriet's flush matched the blooms in her basket. "I suppose you expect me to screech, *What young man?* But you saw him. Very well. I love him." She eyed me defiantly. "But he isn't suitable, is he? Not for the daughter of a railway magnate and stepsister of a baron. He's George's secretary." Her voice weakened, ending on a hopeless note.

"He works for the railway?"

Harriet threw wide her hand with the scissors. "How else do you suppose I met him? I'm scarcely allowed out of the house. If George discovers it, he'll sack Darren—Mr. Amos—and I'll never see him again." Tears beaded her lashes.

"What does your mother say?" I asked gently.

"She doesn't mind his character, and he's a gentleman, but he's poor. A besetting sin, in the eyes of this family."

Harriet's predicament explained some of her petulance, and she stirred my sympathy. "Perhaps, as your mother has much influence with the railway board, she can suggest a position for Mr. Amos with a higher income. If you explain to her what is in your heart, she might understand."

A flicker of hope lit Harriet's eyes, but she remained skeptical. "George will never understand. He's a stiff-necked, pompous prig."

"Her ladyship might be able to help with that. It would not hurt for you to speak to her. Now, you've ruined that basket of flowers—leave them here and cut a few of those early roses instead. Cynthia likes them."

Harriet glanced at the crushed blossoms, made a noise of

annoyance, and dumped the flowers to the ground. Without saying good-bye, she stalked toward the rosebushes, scissors in hand.

"Good day, Mrs. Holloway." Symes halted on the path behind me, resting his rake on the ground and giving me a toothy smile. "Was she impertinent to you?" He nodded toward Harriet as she approached the rosebushes like a hunter stalking a snared animal. "She has a temper, that one does."

"She has much on her mind." I scooted the fallen flowers under the rhododendrons with my foot, where they could become compost. "Tell me, Mr. Symes, does the family cut these bushes often? For the flowers, I mean."

Symes considered then shrugged. "Not that I know. Never seen sign of cutting, except for what I prune."

"You'd notice?"

"'Course I would. I notice everything what goes on in this garden." He leaned closer to me, using the rake for balance. "Can I offer you some nice pole beans, Mrs. Holloway? Just out, sweet as can be."

I backed up a step. "That would be lovely, thank you. Perhaps you can gather them while I have a word with Mrs. Gamble."

"Aye, that I'll do." Symes touched his hat, gave me another large smile, and walked toward the hothouse, whistling.

I entered the house through the back stairs, but I bypassed the kitchen to climb to the main floor. The servants' staircase was dark and enclosed, the walls not well finished. Hatches for maintaining the bellpull system and other things were set haphazardly here and there.

As I emerged into the front hall, I stopped a passing maid, who faced me with her duster as though she'd battle me with it.

"Will you tell Lady Cynthia that Mrs. Holloway is here, please? I'll wait."

"You should be in the kitchen, missus," the maid said coldly. "But I'll go up."

She turned away and ascended the stairs. I saw what Inspector McGregor meant about being treated as though he were dung on their shoes.

Cynthia skimmed down the stairs a few moments later, her smile canceling the irritation of Harriet and the sourness of the maid. "Glad to see you, Mrs. H. There are storms a-brewing."

"What sort of storms?" I asked in hushed tones.

Cynthia drew me aside. She wore a light gray frock, slim fitting and simple—I saw Miss Townsend's influence in the design. "Good old George is threatening to turn everyone out. Says it's his house now, and Lady Covington and her brood must go. He blames them for his sister's death. Not that he gave much thought to her when she was alive, Jonathan tells me."

"Can he do that?" I glanced at the high-ceilinged, hushed, and empty hall. The house exuded all the luxury money could buy, and yet, so much coldness lived here.

"He can, since this house is part of the entail. But whether Lady Covington will stand for it is another matter. Dear George could have his solicitor force them out, but then he'd have to deal with public opinion. Lady Covington is much loved. If George casts a mother and children into the street— even with the children grown—the newspapers will vilify him." She finished with relish, her blue eyes dancing.

Thinking of Lady Covington's formidable character, I doubted George would prevail. "Will you ask if Lady Covington will see me?"

"I'm certain she'll be delighted. Come with me." Cynthia hooked her arm through mine and strode with me toward the closed double doors of the drawing room.

She opened one door to usher me inside, interrupting a furious and low-voiced conversation between Lady Covington and Jepson, her lady's maid. Jepson jerked around and glared daggers at me.

Lady Covington rose. Her mourning black made her face wan, the gray in her hair more prominent. She was a woman grown haggard by worry and guilt.

"Good morning, Mrs. Holloway. I was about to send for you."

Cynthia led me forward, but Jepson stood firmly between us and her ladyship.

Lady Covington sighed. "Jepson is trying to convince me to leave London. I am to go anywhere, she insists; the Continent perhaps. She believes I will be the next victim."

"A jolly good idea." Cynthia made a decided nod. "Find someplace with sunshine and put all this behind you."

I had to agree, but I didn't trust Jepson. If Lady Covington holed up somewhere in Southern France alone with Jepson, would she survive the retreat?

"She wishes me to go without Harriet and Jonathan." Lady Covington's lips tightened. "A thing I cannot do. They need me."

"If they put a dollop of poison into your breakfast tea, it won't matter, will it?" Jepson demanded.

"I will not flee, and I will not hide. The solution is to find out who is doing this and stop them. Do you not agree, Mrs. Holloway?"

"I do," I had to say. "May I speak openly, your ladyship?"

Lady Covington waved a thin hand at me. Though she resumed her chair, she remained upright on it, her back ramrod straight. "You may leave us, Jepson."

"Not likely." Jepson firmed her jaw and faced me. "If she stays, I do. I don't trust this cook."

"It doesn't matter," Lady Covington said wearily. "What did you wish to say, Mrs. Holloway?"

I began as delicately as I could. "That as long as your children are fully dependent on you, and his lordship fears to make a decision without you, you might be in danger. If your family felt more freedom to decide their own fate—"

Lady Covington cut me off with a snort. "If you are ever gifted with children, Mrs. Holloway, and you too, Cynthia, you will understand. I wish my children's lives to be comfortable and prosperous, believe me. But if I loosen the reins on Harriet, she will throw herself at a poor nobody who will take her to live in wretched rooms in some run-down house. How do you believe she will fare? Within a year, she will be back here, her marriage in ruins, and no more prospects for a better one. I love Jonathan dearly—he is a good boy—but I am not a fool. He gives money away, helping his friends mostly, but his generosity will be his downfall."

Jepson stared at her in disbelief. "Helping his friends? I beg your pardon, my lady, for speaking out of turn, but he gambles that money away. In the clubs and at the racing meets."

"Gossip." Lady Covington's voice turned hard. "I thought you of all people would know better than to listen to it, Jepson. His friends are softheaded with money and get themselves into trouble, time and again. Jonathan is too kind to them."

I recalled the cook's assessment of Jonathan and rather agreed with Jepson. I loved Grace dearly, but I hoped I would not be so blinded if she suddenly turned into a reckless young woman who got herself into gambling scrapes.

"As for George." Lady Covington looked exasperated. "Giving him his head would be the worst thing I could do. He has no idea how to run a business. Thank heavens there are a few others on the board with sense. Even Mr. Amos, the secretary Harriet is potty about, is far wiser than George."

"Perhaps Mr. Amos should be given more to do," I suggested gently. "If he is an intelligent young man, if he had more say in the company . . . I have no idea how railways are run, but he might go far if you let him."

"Excellent idea," Cynthia agreed. "If you're not careful, Harriet will elope with this fellow. Nothing makes a gentleman more enticing than a parent telling her he's unsuitable." She spoke with the great confidence of one who'd never, ever fall for an unsuitable gentleman.

Lady Covington closed her eyes. "You have a point, my dear. I will consider it. However, the board, including George, would have to go along with a promotion."

"You could talk them 'round," Cynthia said with confidence. "Save you a good deal of bother."

"Perhaps." Lady Covington opened her eyes and skewered me with her gaze. "What else will you bluntly tell me, Mrs. Holloway?"

"I'm afraid I must ask about something that might be painful." I drew on my courage as Jepson scowled at me. "The train accident in Heyford."

Lady Covington's face was brittle. "The one that killed Mr. Morris."

I nodded. "Did anyone who was hurt in that accident, or who lost a loved one in it . . . Did they blame your husband?"

"Of course they did." Lady Covington remained rigid, but her lip trembled once. "There was an inquiry and a judge who went over the case. Wheels on one car were faulty, which was found to be the responsibility of the wheel manufacturer. But the railway line was also held responsible, for not having enough inspections that would have discovered the problem. My husband was excoriated in the newspapers, even after he'd lost his life."

"Newspapermen are a cruel lot," Jepson broke in. "They even hounded her ladyship. Was angry at her for not claiming her husband was an incompetent idiot. No mention of the plenty of others who ran the railway." She cast her glare at the painting of the haughty, late Lord Covington, whose bearded countenance gazed down at us imperiously.

"The newspapers were angry with me for standing up for my husband," Lady Covington explained. "I told them pointedly that Mr. Morris had been a good man, and the mistakes of others were not his fault. Those hurt in the accident were compensated, as well as pensions made for those who lost members of their family. I received a pension as well, for Mr. Morris's death, and the newspapers stabbed me for that too. I gave the money to a widow and orphan fund, and even that did not relieve me of denigration. I had to sue several of the newspapers."

"Forgive me if this is even more painful," I said. "But could either of your children resent you for what happened to their father? Or for you giving away the money that they thought should come to them for losing him?"

Lady Covington drew a breath for an angry retort, then she stopped. "I hadn't thought of that when I donated the pension, I admit. But yes, they were very angry at me."

"And your stepchildren. Were they resentful when you married their father?"

"That is natural. They doted on their mother, though she was rather heavy-handed. They also hadn't liked Mr. Morris, this is true. He could be a difficult man, though I never found him so. Lord Covington and I were happy together. Once George and Erica saw this, they came around."

Or perhaps they'd hidden their feelings, knowing it did no good to object. Both sets of children had had domineering parents, but now all those parents were dead—except Lady Covington.

"I will cease my questions, your ladyship," I said. "I am truly sorry for stirring painful memories. However . . . may I have leave to look through Mrs. Hume's bedchamber?" I was still mystified by who Henry was, and perhaps I could find some clue to his identity. I hesitated to mention the name to Lady Covington, though as I'd been openly asking the staff about him, she might already have heard.

I was trying to think of a plausible reason to give her for my request when Lady Covington heaved a long sigh and waved her hand. "Of course you may have leave. Jepson, please bring me some tea and tell Cook to add seedcake. I am hungry. Lady Cynthia, please remain and take tea with me. I feel the need to speak to someone with a good head on her shoulders."

I had hoped Cynthia could help me in Erica's bedchamber, but I was in no position to argue. I curtsied and followed Jepson out the door.

As soon as Jepson and I were alone in the hall, she seized my arm and dragged me to the staircase. I jerked from her painful grip as we reached its foot.

Jepson did not try to grab me again but shoved her face to mine. "What call do you have bringing up her ladyship's husband? Making her suffer it all over again? Who are you to question her about it?"

I already felt terrible about having to prod Lady Covington's memories, but I maintained my temper by reminding myself that Jepson might be a crazed poisoner.

"Her ladyship has asked me to discover who is trying to harm her," I said firmly. "That is all. To do so, I must find out who would be willing to kill her and why. Naturally, a few skeletons in the closet must be rattled."

"Just so you don't end up one of those skeletons." Jepson bared teeth that were stained from a lifetime of drinking tea. "Nor does her ladyship."

"This is what I am trying to prevent," I said with exaggerated patience. "Which is Mrs. Hume's bedchamber?" I scanned the stairs, wondering where in this vast house it lay.

"Find it yourself." Jepson turned on her heel and strode to the door to the back stairs, yanked it open, marched through, and slammed it shut.

The sound carried through the house, then silence reigned once more in the hall, the dust motes settling into their regular patterns.

I let out a slow breath. Jepson was a strange one, and I'd met many servants with peculiarities. One moment I was certain she was the poisoner; the next, she'd be guarding Lady Covington like a lion. If Erica had been the true target and Jepson the killer, then her behavior would make more sense, I reminded myself, and went up the stairs.

The wide staircase led to a hall as enormous as the one below it. A large gaslight chandelier, dark now, hung from a dome of stained glass far above.

The carpeted hall led to the north and south ends of the house, and the east and west walls held windows. One bowed out in the nook I'd seen over the doorway from the street, with a view over Park Lane and Hyde Park. I remembered spying a person in this window when I'd first approached the house, and I wondered anew who it had been. Not Lady Covington, who'd been in the garden. Erica, perhaps? The thought made me sad. Or Harriet, wondering who stared up at the house?

The long hall held doors, all polished walnut, all closed. Nothing distinguished any from another.

As I debated which door to approach first, one flew open, and a maid emerged with an armful of folded sheets. I saw behind her an airy bedroom in which another maid fluffed blankets over the bed while a young boy scrubbed blacking onto andirons at the fireplace.

The maid with the sheets kicked the door shut, hiding the flurry of activity.

I approached her and asked the way to Mrs. Hume's bed-chamber, explaining that her mistress had said I could look it over. The maid, after a sullen stare, led me down the hall to the south wing of the house.

She set the sheets on a table, took a key from her apron pocket, and opened a door to reveal a room similar to the one she'd left—light-colored paneling, a carved bedstead, a fire-place instead of a stove, and a large window overlooking the garden.

I thanked the maid. She said nothing at all, and once I'd entered, she closed the door hard behind me. I half thought she'd lock it, shutting me in, but I heard no click of a key, just the thump of her feet as she stalked away.

I took a calming breath and scanned the room.

The bed had been stripped, the bare tick mattress exposed. The wardrobe I opened held Erica's gowns and a coat that had been wrapped in paper, put away for summer. Another cup-board held her boots. Her clothes and shoes were elegantly made of expensive fabrics, the shoes of soft leather, but all

were in muted colors, the trim either plain piping or nonex-
istent.

I'd worked for matrons and widows who, within the bound-
aries of what was appropriate, decorated themselves without
worry. They might be expected to wear dark blues, grays, and
maroons, but they fitted out their gowns with laces, ribbons,
feathers, and beading that flaunted their wealth or taste.

Erica had been like a subdued wren, trying to efface herself
to the point of absurdity. Her marriage had been unhappy—
perhaps she preferred people not to notice her and remind her
of it.

I closed the wardrobe and moved to the small desk, a delicate thing on slender legs that could be moved from place to
place. It sat against the wall with no seat before it, and I imagined Erica had had it carried to the cushioned chair near the
fireplace when she'd wanted to use it.

The desk was locked, but a small key on a ribbon dangled
from a nail on the desk's side. I inserted the key into the lock
then lowered the desk's lid, which formed the writing surface.

"Mrs. Cook, is it?" a male voice said behind me. "Does
Mama know you're here rummaging through poor old Erica's
things? Perhaps I ought to take you downstairs and let her
shake some respect into you."

I swung around to behold the handsome Jonathan, a half
smile on his face as he thoroughly blocked any escape through
the door.

23

I remained where I was at the desk, stemming my uneasiness. "Lady Covington gave me leave to be here, yes."

"What are you looking for? A stray bit of cash to line your pocket? A trinket to sell?"

Jonathan advanced, menace in every line of him in spite of the smile. His dark hair was neat enough to gain approving looks from mothers but tousled enough to charm their daughters.

"Of course not," I told him in indignation. "I am trying to discover who murdered Mrs. Hume. I believe it was murder, not an accident."

"Oh?" Jonathan came closer. He was tall, and I imagined strong. "Do the police hire cooks now? I mean, to do policing, not cooking." He laughed but the laughter did not reach his eyes.

"I am acquainted with Detective Inspector McGregor," I said, standing my ground.

"Who is he, when he's at home? Oh, wait, he's that ungainly, bad-tempered copper who came to question Mama, isn't he? Old Jepson showed him the door. She hates the police, does Jepson. I imagine her as a member of some secret criminal society—in odd moments when I have nothing to do."

He unnerved me, and I was very aware of being alone with him. If I shouted, would the other servants hear me? Would they come to help me or decide I would only receive what I deserved?

"Do you not wish to discover who killed your sister?" I asked, trying to hide my nervousness.

"Stepsister. I never liked her. Fair—because she never liked me." Jonathan ran a hand through his hair, rumpling it further. "Though I hated to see the poor thing go like that. But yes, I'd like to find out who this mad poisoner is before I feel funny after eating my veal stew. I've been taking all my meals at my club since Erica died. It's not one that lets in affected sticks like my stepbrother, so I'm safe from him."

"Do you believe Lord Covington is doing this?"

Jonathan, who didn't seem to be able to keep his hands still, clutched the lapels of his frock coat. "I wouldn't put it past George. If he rids the world of Mama and then the rest of us, he inherits the lot. Then he can rush off to the South of France with his lover."

"His lover?" I thought of the stiff, slightly balding George—*good old George*, as Lady Cynthia referred to him—and tried to imagine him whispering sweet words into a lady's ear. I could not.

Jonathan moved abruptly to the door. I wondered why he was leaving so suddenly—and was relieved that he was—when he shut it and returned to me.

"Prying ears," he said quietly. "Servants in this house snoop atrociously, but I know secrets they don't. My dear, George's lover is not a lady."

I blinked, then I understood. "Ah."

"*Ah*, indeed." Jonathan's laugh was breathy. "You'd never think such a pompous prick would attract anyone of either sex, but apparently, he's been carrying on with this chap for ages. If George is happy, fine with me, but of course, no one can know."

"He could be arrested," I said in alarm. Such a thing was illegal, a hanging offense.

"True, but fortunately for George, it must be proved beyond all doubt, which means witnesses to the act. I can't imagine *that* would be pleasant, seeing George in such a position." Jonathan shuddered. "I meant no one must know because even if George wasn't arrested, he'd be dismissed from his precious railway board and break Mama's heart. She loves the railway. I think she married Covington when Papa died so she could stay close to it, no other reason. Not that she's fond of trains and steam engines and that sort of thing, like an enthusiast. She simply likes the money and the power. That's why I believe George is trying to kill her. She won't let him run the business without her guidance—wise of her, because George is an idiot—but the man has his pride."

What Jonathan said made much sense. However, proving George had put ground pieces of rhododendron into the food Erica had eaten would not be simple.

"Poor Erica." Jonathan glanced about the room, true pity in his voice. "She didn't leave much, did she? Never really alive, the hapless girl."

"If you know secrets," I said on impulse, "can you tell me who Henry is?"

Jonathan started then sent me a broad smile. "Of course I can. I know all the messy little scandals of this family. I followed Erica one day, you see. She made mysterious outings, and I am naturally curious."

He stepped past me to the desk, amused when I scuttled out of his way. He pulled out a small drawer inside the desk and set it aside. It contained letters, I saw, folded carefully.

Jonathan put his hand into the niche the drawer had left. "Now where . . . ? Aha." He poked at something, and another drawer, which had been fitted seamlessly into the polished wood, popped from the side of the desk.

Jonathan removed it and plopped himself down on the padded bench at the foot of the bed. He patted the cushion beside him. "Come and sit. I won't bite."

I had many reservations about putting myself near Jonathan, but I was too curious to refuse. I sat on the bench, leaving at least a foot of space between us.

The drawer contained photographs and folded bits of paper. Jonathan removed one photograph that had faded, the grays and blacks lighter than those of a freshly developed picture.

Jonathan handed it to me. "*That* is Henry."

A child, small and spindly, leaned against a chair that dwarfed him. His lips were parted, and he stared at the camera as though afraid of it.

"Henry is a little boy?" I asked in amazement. "How old is this photograph?"

"It was taken five years or so ago. Henry is about nine now. My nephew. Or, step-nephew, I suppose."

"Mrs. Hume's secret is a *child*?" I thought of the frantic note in Erica's voice when she'd caught my hand, her plea. *Look af-*

ter him for me. It was a mother's fear for a son, not a woman's for a lover. I'd say the same if I were dying—my last thoughts would be for Grace. "But . . ."

"She was married, so why is it secret?" Jonathan took the photograph from my hand and showed me another of the same boy, slightly older, but no less frightened. "Think, Mrs. Holloway. She was married at the time, yes, but Henry did not come from the loins of Mr. Hume."

I plucked up one of the papers, its creases dark, and unfolded it to find a copy of a birth record. The baby's name was given as *Henry Stephen Hume*, with *Erica Hume, née Broadhurst* as the mother, and *Jeremiah Hume* as the father.

"Of course she'd use her husband's name," Jonathan said as I studied the page. "She wouldn't want the little tyke to be fatherless. But Jeremiah did not know about this child. Too busy leaving his own offspring on the wrong side of the blanket to realize his wife had decided that what was good for the gander was good for the goose."

Erica, so stiff, so brittle, had carried this secret in her heart. I wondered who the unknown father was, and if he was aware he had a son.

"How do you know all this?" I asked Jonathan.

"I pried it out of her, oh, about six months ago. When I followed her to the house where this little chap lives with a nanny, she saw me. She was terrified I'd tell George, or my mother. I assured her I wouldn't—and I haven't. I, Jonathan Junior, keep my word. She spilled everything. A relief to tell someone, I think." He let out a pitying sigh as he gazed at the boy in the photograph. "Doesn't matter now, does it?"

"It will to Henry." I touched the boy's face. "Who is the father?"

"Sadly, Erica would not tell me. Claimed he was dead, and

he might be. Erica always wore mourning or half mourning, and I'll wager it wasn't because of Jeremiah Hume."

"You will have to tell me where the house is," I said. "I promised Mrs. Hume I would make certain Henry was well."

"Of course." Jonathan took the photograph and paper from me and dropped them back into the box. "We'll go together." He winked at me.

"You ought to tell your mother about Henry," I said sternly. "She can make certain he's cared for. Perhaps bring him to live here."

"Ugh, why do such a horrible thing to the poor little chap? But yes, I'll tell you where to find him. I wager Mama would even understand. She always felt sorry for Erica. Harriet and George, now, they won't understand at all."

"But they have secrets too." Harriet meeting for kisses with Mr. Amos in the darkness of the Crystal Palace, and George with his very scandalous lover.

"True. Most damning secrets. Perhaps we can convince them to see things our way." Jonathan rubbed his palms together, almost comical in his machinations.

"Do you always speak as though you're in a melodrama, Mr. Morris?"

"In this house, how could I not? Besides, I go to the theatre quite often. Nothing else to do," Jonathan finished glumly.

He fished for my compassion, but I sent him a severe look. "When you are not helping your friends out of their scrapes?"

Jonathan's amusement returned. "Mama told you that, did she? It's true, I do help a fellow out now and again. Old school friends, you know. Can't turn them down. I suppose Jepson told you I was a reprobate squandering all I have on the gee-gees."

"Yes," I said. "Which is it?"

"Helping the friends, of course." Jonathan gave me another wink. "I can prove it, but it's a lot of bother. Mama is probably wise not to give me a larger allowance. My kind heart can't tell a friend no."

I did not answer. Jonathan was very charming, but that did not mean Jepson was wrong about him.

"I say." Jonathan had set aside the drawer and moved closer to me as I ruminated. "You are a beautiful woman, Mrs. Holloway. For a cook." I was not flattered. He leaned closer still, his breath hot on my cheek. "A kiss would not be a bad thing, would it?"

I jumped to my feet. "It certainly would be."

My voice rang with indignation, nothing of the timid maiden about it. Jonathan frowned in disappointment as he rose.

"Why? Is there a Mr. Holloway?"

My husband's name had not been Holloway—that was my maiden name—and so Mr. Holloway technically did not exist, but I saw no reason to explain this to Jonathan. "He is deceased," I said truthfully.

Something in my face must have showed the pain that death had caused me, because Jonathan's voice softened. "Oh, bad show. I beg your pardon, Mrs. Holloway. I will take you to Henry whenever you'd like. If you'd prefer I didn't kiss you, then I will turn my broken heart to Lady Cynthia. Now *she* can stir a man to picking flowers and writing poetry."

He took on a dreamy expression that was so farcical that I could not help a smile. Jonathan could be quite winsome, I conceded, but I refused to let my guard down around him.

"Thank you, Mr. Morris. I will warn Lady Cynthia to expect flowers and verses from you."

Jonathan burst out laughing in genuine mirth. "You are a

treasure, Mrs. Holloway. Perhaps one day I'll be wealthy beyond measure, and you can come and cook for me." His laughter died. "And perhaps one day, I won't be afraid to eat a meal served in my own home." He gave me a serious look. "Do find out who is poisoning us and tell that police chappie. I'll be here to help tackle George when the inspector comes to arrest him."

"You are convinced it is your stepbrother?"

"I am. He's the sort of tick who'd watch his own sister die and say nothing at all."

The chill of the house returned. "I will keep it in mind," I said.

"And take care." Jonathan walked me to the door, pausing as his hand rested on its handle. "George is beastly. Looks like a harmless dullard, but he's cunning and nasty."

With that, he opened the door and ushered me out. The maid who'd admitted me just then emerged from another bedroom with a stack of towels. She caught sight of me with Jonathan and gave me a glare that tried to sink me through the floor. I nodded to her coolly and marched down the stairs, my mind filled with all I had learned.

When I returned home, it was to find a frantic James lurking outside the scullery stairs. "Dad's holed up in Mr. Thanos's rooms," James told me as I stopped to greet him. "He's wild to see you."

I doubted the maddeningly calm Daniel was wild about anything, but James's eyes held worry.

"I must take these in and see to supper. Can he wait?"

"Don't know. Said I should fetch you, sharpish."

Now I grew troubled. Why was Daniel in London, if the

duke's house party was to have gone on through the weekend? Lord Clifford had returned, but that was to keep himself out of the way so Mr. Fielding could take over with the necklace ruse, though I'd believed Lord Clifford when he'd said he'd wanted to return to his wife. Had something gone wrong with the scheme?

"I will be as quick as I can," I said. "Do you want to wait for me? Or run back and tell him?"

"I'll wait." James leaned on the railing. "If it grows dark, and I let you walk alone . . ." He trailed off, his expression telling me dire things would happen to him.

It wouldn't be dark for hours yet, but I nodded to him and hurried down the stairs.

Before I'd departed Lady Covington's, I'd stepped into the garden and taken Symes's offer of the pole beans. While he'd ducked into the hothouse to fetch them, I'd taken a cutting from the nearest rhododendron bush and stuffed the leaves into my basket. I'd carefully laid a cloth over them so they'd not touch the beans and extra herbs and greens that Symes brought to me, beaming with pride. I'd thanked him for giving me so much and departed before he could take my thanks for anything more than simple gratitude.

I sorted the herbs—parsley, thyme, and dill—and the greens—spring onions, leaf lettuce, carrot tops, and radishes. I eyed the radishes, imagining their cool crunch with a bite of vinegar and a sprinkling of dill.

I instructed Tess to wash and prepare the vegetables, telling her we'd do a large salad and then a sauce of onions and thickly reduced stock, well seasoned with the fresh thyme.

Meanwhile, I carried the basket down the hall and hid the rhododendron leaves and stems I'd cut in a box on a bottom shelf, well behind the empty crates that rested there, where no one would come across them.

I'd brought the specimens home so I could decide how someone would get them into the food coming out of the kitchen or into the hamper that had accompanied the family on the train. The leaves or stems must have been chopped fine, or ground, or perhaps soaked in water for a long time and the water sprinkled over the food. I would have to ponder how it could have been done.

I hated to leave Tess on her own, but when I told her Daniel wanted to see me, she waved me off with a bright green carrot top. "I know how to cook all this." She indicated the table. "Off ya go, Mrs. H. It's why you have an assistant. Specially one as good as me." Tess grinned, her nose wrinkling. "But you have to tell me *everything* when you come home."

"Of course." I prepared a basket of tea cakes for Mr. Thanos then snatched up my coat and headed upstairs. The spring afternoon was balmy, but I knew from experience that at this time of year, cold could sweep down upon London without warning.

James paced near the railings, looking relieved when I emerged. We hurried arm in arm along Mount Street to Davies Street, then northward to Brook Street and east through Hanover Square to the busy thoroughfare of Regent Street.

Mr. Thanos's landlady knew James and me by now and welcomed us with a smile. James rapped his knuckles on the door of the upstairs landing and opened it before any could come to answer. Inside we found Mr. Thanos, Daniel, Mr. Fielding, and Lady Cynthia, all rising to greet us.

Before Daniel, who was still in his suit as Mr. Lancaster, could speak, Mr. Fielding stepped forward.

"Dear Mrs. Holloway. Would you be so kind as to reprise your role as Mrs. Holtmann from Amsterdam? We believe the duplicitous duke would be amenable to taking money offered for the necklace from *you*. He certainly isn't interested in any from a dithering but well-meaning vicar."

24

‹——————›

I stared in bafflement at my friends, who clearly expected me to switch my frock for a finer one on the moment and parade back to Surrey. All except Mr. Thanos, who sent me an apologetic look.

"Only if you are willing, Mrs. Holloway," Mr. Thanos said gently. "They explained things to me, and I said it was too much risk to you. I can always pretend to be a collector who understands nothing about expense, if you like."

Daniel came to me. I saw fury in his eyes, suppressed with difficulty. "I'm afraid I'm rather in a corner, Kat."

"May I guess who put you in that corner?" I shot a glance at Mr. Fielding, who rubbed his beard.

"Nothing I could do," Mr. Fielding said. "Our duke professed to be uninterested in selling the necklace he bought from Lord Clifford. I told him I had a friend who would offer a very good price, but Daventry hems and haws. I'm beginning to think he has nothing to do with anarchists, but Daniel believes otherwise."

As Daniel was usually right about these things, I did not argue. Daniel must have discovered solid information about the duke but still was at a loss as to how to prove it. The case had to be incontrovertible before Daniel could speak out.

"None of this explains why you wish *me* to return to Surrey and playact again," I said.

"Not Surrey," Daniel said. "Berkeley Square. The duke and his wife have retreated there, the house party over."

I widened my eyes. "I cannot go to Berkeley Square and pretend to be a lady I am not. That is hardly any distance from Mount Street. Someone will recognize me."

"Not necessarily," Mr. Fielding said quickly. "No one notices servants. They drudge in the shadows while the master and mistress see nothing but hands that give them things or take away what isn't wanted." He trailed off bitterly. "If you worry about the other servants, we'll keep them away from you."

"You still have not explained why *I* must go," I said impatiently. "Why should the duke want to sell the necklace to me?"

"He is reluctant to use Errol as a go-between," Daniel answered. "He's not met the gentleman Errol says is interested in putting up the money for the necklace—because the gentleman doesn't exist, of course. The duke is careful, and prefers to deal directly with people instead of using intermediaries. Considering what he gets up to, that is not surprising."

"And I, er, might have mentioned that Mr. Lancaster's lovely fiancée could be interested in purchasing the diamonds," Mr. Fielding finished.

"Oh, did you?" I sent him a glare. "Thank you very much."

"I would not ask you, Kat." Daniel faced me, shutting out

my view of the others. "I hardly want you in danger, but I am running out of time—I've had word that another attempt at murdering British government officials might happen soon, with the duke providing the funds. I need to catch him at it and thwart his scheme."

I understood why Daniel was in this predicament, though I did not like to say so out loud. The cold-eyed Mr. Monaghan had demanded a result, and Daniel would have to do anything he could to get it.

Mr. Fielding broke in. "As soon as I made the suggestion, the duke brightened. Said you were a fine lady he could trust, and as he had no use for the necklace, he would be willing to sell it to you. His wife is very particular about the jewels she wears, and she was not happy with him for handing Lord Clifford two hundred guineas."

I recalled meeting the small, smiling duchess and hoped she knew nothing of her husband's perfidy. She must be exasperated with what she saw as his kind heart getting the better of him when he'd purchased the necklace from Lord Clifford.

"The duke took her admonishment as a cue to sell the necklace for a good price," Daniel said. "He does want the money—he is simply being cautious as to how he obtains it." He cleared his throat. "I made certain to imply, in a roundabout, vague manner, that you might be sympathetic to his cause, which made him all the more keen."

I thought this over while Daniel and Mr. Fielding watched me closely, Mr. Thanos and Cynthia more dubious.

Finally, I heaved a sigh. "Very well. I will give up my half day out tomorrow and help you."

"I'm afraid it must be tonight, Kat. I left the Berkeley Square house saying I'd look you up at your hotel and bring you back for a meal. The duchess offered you hospitality for the night—

or as long as you wish to stay—but you will be modest and insist on returning to your hotel after your transaction with the duke."

"So I should hope." Sudden apprehension made my limbs watery. "I left the gown at Miss Townsend's."

"Doesn't matter," Cynthia said, breaking her silence. "I have another for you, plus all the trimmings—I stopped by Miss Townsend's and fetched them. We thought you'd be less noticeable going in and out here."

My apprehension grew. "Except by Mr. Thanos's landlady. What will she think of my transformation?"

"I will distract her while you slip away," Mr. Fielding promised. "A vicar is always ready to bend a housewife's ear about good works."

An hour later saw me once more in a graceful frock that Miss Townsend had supplied. According to Cynthia, her friend had wanted to be rid of several gowns, and Miss Townsend had altered them for me. She, being familiar with Daniel's work, likely had guessed my role would have to be played more than once.

This gown was a peach-colored evening dress, with creamy lace on the bodice, bustle, and hem. The décolletage bared my shoulders an unnerving amount, and I kept trying to raise the wide band of the neckline to cover what I considered a daring expanse of bare skin.

"You are beautiful, Mrs. Holloway," Cynthia assured me as we stood before a looking glass in Mr. Thanos's bedchamber. "No need to fuss."

"I've never shown my shoulders in my life," I said, tugging up the neckline again.

"Well, you ought to more often. You have lovely skin."

"A right fool I'd look in the kitchen with my frock down to my bosom." I declared.

"Take this." Cynthia wound a lace shawl about my arms, which, in my opinion, did very little to cover me. I felt a definite draft on my back.

White silk gloves completed the costume, soft against my work-roughened fingers. Cynthia pinned up my hair, letting one lock stray down to rest on the shawl. I resisted tucking it into the coiffure again.

Cynthia led me out. "Gentlemen, I give you Mrs. Katharine Holtmann, belle of Amsterdam."

"Don't be silly," I whispered as I stepped into the front room.

The three men sprang to their feet. Mr. Fielding made a comical, old-fashioned bow, extending his leg. "Your servant, my lady."

Daniel's gaze met mine in amusement at his brother's ridiculousness. His eyes held admiration, and I will stoop to admitting that the admiration pleased me.

Mr. Thanos stared at me without embarrassment, his mouth agape. "Jove, Mrs. Holloway, I'd never know you were the same person. Or that you could make such excellent tea cakes." The packet of them was open on his desk, one already reduced to crumbs.

"I have decided I'd rather be known for skill in cooking than for being a dressmaker's doll," I told him. "Having nothing to do all day but keep my clothes clean would be tedious."

"Now you know what I face, Mrs. H.," Cynthia said wryly. "Lord save me from it."

Mr. Thanos's gaze went to Cynthia and remained there, his expression thoughtful. I wondered if he'd approached her yet about her acting as his assistant. I hoped he would, and also hoped that, when they were thrown together day after day, he'd ask her an even more important question.

Daniel offered his arm. "Shall we adjourn to Berkeley Square?"

I slid my hand through the crook of his elbow, trying not to like the feeling of his strong arm beneath the cashmere sleeve. "We may as well. I do hope Mr. Lancaster's inanities will not make me too ill."

Daniel chuckled. "I will endeavor to spare your digestion."

I allowed Daniel to escort me out. Mr. Fielding bustled past us to keep his word to distract the landlady if necessary. That left Mr. Thanos and Cynthia alone on the landing.

"Suppose I should go," I heard Cynthia say.

Mr. Thanos paused a long while before he spoke. "I suppose it is best." He sounded regretful. "But, erm ... Would you—that is, would you be so kind as to visit me tomorrow? At the Polytechnic," he added hastily. "At my office. To talk about my lectures."

"Of course," Cynthia said, making her voice extra breezy. "Sounds a treat. Good night, Mr. Thanos."

I was pleased to find when we arrived at the mansion in Berkeley Square that I would not have to sit down to a formal supper at all. Because of the late hour, and the fact that the duke and duchess had traveled from Surrey that afternoon, a light meal was set on the dining room sideboard for us to partake of as we wished. The staff, who'd been given a holiday for the weekend, was reduced to one footman in the dining room and a maid to take our wraps. Fortunately, I knew neither of them.

Mr. Fielding, acting the solicitous gentleman, offered to fill my plate while I seated myself at the table, as my negligent fiancé seemed unable to remember to assist me. Daniel piled a mountain of cold meat, soft rolls, and gooseberry pudding onto his plate and sat town to tackle it.

The duchess, with lines of tiredness about her eyes, sent me an understanding smile as Mr. Fielding, instead of Daniel, served me. Her flick of gaze at Daniel held even more amusement. She must be wondering why I'd chosen to marry this rather thick gentleman.

"I am sorry if the sun was too much for you on Thursday, Mrs. Holtmann," the duchess said as we ate. "I hope you feel better."

"Oh yes," I said, recalling the excuse for my retreat. "I needed only a little rest."

Daniel chewed robustly through his food and pretended to ignore me.

The meal was not one that would win the cook any praises, even if it was warmed-over leavings from the week. The slices of veal and mutton were dry, and the lobster sauce over the equally dry salmon was too salty. As Mr. Fielding had put a dab of everything on my plate, I could tell that the cook had no talent in any area. The gooseberry pudding was watery, the jam tart sour.

I could charitably believe the meal had been thrown together by a harried underling instead of the cook herself, but the first round of these dishes must have been less than satisfactory. Well-prepared food will taste as good, and in some cases even better, after a day or two.

I ate carefully, happy to see there were only a few pieces of cutlery to navigate. While Mr. Davis would have known the names of each fork and spoon in an eight-piece place setting and when they were to be used, I had never before found my-self on this side of the culinary system.

The footman poured wine, a crisp white and a robust red— Mr. Davis would have approved of both. I deduced the house had a good butler but a mediocre cook.

I was not called upon to offer opinions of any kind on any subject, I soon understood. The duke seemed to be of the mind that ladies were to silently adorn and inspire while gentlemen talked about any inanity they liked. The duchess, who must have been long accustomed to her husband, ate, drank, smiled, and occasionally nodded or interjected a "Yes, of course, dear," when called upon to do so.

I said not a word. No one mentioned necklaces or the pur-chase of them, or anarchists, or Ireland.

I had not quite finished my meal when the duchess set aside her napkin, said, "Mrs. Holtmann, shall we leave the gen-tlemen to their port?" rose, and glided out of the dining room.

I could only lay down my fork, surreptitiously chew my last mouthful, nod at the gentlemen, and follow her. Mr. Fielding caught my eye and sent me an encouraging smile, while Daniel, true to his character, pretended not to notice my leaving.

The duke's house was enormous, an older mansion built when this area had begun developing more than a hundred years before. The ground floor hall held a long staircase, with rooms opening on either side of it. Most London town houses were one room wide plus the staircase hall, though the houses could run deep into the property. This two-room wide home flaunted its vastness. The hall was paneled with old-fashioned mahogany wainscoting below a mural of ladies and gentle-men dressed in clothes of the last century wandering through an idyllic park.

I contrasted this abode to Lady Covington's as I followed the duchess to the drawing room. The Park Lane house was much more modern with its lavishly carved staircase, thick carpets that absorbed all sound, and domed skylight of stained glass. I thought I preferred this house, whose bare wood floors and tasteful Oriental rugs were understated and graceful.

In the drawing room, the duchess settled herself on a gilded chair upholstered in salmon and cream stripes and gestured for me to relax on the matching settee.

"They'll be some time, my dear," she warned. "My husband can go on a bit, and the vicar is as long-winded."

I hid my smile at her assessment of Mr. Fielding. "It is no matter."

The duchess lifted one thin finger to signal the maid who hovered outside the door. The maid curtsied and disappeared. "Now, then, His Grace will dance around a point," the duchess said to me in her gentle tones, "but I am certain you are anxious to view this necklace."

I started, then stifled my surprise at her bluntness. "Mr. Fielding has told me about it," I said carefully.

"It is a nice little bauble. Though not a style I wear, I am certain it will suit you. When Mr. Fielding said you might be interested, I thought it a perfect solution. The duke bought it from Lord Clifford as a favor."

I saw the flicker of annoyance at her husband in the duchess's eyes, and I wondered if she was the financial negotiator of the family, as some women were when the husband had no head for it. Lord Clifford had easily talked the duke out of two hundred guineas, so perhaps that was the case here.

"I am interested," I said. "I like to find the exact piece to match a gown." I hoped I sounded like the vain, frivolous creature I pretended to be.

"You are wearing no jewels tonight." The duchess broke off as the maid carried in a full tea tray, set it on the low table between us, and swiftly departed. The duchess paid her less attention than she would a fly, and I remembered Mr. Fielding grumbling that the upper classes saw only a pair of hands bringing them what they wished.

"I left most of my jewelry behind at home, of course," I said to explain my lack of it. "Safer for traveling."

"Very wise. And that gown is pretty with all the lace. No need for further adornment, is there?"

"I thought so," I said sincerely.

The duchess poured tea into a dainty cup decorated with sprays of purple flowers with gold leaf on the rim and handle. She handed the cup and saucer to me before she poured tea for herself. She did not offer sugar or cream, and I did not mention them. Excellent tea needed no embellishment, and this tea was quite good, I found as I sipped. The duchess might not have hired a talented cook, but she could choose a tea.

"Tell me, my dear," the duchess said, cup in hand. "Are you from Ireland?"

I blinked, stilling myself before a drop of tea could fall on the beautiful gown. "No," I said. "Amsterdam. Did Mr. Lancaster not tell you this?"

"Ah, yes, so he did. Where in Amsterdam? I am curious."

Her tone held only vague interest, as though she made polite conversation, but my heart beat faster in worry.

Fortunately, Daniel, on our train ride to Esher, had instructed me on what to say if questioned. He'd prepared a thorough story for the traveling Mrs. Holtmann.

"On the Amstel," I said. "A house, left by my husband." The

Amstel was a long canal and river, Daniel had told me, so a safe answer. He'd also told me what lanes to name if pressed, but to never give up more information than exactly what was asked.

The duchess nodded as though she did not care one way or the other. "A lovely city, is Amsterdam. Or can be. Rather smelly."

"Indeed," I murmured.

"Ireland can be a dirty place as well. Cities with lanes of filth. And then one turns and beholds fields so green they will break your heart."

"That sounds very nice." I took another sip of tea to cover my unease.

"I lived in Ireland as a girl." The duchess had finished half her tea and lifted the pot to pour more. "It is where I met the duke. I resided near Dublin, on a grand estate. My mother passed away when I was very young, and my father and I looked after each other." She smiled in fond memory.

"I am sorry to hear of your loss," I said, as she seemed to wait for my answer.

The duchess nodded her acknowledgment, set down the teapot, and carried on. "When I was twenty years old, in 1830, my father was accused of siding with farmers who were rioting over having to tithe to the Church of Ireland—they were devout Catholics, you see, and being forced to support the Protestant church was anathema to them. My father did have sympathy and tried to help by paying most of the tithes of his tenants himself, only requiring that they give him a small amount so the officials wouldn't investigate. But he was found out."

She paused to take a sip of tea. My mouth was too dry to comment, but the duchess did not note my silence.

"Too many men in high places detested my father," she went on. "And so he was tried, found guilty, and stripped of his wealth and estate. He killed himself while under house arrest. I found him. Then the English turned me out and burned the house around his dead body."

25

I sat very still. The duchess spoke in a matter-of-fact tone, but I saw the fires of rage deep in her eyes. The smiling, sweet lady was the facade, while a fierce dragon burned inside.

"How dreadful," I said when I could find my voice. I set down my teacup, hands shaking.

"So you see why we need your four thousand guineas. My husband will not ask you directly, but I am more to the point than he is. We ladies usually are. Don't you agree?"

"Yes, of course," I said breathlessly. Had she seen through me? Through Daniel?

My heart banged as the elegant parlor took on a new menace. The door we'd entered through led to the hall, and another door stood in the rear of the room, nearer to the sofa. Was it locked? Could I reach it before she . . . what? I could not picture this small, elderly woman tackling me to the floor.

The duchess calmly sipped tea, not at all behaving as though she'd have a go at me.

"Mr. Lancaster, I beg your pardon for saying, is a bit thick-witted," she said with a weary air. "But he let slip a few things that told my husband you would be sympathetic. Are you? Though you've never set foot in Ireland, you say."

I thought rapidly. How did I feign sympathy for those who banded together to organize the murders of other gentlemen?

"I do understand their plight," I said tentatively. "They work very hard for English landlords who grow rich and spend all their money here in London. When there is no food, they have nowhere to turn. Their faith, which is a comfort, is denied them, or at least highly discouraged." So I understood from all I'd read of Ireland plus conversations I'd had with servants who hailed from there.

"Exactly. Are you a Catholic, Mrs. Holtmann?"

"Oh, I . . ." I glanced nervously at the door behind her.

"I understand. It's a risky thing to be, even these days. It's no longer forbidden to be of the true faith, but it can be a social death knell. I advise you to keep it to yourself, as I do."

"Yes, indeed."

"My mother was Catholic, you see. My father attended the Church of Ireland, but my mother secretly converted him. She was the daughter of one of my grandfather's tenants, and she and my father married when they fell madly in love. Do you know how she died? An English soldier came upon her one evening as she walked and, mistaking her for a peasant, tried to force himself upon her. When she fought him, very hard by the look of things, he killed her. She had her revenge though. When she was dying, she wrested his pistol from him and shot him through the heart."

The duchess smiled proudly and drank more tea.

"I am so sorry, Your Grace," I said in a near whisper. To live through such things would unhinge my mind. I had the feeling it had unhinged hers.

"The duke met me after my home was burned. I was rather frenzied, as you can imagine. He nursed me, fell in love with me, and I married him. He is a rather weak man, John is. But I am not weak."

I saw in a flash what she meant. The kind-looking, tiny woman with the warm smile had her iron fist around the duke. Instead of being a deliberate traitor to his country, he was under the thrall of this woman and could not resist her.

"I found my revenge," the duchess continued. "I had won the heart of a duke, one of the highest men in Britain, prominent in their government. He had plenty of money and influence and no idea what to do with either. I told him. He knew my story and sympathized, as you do, and he has helped men and women in Ireland plan and act for the day we throw off our shackles. It won't be long now." She heaved a sigh and set down her tea, the wild light in her eyes fading.

"Thank you for letting me unburden myself to you, my dear. You are very easy to speak to. Give me the four thousand guineas now, please—less embarrassing than negotiating with my husband, who will prevaricate and say everything but what he means. So tiresome." She leaned to me conspiratorially. "I will tell you that the necklace is worthless, but it is a good pretense as to why you are giving us the money. The vicar has no idea it's only paste, but that's the English clergy for you. Fools, the lot of them, and they are supposed to lead us to salvation."

I picked up my tea and took a casual sip. I certainly did not have four thousand guineas in my pocket, and I cast about for what to tell her.

"The money is at my hotel," I said carefully. "I wanted a look at the necklace first."

"Ah well." The duchess waved her hand. "We can send for it." She rose to reach for a bell sitting on a table near the fireplace.

Blast. If she summoned her footman, what would I tell him? There was no hotel, no cash for him to run for. I toyed with the idea of directing an errand runner to Miss Townsend's house instead. She was a quick thinker and could decide what to do.

Before the duchess reached the bell, she glanced behind her and saw my face. She stilled.

This woman had lived her entire life with subterfuge, secretly funding societies through her husband to take her vengeance on those who'd murdered her mother and destroyed her father. She had believed my story and Daniel's thus far, but my indecisiveness must have shown in my expression in one unguarded moment.

"You bloody . . ." The duchess broke off her snarl and ran for the door at the back of the room.

If she got through it, if she summoned her husband and whatever servants were within shouting distance, she'd expose me, and through me, Daniel and Mr. Fielding.

At best, the duke and duchess would slip Daniel's net, and he'd be blamed for their escape. I shuddered to think what Mr. Monaghan would do to Daniel for that.

At worst, Daniel and Mr. Fielding could be in very great danger. The men the duchess assisted thought nothing of stabbing important aristocrats to death—she'd not care about the lives of a pair of Englishmen from London's backstreets.

I leapt at the duchess and seized her before she could reach the door. She struggled, spitting language that no genteel lady should know.

Quick as a snake, she whipped from my grasp and came at me, a slender knife in her hand.

I sidestepped and spun away, my lace shawl fluttering to the carpet. I decided to make for the hall and scream for someone to help me with this madwoman.

Somehow, the duchess was in front of me, skirts bunched in one hand, the other competently wielding the knife. I had a flash of vision of this woman in her younger years. Angry, nurturing hatred, in the midst of a mob, shouting her fury, fighting. Someone had taught her to brawl like a child of darkest London.

She was much older now, but wiry and quick. Elderly does not equal feeble, in my experience.

She came at me until I had to retreat to the window. The thick velvet drapes were closed, so no one on the square would notice me battling a crazed woman with a knife.

"*Daniel!*" I shouted at the top of my voice.

If the name confused her, the duchess made no sign. I caught her knife hand, but the knife jerked upward, the blade slashing across the neckband of my pretty peach gown and across my upper chest and shoulder.

An angry red crease opened across my skin, and blood spilled onto the bodice.

The sudden streak of pain coupled with the heat of the battle stripped me of any genteelness I'd ever learned. The professional cook who struggled for respectability fled, and the girl from Bow Lane emerged.

"You've ruined me dress, you owd bitch!"

It was a shriek worthy of Tess at her most enraged. I seized the duchess, clamping hard on her wrist while I wrested the knife from her grasp. She fought me fiercely, another cut slicing across the bodice, this one stopped by my thick and sensible corset. I hadn't taken the time to change into the pretty one.

I lifted the knife out of the duchess's reach, and she danced backward, a look of cunning on her face.

"Help!" she cried. "She's attacking me. She's gone mad!"

I brought the knife low, keeping her at bay. "No, missus, *you're* the barmy one."

Both doors crashed open, and a number of people poured in. Mr. Fielding was the first to reach the duchess. He cast a glance at me and the knife, then twisted the duchess' arms behind her back, holding her competently as she thrashed and screamed.

"What are you doing?" she screeched. "She's trying to kill me!"

"That's porkies, that is," I raged. Mr. Fielding understood. *Pork pies—lies.* "And you've no notion how to hire a decent cook," I snapped at the duchess, my ire high.

Daniel came straight to me. I felt his touch on my back, and he pressed a handkerchief to my bleeding chest. "Kat." His voice, warm in my ear, shook.

"I'm fine," I assured him, though my legs wobbled and my throat was tight. "It's only a scratch." One that hurt like the devil.

Daniel had me on the settee, sinking down next to me. The duke stood in the middle of the room, his mouth open. Several footmen hovered nearby, a few without livery, likely just returned from their day out. They turned to the duke for instruction, but he stood as one stunned.

"Ciara," he whispered.

I took that to be the duchess's name. She continued to struggle against Mr. Fielding, wrath in her eyes. Mr. Fielding showed no worries about injuring the woman as he tightened his grip.

"The police, I think," Mr. Fielding said.

"Do not let those bloody bastards into my house," the duchess shouted. "John, stop them."

The duke only stared at her. "Ciara, what have you done?"

"Confessed to funding illegal organizations plotting against the British crown and carrying out assassinations," Daniel said grimly. He remained with me, his handkerchief now stained crimson. "I'm so sorry, Kat. I wanted to rush in right away, but Errol insisted we wait and hear her tell you all, with witnesses."

He glanced at the footmen, who watched in shock. Apparently, they were as surprised as I to find that the duchess was duplicitous.

"I will summon our solicitor," the duke said in a subdued voice.

"You should," Daniel said quietly. "The police will be here soon."

"Will they?" Mr. Fielding asked as the duchess struggled anew. "How will they have heard? Ah . . ." He gazed at Daniel with new respect. "I might have known."

I had no idea what he meant, but Daniel explained to me. "I have men stationed outside, and I sent them a signal."

"Of course you did," Mr. Fielding said.

"We have a few minutes, that is all." Daniel held out his hand, and I put the knife, which I still clutched, into it. "I do not want you here when they arrive," he said to me.

"But I am a witness." My ability to speak in more neutral tones had returned.

"No. Errol and I are."

Daniel helped me to my feet and began to steer me toward the door in the back of the room. It led to a smaller chamber, I saw, a writing room, very neat and cozy. Daniel shut the door, blocking the view of the drawing room and its strange tableau.

"Not only the police will come," Daniel continued.

I thought of the tall man with the icy gaze. "Your Mr. Monaghan will be with them."

"I do not want him to know about you."

"I understand." I'd never spoken to the man, but I sensed that Mr. Monaghan, if he knew of our friendship, might use me to tighten his hold over Daniel. "The duke and duchess, never mind the servants, will tell the police about me."

"Yes, but I can deflect Monaghan's attention from you, and Errol will help me. Now, you must be gone."

"Indeed." I glanced at myself, mourning the ruin of the lovely silk. "I cannot go home in this state." I'd decided where I would seek refuge, but Daniel did not ask me. He trusted me to take care of myself, which gave me a warm feeling through my shock. "I will need a hansom," I continued. "Or I might be arrested walking about like this, or at least stopped by a concerned person."

I started to turn away, but Daniel pulled me back. I landed against him, my bloody frock ruining his cashmere coat.

"Damnation, Kat." He kissed me. It was a hard kiss, Daniel's mouth a point of heat. I clung to him, feeling his solid strength, and let him kiss me for as long as he liked.

When Daniel at last ushered me out of the house, a hansom, with Lewis driving, waited. I supposed Daniel had signaled him too. Daniel helped me into it, his tender expression evaporating and the forbidding one returning as he made once more for the house.

I did not envy the duke and duchess. The duke might be a lofty man, but he was about to face Mr. Monaghan, who I gathered would not care one whit about the duke's status.

I asked Lewis to please take me to Upper Brook Street. I found Cynthia there with Miss Townsend and Bobby, as I'd suspected I would.

The three ladies were horrified at my injury and fussed over me with flattering attention. Bobby capably cleaned the wound and dressed it with a pad of cloth. Miss Townsend, who held the basin of water for her, waved away the destruction of the gown and said she'd give me another.

I scarcely wanted it. My days of playing a well-bred young lady were finished.

Cynthia had brought my work frock that I'd left at Mr. Thanos's, and she helped me into it, careful of my wound. The cut wasn't deep, Bobby said, and would soon heal, if I took care. I had enough knowledge of poultices and the benefits of clean water that I knew I could keep it from becoming septic.

Exhausted, I took my basket, which Cynthia had also brought, and walked home. Miss Townsend wanted to fetch another hansom for me, but I said it would look more natural if I arrived on foot, basket over my arm, as though I'd simply run out to a shop. Besides, it wasn't far.

Cynthia accompanied me. Though she wore a frock tonight, she walked with a free stride, her skirt cut to hang straight, with no bustle or crinoline.

It was with relief I stepped into my own kitchen, set down my basket, and hung up my coat. Elsie washed dishes with fervor, anxious to finish so she could go to bed. Tess stirred flour and water that would ferment overnight for bread dough in the morning. Mr. Davis was removing his coat, ready to sit at the kitchen table with his lump of meat pie, while the footmen and maids chattered loudly in the servants' hall. Mrs. Redfern shushed those who grew too voluble.

I inhaled the scents of roasted meat, thickened gravy, piles of herbs and greens, carbolic from Elsie's sink, and the underlying mellow tang of fresh-baked bread that never quite went away.

I belonged here, I knew as I donned my apron and moved to the larder. I was not hungry, as I'd eaten at the Berkeley Square house, though that unsatisfactory meal seemed a long time ago. A portion of meat pie waited under a cloth, and I cut a piece and put it on a crockery plate. The plain food would taste good at the moment.

As I turned to leave, my gaze fell on the crates behind which I'd hidden the rhododendron clippings. I bent to peer at them, but they seemed untouched.

Carrying the plate back to the kitchen in shaking hands, I entered to hear Mr. Davis say, "A clerk at Mansion House has gone and stolen one pound eleven from his employers." He clicked his tongue. "What is the world coming to?"

Tess finished stirring the flour mixture and returned to the table, wiping her hands. Her eyes held curiosity, but she would not ask me where James had rushed me to in front of Mr. Davis and the others.

"I done the greens." Tess pointed to three small baskets on the sideboard with lettuce, more of the carrot tops, and mixtures of fresh herbs in them. "All rinsed and the dirt shaken out. I didn't tear them up yet, 'cause I remembered you said they stayed crisp and bright if you don't until the last minute."

"Well done, Tess," I said with true approval. "Thank you."

"Bit of a dustup at the dining table," Mr. Davis said, raising his head from the newspaper. "Mrs. Bywater has been insisting Lady Clifford take the first helping of everything, saying you must lay the best pieces of fish or meat on top. I suppose she believed you even put the best ladleful of soup on top as well. Mr. Bywater said that was rot and the bottom piece was no different from the first. I was called upon to give my opinion."

I sat down at the table, my legs no longer wanting to hold me. If I kept on in this state, I'd fall to weeping. I held myself together with effort. "And what did you answer, Mr. Davis?"

"That of course every slice of meat and spoonful of custard you prepare is as excellent as the last. But it was proper that Lady Clifford, as the highest ranking lady guest, should of course have first choice." Mr. Davis turned a page of the paper. "That satisfied all present. The upstairs was pleased with me tonight." He snorted. "As if you would bury a bad piece of meat at the bottom of the platter. You'd take it out and not serve it at all."

I scarcely heard this last. As I studied the baskets overflowing with fragrant greens, and Mr. Davis began to read aloud how the Mahdi in the Sudan was trying to throw all Egyptians out of his realm, it came to me exactly how someone could have poisoned the dinner at Lady Covington's house. And likely was still doing it.

26

—◆——◆—

In the morning, I saw absolutely nothing in the newspaper about the duke and duchess, nor any mention of a disturbance in Berkeley Square. Whatever Daniel's Mr. Monaghan had done, he'd been very discreet.

In any case, dukes didn't get hauled to Newgate, nor made to trot through the tunnel connecting it with the Old Bailey to stand in the dock in front of an ordinary crowd. Dukes were tried in the House of Lords, if they came to trial at all. A man with as much wealth, power, and influence as the Duke of Daventry might never be forced to publicly admit he helped his wife with her vengeance against the English government.

I sympathized with the duchess when I wasn't reliving the fear of her slashing at me with her knife. I knew full well that those of the lower orders could be trampled upon without compunction, the poor blamed for being poor. If one was an Irish Catholic peasant and punished for it, well then, one shouldn't be an Irish Catholic peasant, should one? Such logic filled the minds of those whose greatest worry was whether their valet would be at their bedside with coffee the instant they woke.

But did killing make anything right? Very evil and wicked people needed to be punished, certainly, but when innocents were caught up in someone else's vengeance on those evil and wicked people—where did it end?

Which brought me around to my errand today.

I debated taking tea cakes or some other treat to soften the blow I would deliver, but decided not to. This would not be a convivial visit.

I summoned James, who'd been relieved Daniel and I had emerged well and whole but was a bit sorry to have missed the excitement. I gave him messages to deliver for me. His eyes widened, and his mouth opened for questions, but I sent him off.

Today was my half day out. I'd go to Lady Covington's first, though I was tempted to see Grace beforehand. I longed to be with my daughter, but I decided I'd prefer to spend the rest of my afternoon with her after my difficult task was finished.

Cynthia agreed to walk with me. "Are you certain?" she asked in perplexity as I told her what I'd concluded.

"*Almost* certain," I admitted. "But it is the only explanation."

We continued in silence. Cynthia headed for the front entrance of the Park Lane house once we'd reached it, and I parted from her and went around to the back garden.

"Good afternoon, Mr. Symes," I said as I entered through the gate.

Symes looked up from raking the walk, brows rising under his cap. "You come here quite often these days, Mrs. Holloway. I wish I could believe it were to see me."

I kept my basket in front of me like a barrier. "You have been very kind, Mr. Symes."

"Ah, kindness." He shook his head in regret. "Well, I suppose that's all a body can hope for."

"I am popping down to the kitchen. Do carry on."

Symes touched his cap in salute. "Right you are, missus."

I tramped down the stairs to the door and inside the cool, slate-floored hall. I turned to the right, into the kitchen, where Mrs. Gamble stirred something on the stove.

"Good afternoon, Mrs. Gamble," I sang cheerily.

Mrs. Gamble turned around, not startled. "I heard you up in the garden, love. I have a kettle on. Would you like a cuppa? Or did Lady Covington summon you?"

"Lady Cynthia is visiting with her ladyship. I came to ask you a few questions—about how things are done in your kitchen."

Mrs. Gamble wrapped a towel around the kettle and carried it to the table, where she poured steaming water into a teapot. "Is this about who tainted my food and killed Mrs. Hume? Well, sit yourself down, and we'll have a chat. I'll help any way I can."

"Thank you." I took a stool at the table, happy to rest my feet. I'd been doing much walking lately.

Mrs. Gamble brought two cups from the sideboard and also a plate of lemon cake. "The family do love this cake." She set everything on the table. "I thank you a thousand times for the recipe."

"You are most welcome," I said modestly. "It isn't much, really."

"Ah, but the proportions are so exact, it's almost magical. Such a lovely taste."

Once the tea had steeped, she poured it out into cups. "I have sugar and cream if you'd like." She dropped a broken piece of a sugar loaf into her cup, followed by a thick stream of cream from a pot.

"No, thank you. I've learned to take it plain." I sipped, trying not to make a face. Tea for servants was usually cheap, the leftover twigs and dust from finer leaves. I'd learned how to seek out the best of the inexpensive teas, but this was far from that.

Mrs. Gamble finished turning her tea into cream and sugar soup, sipped, and made a noise of satisfaction. She lifted a crumb from the lemon cake plate and nibbled it.

"Have you brought something for Lady Covington?" she asked, peering at my basket.

"Not today. As I said, I've come to ask how you do things in your kitchen." I turned my cup around in its saucer. "In mine, we wash and leave the greens either in the larder or on the dresser, depending on how hot the kitchen is, so that they'll be handy when we want to pop some into a dish, or start a soup, or make a salad."

Mrs. Gamble nodded. "I do the same. I don't have an assistant, which is a pity, but I do sort everything and then have it handy. I never know what his lordship is going to demand, or what her ladyship will need."

"Precisely." I scanned the boxes of produce on her shelves—radishes, asparagus, and plenty of leafy lettuce and herbs from Symes's careful tending. The mortar and pestle I'd spied on my previous visit rested on a table below the herbs. "It must be nice to have the garden handy."

"It does save a journey to Covent Garden." Mrs. Gamble took another sip. "You walk all that way and then the stalls are out of what you've gone for. Most annoying. Greengrocers don't always have the best foodstuffs either."

"Very true," I said with feeling. "They'll sell radish tops as parsley or fennel for onions, thinking we don't know the difference."

Mrs. Gamble chuckled her acknowledgment. "They will indeed. Mr. Symes, now, he understands what's what and sends me down exactly what I ask for."

"He is a good gardener, is Mr. Symes."

"Aye." Mrs. Gamble glanced again at my basket, and I decided to relieve her curiosity.

"I obtained these from your garden." I lifted the cloth to reveal long green leaves on darker green stems.

Mrs. Gamble stared in bewilderment. "You did? Whatever for?"

"I fancied them," I said. "Shall I gather them with some of your herbs and make us a salad?"

Mrs. Gamble pulled back. "Them's rhodies, Mrs. Holloway. They're poisonous." Her brow cleared. "Are you saying this is what was used to try to kill her ladyship?"

"Yes." I sipped more tea. "You recognize them."

"Well, of course I do. They grow right outside the back door." Mrs. Gamble took a plate from a stack at the end of the table and cut a piece of the lemon cake. She placed it in front of me and laid a fork beside it.

I continued. "What I mean is, if someone who wanted to poison Lady Covington sneaked these leaves into your kitchen and mixed them with the chervil or the basil, you would notice."

"Aye." She frowned in puzzlement.

"I've thought and thought about how someone could be poisoning your food. They could gather the rhodie cuttings and grind them up with a mortar and pestle." I waved a hand at hers, a utensil found in every kitchen. "The poison is rubbed onto the very top fillet or slice of meat or mixed into the top dollop of a vegetable platter. Lady Covington always takes the first helping of every dish—a person could watch for a time and see what piece she favors. The poison could be added to her food right here in the kitchen, or surreptitiously in the dining room as the dishes sit on the sideboard before a meal. Or the dumbwaiter could be stopped between floors and the poison added there."

Mrs. Gamble stared at me, round-eyed. "How could it?"

"This house has many pipes and wires for bellpulls and gas and plumbing behind the walls. It's a modern house, with conveniences not found in older homes in Mayfair." I'd noticed last evening that the Berkeley Square house did not have a dumbwaiter—the overworked footman carried in and took out all the dishes. The duchess had reached for a silver handbell while Lady Covington had buttons she could use to summon whichever servant she wished. "The dining room here is five steps up from the main floor, and those steps run next to the central staircase. The dumbwaiter goes straight to the dining room, but there is a maintenance hatch through which one can access it in the servants' back stairs."

I did not offer to leap up and show her, and Mrs. Gamble showed no inclination for me to do so.

"Goodness," she said. "Then anyone in the house could have done it. All the servants use the back stairs, and Mr. Jonathan and Miss Harriet run down here anytime they're feeling peckish."

"No," I said slowly. "Not anyone." I scanned the kitchen once more, noting the spacious feel of it, but also how quiet it was, how lonely. The faded photograph of the man tacked onto the wall surveyed us mournfully. "I realized, as I thought things through in my kitchen last night, that the person who would have the easiest time poisoning the food is *you*."

Mrs. Gamble clenched her teacup and stared in bewilderment. *"Me?* If you are joking, Mrs. Holloway, it is in poor taste."

"I admit, I highly suspected Jepson of doctoring Lady Covington's powders," I said. "But only some of them. The packet Lady Cynthia had tested was a simple laxative."

"Her ladyship does have trouble with her digestion, it is true," Mrs. Gamble said. "But it could *not* have been me, as you know, so please rid yourself of that notion. Whenever I cook food for Lady Covington alone, she's as right as rain. No sickness whatsoever."

"Of course not." I nodded. "If a meal you made only for Lady Covington killed her, everyone would immediately suspect you. So those meals had to be perfectly good. You wanted the poison to seep in when she ate what everyone else did, so that it could be seen as accidental, or done by someone poisoning the food once it left the kitchen."

This idea had come to me last night as I'd mused. The cook would have the easiest time poisoning the food, but of course, she'd be the first suspected. I'd stumbled over the fact that the meals Mrs. Gamble fixed for Lady Covington alone held no poison at all, but then realized it was very convenient that they did *not* make her ill. Someone other than Mrs. Gamble trying to kill Lady Covington would surely take the opportunity to poison any meal they could, especially one they'd not partake in. Jepson could have dropped the ground rhodies into a dish while she attended Lady Covington in her chamber. Harriet or Jonathan could pop in to visit their mother as she ate and introduce it to the food when she was distracted. Even George might have found an excuse to speak to Lady Covington when she took one of these private meals.

Mrs. Gamble had ensured that nothing happened to her

mistress at all when she prepared the special dinners, deflecting all suspicion from her.

Mrs. Gamble sat very still, her hand with the teacup suspended. "That hamper on the train. It was supposed to be for her ladyship. She weren't supposed to share it. So how, if I did nothing to what I made for her alone, did *that* food get poisoned?"

"Because you poisoned it," I said bluntly. "Lady Covington had grown suspicious of her bouts of illness and, when she met me at the Crystal Palace, asked for my help. My friend Mr. McAdam coming around and asking you about it likely put the wind up as well. Lady Covington had heard of me helping solve a theft and a poisoning not far from this house. When I started poking about, asking you, Jepson, and Mr. Symes many questions, you realized I might expose you. And so you struck. Sending off a hamper of food that would be passed through several hands and could have been tampered with at any time. Meanwhile, you are shocked and protest your innocence." I leaned to her, just missing the plate of lemon cake. "The horrible thing is, you didn't mind if those Lady Covington shared the food with grew ill or even died. You murdered Mrs. Hume. She had a child, who is now both motherless and fatherless."

"A child?" Mrs. Gamble drew back, stunned. "What are you talking about? She had no children."

"Mrs. Hume had a little boy in secret, who will never understand what happened to his mother. Or perhaps one day he will. Will he seek revenge as well, I wonder?"

Mrs. Gamble's shock gradually faded. She tapped my plate. "Eat the lemon cake, Mrs. Holloway, while you tell me this rigmarole. It will go to waste otherwise."

I did not touch the fork. "Is that what it was about, Mrs.

Gamble? Revenge?" I glanced at the photograph once more. Cooks were discouraged, even forbidden, depending on one's mistress, from having personal belongings in kitchens. The man in the photograph must be quite dear to her.

I thought she would not answer me, which would be unfortunate, but at my last word, Mrs. Gamble's artlessness fell away, and her voice went hard. "Yes."

"Because of the railway accident?"

Mrs. Gamble's chest rose with her quick breath. "The train that wrecked at Heyford. January twenty-second, 1875." She said this without inflection, as though she'd repeated the facts time and again.

"You worked in a house in Oxfordshire, I remember you saying." I gentled my tone. "Who did you lose in the crash?"

"My husband and my son." Her voice was a rasp. "They'd gone to Oxford, to see my husband's mum. They caught that train on the way home." Mrs. Gamble gripped her teacup, rocking in her chair, her gaze faraway. "A few faulty wheels, they said. How could one set of wheels tip over an entire train? There was Lord Covington, who never had any family on that train, saying to people that it wasn't the railway's fault. Why, even Mr. Morris, who should have looked into such things, had been killed. The fault was with the brakeman who didn't stop the train, his lordship claimed. The brakeman was hurt so badly he died too, and couldn't answer for himself."

"But those who investigated the crash said the railway *was* at fault," I pointed out. "The board had to stop that service and pay out to the families."

"They did." Mrs. Gamble acknowledged this with a nod. "You know what I received? Ten pound." Her lip curled. "Ten pound, for the loss of me husband and me beloved little boy, while Lord Covington marries Mr. Morris's widow and brings her to this great house. She loudly says her husband was innocent of all that blood. That Lord Covington was too. Both those men were dead by the time I was able to be hired here, but I could get at *her*."

I said nothing as her words rang out, her grief and rage filling the space. "I understand," I said quietly. "It's a helpless feeling, when we can't protect our children. When we *should* protect them. But you killed an innocent, Mrs. Gamble. One who tried to protect *her* child."

"Mrs. Hume didn't have no children," Mrs. Gamble insisted.

"She did. She kept it very private." I let Mrs. Gamble contemplate that for a moment. "Last night I was made to realize how anger and sorrow, nursed for years, can emerge as bitter hatred. How they can twist a good person inside until there is nothing left of her. I also realized how dangerous vengeance can be. One death avenged can lead to revenge for that one, and on it goes. It must stop, Mrs. Gamble."

"She ought to pay." Large tears formed in Mrs. Gamble's eyes and spilled down her cheeks. "Her ladyship's husband cost me my man, and my *son*, and she goes on and on about how good her husband was, what a grand thing it is to run a railway. I got ten pound for me flesh and blood, and she and those like her reaped a huge reward. She deserves to die."

"She lost both her husbands, and now a stepdaughter," I reminded her.

"She should lose it *all*."

Mrs. Gamble dashed her teacup to the table. It shattered, splashing me with warm tea and shards of porcelain. I rose quickly and stepped away, and Mrs. Gamble snatched up the plate of lemon cake and flung it to the floor. The plate broke into several pieces, the cake spattering across my boots.

"Yes, I did it, Mrs. Holloway," she said, climbing to her feet. "I ground up the rhodies like you said, and laced her lady-ship's favorite foods with it. I was patient—when I was first hired here, I'd sneak up to the dining room and watch what she did at table, how she took the top portion of every dish like it was her due, and the rest of the family sat back and let her. Lady Covington must have the first, and best, of every-thing. I watched and noted and started to experiment. I put in only a little at first so if the wrong person took the food, they wouldn't die. But she ate the poisoned fish or piece of chicken I'd coated with herbs mixed with the rhodies and grew ill. It was a happy day when the experiment succeeded. I wasn't quite prepared to kill her at first—it pleased me to see her sick and miserable. She needed to suffer, like I had. I'd have kept on like that, but she then decided her illness was from more than her digestion, and she had to go and bring you in. By then, I wanted her to die. Her being sick weren't enough any-more. She was supposed to eat all that lemon cake I packed in the hamper. She couldn't stop praising it, first good word she's ever had about my cooking—and it were *your* recipe. It ain't my fault that Mrs. Hume, who I now learn was a hussy after all, gobbled down the lot."

Mrs. Gamble rushed around the table but not to attack me. She headed for the back door, trying to make her escape.

I could not seize her in time, but I did not need to. That door flew open, and Inspector McGregor, followed by Symes, Daniel, and Caleb, barreled into the room, Symes wearing a thunderous expression.

Mrs. Gamble snarled and headed for the back stairs, but Jonathan darted out from the servants' hall and caught her. Mrs. Gamble fought him, and Caleb and Daniel rushed to Jon-athan's aid.

"Mrs. Silas Gamble," Inspector McGregor intoned as she struggled against the three men, "I am arresting you on suspicion of the murder of Mrs. Jeremiah Hume. I will inform your mistress, who will help you find a solicitor."

"I don't want nothing from her," Mrs. Gamble shouted. "I want her *dead*."

After she screamed the word, the fight went out of her. She collapsed into Caleb, who was trying to put cuffs on her wrists. Jonathan held her upright, a look of surprising compassion on his face.

"Take her out, Constable," Inspector McGregor said to Caleb. "Yes, Mrs. Holloway, I heard it all."

"So did I, by Jove," Jonathan said. "I nipped down here for a bit of quiet and to pinch something from the larder. Then Gamble starts raving about railway accidents and how she tried to poison my mother."

"I hope you did not eat the lemon cake," I said in alarm. "Inspector, you should gather up the remains. There is rhododendron poison in it."

Mrs. Gamble glared at me as Caleb and Daniel guided her to the back door. "Why wouldn't you eat the bloody cake, Mrs. Holloway? You'd have died when you got home and saved me a world of trouble."

"Because I've made a dozen batches of it since Lady Covington demanded the recipe," I said, keeping my voice steady. "I've quite gone off it."

27

❖

hank you." Lady Covington, in her cavernous and silent parlor upstairs, clasped her hands held against her abdomen. "You have relieved my mind as well as saved my life. I'd thought I was a madwoman." She waved me to a chair. "Please sit, Mrs. Holloway. Lady Cynthia. I cannot express my gratitude enough."

She'd softened a long way since I had come upstairs to explain what the commotion downstairs had been about. Daniel had departed with Inspector McGregor and Caleb, all of whom I'd summoned via James. I'd had no wish to confront a murderer without them on hand both to hear her admit her guilt and arrest her.

Jonathan had ushered us upstairs to where his mother sat in the parlor with Harriet and Lady Cynthia, and he'd filled in my story with excitement.

"She deliberately came to this house with intent to kill me?" Lady Covington asked now. Jepson carried in a tea tray, which she set on the table before Lady Covington. Her lips were set in anger, as usual, but she didn't sneer at me as fiercely as before.

"She did," I said. "She was willing to wait as long as it took to procure the post. Poor woman. Her tragedy broke her."

"I think Mrs. Holloway is jolly brave," Jonathan declared. "She sat down with a murderess and drank tea she poured."

"It came from the same pot, and I waited for her to drink first," I said. "I suspected the cream and sugar, but those were fine as well. I didn't eat the cake, because while she nibbled a crumb, that crumb could have come from a previous slice, or she knew such a tiny amount wouldn't hurt her."

"Why didn't she come to me?" Lady Covington broke in. "Why didn't she tell me what she'd suffered? I too lost a husband in that accident. I know no one believes it, but my heart was broken. I was a long time recovering. Lord Covington's kindness and understanding about it is why I married him, once I could breathe again."

She glanced up at his portrait. Lord Covington gazed down at us no less formidably, but I fancied I saw a gleam of relief in his eyes.

"She was treated a bit unfairly," I said, accepting a cup of tea Lady Covington herself poured. Jepson, instead of departing, planted herself next to the sofa. I sipped the tea, pleased to find it of much better quality than what I'd been served downstairs. "As is usual. Those with more to lose are less compensated."

"Well, I'd have done right by her. Poor woman, indeed. To have lost a son." Lady Covington glanced swiftly at Jonathan and shook her head, her eyes holding sadness. "I must apologize to you, Mrs. Holloway, and to you, Lady Cynthia, for my behavior and short temper these last weeks. Not knowing when you will take poison and who is administering it made me quite cross. But you soldiered through. I am grateful. Please believe me."

"Good riddance, I say," Jepson snapped. "You can feel sorry for her all you like, your ladyship, but she made you and your brother quite ill and killed poor Mrs. Hume. Thank heavens Sir Arthur has a strong constitution and weren't harmed by it. She's wicked and will get what she deserves."

"There is some truth to what you say," Lady Covington admitted. "But if I'd known, if I'd found out more about her, Erica might have been spared."

"Perhaps," Jepson said with a shrug. "I think she was eaten up with anger, and it wouldn't have made a difference if you'd tried to help her. I never liked that woman." She sent a glare to me, as though daring me to argue.

I pretended to ignore her. "Your ladyship, if I could be so impertinent as to ask a boon? Not for me, but for Mrs. Hume."

Lady Covington raised her brows, but Jonathan cleared his throat. "I already told her, Mrs. Holloway. About Henry."

Lady Covington inclined her head. "I was shocked, naturally, but thinking it through, it is not so surprising. Erica's husband treated her dreadfully, and so she sought comfort elsewhere. I will meet Henry and do all I can for him. After all, he is part of the family."

I let out a breath, relaxing. I'd come to know that Lady Covington had a good heart beneath her imperious manner.

Jonathan sent me a wink over his raised teacup. "I've also talked her and George into giving Mr. Amos a promotion."

Harriet gasped, her face going crimson. *"Jonathan."*

Lady Covington bathed Jonathan in a disapproving look. "I was not going to state it so bluntly until the deed was done, but yes. Mr. Amos will assist another member of the board who oversees its finances. Mr. Amos is clever with numbers, apparently."

"George approved of this?" Harriet asked in amazement.

Jonathan grinned. "Let us say I put it to him in terms he could not dismiss. He was quite agreeable, in the end."

He shot me a sly look, confirming that he'd used his knowledge of George's private life to leverage Mr. Amos's promotion. I was glad of George's capitulation for Harriet's and Mr. Amos's sake but not certain I liked Jonathan's methods of going about it.

I finished the polite tea with Lady Covington, who looked thankful to put her worries about the poisoner behind her, and then I departed the overly elegant and muffled house, leaving Cynthia to continue her visit. I had a more pressing appointment to keep.

I spent the remainder of my afternoon with Grace, squeezing her hard when I greeted her. Grace held me tightly in return, always sensing when I was in distress.

We took a short stroll together, and I held her hand the entire time. The tale of the railway crash had stirred my deepest fears. How could I keep Grace safe when I could not be with her at all times? If she journeyed on a train without me, would I be approached by a constable telling me of a railway accident that had taken her from me?

Any accident could do that, I knew, from the carts that rumbled past us on the road to the bricks falling from a building undergoing repair. I could never guarantee my daughter's safety, and that had me clinging to her today.

I kissed Grace good-bye at the end of the afternoon and went home, tears in my eyes.

I had little to tell Tess when I reached the house, because Caleb had stopped to see her and had given her the entire tale. Tess surprised me with tea already prepared and tea cakes made specially for me—no lemon in them at all.

Mrs. Redfern, who had no notion of my adventures, came down while Tess and I prepared supper, to inform me that Lord and Lady Clifford had decided to stay in Town, in this house, for the remainder of the Season. They'd postpone deciding what to do about Cynthia until late in June, when they would return to the country.

Mr. Davis, hearing this news, muttered that he'd better lock up the wine, and hastened down the hall.

Daniel did not come. I badly wanted to see him, but James stopped in with a message that Daniel had returned to Scotland Yard and was working through the aftermath of the duke's admission to his crimes. The duke and duchess hadn't exactly been arrested, James said, which was no surprise to me, but Daniel and his guv'nor were speaking to each of them for hours at a time.

I realized that Daniel and Mr. Monaghan would use the duke's knowledge to find others in his organization. They'd interrogate him about who the leaders were and whether other plots were brewing. If the duke feared exposure and accusations of treason, he might be willing to tell all he knew.

I imagined being the recipient of the icy gray stare of Mr. Monaghan. The duke would confess all just to get away from it, I wagered.

I was not certain the duchess would be as yielding. The fire inside her had burned long and deeply.

What would those in the secret society the duke funded do now? I wondered as I worked. Disband and flee? Or try to silence the duke? The last possibility made me shiver, and I worried for Daniel's safety. These men would blame Daniel for the duke's capture, and I hoped they never had to know about him.

I was very busy the rest of that week, as Lady Clifford decided to use her time in London to renew old acquaintances. She had a supper party almost every night, to the delight of Mrs. Bywater, who basked in the company of aristocrats, and the dismay of Mr. Bywater, who preferred quiet and uncomplicated meals.

Tess and I made lobster pancakes, fish with champagne sauce, soups of Symes's beans and tender spring greens, roasted lamb and beef, gooseberry tarts, my Antiguan custards, asparagus every way imaginable, strawberry soufflé, and when Mrs. Bywater demanded it, the lemon cake.

On Wednesday afternoon, Cynthia entered the kitchen in one of her new, trimmer frocks, a spring in her step. She smiled widely at me as she leaned her hands on the kitchen table, right in the middle of a dusting of flour.

"I know this was your doing, Mrs. H."

I looked up from crushing parsley and dill in my mortar, the herbs releasing their pungent fragrance. "What was?"

Cynthia stood up. She thumped her hand to her chest, leaving a smear of flour on the dark blue fabric. "I would like you to greet Mr. Elgin Thanos's new assistant for his mathematics lectures." She spread her arms, her eyes sparkling.

"Excellent." I laid down the pestle, forcing myself to remain on my side of the table. It would never do for me to rush around and embrace her. "I am pleased he talked Sir Arthur into it."

"He jolly well did. Sir Arthur's brush with death has made him an agreeable and affable man. He thought it a grand idea to have me help Thanos keep his equations straight. Truth to tell, I imagine he saw what a muddle Thanos started to get

himself into at the lecture last week and leapt at the solution."
Cynthia leaned toward me again. "I thank you, Mrs. Holloway.
Truly."

"I only wished to help," I said, trying to sound innocent.

Cynthia straightened up once more, sending me a sly look.
"You forget that I grew up in the house of a confidence trickster. You are up to something." A grin split her face. "But I
don't mind. I am happy to be useful, and to help out dear Thanos. I am glad to call you friend."

She swallowed, and my eyes grew moist.

Before either of us could dissolve into sentimentality, she
spun away and ran off, her loose skirts swinging.

"Well, that is that," I murmured, and returned to crushing
herbs for my sauce.

On Thursday morning, Mrs. Bywater came to the kitchen
to suggest I forgo my day out, as Lady Clifford had more
guests coming for supper and card playing. Tess looked hurt,
as Mrs. Bywater clearly did not believe her up to the challenge
of preparing a large meal by herself.

But my Thursdays were sacrosanct. I told Mrs. Bywater
without flinching that to give up Thursday would mean the
end of my employment. Not even the offer of a whole day
Monday instead could move me. I saw Grace two days a week—
though Mrs. Bywater did not know of the reason for my
inflexibility—and that was the end of it.

I stoutly declared that Tess would do fine until my return
this evening, and to my surprise, both Mr. Davis and Mrs.
Redfern agreed with me. Tess wilted in gratitude, and then
almost spoiled it by puffing herself up after Mrs. Bywater departed and proclaiming that she commanded the kitchen
now. I left her to it, knowing Mr. Davis and Mrs. Redfern would
not let her head swell too much.

I donned my hat and light spring coat and made my way via omnibuses and by foot to Cheapside, and so to the Millburns and Grace.

"I have a treat for you today," I told Grace after I greeted her and the family. "We are going back to the Crystal Palace, to see more of its wonders." It had been a place of tragedy, but I did not want to shun it. With an excited Grace, who was eager to go, I could weave happier memories around it.

We departed at once and boarded a train to take us south. We rode third-class this time, and I felt much more at home, the conductor brusque but in a cheerful way. We shared our compartment with a good-natured woman and her grown daughter, a young man off to work on the coast, and an older man heading to the Crystal Palace to stroll the park.

I did my best not to think of failing wheels and carriages twisting from the track as we traveled, and we alighted at the Crystal Palace station without a mishap.

A man in a work-worn brown coat and cap, with dark hair and warm blue eyes, met us on the platform. My heart lightened as Daniel greeted Grace and me, took my arm, and led us onward.

We strolled the vast park for a time, as the weather was fine, before entering the Crystal Palace itself. Sun in a blue sky slanted through the glass building, warming it through.

"May we look again at the Egyptian Court?" Grace asked after luncheon as we moved down the nave past fountains and vast statues of kings and prominent gentlemen. "I did not see enough of it last time. I want to go to Egypt. I've been reading about it in Mrs. Millburn's history books."

"Perhaps one day you will," Daniel said with enthusiasm. "You could be an archaeologist."

I had only a vague idea about how one went about becoming an archaeologist, but Grace looked pleased, so I did not blight her interest with practical thinking.

Daniel and I led Grace to the Egyptian exhibit and then, when we'd exhausted that, the nearby Greek one. The medieval courts were worth a look as well, so elegant and mysteriously ancient.

While Grace admired suits of armor, Daniel and I reposed on a bench to keep watch over her. He and I sat very close but didn't touch each other.

"Daventry and his wife are making a journey to Rome," Daniel told me in a low voice. We'd not discussed the duke or the poisoning during luncheon, as we'd been surrounded by other diners, and I'd preferred to keep the conversation cheerful in front of Grace. "Likely a permanent one."

I was not surprised. I'd known in my bones that the duke and duchess would never be imprisoned. Arresting a distinguished duke would raise too many questions, but a discreet exit from the country could be attributed to anything, including ill health.

"Will they be watched?" I did not believe Mr. Monaghan would let them go so easily.

"They'll be guests of a man Monaghan trusts," Daniel rumbled.

"Which means they'll be watched very closely."

Daniel gave me a nod. "As you say."

I studied the carved stone of the false castle courtyard surrounding us. "Who is he, this Mr. Monaghan?"

Daniel's lips twitched. "No one I can discuss in a public place."

We'd spoken in quiet voices, but yes, anyone could be listening. The statuary and greenery afforded hiding places for eavesdroppers. I'd never thought about such things before I'd met Daniel.

"Caleb has kept Tess informed about the poison case," I said. "Caleb says the barrister might put it to the judge that her mind is unhinged."

"It very nearly is," Daniel said. "I saw her initial interview with Inspector McGregor. Her grief drove her to it, she said. She knew she might harm others in the house, but it didn't matter to her, as long as Lady Covington sickened and eventually died. She's confessed all and does not want the bother of a trial, says Inspector McGregor, but her solicitor is being very careful."

"I feel sorry for her, but at the same time—she had to be stopped."

"Evil is not solved by evil," Daniel said. "It only expands the problem. And then it never ends."

"Very cheering." I reached to him and squeezed his hand. "Let us speak no more of it. Except for me to admit that at first I thought it quite likely Jonathan Morris was the culprit. Or Jepson. But I've come to see she is devoted to Lady Covington, fanatically so."

"Young Morris likes to play the ne'er-do-well." Daniel captured my fingers and twined his through them. "When I saw Thanos yesterday, he told me a story he remembered about Jonathan. A chap Thanos knew at school had gotten into debt with a bad man. Owed the bloke several thousand pounds, and the man was going to send a thug to beat it out of him. Jonathan, a friend of the chap, intervened and paid the debt to spare his friend getting beaten. Jonathan was skint for months afterward. Lady Covington, who thought he'd lost the money on horses, curtailed his allowance for a time, until he won her over again." Daniel paused. "It takes a generous heart for a man to help a friend like that."

I leaned back, enjoying the sunlight washing us, the warmth of Daniel's hand in mine. "Lady Covington said from the beginning that Jonathan would never harm anyone. I am glad for her that she is right."

"It also takes a generous heart for a woman to give up her precious little time to help a lady in distress. To see it through until the end. And to put on a gown and pretend to be a man's fiancée so he can catch a criminal." Daniel ran a thumb over my gloved hand, which started a tingle of fire low in my abdomen.

I spoke quickly to cover my sudden fluster. "I would say I was happy to help you, but I was not. I was frightened every minute I'd be found out. I do not know how you retain your equilibrium in your disguises, my friend. In the end, I could be no one but myself. My true self, the one I'd forgotten existed." I gave a little laugh.

Daniel was suddenly closer to me. "I'll never forgive myself for it." He glanced at my shoulder where the knife had cut it. "How are you?"

"I told you, it was only a scratch." It had hurt badly, and now it itched, but I was not one to give in to physical discomfort. "Bobby cleaned it up nicely. She ought to be a doctor. Or a medic's assistant, or something of the sort."

"Mmm. I believe her family, who can put up with her dressing as a man and smoking cigars, would faint with horror if she took up work."

"A waste, if that is true," I said. "A woman can work as hard as any man. Why shouldn't we?"

"Because you are made to be beautiful and to inspire us to

goodness." Daniel turned his wide smile on me to show me he was joking.

I remembered, however, how he'd gazed at me when I'd appeared in the lovely gowns, as though he'd wanted me to stand still so he could admire me all day. I'd been far too pleased he thought I looked well, but the gowns and high-heeled shoes had been a bit impractical.

"Absolute nonsense," I said, but I softened my tone. "There are plenty of comely young ladies in the world, but I don't notice all the gentlemen rushing into goodness."

Daniel chuckled. "Ah, my cynical Kat."

"Your sensible Kat. I look at the world as it is."

"You do." His laughter faded, and his eyes grew still. "I am pleased you said *your*."

"Did I?" My heart made a small flutter. "I was practicing good rhetoric. A trick of speech."

"Is that all it was?" The amusement had left Daniel's voice, as had the flirtatiousness.

I wound my fingers more tightly through his. "No."

"I am very glad to hear it, Kat."

I decided to say no more. We sat, two upright people watching a young girl study the scenery, but Daniel's arm touched the length of mine and his warmth covered me more than that.

I could have sat thus all day. No awkwardness between us, just acknowledgment and acceptance. I was Kat and he was Daniel, as it should be.

Grace turned and waved to us, her smile wide. She was my world, and with Daniel beside me, it was complete.

Photo by Silvio Portrait Design

Jennifer Ashley is the *New York Times* bestselling author of more than one hundred novels and novellas in mystery, romance, and historical fiction. Jennifer's books have been translated into more than a dozen languages and have earned starred reviews in *Publishers Weekly* and *Booklist*. When she isn't writing, Jennifer enjoys playing music (guitar, piano, flute), reading, hiking, gardening, and building dollhouse miniatures.

CONNECT ONLINE

JenniferAshley.com

JenniferAshleyAllysonJamesAshleyGardner

JennAllyson

Ready to find
your next great read?

Let us help.

Visit prh.com/nextread

Penguin
Random
House